Matt Roe

Life, as we know, ouur [illegible] as with sharp twists and turns — sometimes unpleasant.

How we respond shapes the rest of our lives and our legacy.

In this history-rich book, savor the ways in which memorable people deal with the unexpected — and offer lasting lessons on how we can live our own lives.

To add to your reading enjoyment first read Acknowledgements on Page 376.

Your former colleague and friend ever,

Mike Johnson

North Canton, Ohio

Long Journey To Destiny

Mike Johnson

authorHOUSE®

AuthorHouse™
1663 Liberty Drive
Bloomington, IN 47403
www.authorhouse.com
Phone: 1-800-839-8640

© 2012 Mike Johnson. All rights reserved.

No part of this book may be reproduced, stored in a retrieval system, or transmitted by any means without the written permission of the author.

Published by AuthorHouse 2/7/2012

ISBN: 978-1-4685-4660-6 (sc)
ISBN: 978-1-4685-4659-0 (hc)
ISBN: 978-1-4685-4658-3 (e)

Library of Congress Control Number: 2012901601

Any people depicted in stock imagery provided by Thinkstock are models, and such images are being used for illustrative purposes only. Certain stock imagery © Thinkstock.

This book is printed on acid-free paper.

Because of the dynamic nature of the Internet, any web addresses or links contained in this book may have changed since publication and may no longer be valid. The views expressed in this work are solely those of the author and do not necessarily reflect the views of the publisher, and the publisher hereby disclaims any responsibility for them.

This is a historical novel. The story combines real-life historical figures (roster shown at book's rear) with fictional characters. All names of ships are historically accurate. All locales are authentic, and cited statistics are accurate in so far as my research shows. References to actual historical events and real people as well as locales are intended to give the fiction a stronger sense of authenticity. The chronology of the story also is historically accurate.

Also by Mike Johnson

Warrior Priest

Fate of the Warriors

God's Perfect Scar

Mascot, Minister, Man of Steel – The Final Reunion

Shadows of War

For

Henk Deys & Jeanne Deys-Trijssenaar

Peter Verveen & Jose Verveen-Koopman

(The Deys and Verveens are Dutch, and in The Netherlands when
a wife uses her maiden name, it follows her married name)

CHAPTER 1

"They have Jews."

"Who doesn't?"

"More than one hundred forty thousand," Paul Joseph Goebbels said calmly, confident of his statistics.

"We can rid them of that contamination," Adolf Hitler said with deceptive casualness. He was smoothing his hair repetitively, as though primping for a portrait-painting session.

"So you think well of the Dutch," said Goebbels, son of peasants who had risen to become Hitler's propaganda chief.

"Except for their Jews," replied Hitler, "they are Aryan. I see them becoming partners in our Reich, part of a Greater Germany."

"The Dutch are a stubborn lot," said Hermann Goering, head of Hitler's expanding Luftwaffe and then directing the overall buildup of Germany's war industry. "They are likely to resist an invasion."

"They were neutral in the First World War," Goebbels observed. "They would likely prefer to stay that way."

"We might not be able to grant them that option," Hitler replied thoughtfully, forefinger and thumb massaging his narrow mustache. "We might not be able to afford to, not if it is incompatible with our strategy. We want the Dutch on our side. They must be. Their location on the North Sea and English Channel and their ports, especially Rotterdam, demand they be our allies. The situation must be managed smartly." Hitler paused briefly. "Their queen…how long has Wilhelmina been on the throne?"

"Since 1890," Goebbels answered, "when she was just ten years old. And she has a reputation for being strong-willed."

Hitler's lips pursed and he sighed. "She could be difficult to deal with."

"She has not spoken kindly about our party or our movement," observed Goebbels.

"We would need to defeat the Dutch quickly," said Goering, a highly decorated German pilot in the First World War who clothed himself with ornately decorated uniforms and relished lavish entertainment and expensive art. "Our air power could do that."

"Not alone," said Hitler, lips tightened, head shaking slightly. "We would have to commit ground forces. Your Luftwaffe could create terror and inflict heavy damage. But to actually defeat the Dutch – or any determined army – we would need overwhelming ground forces – armor, artillery, infantry." Another pause, then Hitler smiled indulgently. "You will remember I was a foot soldier in The Great War."

"Of course," Goering replied with genuine respect, one warrior to another, "and decorated with an iron cross." Goering projected a jovial personality but acted ruthlessly against opponents and rivals.

Hitler had convened this meeting in his Reich Chancellery office. Hitler's chief architect Albert Speer had designed the massive, ornate building on Vosstrasse as the Reich's seat of government and a tribute to Hitler's self-described greatness. Hitler's office was immense and intended to awe and intimidate visitors. It measured approximately 75 feet long and 40 feet wide. The ceiling and doors were high enough to shrink a visitor's self-confidence. The walls themselves were covered with a brownish marble that visitors vaguely sensed could crush them if Hitler so much as wished it. Surprisingly his guest chairs were smartly upholstered and comfortable with arms.

At the far end of his office and far from his desk were arranged a light blue sofa flanked by matching blue chairs and facing three beige chairs. Behind the guest chairs stood a fireplace with unexpectedly modest dimensions.

The large open space between Hitler's desk and the sofa and chairs served the fuhrer well when he felt a need to pace. It also could unnerve some visitors who felt exposed and vulnerable traversing from one end to the other.

"But we are getting ahead of ourselves," Hitler said, semi-smiling. "Talk of invasion at this point is premature, in particular talk of any detailed planning. Our chief purpose today is when and how to announce my renunciation of the Treaty of Versailles. As you well know, it is unfairly punitive and locked our people in poverty."

The meeting was taking place on March 15, 1935, and Hitler was referring to the treaty that had brought closure to Great – or First World – War hostilities. The treaty had been signed on June 28, 1919, in the Hall of Mirrors at the lavishly ornate Palace of Versailles, west of Paris. Representatives from 32 Allied nations had participated in crafting the treaty. But only three – the so-called Big Three – United States President Woodrow Wilson, Britain's Prime Minister David Lloyd George and France's President Georges Clemenceau – had actually controlled negotiations. In the end, the United States Senate had refused to ratify the treaty, and the U.S. then signed its own treaty with Germany in 1921.

"Our people detest the treaty," Goebbels observed accurately.

"And rightly so," said Hitler, rising from his desk chair. "There was no good-faith negotiating. The treaty is a dictate. It was forced on us."

He was right. The Allies felt, with justification, that Germany not only deserved punishment for its wanton aggression but required strong deterrents from launching still another war against European neighbors keenly aware of Germany's legendary war-like tendencies. As a result the treaty stripped Germany of its western province of Alsace and gave it and the previously German-controlled portion of Lorraine to France. It also cleaved a slice of eastern Germany that gave Poland a corridor to the Baltic Sea. In addition, the treaty carved out other German-held territory that became provinces of Denmark, Belgium, Czechoslovakia and Lithuania. Most vexing of all to Hitler, the treaty virtually eviscerated Germany's military, reducing its army to 100,000 men and forbidding it from including tanks or an air force. Germany's navy was permitted only six capital ships and no submarines. To further assure Germany's good behavior, its western Rhineland region was to be demilitarized entirely and occupied by French and Belgian forces for up to 15 years. Lastly, the treaty imposed stiff – some believed disastrously punitive – reparations on Germany and its crippled economy and created the League of Nations as a global watchdog.

"Tomorrow," Hitler said, standing behind his desk chair, hands on hips, dark eyes peering resolutely past his senior staff, "I will publicly renounce the treaty's disarmament clauses, and I will announce the existence of our Luftwaffe. I will also announce that we will be resuming compulsory military service."

"Do you think it wise to speak so boldly and so soon?" quietly asked Rudolf Hess, Hitler's secretary and deputy. Hess was alluding to the fact that fewer than two years had passed since Hitler had taken full control of Germany's government.

"I understand your concern." Hitler re-seated himself. "But if there is one thing I am supremely confident about it is the desire of the Allies – especially France and Britain – to avoid committing themselves to another war. Certainly not now and not anytime soon. As for the United States, President Wilson took a major political risk by involving America in The Great War. I simply cannot see the Jew-loving President Roosevelt taking America to war again in Europe. With the economic great depression, he has much to worry about at home. No, gentlemen," he said, eyes moving from Goebbels to Goering and Hess, "tomorrow is precisely the right time to inform our people that the Treaty of Versailles henceforth is without practical effect." Hitler breathed deeply before continuing. "Remember this day. Remember this meeting. We are creating history. Our people will cheer my announcement, and they will be forever grateful."

CHAPTER 2

Father Titus Brandsma wasn't feeling grateful. On March 17, 1935, in his office at Catholic University (now Radboud University) in Nijmegen, The Netherlands, he was leaning back in his desk chair, reading a newspaper article trumpeted by the headline:

HITLER DENOUNCES TREATY OF VERSAILLES; GERMAN LEADER REVEALS FORMATION OF AIR FORCE

The 54-year-old Carmelite priest detested Adolf Hitler's dogma, in particular its virulent anti-Semitism. To Father Brandsma, the word Catholic literally meant universal and embracing.

He finished the article and nearly slammed the newspaper down on his desk. Hitler has a special talent for angering me, he reflected. Father Brandsma stood, breathed deeply and exited his office. Outside he went walking briskly across campus, his black cassock swishing at his ankles. His right hand tugged at his tight, white Roman collar. I need to walk off my abhorrence of Hitler before it consumes me. Hitler's mind, the priest continued thinking, is clearly a repository of evil. I am no intellectual giant, but I can easily foresee Hitler imposing his hatred of all so-called non-Aryans throughout Germany and beyond its borders. The man's ambition is limitless and naked. If ever I should meet Hitler, he told himself, I would look into his eyes for signs of a soul. I am not confident that I would see one.

Father Brandsma was born in the Dutch town of Bolsward on February 23, 1881, and was ordained in 1905 when he took the religious name Titus. Any name, he had smiled inwardly, would be an improvement on my given name – Anno Sjoerd Brandsma. Even for us Dutch that is a mouthful.

Physically unimposing, his hair was thick and combed straight back. His forehead was high, eyes kind and smile warm. His intellect, though, self-doubt notwithstanding, was in fact inspiring, and it led him to a range of pursuits. In 1909 in Rome he had earned a doctorate in philosophy. Subsequently he had taught in various schools in his native Netherlands. He also worked as a journalist, a job that gave him a bully pulpit from which to voice his disdain for Nazi doctrine and to press his case for stronger freedom of the press. It wasn't long before his writings were brought to the attention of Hitler and his senior leaders.

Still, it wasn't Father Brandsma's journalistic achievements or scholarly work as a professor that most earned him widespread respect and affection. Instead it was his nearly constant availability to any and all who sought his thinking and counsel. Students didn't hesitate to approach him, and he was patient with their questions and comments. The wise professor, he reminded himself, can and should learn from his students. As iron-minded as he was in his beliefs, Father Brandsma was a kindly, sympathetic man whose persona was magnetic.

CHAPTER 3

"Bliss, are you keen to go to the Red Barn today? Saddle up a pair of horses?"

On that Saturday in 1935, Meredith Forbes was directing her questions to Joshua Bliss. Fewer than three years earlier, given their vastly different upbringings, neither would have imagined being together on that sun-splashed morning.

"Well, let's see. I've had breakfast, and I could stand some time away from the books."

"Great!" Meredith smiled exultantly. "It's a perfect day for riding."

As a young girl Meredith Forbes had never sat a horse. Born in 1915, she was a Manhattanite. Blond with sparkling blue eyes, her five feet four inches carried 108 pounds. She was the youngest of three daughters of New York banker Russell Forbes and his wife Victoria, who when not mothering their girls, helped raise funds for area charities. Meredith's older sisters were Clarisse and Christine, born in 1910 and 1913, respectively.

The family lived in a handsome brownstone on East 72nd street, only a block removed from Fifth Avenue and Central Park. The girls' world orbited around the park where they learned to ice skate on the frozen surfaces of the reservoir and the lake, Fifth Avenue stores, museums and Rockefeller Center's Radio City Music Hall with its magnificent productions and 6,000 seats. More than once Russell had treated the entire family, including two sons-in-law, to dinner in the Rainbow Room on the 65th floor of the RCA Building –widely regarded as the gem of the 14 art deco buildings comprising Rockefeller Center.

Had the youthful mind and eyes of Meredith been apprised of a Joshua Bliss, she might well have imagined him born on a distant planet. In actuality he was born and raised on a farm on Funk Road, just a couple miles west of Shelby, Ohio. Sandy haired, he stood six feet tall, and his 185 pounds had been sculpted and hardened by daily farm labor. Also born in 1915, he was the younger brother of Paul who was four years older. There was just one remarkable aspect of Joshua's appearance; by age 19 his hair had begun thinning.

The boys' parents, Noah and Goldie, plowed, planted, harvested and prospered on 300 acres. Their house, barn and grain silos all were white washed and proudly maintained. In addition to growing wheat and corn, they kept chickens to provide fresh eggs, pigs for pork and bacon and a single extravagance – a pair of riding horses for Paul and Joshua. The horses, which the brothers had named Beau and Duke, were both brown geldings and products of undistinguished bloodlines. But they were sturdy, dependable mounts and much loved by the brothers Bliss, both of whom became skilled horsemen.

Meredith and Joshua had connected in a way decidedly unlikely for the early 1930s when few Americans traveled long distances. Many roads remained unpaved, buses were cramped and broke down frequently, and airline service was nascent and regarded as dangerous and even foolhardy. Only trains moved smoothly and reliably.

Clarisse and Christine had shown no interest in higher education, and Russell and Victoria had not urged them to pursue formal studies beyond high school. Marrying well and bearing babies were their highest priorities. Clarisse already was married to George Morgan. Christine was engaged to Donald Halston. Meredith, to her parents' surprise, had acquired a strong spirit of adventure and exploration.

"Father. Mother. I want to go to college," she had told them one night at dinner in the autumn of her senior high school year. The table was covered by exquisite linen and set with fine china and silver. Dress was typically formal.

Christine wasn't surprised. Meredith had confided in her. Knowing what was coming, Christine knew she would have to conceal her enjoyment over the coming conversation.

"That's wonderful, dear," replied Victoria. "I know that some of your girlfriends are going to college. And there are some most reputable choices available to you. Isn't that right, Russell?"

"Quite right, dear," he said, not at all sure where this conversation was heading, but mindful that Meredith often thought differently from his wife and two older daughters.

"You see, Meredith, your father and I agree. Vassar, Wellesley, Barnard and Marymount right here in Manhattan. Any of them would give you a marvelous college education."

Meredith's eyes closed and her chin rose in contemplation. Then her eyes opened flintily and she spoke. "Stanford."

Victoria's eyes widened in shock. Her mouth opened to reply, then closed and opened again. "Stanford," she spluttered. "Why, why, isn't that in California?"

"Yes, Mother," Meredith said evenly. "In Palo Alto, near San Francisco."

Victoria shuddered. Russell smiled inwardly, amused by this unexpected mother-daughter dialogue. He shot a glance at Christine and thought he detected foreknowledge and sisterly support.

"Stanford," Victoria said again, her dismay obvious, "isn't that a new school?"

"Newer than eastern schools," Meredith said.

"And isn't it, uh…?"

"Yes," Meredith interjected helpfully, "it's co-educational. Has been from the beginning."

"Oh my," preceded a long pause. "Well, dear, we have indulged you often, more often than your sisters. But I am afraid Stanford – California – is entirely out of the question. My God, it's at the other end of the continent. No, I am afraid it's entirely unacceptable. Don't you agree?" she said, turning toward Russell.

Meredith's face swiveled toward her father. Her eyes were silently pleading.

Russell smiled. "Well, dear, I think it might be wise to let Meredith choose."

Victoria's eyes widened again. She was distressed – both by Meredith's thinking and Russell's disagreement with her. Victoria was strong-minded but consistently deferred to her husband's judgment on all matters of significance. Not always willingly and certainly not in this matter. She swallowed her defeat and looked down at her dinner plate.

Russell smiled again, first to his wife and then each daughter, and the deal was done.

On the Bliss farm, Joshua had encountered no resistance. Stanford hadn't even been his idea. To him, as high schooler, Stanford had been nothing more than college football scores. His grades – he had ranked first in his 1933 Shelby High School class – and athletic ability – he had been named an All-Ohio halfback by Associated Press – had led a Stanford assistant football coach to the family farm.

"Young man," the coach had told Joshua, his parents and brother, "you are precisely the kind of football player we prefer. One who is a crack student with a strong work ethic and superior athletic skills. I am prepared to offer you an all-expenses paid scholarship."

The offer was unexpected but not unprecedented. Ohio State University had extended a similar offer and Joshua was flattered. But the Stanford coach's photos of the campus, surrounded by towering deciduous trees, waving palm trees and desert cacti with mountains in the distance, exerted the stronger pull, and in the summer of 1933 Joshua found himself first on a Baltimore & Ohio train to Cleveland's Union Station, deep in the bowels of the soaring Terminal Tower. There he boarded the Lake Shore Limited to Chicago where he switched to the Super Chief for the long journey to California.

Stanford's life had sprung from death. In 1884 Leland Stanford Jr. was stricken with typhoid fever while on a European tour. He died just before his 16th birthday.

His father was president of the Central Pacific Railroad and in 1869 had pounded the golden spike at Promontory, Utah, completing the transcontinental railroad. Leland Stanford also had served as governor of California during the Civil War and later became a United States senator.

Leland Stanford thought big. Within weeks after his son's death, he and wife Jane decided to found a world-class university in their son's honor. Their goal, they declared, was to employ their considerable wealth to do something for "other people's" children.

Their university's doors didn't open until 1891, which in fact made the school far younger than its eastern counterparts. But to Meredith and Joshua, sophomores in the spring of 1935, Stanford – officially named Leland Stanford Junior University – conferred advantages unmatched by any other school.

First, there was the university's location – just 37 miles south of spectacular San Francisco. And there was its sprawl – 8,180 acres that stretched westward across the San Francisco Bay peninsula into the foothills of the Santa Cruz Mountains beyond which glistened the blue Pacific Ocean. The acreage came cheap to the university; it had been the site of Leland Stanford's horse farm and hence the school's instant and enduring nickname – The Farm.

Then there was the university's tuition. It had remained zero – free to any and all students – into the 1930s. That was of little moment to Joshua who arrived on his full athletic scholarship. Meredith's father,

Russell, easily could have afforded any tuition. But his banker's mentality appreciated the bargain that accompanied his daughter's choice of a distant university that was quickly earning a reputation for academic excellence.

Campus architecture was inviting and unlike any to be found east of the Mississippi River. In 1935 the campus included the Main Quad, its inner courtyard surrounded by classrooms and laboratories, dormitories and library connected by arches and long arcades and Memorial Church with its stunning façade – a mural with a white-and-blue-robed Christ, arms upraised, flanked by followers in their own colorful robes. Forming a backdrop for the church were those Santa Cruz Mountain foothills. All campus buildings featured sandstone exteriors and red tile roofs.

The Stanford family mausoleum was situated to the north of the central campus, closer to downtown Palo Alto.

Leland Stanford had decreed that the land could never be sold and envisioned that much of the acreage would never be tamed. In addition, some 1,000 acres were designated for income-producing uses.

And then, for Joshua and Meredith, there was the Red Barn with its adjacent stables on the campus' western fringe. The two youngsters had connected soon after arriving as wide-eyed freshmen in September 1933. They had met at a freshman mixer and taken a quick liking to each other. Romance soon took root and blossomed.

Joshua had decided to major in economics, mainly because he wanted a deeper understanding of the forces that were buffeting many of the families he knew in Shelby, a town of about 9,000 people that combined a robust industrial base with a strong agricultural presence. Meredith was majoring in English and hoped to teach in a New York high school.

By mid-November of their first year, Joshua's freshman football season had ended. On Friday afternoon after the week's last class, Joshua and Meredith were strolling through the university's Arizona Garden, so named because it was planted with cacti by Leland and Jane in the 1880s near where the mausoleum later would be built.

"Any plans for the weekend?" Joshua had asked.

"Well, there's the big game against Cal," Meredith replied. "You wouldn't want to miss that, would you?"

"No, I wouldn't miss a varsity game, especially our biggest rivalry game." Joshua was referring to the upcoming contest with the University of California at Berkeley, only about 40 miles northeast of Stanford. "But the kickoff isn't till two o'clock."

"Do you have something else in mind?"

"Do you wanna ride?"

"Ride?"

"Horses."

Her eyes widened in surprise. "I've never even been on a horse. I've seen mounted police, and the carriage horses around Central Park. But ride? I never saw cows and pigs for that matter – until my train was west of the Hudson River."

"You poor, deprived woman." Joshua grinned. "Look, city girl, the question is, Do you want to try riding?"

Meredith's head shook slightly and her lips turned downward in deliberation. "I guess if I could travel all the way to California, I should try being a cowgirl."

Early the next morning Joshua took Meredith's hand and led her to the stables beside the Red Barn. Minutes later he had saddled two horses – a gelding and a gentle mare.

"What now?" Meredith asked dubiously.

"Get on her left side. I'll be right behind you." Meredith stepped behind and around to the mare's left. "Now put your left hand on the pommel and grip it firmly. Now put your shoe in the stirrup. Bend your right leg and spring up."

As Meredith rose Joshua patted her bottom. "Not bad."

"Hey, Bliss. Watch that stuff, cowboy."

"Just checking the stock, ma'am."

"Is it fit for the trail?"

"Seems firm enough for a long ride."

Minutes later Meredith whooped and laughed. "Aren't I just the picture of grace? I feel like I'm a rubber ball bouncing on a sidewalk." She was wearing a black-and-white-checked blouse, light wool blue slacks, sharply creased, and a blue woolen sweater to ward off the morning chill. Her shoes were black pumps.

"You'll get the hang of it."

Which is exactly what she soon did. Her fondness for riding grew fast, strong and lasting. Now, 17 months later on this March Saturday in 1935, Meredith was eager to ride.

"Where to?" Joshua asked.

Meredith extended her left arm and, with forefinger pointing upward, said, "There. The crest of the foothills. I've always wanted to see the view from up there."

"All right, cowgirl, let's head out."

They both tapped their horses' flanks with their heels and the mounts stepped away from the stables.

"The climb looks pretty steep," said Meredith. "Do you think it's too much for the horses?"

"No. Not as long as we don't push them too hard. It's the ride back down that will be dicey."

"Oh, great. I didn't think about that."

"Not to worry. If need be we'll dismount and lead the horses down."

"And ruin my shoes," she whined half-seriously.

Joshua laughed. "Scuffed shoes. A tragedy of epic proportions."

Meredith laughed at herself, a trait Joshua found endearing.

Two hours later they were sitting their horses atop the crest of the highest hill.

"Oh my," Meredith marveled. "What a view! It is spectacular. We can see the bay and even a glimpse of the Pacific. And the campus below, the buildings look tiny."

"Get down," said Joshua. "Let's give the horses a breather."

Meredith dismounted and breathed deeply. She ran her hands back through her blond hair. "I've seen the view from a New York skyscraper, and it's impressive. You can see both the Hudson and East Rivers. But that's nothing compared to this. It's absolutely inspiring."

"I'm thinking it might inspire a kiss," Joshua smiled.

"Is that all?"

"We wouldn't want to spook the horses."

"They have reins. Let's tie them to a tree branch."

"We might miss lunch," he grinned.

"I'm sure we'll find something to nibble on up here."

"I don't see anything resembling a mattress or even a pillow."

Meredith surveyed their surroundings. "Well, Bliss, the saddle blankets might do nicely. Roll one up for a pillow."

"What would your mother think?"

"If she's telepathic, she's already fainted." A pause. "I sometimes wonder if she and Father ever made out."

They both laughed.

"You've come a long way from Manhattan, city girl."

"I have at that, haven't I, farm boy?"

CHAPTER 4

On two adjoining farms some 8,000 miles to the east of Stanford, two teenage girls were following plodding oxen. The grimy, grim-faced youths were gripping the handles of plows that were turning moist spring earth. Although the morning temperature was cool, their exertion had both girls sweating profusely.

They were wearing faded, threadbare ankle-length dresses. One was brown, the other blue. Their feet were shod in leaky leather shoes on the verge of disintegration. Each wore a sweat-stained kerchief – also blue and brown – around their heads to keep salty sweat from stinging their eyes.

Raluca Johnescu and Alicia Domian were both 15 years old. Raluca stood five-feet five inches, two inches taller than Alicia. Both were pretty with dark brown hair, brown eyes and olive-tinged skin. Both were slender, almost stick thin.

Their parents' neighboring farms were typically small, each about eight acres. They were located west of Apahida, a town of about 7,000 nestled at the base of foothills of the Apuseni Mountains, part of the Carpathian Mountains in Romania's northwest corner. Apuseni peaks ranged from 1,600 to 2,300 feet. The Carpathians stretched some 930 miles across Czechoslovakia, Poland, Hungary, Ukraine and Romania.

The city nearest Apahida was Cluj, eight miles to the southwest with a population of about 300,000 and some 280 miles northwest of Romania's Black Sea beaches. Given the primitive state of Romanian roads, traversed mostly by ox- and horse-drawn wagons, those beaches rarely welcomed Apahida-area residents. Only the few relatively affluent could afford train travel.

Raluca had a younger brother, Dan, and Alicia two younger brothers, Nicolae and Leo. The girls were expected to do the heavy chores until the boys gained sufficient size and strength.

At one point in their labors, Raluca caught Alicia's eye and waved tiredly but with a hint of a smile. Alicia returned the greeting. An hour later the girls had completed their work. They freed the oxen from the plows and led the hulking beasts back to their pens outside the two small barns with thatched roofs. Now the girls were reclining against the base of an ancient, towering tree on the border between their farms.

Raluca removed her sweaty kerchief and shook her dark hair. She hiked her dress above her knees to let cooling air reach her thighs and crotch.

"Look at the mountains. They are beginning to green. Spring will be here soon. Crocuses will be popping up any day now."

Alicia pulled up her dress and smiled at her friend. "Are you dreaming again?"

"Yes."

"About what?"

"A better life."

"This is our life."

"Don't you wish for more?"

"No." Alicia noisily sucked in a breath. Slowly she let it escape her lungs. "Well, sometimes. But what good is dreaming about the impossible?"

"We are poor. I am so tired of being poor."

"But," said Alicia, "everyone is poor."

"Not everyone."

"No. But almost everyone in Apahida. And on the farms."

"Yes," Raluca said, her voice hardening, "and look at what being poor does."

"What do you mean?"

"Look at us. We are young. We are dirty. We wear clothes that are not much nicer than rags. People here have no spirit, no hope. They do not dream. Even the young have old eyes."

"That is our fate."

"I want to change our fate."

"Change it? How? Is it possible?"

"Yes, if we leave." Raluca spoke those four words in a way that had them taking on the hardness of iron.

"Leave?" Alicia's bafflement was complete. "To where?"

"Paris."

"Paris?" Alicia asked her voice rising in surprise on the brink of shock. "Why?"

"Because it is called the city of light. Perhaps there is light there for us."

"Us?"

"Of course. We are best friends. You would go with me."

Alicia smiled warmly. "I have always followed you, haven't I?"

Raluca grinned slyly. "That is because I am a whole, entire two months older than you."

The girls laughed. Then Alicia turned thoughtful. "We are farm girls. We can plow fields and plant crops. We can harvest them. We can milk cows and sheer sheep. What need is there for that in Paris?"

"None, probably."

"Then what? What would we do? We would need money."

"We would look for jobs. Maybe as seamstresses or maids."

"And if we do not find such jobs?"

"I think we are both pretty. Perhaps we could be models. Pose for artists, painters, sculptors."

"But that will take time. And we must keep eating."

"Yes. You are right." Raluca closed her eyes and gulped in cool air. "We might have to sell."

"Sell? What would we sell?"

Raluca let her head rock back gently against the tree trunk. "Ourselves."

Alicia stared uncomprehendingly at her friend. Raluca returned her gaze. Then understanding began dawning. "I cannot believe you are saying this," Alicia spluttered. "Or even thinking it. It is wrong. It is a sin. We would be condemned to hell. And we are too young." A pause. "Aren't we?"

Raluca laughed. "You said it yourself. We are farm girls. We know how it works. We have seen the sheep do it."

"Eww." Alicia's nose crinkled and she shivered in disgust. "Our parents. What would they say?"

"You mean, what would we tell them?"

"Yes."

"We would think of something. Not the entire truth but not a lie."

"What if men in Paris don't think we are pretty?" Alicia asked.

"Then we would go to Amsterdam."

"Amsterdam! Holland! That is so far. Why there?"

"Because in Cluj I have heard men talking."

"Where?"

"On the streets. Near the taverns and inns."

"What do they say?"

"They say there is a big demand in Amsterdam for young women who are willing to serve men."

"I cannot imagine myself doing that. Never! It sounds...It sounds so ugly."

Raluca's next words took on a tone of severity. "Alicia, do you prefer to imagine yourself living here? Forever? Poor. Wearing rags. Working in the fields. Being twenty but looking forty – if you live that long."

"I do not want to think about that," she said petulantly.

"No. But you should. I heard the men say that prostitutes-"

"I do not want to hear that word."

Raluca's head shook wearily. "I understand. But you need to listen.

14

Prostitutes are treated well in Amsterdam. They have their own quarter of the city. There is no crime. No shame. It is business."

"A filthy business. And there would be sin. Our sin."

"We could pray for forgiveness. And once we saved money, we can enter another business."

"What business?"

"I think we will find it. Perhaps open our own Romanian restaurant. Look, it might not be so bad. Maybe we will have success in Paris."

Alicia's visage brightened. "Yes, maybe you will become a famous model. And rich. And I will open a restaurant and use Mother's recipes." The girls laughed. Then Alicia's eyes focused on the ground between her legs. "Your dream," she said somberly, "is scary."

"I think sometimes dreams are." A pause. "We have worked hard today. We should not be feeling scared or sad. Come on," Raluca said, springing to her feet, "let's walk up the hill. To the top. We can admire the view."

"Maybe we can see Paris," Alicia teased, "or our future."

With renewed energy Raluca and Alicia started the climb up an oft-trod trail toward the 570-foot summit. At about 425 feet, Alicia said, "I need to pee."

The girls stopped and Alicia stepped off the trail into high ground cover. She lifted her long dress, lowered her cotton underpants, squatted and urinated. Moments later she stepped back onto the trail.

They took two more steps up the trail and hesitated. They heard rustling in the ground cover. They strained to hear. In the next instant the girls heard snorting and froze. They looked at each other, eyes widening in fear. Before they could turn, a wild boar, coarse black hairs bristling, came crashing from the ground cover some 15 feet in front of them. Unknowingly Alicia had picked the wrong spot to pee. The boar was snorting her anger at two humans who had neared her three helpless young.

The girls shrieked, turned and began running down the twisting trail. The boar was following noisily. Then after a rapid descent of some 60 feet, the boar skidded to a stop. She sniffed and seemed to raise her head in victory.

Raluca and Alicia kept running another 30 feet before looking back over their shoulders. Then they stopped. They watched as the boar pivoted and began trotting up the trail. Each girl gulped in air and blew it out forcefully. They looked at each other with both relief and elation – and then erupted in gales of laughter.

"In Paris," Alicia said, her right hand brushing tears born of merriment from her cheeks, "we would not have wild boars chasing us. Of course we wouldn't be peeing in a forest."

Raluca chuckled and then said thoughtfully, "We need freedom. Freedom from drudgery and dirt. Freedom from poverty and the way it kills dreams and deadens spirits."

CHAPTER 5

The boy was chasing, arms pumping emphatically, and the girls were shrieking as they went racing along one of the more than 100 canals of varying lengths and widths that crisscrossed Amsterdam. Those channels continuously drained the city's land that sat slightly below sea level.

The boy was Aaron Folleck and he was nine years old in 1935. The girls he was pursuing in a spirited game of tag were his sister, Mariah, age nine, and the Frank sisters, Margot, nine, and Anne, six. Aaron's second sister, Julia, only four, was too young to keep up with the other kids. But she was jumping repeatedly, delighting in watching their antics.

Aaron tagged Anne who nearly lost her balance. She managed to right herself before tumbling into the canal.

"I will tag you back," cried Anne. She was winded but determined to show she could run down a boy. Aaron laughed and bolted off, pulling away from Anne and quickly overtaking Mariah and Margot.

The Follecks had immigrated to The Netherlands in 1933, soon after Hitler came to power. They were among the first of some 300,000 Jews who would flee Hitler's Reich before 1939 when the exits from Germany slammed shut.

Aaron's father, Samuel, born in 1904, had prospered as a retailer – men's wear – in Frankfurt in western Germany. After arriving in Amsterdam with his wife Miriam, born in 1905, and their three children, Samuel bought a men's wear shop on Merwede Square. He quickly saw potential for growth that would result from Amsterdam's status as a major maritime hub. Samuel expanded the shop's offerings to include apparel worn by the legions of sailors – woolen sweaters, scarves, socks, caps, thick leather gloves and jackets. Miriam helped with bookkeeping and other paperwork in the family's apartment above the shop.

Only two doors away from Samuel's shop lived another recently arrived Jewish family. The Sevels – Guillermo, Juanita and their children, Maribel, 10, Jorge, nine – had fled Spain during the turmoil that preceded the outbreak of civil war on July 17, 1936. Riots had erupted in December 1933, and Hitler had begun supporting Spain's rebels. Given Hitler's increasing oppression of Jews in Germany, the Sevels decided to join an early exodus to other nations deemed more hospitable, or less antagonistic, to Jews.

Guillermo had opened a tobacco shop on Merwede Square, and he and Samuel and their families had become friends. Their sons, Aaron and Jorge, had become virtually inseparable.

CHAPTER 6

On March 7, 1936, Hitler continued his mockery of the Versailles Treaty. He ordered Wehrmacht troops to reoccupy the demilitarized Rhineland, the region bordering northeastern France, Luxembourg, Belgium and The Netherlands. His generals had opposed the move as too risky. Hitler tempered his boldness by promising them that he would withdraw Wehrmacht troops quickly at the first sign of intervention by French forces.

Soon after dawn, 19 German infantry battalions went marching into the Rhineland. A few Luftwaffe fighter planes provided close air cover. By 11 a.m., the troops had penetrated deeply enough to take up defensive positions.

Word reached Hitler that French troops were assembling to the west. Instead of ordering immediate withdrawal, Hitler asked, "Have they crossed the border?"

"No," replied his chief of staff who then encouraged the fuhrer to stay the course.

Hitler had believed, correctly, that France – and England – would be unwilling to commit to another European war. This resounding success further strengthened Hitler's belief in himself as a political and military genius. Still, Hitler later confided to his staff, "The forty-eight hours after the march into the Rhineland were the most nerve-wracking in my life. If the French had then marched into the Rhineland, we would have had to withdraw with our tails between our legs, for the military resources at our disposal would have been wholly inadequate for even a moderate resistance."

Father Titus Brandsma, clad in his black cassock with white collar, was striding across the campus of Catholic University. He was lost in thought about what he might say in his sermon on the coming Sunday.

"Father Brandsma!" a voice called out excitedly. "Father!"

Father Brandsma looked up and stopped. Two male students were running toward him. They stopped three feet in front of him. "Yes?" he smiled, eyes twinkling. "What has you racing across campus? Are you late for a class?" he teased. "Or are you so eager to learn what I will be saying on Sunday?"

"No, Father," one of the young men replied earnestly. "Have you listened to the radio this morning?"

"I am afraid not. But I have a feeling," he grinned, "that you are about to give me a personal report."

The student nodded. "German troops have moved into the Rhineland."

All signs of levity vanished from Father Brandsma's mien. "Has there been fighting?"

"The radio said no fighting."

He sighed. "Did it say how many troops?"

"Thousands. But not how many thousands. Plus some airplanes."

"Nothing about the French?"

"No."

Father Brandsma sighed again. "Thank you, son." A brief pause. "I need to think."

Minutes later, Father Brandsma wasn't thinking. He was in his office, kneeling beside his desk and praying softly. "Dear Lord, please keep the world safe from Adolf Hitler. He has spoken openly about Germany needing more living space, and now he has taken the first action. I feel certain it won't be his last. If only one of my prayers is to be answered, let it be this one. Amen."

That same day at Stanford, Joshua Bliss and Meredith Forbes were strolling across Main Quad's brick-paved courtyard in front of Memorial Church. The temperature was just cool enough for sweaters. Meredith was wearing a navy blue cardigan, while Joshua was wearing his football letter sweater in the school colors – white with cardinal red letters.

"Test tomorrow," Joshua said.

"On?" Meredith asked.

"Economies of the world. It'll be tough."

"You'll do fine, Bliss," Meredith said reassuringly. "You always stay up with your studies. The rest of us mere mortals have to cram."

"It's probably my farm boy work ethic," he grinned.

She took his left arm in her hands. "You're some farm boy, cowboy."

He laughed. "You're right, you know. I am ready for the test. So tonight let's take in a movie."

"Boy, Bliss, you are confident. What do you want to see?"

"*Mutiny on the Bounty* is showing at the Stanford. Clark Gable and Charles Laughton. I've heard good things about it. Supposed to be exciting."

"I should have known," Meredith said teasingly.

"Huh?"

"It's a movie set on the ocean."

"Yeah," he smiled slightly sheepishly.

Downtown Palo Alto was about a 15-minute stroll from the Main Quad along arrow-straight Palm Drive. Palo Alto was a picture-perfect college town. Narrow streets bordered by trees, shops and bicycle racks. Students sipping Coca Colas at drug store soda fountains. Young men puffing pipes outside a tobacconist shop. The main street, University Avenue, boasted two movie emporiums – the Stanford Theater that had opened in 1925 and the Varsity Theater that had debuted two years later.

Joshua found *Mutiny on the Bounty* riveting. He thrilled to the high seas action scenes – filmed on a Hollywood studio backlot pond.

After the movie ended and the curtain closed, Joshua and Meredith exited the theater. They turned right to begin returning to campus. Joshua took Meredith's right hand in his left and squeezed gently.

"Feeling romantic, Bliss?"

He looked down at her, smiled but said nothing. Back on campus, still holding hands, they were approaching The Oval, a flower garden inside an egg-shaped split in Palm Drive and just across Serra Street from Main Quad.

Joshua stopped and peered up at the star-spangled sky. Meredith, eight inches shorter, looked up at him. Still, he said nothing.

"A penny for your thoughts, Bliss."

Joshua lowered his head and smiled. Still holding her hand, he dropped to one knee. He looked up into Meredith's blue eyes.

"Whoa," she said lowly, visibly shocked. "Is this what I think it is?"

"Unless you've gone suddenly dense, it is. Look, I don't have much money. I don't even have a ring for you. But I love you and-"

"Shut up, Bliss," she commanded sharply. "The answer is yes."

"It is?"

"Do I need to repeat it?"

"It would help."

"Yes, I will marry you."

"That was too easy," he chortled. He rose, released her hand and pulled her close. "I know it makes sense to wait till graduation, but-"

"We will marry in Shelby," she said decisively, cutting him off again. "Not in New York."

"Why?"

"Because it's easier for a banker and his socialite wife to travel than it is for farmers, right?"

"Uh, right."

"Besides, I've never seen your hometown, and I've never seen a farm. It's high time I did both. Now that I think about it, I'll bet Mother and Father have never seen a farm either. It'll do them good to get out of their Manhattan cocoon."

"They will get their first whiff of country cologne," Josh grinned.

"What's that?" Meredith asked.

"You'll see – or smell."

"When?" she asked. "When is the wedding? You have thought about it, haven't you?"

"I was thinking maybe during the Christmas holidays."

"Perfect! This Christmas will be my happiest ever."

Sadness was prevailing at the railroad station in Cluj. Raluca and Alicia were standing on a concrete platform, arms straight at their sides, tears coursing down their cheeks. At the girls' feet were two heavy cloth bags, each with red roses embroidered on the sides. Except for the clothes that Raluca and Alicia were wearing – their only nice dresses, saved for the most special of occasions – the bags contained all the girls thought they would need on the long journey. Over the dresses each was wearing a simple cloth coat, blue for Raluca, brown for Alicia. They were hand-me-downs from their mothers and though not shabby showed signs of frequent use.

Both girls' families were there and all – parents and siblings – were weeping. Raluca's younger brother Dan had his sister's arms pinned to her sides in a fierce hug that seemed destined to end only when the conductor cried, "All aboard."

"I am afraid we will never see you again," groaned Raluca's mother, Magdalena. Her distress was understandable. Rarely did young people leave Apahida and its neighboring farms. What Raluca and Alicia were doing was unprecedented, at least within the community's living memory.

When the girls broke the news of their plan to their parents, anger quickly followed shock, and recriminations wounded all. But the parents gradually came to understand their daughters' determination to break the chains of poverty and acceptance surfaced. The two sets of parents had conferred at length in the Johnescu's small house and then called for the girls to join them.

"Please sit down," Gheorghe had said to Raluca and Alicia. The girls sat next to Livia on a flower-patterned sofa that was draped by a folded violet blanket to cover rips in the upholstery. Magdalena and Ion were seated on the room's only two chairs, and Gheorghe was standing about 12 feet opposite the sofa. It was about 7 p.m., and darkness was closing in as the sun had slipped below the mountains.

"We," said Gheorghe motioning with his right hand to the other parents, "have been talking and we have agreed." Instant stabs of uncertainty tightened the girls' chests. Were their parents mounting a united stand against their departure? Absolutely forbid them to leave? "We don't have much money and neither do you. We believe you need more."

With that, Gheorghe reached into a pocket of his worn brown trousers and extracted folded lei. He walked across the room and handed the money to Raluca. "Here."

Raluca stood, tears misting her brown eyes. "No, Father, we can't take your money. Not yours, not Alicia's parents.'"

"We are simple farmers," Gheorghe said, pressing the lei into his daughter's left hand. "That is all we have been for generations. But we have talked, and we do understand your desire – your need – to find a different life in a different place."

Raluca extended her hand holding the lei. "Father-"

"Keep the money," he said. "We will be worrying about you – both of you – while you are away. But we will worry less if we know you have this money."

"Dear," Magdalena said softly. "You and Alicia are our only daughters, and you are so young. Only just turned sixteen. But your father is right. We don't want to stand in your way. You are like young birds. You have wings and you have decided to fledge and leave the nest. Go and know that we will always love you."

Now, on the station's platform with the locomotive wheezing noisily, Raluca sniffled and struggled to release herself from Dan's grip. She then stepped forward and embraced Magdalena. "I will return. I don't know when. But I will. I promise."

Her father Gheorghe was struggling to smile. Raluca leaned toward him and placed her face against his chest. No words were spoken.

Alicia then locked herself in a group hug with her parents, Ion and Livia, and her two younger brothers, Nicolae and Leo. "I make the same promise," Alicia murmured, barely audibly. "Some day I will come back. Our farm will always be my home."

Sooty smoke was billowing from the locomotive's stack. The conductor was watching the farewell scene. Instead of shouting "All aboard," he stepped to within a few feet of the distraught group and quietly said, "It is time to go. Please get on the train."

Hugs were slowly released and Raluca and Alicia picked up their bags. They turned, still sniffling, stepped up and onto the second-class car. From Cluj their journey would take them first to Budapest, then Vienna, Munich, Strasbourg and Paris. As the train began inching westward, the girls were grateful that the weather was cool enough to keep windows closed and soot out.

Hours were crawling by with the soothing rhythm of steel wheels cruising over steel rails lulling Raluca and Alicia. They were staring out a grime-coated window in silence at the passing countryside. The train had left Romania and was steaming northwest through Hungary toward Budapest.

At last Raluca ended their reverie. "What are you thinking?"

"I am thinking we must be brave."

"Why?"

"Because we are frightened, and we are still doing it."

"You might be right."

Alicia, in the window seat, turned toward her friend. "Do you want to come back?"

"Some day, yes. But not poor."

"Do you think we will come back?"

Raluca sighed and gazed at the back of the seat in front of her. "I don't know."

On that March 7 in Amsterdam, Aaron Folleck and Jorge Sevel were energetically kicking a scuffed, white leather soccer ball. Both boys at age nine were developing impressive ball control skills. Their unfettered joy was magnetic.

Watching were their fathers, Samuel and Guillermo.

"They are happy," said Guillermo, puffing a black briar pipe outside his tobacco shop.

"And I think they are quite good," said Samuel.

"I agree. Perhaps one day they will play professionally – or even for our national team."

Aaron and Jorge were using the expanse of Merwede Square for their play. They were little concerned with traffic. Few cars were driving through Amsterdam in 1935, and the boys were easily able to avoid collisions with slow-moving, horse-drawn carriages and freight wagons.

"That is a nice dream, my friend," said Samuel. "Representing The Netherlands on the international stage, I would happily pay guilders worth a month of my sales to see that."

"Let's hope we both live long enough to see that. If it's Aaron, I will be there to cheer him."

"Likewise," said Samuel. "If it is Jorge who reaches that level."

An errant kick sent the ball bouncing off the forehead of a startled carriage horse. The two fathers laughed. The ball rolled to a stop near their feet. Gracefully and expertly with his right foot, Guillermo struck the ball, sending it back to his son across the square.

"Nicely done," Samuel said, his admiration obvious. "Perhaps," he kidded, "there is a spot for you on the national team."

"There was a time," Guillermo said with a distant look, "there was a time." Then he went about relighting his pipe.

Samuel nodded. "Let's hope there is time enough for our boys."

CHAPTER 7

It was summer in the city of light, and Raluca and Alicia still were in awe of the sights, sounds and smells of their new home. And they were beginning to think of Paris as their home, albeit one not entirely pleasant.

Three months earlier, when their train from Cluj had arrived at cavernous Gare de l' Est, the girls stepped tentatively outside the cavernous station, and Raluca immediately put to use her most rudimentary of French. She and Alicia, each toting their cloth bag, began walking south on tree-lined Boulevard de Strasbourg which, at the intersection with Boulevard St. Martin, became Boulevard de Sebastopol. With the boulevards sloping slightly downward toward the Seine, their walk required little exertion.

After covering about one and half miles, gawking along the way, they arrived at the Pont Notre Dame. Across that bridge spanning the Seine, they looked to their left and saw the twin towers crowning stately Notre Dame. They crossed onto little Ile de la Cite where Paris first had been settled more than 2,000 years ago. In 52 B.C., invading Roman soldiers found fishermen on the small island. They were Celtic tribesmen known as Parisii. Colonizing Romans dubbed the settlement Lutetia. It became known as Paris about 300 A.D. Raluca and Alicia made their way to the plaza in front of the cathedral. The massive gothic structure with gracefully carved figures and scowling gargoyles was started in 1163 and completed 150 years later.

Alicia's head shook in wonder. "It is so beautiful, so magnificent. Even the doors, they are so huge." In fact, across the cathedral's front stood three pairs of double doors, each about 18 feet high. "This must be God's favorite house."

"If not his favorite," Raluca smiled beneath elevated eyebrows, "perhaps his most expensive."

"Raluca! Shame on you."

"My dearest friend, how do you think Notre Dame was built? By cheap charity? The architects, the sculptors, the masons, the painters. They all had to be paid and paid handsomely"

"But I am sure they did it for their love of God and Christ."

"No doubt, some did," Raluca observed. "But most saw it as a lifetime job that paid nicely. We should fare so well."

Alicia and Raluca had turned away. They went walking south across the rest of the small island in the river, continued strolling south over a second bridge and found themselves on what Parisians called the Left Bank. Minutes later they were standing on Rue Saint Andre des Artes, a narrow street only about 300 yards long. In a gallery window they saw a print of Henri Matisse's impressionist still life, *Gold Fish & Sculpture*.

Inspiration struck.

"Come," Raluca commanded Alicia, and she pushed open the door to the small gallery. She eyed the proprietor, Christian Fabre. He was short, about Raluca's five feet five inches, and slightly paunchy. He wore wire-rimmed glasses, and his gray hair was just a few strands shy of rendering him bald. From behind his sales counter, Fabre smiled pleasantly at his visitors.

"Good morning, ladies," he said cheerfully. Fabre could see at a glance that the pair were not serious art buyers. More likely newly arrived students from some distant spot on the globe, come to study painting at the world's mecca for art and art students. In fact, he was thinking, they look young enough to be my daughters. Fabre was at heart a nice man and instantly decided to be nice to Raluca and Alicia.

"Bonjour," Raluca said. With her right hand she motioned Fabre to join her at his window display. Raluca pointed to the reclining woman in Matisse's painting. She was lying next to a vase holding red and green flowers and a bowl with three reddish fish swimming languidly. Then Raluca pointed to herself. She opened her right hand and slowly passed it from her face down past her small breasts and abdomen. Then she smiled at Fabre, hoping that her amateurish charade had created understanding.

She had succeeded. "Model," Fabre said, smiling. "You want work as a model."

"Raluca!" cried Alicia. She was aghast, her voice rising to near panic. "That woman is naked!"

"She is," Raluca replied, smiling agreeably. "But you can't make out her face. No eyes, no nose or mouth. Only a blank area. And her breasts, you can see only one nipple and just barely."

"But the model," Alicia protested, "she had to lay naked for the painter."

"True, but with nice flowers and pretty little fish to look at. The work does not look so hard." She smiled wryly at her friend. "Not at all like following oxen through a muddy field."

25

Alicia wasn't so fortunate in finding work. Though pretty, her five feet two inches were less appealing to artists who much preferred posing Raluca's lithe three additional inches, all in her slender legs. Instead, Alicia found labor along the nearby Seine, unloading cargos of grain and milled flour from boats arriving from French farms. The work was steady but hard. With each lift, sometimes 50 to 60 pounds, Alicia grunted. She wore a black wool cap with a short bill, her brown cloth coat and heavy black pants. She didn't try to mask her gender, but as one of few women working on the quay she didn't want to dress in a way that would encourage unwanted attention from rough-looking men who spoke coarsely and cursed often.

Raluca's modeling proved unsteady and, through one of the neighborhood artists, she found work clerking a few hours a week in one of Paris' ubiquitous flower shops.

Their apartment was on Rue Suger, a tiny street no longer or wider than an alley and squeezed in just two blocks south of the Seine. The cramped flat the girls occupied was scarcely more spacious than a large closet. They shared a bathroom at the end of the hallway with their neighbors. Privacy was at a premium, and accommodation a necessity. Glimpses of neighbors' bare bottoms and genitals occasioned embarrassment. Still, in those early months, Raluca and Alicia were thrilling to their new environment. In free time they sunned themselves in the Tuileries Gardens that stretched for blocks just across the Seine from their own cozy neighborhood. They visited the Louvre, marveling at its vast array of masterful creations. They relished strolling the sidewalks on either side of the broad Champs Elysees. Fashionably attired Parisians aroused envy but also heightened hope and determination to better their station. Raluca and Alicia stood in wonderment, their eyes following upward the graceful lines of the Eiffel Tower. "She would put me to shame as a model," Raluca said reverentially. "Stylish, long legs. A small waist. But," she smiled self-deprecatingly, "hips no bigger than mine."

Early one practically perfect Saturday morning, the girls had gone hiking up to Sacre Couer, the stunning white church with the Byzantine dome that majestically crowned Montmarte, the highest point of land in Paris.

At the summit the girls were short of breath and perspiring. "It was a long and steep climb, like the hills behind our farms," Alicia said.

"But no wild boars," Raluca smiled.

They then fell silent. They raptly took in the broad panorama that now lay far below their feet. Straight ahead, two miles distant, Notre Dame rose from the island in the Seine. Their eyes easily spotted the Eiffel Tower, some three miles to the southwest.

After several minutes, Alicia murmured, "Did you ever imagine you could see so many beautiful sights that are free?"

"No," said Raluca, "but that price is the most we can afford."

Prices were never a concern for Meredith Forbes. Her tastes were far from extravagant, and she had taken care to not let ostentation rise as a barrier between her and Joshua and his more modest means.

Still, Meredith wanted for nothing material. Her father Russell was unfailingly generous with all three daughters. He often impressed Meredith with his prescience; he frequently anticipated her desires and needs and didn't wait to be asked to satisfy them. Indeed, Meredith had seldom asked for anything. Occasionally she took pleasure in substituting creativity for gaudy expenditure. That was evidenced on October 31, 1936.

Some decidedly non-academic traditions had taken root at Stanford. One centered on Halloween. Each year students delighted in staging a raucous, costume party at the Stanford family's on-campus mausoleum. The imposing structure resembled a Greek temple. Flanking the steps to the entrance was a pair of reclining male sphinxes. At the mausoleum's rear was a pair of female sphinxes with bare breasts.

Masks hid identities, costumes sometimes confused genders and beer fueled whimsy. Slow-burning torches provided just enough illumination to lend the scene a ghostly aura.

"You want me to go as what?" Joshua asked incredulously.

"We'll make the perfect couple," Meredith replied cheerily. "A classic study in polar opposites."

Meredith proceeded to fashion white sheets into a silly looking gown. The hem was ragged, the neckline an off-center V. From thick, red paper she created a crown with uneven points. She applied deep crimson lipstick above and below her eyes. She then smeared it generously on, below and above her lips, with streaks rising to the outside edges of her eyes. She studied herself in a dorm room mirror affixed to the back of her closet door. "There," she said, laughing giddily, "you now see Princess Devilette."

She walked to the Main Quad's courtyard and awaited Joshua's arrival. Minutes later she saw him approaching with a suitable swagger.

"Perfect, Bliss! Just perfect."

"I guess so — if I were going to be terrorizing children in a country town."

Joshua was a study in black. Boots, pants, shirt and a broad-brimmed sombrero – all from a Palo Alto costume shop that loved outfitting a Stanford Indian football player, free of charge. (Decades later, in a move born of political correctness or racial sensitivity, the school would change the nickname of its athletic teams to the Cardinal – singular not plural.) Joshua had smudged his eyes – above them as well as below – with the burnt cork he used to reduce the sun's glare during Saturday afternoon football games. Across his nose and mouth was a black kerchief tied behind his head.

"I anoint you the The Blackheart Kid," Meredith giggled. "The baddest of silver screen bad guys."

Joshua extended his right arm, bent at the elbow. He pointed his forefinger and cocked his thumb. "Stick 'em up, Princess," he growled menacingly, "or I'll pump you full of lead."

"Oh, gracious me," she pleaded in mock terror, "please put your gun away. I will do your bidding, Kid Blackheart. Just don't hurt me."

"I like my women saucy. Do you have sauce?"

"I buy it by the barrel and slather it on my steak every day."

"Steak? I'm a chicken and fish kind of guy."

"Then let's go fishing. You bring the bait and I'll bring the sauce."

"You," Joshua glared, "are the sauce – and the bait."

"So you will catch me and eat me too?"

"And love every nibble."

The party proved cathartic. For both Joshua and Meredith it served as a welcome break from the rigors of studying. For Joshua it also brought a gleeful respite from a football team rule prohibiting alcohol consumption. Beer kegs abounded and liquor bottles lined the steps of the mausoleum. And they were legal as the 18th – or Prohibition – Amendment to the U.S. Constitution had been repealed fewer than two years earlier in December 1933. But during nearly 15 years of Prohibition, alcohol consumption at Stanford hadn't noticeably waned. Students had shown themselves creative and determined purchasing agents.

Joshua knocked back several sudsy brews, said little, belched several times and was confident his identity would remain a Halloween mystery.

Princess Devilette matched The Blackheart Kid beer for frothy beer.

Shortly after midnight, the Princess and The Kid shuffled and stumbled their way back across campus to the Main Quad. In the courtyard Princess Devilette fell against The Blackheart Kid's chest. She burped loudly and giggled.

"You are tight," Joshua mumbled. "You are pie-eyed tight."

"You're darn tootin' I am, Bliss."

After a long moment, Meredith raised her head. "You jus' wait," she said, slurring and swallowing letters. "This princess and bad guy will live happly ever after." She sniffed with faux haughtiness. "Tha's the way fairy tales sposed to end."

CHAPTER 8

Christmas season, 1936.

Cold, wet and windy described the weather in Paris the week before Christmas. Alicia Domian was feeling its brunt. On the Seine's south side quay, she was helping unload sacks of flour from a riverboat. In the wind-whipped mist, the work took on an extra measure of difficulty. To keep the sacks as dry as possible, she and her fellow laborers had to move quickly, removing protective canvas tarpaulins, loading the sacks onto the high beds of horse-drawn wagons and then quickly re-covering the bags with the tarps. She was grateful whenever motorized trucks with enclosed rears made the pickups. They meant less arduous lifting and no need to cover sacks on rainy days. The work was draining and the pay unremarkable.

On this day, her work completed, at 2 p.m., Alicia stood, wet hands resting against her hips. She looked across the Seine at Notre Dame's gray towers. Our dear mother in heaven, she reflected, I am far from home for the first time at Christmas. I am grateful for the freedom that is Paris. I have seen and learned much. But I fear this work will make me old as fast as farming in Romania. What should I do?

It was seven hours earlier in Shelby and smiles abounded. Joshua and Meredith were standing before the altar inside expansive and ornate Most Pure Heart of Mary Church. Father Albert Fate was presiding – after he had facilitated, in his experience, an unprecedented long-distance conversion of Meredith from Presbyterianism to Catholicism. Exchanges of telegrams and letters had replaced in-person instruction. Father Fate, a strong adherent of Catholic dogma and church rules and typically unbending, wavered after receiving a rare long-distance phone call. It had come from Russell Forbes who had emphasized how important it was to his Protestant daughter to wed Joshua in his hometown Catholic church. Russell then had suggested to Father Fate, gently but clearly, that he would like to contribute significantly to helping reduce the massive debt the parish had incurred when the dictatorial priest had accomplished his grand goal of building what amounted to a cathedral in the small town.

The lovingly painted, heavy-beamed ceiling peaked more than 50 feet from the floor. The interior was eye-popping. The mammoth center altar, the three smaller side altars and the statues above them and the communion rail all were sculpted from polished Italian white marble. The floors of the three long aisles were pink and gray marble. Eight massive granite pillars, each with the girth of a mature sugar maple tree, lined each side of the church's main body. Paintings were everywhere. All were done by European artists Father Fate had brought to the U.S. Along each sidewall were two banks of soaring stained glass windows. In 1924 parishioners had seen his plan as excessive zeal at best and, at worst, outright lunacy. Congregants had pressured him to develop a more modest alternative. They had failed. The church had been dedicated on June 15, 1928.

Meredith's sister Clarisse was flanking her. Joshua's brother Paul was serving as best man. Russell, Victoria and Christine were sitting in the front row on the left side – facing the altar – of the center aisle. With them were Clarisse's husband, George Morgan, and Christine's, Donald Halston. Joshua's parents, Noah and Goldie, were seated in the front row opposite.

Victoria couldn't help gawking. She had expected the wedding venue in this rural, midwest community to be a sorry excuse for a house of worship, not at all suitable for her youngest daughter's nuptials. Father Fate, she concluded quickly, was a man of vision, sorely out of place in a small town that she regarded as bumkinesque. He needs to be in New York, she was thinking.

Raluca was lying naked on a settee and she was chilly. The raw, wet wind was penetrating the cramped studio's windows. "How much longer until we finish today?" she asked.

"Perhaps another thirty minutes," Jean-Claude Romaine replied. In his mid-40s, he was darkly handsome, black-haired and sported a thick mustache streaked with the same gray that was coloring his temples. He was painting a landscape in which a nude was reclining beside a narrow stream. Not terribly original work was Raluca's verdict, but he was paying her. "The light is fading fast," said Jean-Claude.

"Not fast enough," Raluca grumbled. She shivered.

Romaine stepped away from his canvas. He carried his stool to the settee, put it down and sat. He studied Raluca's form. Nothing unusual about that and Raluca had become accustomed to having artists scrutinize her body and instruct her on the nuances of poses they wanted. They were consistently very detailed – "picky," thought Raluca. He reached down and cupped her chin between his forefinger and thumb. That was unusual. "I am thinking," he said slowly, "that perhaps we should end now."

"Good," said Raluca, starting to rise.

Romaine moved his hand from her chin to her small right breast and applied gentle, firm pressure. "It is the holiday season," he said, "and we should share some good cheer."

Raluca's right hand pushed against his. He resisted. She was torn. In surging anger she wanted to strike his face. But he employed her often and paid her promptly if not generously. She controlled her ire.

"Sex," she said firmly, "is not part of our agreement."

"A virgin?"

"Yes."

"In Paris. But why?"

"Because I am worth more than you are paying me."

"What if I paid you more?"

"I don't think you could afford me."

"Shall we discuss price?"

"Not now." She paused, her mind racing. "After Christmas."

The Forbes family was staying at the Hotel Shelbian on North Gamble Street. The wedding reception was being held in the hotel's modest ballroom.

After dinner Russell asked Joshua to step outside. Fronting the hotel was a covered porch that spanned its width.

"Would you like to try one of my cigars?"

"Never smoked one."

Russell smiled kindly. "Seems like a fine occasion to be initiated into one of life's more sublime pleasures."

"You are very persuasive."

"Bankers need to be," Russell chortled self-deprecatingly. His right hand slipped beneath his suit jacket to an inside pocket. When it emerged it was holding two cigars. "Macanudos. The best."

"I would be expecting nothing but the best from a successful banker. No sarcasm intended."

"None taken." Russell was a senior vice president and officer of Chemical Bank, headquartered at 277 Park Avenue in midtown Manhattan. Founded in 1824, the bank originally was a division of New York Chemical Manufacturing Company that had made blue vitriol, alum, nitric acid, camphor, saltpeter, medicine, paints and dyes. After the bank was spun off, it invested in numerous industries and later bought Red Star Line, a shipping company based in Amsterdam.

"I confess," Joshua said lightly, "that I've never smoked anything. Not even the first cigarette. I was tempted to try a pipe because they smelled so good when my friends smoked them."

Russell fished in his left suit jacket pocket and brought out a silver-jacketed Ronson lighter. "Bite off the end of your cigar," he instructed. Joshua did so and spit the nub onto the sidewalk. Russell snapped open the lighter and a flame leaped up. "Hold your cigar to the flame and draw on it. Don't inhale, though. No need for that." Again, Joshua did as told. "Now," Russell coached him, "let the smoke escape your mouth and blow gently." Joshua did so, and a bluish ring of smoke drifted upward. "Take another puff and let it out." Russell waited for Joshua to repeat the procedure. "Well?"

"I like it. Tastes darned good. Very rich tasting."

"Ah, glad you like it." A pause while Russell lit his own Macanudo. "Cuban," he smiled after drawing on the flame and expelling the richly scented smoke. "The best. I don't mean to be nosy, although you could argue I am, but what are your plans after graduating?"

"I'm not sure yet. Maybe stay in California." He puffed the cigar again. "It's growing rapidly. I don't see myself coming back to Shelby. I don't think that would be fair to Meredith. She's a city girl."

"I don't disagree with that," Russell smiled. "You might want to keep New York in mind. Or at least don't rule it out yet."

"Fair enough."

"Good. Look, if you two do come to New York, I'm certain we could find a good spot at the bank for a Stanford economics major. Especially," he grinned, "one who appreciates a fine cigar."

"Or," Joshua grinned, "who has married the boss's daughter."

Russell raised his right hand, the one holding his cigar, and gestured as though signaling caution. "Just one of the bosses. I'm not the president."

"Not yet," Joshua replied. "Your offer is very kind, but for now I'd prefer to say, 'We'll see.'"

"Understood," Russell said and he did. "You want to make your own way on your own terms. Very commendable. But do keep in mind that I have contacts virtually everywhere – other banks, accounting firms, shipping lines – we own Red Star – trading companies. Lots of different firms."

"Well, sir-"

"Russell. Please call me Russell."

"Okay. I have six months to go before graduation. I'll talk all this over with Meredith and then we'll decide."

"That's fine."

"We'll try to have a decision made by the end of March – after spring break."

"Alicia, we should write letters – Christmas letters – to our families."

"I have never written a letter."

The two girls, now nearing 17, were sitting in their tiny apartment. The building was ill-heated, and both were wearing their caps, coats and gloves.

"Neither have I. But then," Raluca smiled, "we've been doing lots of things we had never done before."

"I'm not sure I could write a letter. It sounds difficult."

"Not to worry. Tomorrow we will go to a stationery shop and buy paper and envelopes."

"And a pen and ink?"

"Of course, we must. We wouldn't want to write our first letters with a cheap pencil. Then you will tell me what you want to say to your parents and your brothers, and I will write it. They will be thrilled."

After the Forbes left Shelby for New York on board a New York Central train, Joshua and Meredith stayed on for a few days. After two nights at the Hotel Shelbian, they moved to the Bliss farm where they moved into Joshua's former room.

"Do you feel funny – awkward – sleeping with me in your parents' house?" Meredith asked on their first night.

"Well," Joshua chuckled lowly, "it does make for an unusual honeymoon. We'll do better after we graduate."

"Actually, this seems quite romantic," Meredith whispered in Joshua's left ear. "We'll just be a little quieter than we were at the hotel."

"Hmm, these springs do squeak," Joshua teased. "We wouldn't want Mom or Dad thinking their new daughter-in-law is wild in the sack." A pause. "Even though she is. But I like wild."

"Do you know the real reason I love you?" Meredith asked, eyes twinkling.

"Uh oh. I sense a deep dark secret about to be revealed."

Meredith giggled. "You're thinning and well along to being bald."

"You've noticed." Only a few strands remained atop Joshua's skull.

"Hard not to." A brief pause. "It's good though."

"Why?"

"It shows you don't fake."

"Uh, I don't follow you."

"Some young men losing their hair would let it grow long on the side and comb it over. Or buy a wig."

Joshua chuckled and rolled his head against the feather-filled pillow. "A farm boy wearing a wig. Dad and Paul wouldn't stop razzing me. Even the pigs would probably snort in derision."

"Does it bother you? Going bald so young?"

"It did at first. Then one day Dad saw me putting on a jacket and looking in the hallway mirror. It's like he was reading my mind. He said, 'Hair doesn't make the man.' I knew he was right. So, Meredith Forbes Bliss, let me ask you: Does my baldness bother you? Even a little?"

Her reaction was wordless. She reached over, pulled Joshua's head toward her and kissed its nearly hairless crown.

Raluca placed the second sheet of paper on the bed she and Alicia shared. Then she picked up the first sheet and re-read Alicia's letter aloud.

22 December 1936

Dear Mother and Father,

Paris is such a beautiful place. There are no mountains like the Apuseni and Carpathians, but the cathedral, churches, monuments, gardens and museums are all wonderful. We have taken long walks almost everywhere. This has been a good adventure.

Please do not worry about me. I have steady work, we have enough to eat – lots of wonderful French bread and cheese – and Raluca and I enjoy sharing our little apartment. We live only two blocks from the Seine River.

I miss you and the boys very much. Please tell Nicolae and Leo their big sister said that. I wish you a happy Christmas.

With all my love, your daughter,
Alicia

Raluca handed the letter to Alicia. "Does it still sound the way you want it to? If you are not happy with it, I can do it over. We have more paper – two sheets."

"No. I think it is perfect. Thank you."

"Good. We will fold the letters and put them in these envelopes and seal them. Tomorrow we will go to the post office to buy stamps."

"Wait."

"What is it?"

"Don't seal the envelopes yet."

"Why?"

"There is something I want to talk about."

Funk Road was snow-covered and slippery so the three riders were guiding their horses across the Bliss farm's expansive wheat field.

"I'm glad you got the third horse, Paul," Joshua said. "Maisy makes a nice girlfriend for Beau and Duke."

"Actually," said Paul, "getting her was Mom and Dad's idea. They figured since you were bringing Meredith here we all might want to go riding. Parents. Just when you think they can't surprise you again, wham!"

Joshua laughed. "And who says farm people are boring and predictable?"

"After you guys leave, we'll keep Maisy," Paul said. "Maybe offer riding lessons for Shelby girls."

"That's very sweet of them," said Meredith. "It's really easy to get to like your parents."

The horses were enjoying the winter exercise. Their hoofs were kicking up snow, and they were holding their heads high, forcefully blowing out breaths that crystallized when colliding with the late December air.

"What's after graduation?" Paul asked.

"Could be California but probably New York," Joshua replied. "Hey! Why not come with us?"

"Oh sure. A threesome riding horses across an open field is one thing. But three of us traveling together to New York and you two as newlyweds. Sounds pretty darned crowded to me."

"We could make it work," said Joshua.

"Yes," Meredith said excitedly. "We can get an apartment with an extra bedroom until you get your own place. I could introduce you to some of my friends."

"Uh huh," Paul said dubiously. "What would I do? Remember, I'm a farm boy." A pause, then Paul's voice turned somber. "If I don't keep farming, what will happen after Mom and Dad are too old to keep it going?"

"Sell it," Joshua said.

Paul reacted viscerally, rocking back on his saddle. "That's a terrible thought. It would kill Mom and Dad."

"You mean if farming doesn't?"

Raluca peered intently into Alicia's brown eyes. "What do you want to talk about? What is wrong?" She draped her left arm across Alicia's shoulders.

"I am tired. Cold and tired. My work is hard. I am used to hard work, but this isn't why I left Romania. Not to work hard every day and barely make enough money to help us live on. We have saved only a little."

"Do you want to go home?" Raluca asked softly.

"I don't know. No. Not yet. I am just tired of being tired. And tired of being cold, dirty and still poor."

"I understand."

"I know you do. I am sorry. I won't complain any more."

"Don't be sorry. I am glad you told me."

"Really?"

"Really. You know my modeling doesn't pay much either. There are too many girls willing to pose."

"But not many who are so beautiful as you – and with your long legs and coloring."

"That's a problem."

"What do you mean?"

"Jean-Claude is pressuring me to have sex with him. If I don't he has made it clear that he will tell other artists that I am being difficult and they won't hire me."

"That is awful."

"That is reality."

"If you do – have sex with him, then what?"

"I would be doing it for money. Not love. And if I am going to do it for money, I want it to be for more than a poor painter can afford. And I am like you."

"What do you mean?"

"I am also tired of being cold and poor."

"Your job at the flower shop?"

"I like it. The people are nice. But it is only a few hours a week."

Alicia smiled, turned toward Raluca and reached out. The girls embraced warmly. After releasing each other, Raluca spoke. "I think I now know why you didn't want to seal the letters." Alicia nodded. "We will add – to each letter – that we are leaving Paris."

"For where?"

"Amsterdam."

"Oh. Oh my. You mean-"

"Yes. But we will not be too descriptive in the letters. I doubt if our parents know Amsterdam's reputation. We will simply write that we are moving there for a better opportunity. And that is true. I think we can earn more money."

"But-"

"I know what you are thinking. We talked about it back on the farms. We will do what we have to do, but only as long as necessary."

The crowing rooster again roused Meredith. She yawned widely and snuggled cozily against Joshua. She was wearing a long flannel night gown – courtesy of Goldie – and Joshua his old pajamas that he hadn't needed at Stanford where winter was more like an Ohio spring – cooler and wetter than summer but not requiring heavy night clothes.

"It's barely light out, Bliss," Meredith said with a hint of protest. She blinked several times and yawned again.

"That's the idea. The rooster wants to be sure his hens get an early start in the egg laying department."

"Do they lay every day?"

"Almost always. Some of them sometimes twice a day."

"What do your parents do with all the eggs?"

"Eat some, sell some, give some away."

"They've made quite a life for themselves."

"Do you think Amsterdam will give us the life we are looking for?" Alicia asked. "I mean, eventually."

She and Raluca were striding purposely north from their apartment on Rue Suger. They had crossed the Seine and were carrying their cloth bags beneath a canopy of trees up the grade that was Rue du Fauborg St. Denis toward Gare du Nord. That station accommodated train traffic from and to the north and was only a few hundred yards farther north than Gare de l' Est that served trains steaming from and to the east.

"We can't be certain," Raluca answered, "but we will do our best."

"I am frightened – all over again."

"Me too."

"Sex. Another strange city. Strange food, strange people."

"We will need to be strong."

"So once again we are being brave," Alicia smiled wryly.

"You are a clever girl," Raluca said admiringly. "Brave and clever."

"If we work as prostitutes, I think we will need to be very brave."

"Try not to worry about it," Raluca said soothingly.

"Are you worried?"

"Yes, but I am trying not to be."

Gare du Nord's broad, gray façade was coming into view.

"There is something else," Alicia said. "We have been learning quite a lot of French. Now we must learn another language. Dutch, or English."

"English?"

"Yes. I think many Dutch people speak English. That is what I have heard."

Meredith had finished breakfast. She pulled on a borrowed red stocking cap with white stripes and a heavy gray coat and stepped outside into the bracing air. Joshua still was inside, sipping coffee and chatting with Goldie and Noah.

Paul was emerging from the huge, white barn. "Morning, Meredith!" he said brightly.

"You're up early."

"No earlier than usual. Sleep well?"

"Very. Well, until the rooster crowed."

Paul laughed. "He was just letting us know he and his hens are ready and waiting for their breakfast. Come here."

Meredith followed Paul inside the barn door. He opened the latch on the hinged top of a large wood box. He reached in and lifted a burlap sack.

"What's in it?" Meredith asked.

"Chicken feed," Paul answered.

"Why the latch?"

"Raccoons. They're smart critters. They would have this box open in a flash without the latch. Follow me."

Paul led Meredith about 50 feet to a long white chicken coop fronted by a fenced-in enclosure.

"Why the wire across the top? Raccoons?"

"Yes, and hungry foxes."

Paul opened the gate to the enclosure and immediately was surrounded by madly clucking hens. "Here," he said to Meredith, opening the burlap sack, "make new friends. Grab a handful of the feed and toss it on the ground."

"What is it?"

"Mostly dried corn but chickens will eat most anything and everything. Amazing how most of it comes out as beautiful eggs."

Meredith scooped a handful of the feed and tossed it. The hens, wings flapping, immediately and contentiously began devouring their breakfast.

"We'll come back in a while," said Paul, "and collect eggs inside the coop."

"Are you trying to make a farm girl out of me?"

"You could do worse."

"Now what?"

"Follow me."

Paul led Meredith to a fenced-in pen on the north side of the barn. "Hey, pigs," he called, "time for chow." Then he rustled the bag of feed. In the next instant husky black and white pigs – some 35 in all – came charging and stumbling through a small portal in the barn's wall.

"They're not very polite to each other," Meredith said wryly. "Banging into each other. You need to teach them manners, Paul."

"I'll work on that. Okay," he told Meredith, "reach in the bag and start throwing them feed."

Meredith did as instructed and marveled at the swirling, grunting porcine mass. "Ugly, aren't they?" she asked rhetorically.

"It's their big flat noses and scanty body hair. But, Meredith, I can assure you that a well-fed hog looks mighty handsome to sows."

"You love it here, don't you, Paul?"

"I do."

The train was rolling north from Gare du Nord and would first take Raluca and Alicia through Belgium with stops in Brussels and Antwerp. Then after passing into The Netherlands, the train would cross rivers and canals and stop at Rotterdam and The Hague before arriving in Amsterdam.

"This land," observed Alicia, "it is so flat. Nothing at all like Romania. Not even a Montmarte."

"Agreed," said Raluca, "but Holland seems to have a quiet beauty. Look at the windmills. They are like friendly giants with four arms, waving greetings to us. And look at all the cows in the fields. The Dutch must drink a lot of milk and eat a lot of cheese. I think in the spring we will see more flowers than we have ever seen anywhere. That's what I heard at the flower shop in Paris."

"You see beauty everywhere," Alicia said admiringly.

"I am beginning to think there are people and things of beauty and interest everywhere on earth."

"Well, I hope we find beautiful people in Amsterdam."

CHAPTER 9

In Rotterdam, four blades were skimming across the hard surface of the Noordsingel, a narrow canal about one-half mile south of 24 Jacob Catsstraat, home of Anneke Azijn. It was the day after Chrismas 1936, and she and Stefaan Janssen were ice skating. They were gliding athletically side-by-side and smiling contentedly.

When not atop her white skates, Anneke stood five feet five inches and weighed a trim 115 pounds. Blond hair framed a high cheek-boned face. Blue eyes radiated intelligence and wit. When not smiling, a serious mien reflected her strong work ethic. She had graduated from high school and was working as a secretary for the Holland-America Line that was headquartered at 110 Otto Reuchlinweg, a broad, bulky, four-story red brick building on the waterfront. She was learning English quickly among the multilingual staff.

Stefaan's hair also was northern European blond, but the remainder of his appearance contrasted sharply with Anneke's. He was burly. His five feet seven inches supported 180 solid pounds. They were put to use daily in his job as a stevedore, working the docks in Rotterdam's sprawling port facilities, then the world's busiest. Stefaan was jovial, a personality that seemed to match his open, congenial visage. On skates he flew, often laughing as Anneke tried gamely but futilely to match his powerful, long strides.

Both were 17. They were in love and had been since they had begun dating in high school.

As they went gliding down the canal, Anneke said, "Do you know why I love you?"

"It must be because of my movie-star looks and brilliant mind," Stefaan replied, laughing.

"Ha! Actually it is because of where you live – on Vergeetmijnstraat." Forget-Me-Not Street was about two and a half miles northwest of Anneke's home. "That's the only reason I didn't forget about you after our first date."

"Thank God my parents picked the right street to live on."

"There is one other reason I love you." A pause.

"I am waiting."

"You kiss well." And with that, Anneke leaned toward Stefaan and pushed hard, causing his balance to falter. He went down in a graceless, skidding heap.

Anneke laughed loudly and went skating away. Stefaan quickly regained his footing and shouted, "You will soon have another reason not to forget me." He went racing after her.

That same morning another couple was ice skating. Karl and Hannah Kramer, both born in 1916, were newlyweds, and the skating was serving as a departure from their frequent and spirited conjugal exercise.

"We should give our bed springs a rest," Hannah had joked.

"You are right," Karl had responded. "We should exercise a different set of muscles."

They were skimming the frozen surface of the Dreisam River that bisected their hometown of Freiburg.

The city, situated in the extreme southwest of Germany and just across the Rhine River from France, was founded in 1120. The city's descriptive name translates as Fortified Free Town. It sits in the shadow of the Schlossberg, a forested hill.

Freiburg was renowned as the site of Alfred Ludwig University, and that's where Karl was proceeding toward a degree in history that he expected to complete in another six months – June 1937. His ultimate student goal was a doctorate in history with an emphasis on America's past. The young nation that traced its origins to western Europe intrigued him. That hundreds of thousands of Germans had emigrated to America further heightened his zeal to study its history. After earning his graduate degree, he was hoping to secure a professorship at his alma mater.

Hannah's formal education had ended with high school graduation. She was working as a waitress in a winstub in the town's picturesque central square – stone-paved Augustinerplatz.

Freiburg possessed another distinction – its unusual system of gutters. They were open, shallow, narrow channels – only about three feet wide – that were created to speed the delivery of water for fire fighting and for watering livestock. The Dreisam River continually fed the gutters with fresh water. Officially the gutters were never to be used for carrying away sewage. Violations of that stricture could and did lead to harsh penalties, even as far back as the generally unhygienic Middle Ages. During warm weather, the flowing gutter water cooled the city's air. They also provided another sublime benefit – a pleasant, gurgling sound that promoted sleep for both babies and the elderly.

After some 45 minutes of skating, Karl and Hannah glided to the river bank, stopped, pirouetted and sat. They breathed deeply, exhaled, kissed and smiled. They pulled off their stocking caps and began removing their skates.

"The new year is almost here," said Hannah. "I am sure it will be a happy one."

"For us, yes," Karl replied meditatively.

"But not for everyone?"

"Not for Jews. Hitler and his cronies will see to that."

"You are right, of course," said Hannah. "His persecution of the Jews stains our nation's soul. We all should be ashamed."

"Many of us are," Karl said, "but not enough. Few dare to speak against Hitler. At least in public. He is proving ruthless to dissenters."

"Assassinations and concentration camps. Those are the fates that await brave Germans."

"Those fates are chilling the temptation to openly criticize him," Karl said. "I fear the history of Germany in the 1930s will be a sad commentary on a proud country that let a man of unbridled hatred rule with impunity."

"Where do you think Hitler is taking Germany?"

"Armageddon."

CHAPTER 10

It was a Tuesday morning in February 1937, and Meredith had two hours to spare before her next class. She headed to the apartment that she and Joshua shared above a cozy Italian restaurant – The Golden Bowl – that sat on the east side of University Avenue, just across Camino Real which marked the university's frontier with Palo Alto.

Meredith stepped inside the restaurant's entrance and to her left opened a second door that led to the staircase and their apartment. She inserted her key in the lock and turned it, simultaneously pushing open the door.

Inside she stood open-mouthed. Arrayed around the living room were seven of her student girlfriends. They said nothing but each bore a smile that smacked of eagerly awaited mischief.

Meredith, eyes narrowing, stood silently for a long moment. "Who let you in?"

The girls remained silent except for a lone giggle that escaped one's lips.

"Who told you?" she asked, understanding dawning. "Oh, of course, it was Josh."

At which point Joshua stepped into the living room from a hallway that led to the apartment's kitchen, bath and single bedroom. The girls looked at Joshua and he nodded.

The girls then advanced toward Meredith, shrilling joyously.

"At least," Meredith pleaded, "let me get my clothes off."

"Not on your life," one of the young women shouted.

The seven friends grabbed Meredith's arms and began pulling and pushing her across the room and down the hall.

"No use fighting it," Joshua laughed.

"You...I should have seen it coming."

"Right. I believe in upholding traditions."

The friends forced Meredith into the bathroom. One stepped to the tub and pulled the shower curtain aside. Then she turned the shower handle. Water began cascading forcefully.

"No problems with water pressure here," Joshua called above the girlish din.

The girls then lifted Meredith, fully clothed, into the tub and drew shut the curtain.

"How long do I have to stay in here?"

"Till you're soaked through to your birthday suit."

Thus was another Stanford tradition continued. At the university in the 1930s, tradition demanded that students be dunked in showers fully attired on their birthdays.

After three minutes that to Meredith seemed an eternity, one of the women yelled, "Okay, you can turn off the water."

Meredith complied and a second friend pulled aside the curtain. The women began applauding. Meredith was drenched from her blond hair downward. She broke into giddy laughter. "I'll bet Leland and Jane Stanford never saw a tradition like this taking hold."

From behind the laughing women, Joshua interrupted his chuckling long enough to add, "Their world-class university and high jinks are not proving to be incompatible."

Then Joshua and the women began serenading Meredith with a rousing *Happy Birthday.*

Alicia Domian couldn't help herself. She was staring, eyes wide and mouth agape. Raluca Johnescu gulped and blinked. Both were looking through a large window. Behind the glass, semi-reclining, lounged a nearly nude young woman. She was bathed in a flattering soft red glow. Amsterdam whores had long known that soft red light enhanced their appeal. As early as the 1300s, women carrying red lanterns met sailors arriving at the port.

Only the scantiest piece of pink cloth was covering the prostitute's genitals. She had arranged herself on a small, pink settee, and she was smiling seductively.

"I...I couldn't put myself on display like that," Alicia gasped. "And having sex in full view. I would rather starve."

Before Raluca could comment, a smartly dressed man – dark gray suit, white shirt, navy blue necktie – of middle age stepped past the girls to the window. He lowered his head in an almost imperceptible nod. The woman behind the window rose calmly and moved deliberately to open the door beside the window. The man stepped inside, and the two of them disappeared through a second door.

"They have sex in private," Raluca observed, recovering from her shock.

Alicia let out a long, slow breath. "Still, I could not display myself like that."

"I agree. We will find a brothel."

"What if we can't find one that will take us?"

"We would learn if a window is available or we could walk the streets. You can see others doing that." Which Alicia could, in fact, see clearly.

"That seems so disgusting. What if we find a brothel that will take only one of us – you?"

"We will stay together."

"Promise?"

"Promise."

Amsterdam's red light district, so named for the red bulbs outside brothel entrances, hadn't been difficult for Alicia and Raluca to find. It occupied some 7,000 square yards in the historic heart of the city that was founded about 1204 as a fishing village and had grown to become royal capital of The Netherlands.

The city lies at the junction of the Amstel River and the IJ, an arm of a lake called IJsselmeer. The city's name translates into English as *dam of the Amstel* and refers to a dam built at that junction in the late 1200s.

Amsterdam was situated 34 miles northeast of The Hague, actual seat of The Netherlands' central government, and 47 miles north of Rotterdam.

Raluca and Alicia had needed only 10 minutes walking south from Amsterdam's waterfront Centraal Railroad Station to reach the red light district. Once there red light bulbs signaled a welcome to a warren of narrow, stone-paved streets and alleys that paralleled and crossed canals and wound among buildings dating to the Middle Ages. The district included a stunning moral contradiction. At its center stood Oude Kerk (Dutch for Old Church), a magnificent Gothic house of worship dating to 1306. It was the city's oldest surviving structure. Capping its red brick tower were three tiers. The face of the lowest held a large clock with a handsome black face and gold-colored Roman numerals. The middle tier was circular and surrounded by slender gray stone pillars. The top tier, also constructed of gray stone, was six-sided with six open arches. Inside the tower was Amsterdam's oldest church bell, installed in 1450. Only about 500 yards southwest of Oude Kerk and on the fringe of the red light district sat the Royal Palace. Amsterdammers seemed not at all distressed by the close proximity of prostitution, church and royalty.

In fact prostitution's history in Amsterdam was as long as it was renowned. Prostitution was allowed there in the Middle Ages, but with restrictions. Whores couldn't be married, and married and Jewish men couldn't hire them. Otherwise, civic recognition, understanding and toleration were the municipal watchwords. A 1413 Amsterdam decree stipulated: *Because whores are necessary in big cities and especially in cities of commerce such as ours – indeed, it is far better to have these women than not to have them – and also because the holy church tolerates whores on good grounds, for these reasons the court and sheriff of Amsterdam shall not entirely forbid the keeping of brothels.*

During The Netherlands' golden 1600s when the small country dominated global exploration and trade, prostitution flourished and sexuality was openly on display in paintings and literature.

During the 1700s, Amsterdam prostitutes could have been accused of prudery. In copulating they tolerated only the mission position and standing upright, face-to-face. Taboo were oral sex, anal sex and kissing.

By the early 1900s most Amsterdam prostitutes were white, lower-class women from rural Holland, Belgium, France and northern Germany. Which is to say that most prostitutes looked like a Dutchman believed a proper Dutch woman should look – blond with blue eyes.

By the time Raluca and Alicia arrived, prostitution was regarded as central to Dutch culture. The red light district included some 300 window prostitutes. Many more populated brothels, and streetwalkers offered themselves throughout central Amsterdam. Raluca and Alicia were the vanguard of a stream of young women who would make their way after World War II from ravaged Eastern Europe to The Netherlands to work as whores. Their fundamental goal would be survival – escaping Soviet tyranny and grinding poverty.

In the afternoon Raluca eyed a red light outside a handsome four-story house on Molensteeg. The tree-shaded street originated in front of Oude Kerk and continued eastward across two of the city's narrower canals. The house was only three windows wide, typical in Amsterdam where property taxes were calculated on a building's width. Thrifty Dutch built narrow and high.

Raluca inhaled, pulled open a heavy wooden door and exhaled forcefully. Tentatively she stepped inside, followed closely by Alicia. The narrow but deep sitting room was decorated tastefully in muted colors. Two table lamps dimly illuminated the room.

A smartly dressed woman scrutinized the girls and their embroidered cloth bags. She was blond, shapely and lightly made up. With stylish high heels she stood five feet eight inches. To Raluca she appeared about the age of her mother Magdalena. One difference: This woman was not yet showing the lines that creased Magdalena's visage and resulted from physical labor and daily exposure to the elements.

"Hello," said the woman in Dutch. "I am Madame Clarbout – Anna Clarbout." When she saw the girls' puzzled expressions, Anna switched to French. "Bonjour. Comment vas-tu?"

"Tres bien," Raluca smiled slightly. "Mais fatigue."

"Arriver en train?"

"Oui. De Paris."

"Paris!" Anna's face brightened. "Please, come in and sit. Rest."

Raluca and Alicia placed their bags on the rose-colored carpet and sat on a pale green sofa. "You are French?" Raluca ventured.

"Lyon!" Anna paused. "You have come here looking for work. Is that right?"

The girls nodded, not eagerly as Anna noted. "We are hoping to better our lives."

"You are not French women," Anna observed, not condescendingly but appraisingly.

"We are Romanian."

"Gypsies?" Anna was hoping the answer would be no. As open-minded as she fancied herself, she was certain that few of her clients would buy the services of roving gypsies, and Anna wouldn't lie to her clients. Simply not good business, she knew.

"Romanian Orthodox," said Raluca. "Our families are farmers. They have lived on the same land for many generations."

"Good," Anna said quietly. The offspring of stability, she was thinking, and no doubt imbued with a strong work ethic. "You know the kind of work we do here."

"Yes," said Raluca.

"Are you experienced?" The girls shook their heads. "Nor was I when I came here from Lyon. Are you virgins?"

"Yes," Raluca murmured.

"Do you think you would like working here? For me?"

Raluca and Alicia looked at each other. Their eyes were saying, She seems nice. "Yes," they both answered quietly.

Anna's lips pursed and her eyes narrowed in contemplation. "You are not blond. But your coloring could be intriguing to some of our clients. Many of my clients – especially sailors – have seen and coupled with dark-haired women. So have my British clients – men here on business."

"So," Raluca said quietly, "you will hire us?"

"Yes. Now, here are the arrangements. First, I will buy you some nice new clothes – dresses and underwear. You will repay me from your earnings. That is business. You will work upstairs, mostly late at night. I will help you find rooms to rent in one of the neighborhood houses. That is where you will live."

"Not here?" Raluca asked softly.

"No. You are to regard this house only as your work place. Only I have an apartment here," Anna said, pointing toward the house's rear. "Now usually I permit clients to pick their girls. But because you are virgins, I will choose your first clients, and I will see that they treat you gently. And they will because," she smiled savvily, "I will make it clear that they must if they are to be welcome in my house again. Clear?"

The girls nodded. She is no Magdalena or Livia, Raluca was reflecting, but she does seem caring. "Payment?" Raluca asked timidly.

"Clients will pay me and I you. If your first clients are happy with you, I will want you to stay and so will pay you fairly." She studied their faces for signs of doubt and saw none. "You said you want to better yourselves, and I can help you do that. If you work hard and live frugally, you can save money. I have few rules but you must obey them. They mostly have to do with the way you will be expected to service our clients. Understood?"

"Yes," said both girls.

"Good. Now, first things first. I want you to try on some dresses so I know what sizes to buy. Then I will make a telephone call to check on the availability of rooms for you."

"Thank you," Raluca said.

"One more question," Anna said. "How old are you?"

"Seventeen," Raluca answered. "Both of us. Is that a problem?"

Anna shook her head. Sharp businesswoman though she was, maternal instincts sometimes began surfacing. This was one of those occasions, and she quickly tried quelling her protective urge. Had Raluca and Alicia been any younger, she knew she might have been tempted to tell them they would need to seek employment elsewhere. But, she was smiling inwardly, perhaps it is my mothering nature that has me taking in these refugees from rural dirt and poverty.

Anna had become a mother, once, when she was not yet 20. But the child, Marie, had contracted the flu during the global pandemic of 1918-1919 and died at three. Anna had never confided that fact to any of the prostitutes, not once in the 11 years she had owned the brothel. Nor had she had sex with a client. Bad for business she had concluded.

Anna's young husband had deserted her, and she had begun taking the path now being followed by Raluca and Alicia. "No, not a problem," she told them. "I think we will get along well together."

CHAPTER 11

Joshua pushed open the door to the second-floor apartment on University Avenue. It was 4 p.m. Meredith greeted him with a kiss and a hug. Joshua responded but with a noticeable lack of ardor.

"A penny for your thoughts, Bliss," she smiled. "You seem distracted."

Joshua sighed. "I guess I am."

"By what?"

"Oh, on the walk here from class I was thinking about what happens after graduation."

"My dad's offer?"

"Right. I know he means well, but…"

"You'd prefer to be your own man, make it all happen on your own."

"Do you see a problem with that?"

"Not at all, husband. That's just one of the things I love about you."

Joshua brightened. "Just one? What are the others? All of them?" he asked with a teasing grin.

"You're funny."

"That's me. Farm boy funny."

Meredith chuckled. "Want a glass of cold milk, farm boy? Not freshly squeezed but chilled in the fridge."

"Sounds good. After I take a leak."

"Sure," Meredith laughed, "go leak. And remember to lower the toilet seat when you're done."

"Ah," Joshua said, keeping a straight face, "an early lesson of married life."

He stepped around Meredith and headed down the hall to the bathroom. After urinating and washing and drying his hands – and lowering the toilet seat – he returned to the living room. No Meredith.

"In the bedroom, Bliss."

Joshua pivoted and walked back into the hall. The bedroom door stood slightly ajar. He pushed it open – and grinned, first in amusement and then with faux lasciviousness.

"I wouldn't want you thinking that your new bride is already predictable," Meredith cooed.

"You can bet I won't accuse you of that," Josh said, eyes gleaming.

"Can the milk wait, Bliss?" Meredith asked with the purr of a playful kitten.

"Until it sours," Josh replied.

Meredith was lying on their bed – naked with legs spread wide. "I decided you could use a different kind of refreshment. Not chilled. In fact, warm to the point of being hot."

"I can taste it already."

Raluca and Alicia were sitting on the pastel green sofa in the brothel's sitting room. They were wearing new dresses – white with frilly, high necklines. Beneath the dresses they were wearing fine cotton panties. It was 9:30 p.m.

Anna Clarbout entered the room from her apartment. "Girls," she said to Raluca and Alicia, "come with me."

They rose and followed Anna into her apartment, a sanctuary rarely seen by her whores. She motioned to a sofa – also pastel green. "Please sit." Anna waited while the girls sat and smoothed their dresses. "Tonight you will service your first clients." Immediately, both Raluca and Alicia felt their chests tighten with anxiety. Anna sensed their unease. "Try not to worry. I selected these clients for you as I promised I would. They came here last night, and when I saw them I thought they would be right to help you get started. They are businessmen from Brussels. Both speak French. Actually they also speak English. They were dressed well and seemed refined. I told them about you." Anna paused. The girls fidgeted, trying to calm screaming nerves. "They know you are virgins. I have told them they must be gentle with you – or else. I have told them they will each have only thirty minutes with you. They agreed. In return I told them they could kiss you. You have a responsibility – an obligation – to enjoy the kiss or successfully pretend you do. That is business.

"You will bleed, but don't worry. It is not dangerous because the clients will not be rough. I have put old thick towels in your chambers. They are clean. When you lie down on the bed, be sure to put the towels under your bottom. They will absorb your blood and keep it from staining the sheets. Because you are virgins, I have told the clients they must pay double. They agreed. You will receive your normal pay. The extra money will reimburse me for your new dresses. Understand?"

"Yes," Raluca said, barely above a whisper.

"Now, go upstairs to the third floor and take the two chambers at the end of the hall. I will bring the clients up and review our agreement with them. When they enter, let them take your dresses off." Alicia shuddered. "That also is part of the agreement. But be sure they are hung up neatly. You remove your panties. After the kissing the clients will touch you. If they do it well, it should feel good. And you should not be afraid to let them know it. When they enter you, it will not feel good, not this first time. Try not to cry. If the clients like you, they will return. That will be good business – for you and me."

CHAPTER 12

The celebrating that attended Joshua and Meredith's graduation had ended. They had bussed from Palo Alto to San Francisco where they entrained and crossed the country to New York. Joshua was immersing himself in his job as a loan review specialist.

"It's really risk management," Joshua explained to Meredith. "I get to apply some of my economics studies with straightforward financial management." He had put misgivings aside and accepted Russell Forbes' offer of a job in Chemical Bank's Park Avenue offices.

Meredith was thrilled by the job she had landed quickly. Starting in September she would be teaching ninth and tenth grade English at Loyola School, a smallish high school founded in 1900 by the Jesuits. She also loved the school's location – 980 Park Avenue – only two blocks east from the oasis that was Central Park and just a few blocks' walk from the cozy apartment she and Joshua were renting on tree-shaded East 72nd Street between Third and Second Avenues.

Early on the last Saturday morning in June, Joshua and Meredith had ridden with Russell and Victoria to the Forbes' cottage at Montauk Point, 120 miles east of Manhattan at the tip of Long Island where Long Island Sound met the Atlantic Ocean. So different from Manhattan was its tranquility that it might as well have been on another planet. Once there the foursome had set about preparing the makings for a picnic on the beach.

From the cottage Joshua hefted a large wicker picnic hamper out onto the sand.

"That's what you get for being a college football player," Russell kidded Joshua. "You get to do all the heavy lifting."

Russell carried two bottles of wine and a corkscrew, and Meredith a large blue blanket to spread on the hot sand. Victoria followed with four long-stemmed wine glasses. Russell and Joshua were sporting beige slacks and white shirts open at the collar. Victoria and Meredith were attired in summery linen dresses. Victoria also was wearing a broad-brimmed white bonnet while Meredith was hatless as were the men. All four were wearing white canvas shoes.

The breeze blowing in from the Atlantic was proving a welcome tonic, relieving the group from the suffocating heat and humidity that was drenching denizens of un-air-conditioned Manhattan buildings. The picnic menu included breaded fried chicken, brie, freshly baked bread, newly picked grapes and Riesling from France's Alsace.

"I hear you've been catching on fast at the bank," Russell said.

"Thanks," Joshua smiled. "Word must ride the elevators from my humble office up to mahogany row."

"Yes and they're high-speed elevators," Russell replied. "But I knew a Stanford economics major could handle anything thrown at him."

"My supervisor is a good man. Very knowledgeable and an excellent teacher."

"So I've heard. And," Russell added, turning toward Meredith, "speaking of teaching, have you met with the other teachers at Loyola?"

"Not yet. The principal, Father Walsh, told me we would have staff meetings in early August. I can hardly wait."

"I wish they were paying you more," Victoria said abruptly. "I hear the Jesuits have very healthy bank accounts. They should use them to pay highly qualified teachers salaries commensurate with the elite students they accept." There was no mistaking the acid in her tone.

Joshua's eyes rolled upward. Meredith deftly ignored her mother's jibe.

"Josh and I feel very fortunate to have good jobs when so many Americans are out of work and in bread lines and soup kitchens."

"Well stated," Russell said, complimenting his daughter and avoiding eye contact with Victoria.

"We are blessed with all this food," Joshua said. "And you know what I like best about being here today? Well," he said, grinning, "apart from this fine company."

"I know," Meredith said brightly.

"Give us a clue," Russell smiled.

"Blue," Meredith obliged.

"The ocean?" said Russell.

"The water," Meredith clarified. "Our farm boy became very fond of water while at Stanford."

"She's right," said Joshua. "I wanted to see the Pacific and the bay as much as possible."

"Why?" Victoria asked.

"I think because on the water the horizons aren't interrupted. You can see much farther."

"But," Victoria challenged him, "there's really nothing to see."

Now it was Meredith's eyes that were rolling upward.

"Well actually," Joshua replied calmly, "it's what you can imagine. The water seems to free up my thinking. I think about things differently."

"More creatively?" Russell asked.

"Exactly. When I'm on the water or just looking at it, my mind sees lots of dots and how to connect them."

"Well put, Josh," said Russell. "I have a feeling you are going to connect lots of dots in your life."

"At least it doesn't hurt anymore," said Raluca. "Madame Clarbout was right about the first time."

"I will never forget it," said Alicia. "I am glad the room was almost dark. Just one dim light bulb. When the man took off his clothes and I saw his erection, my insides began shrieking, and I wanted to escape."

The two young prostitutes were sitting in their small, third floor walkup apartment on Molensteeg. It was only a few doors down the street from the brothel. The small sitting room overlooked the street and contained a violet settee, two matching wing chairs and a table lamp with a hurricane-style glass globe adorned with flowers and a blue bird. The bedroom was just big enough to accommodate the bed they shared and a chest of drawers. Raluca and Alicia could barely squeeze into the kitchen together. All the furnishings were worn but clean, what the girls eventually would come to call Dutch clean. As with their Paris apartment, this one required sharing a bathroom, in this case, with the dwellers of three other apartments on their floor.

"And now?"

"It is not so bad," Alicia replied. "Well, actually, it is. I feel like a trash bin for the clients. They are dumping inside me what they no longer need. And some of the men smell. They need a bath." Alicia wrinkled her nose and shuddered. "And you? How are you feeling about our work?"

"It is harder than being a model." Raluca was perched in one of the wing chairs, knees tucked under her chin. "And not nearly so nice as the flower shop."

"Do you enjoy it?" Alicia asked.

"Some of the clients are nice and know how to give me pleasure," Raluca replied softly. "But not many. Most of them only want one thing – to enter me quickly and have their own way. They are too rough."

"I don't know if I could ever face my mother again," Alicia murmured. "I think she would look straight through my eyes into my soul."

"I've had more than enough," Russell said expansively. "Too much to eat and plenty to drink. I'd belch but that would ruffle Victoria's finely tuned sense of propriety."

"Someone has to think about proper etiquette in this family," Victoria sniffed. "If your father didn't need three-piece suits for the bank," she said scornfully, directing her gaze at Meredith, "I think he might have all of us wearing denim overalls and sitting on hay bales."

"She's spot on right," Russell laughed. "But the money does nice things for this family," he added seriously, "and I'm willing to wear what the costume department requires."

Meredith and Joshua both looked at Russell with strengthened admiration.

"Let's get things gathered up," Joshua said, pushing himself up from the blue blanket. "If someone carries the blanket, I think everything else will fit in the hamper, and I can manage that."

The four picnickers stuffed leftover food, empty wine bottles and used glasses into the hamper. Victoria and Meredith picked up the blanket, shook it free of sand and Joshua and Victoria began walking across the sand toward the cottage with Meredith trailing. She took half a dozen steps.

"Meredith," her father called, "wait a second."

She stopped and looked over her right shoulder. "What is it?"

Russell waited until the distance between Meredith and Joshua and Victoria widened by about 20 feet. Then he motioned to Meredith to come to him. "Is everything all right?" he asked.

"What do you mean?"

Russell's right forefinger and thumb rose and rubbed his chin. "Look, I meant what I said about Josh and hearing good things about his work. It's, well, I just don't sense any real passion for his job."

"It's only been three weeks since he started, Dad."

"I know. Maybe I'm reading between the lines when I shouldn't be." A pause. "Josh is a terrific young man, and I think the world of him. I don't want him feeling stuck at the bank if his heart's not in it. Not because he feels he owes me anything for getting him the job."

Meredith's head shook and she smiled lovingly. "You're too much, Dad. I guess I haven't told you in a while, but I do love you."

"Mothers are like that, aren't they?" Raluca said. "They can see right through us. And even when they can't see through us they sense things."

"Do you think we will ever be like that?" Alicia asked.

"Yes, and I wouldn't want to become a mother if I didn't know who the father was," Raluca said emphatically. "This job, this is not our future. It cannot be our future."

"You are right. We must try to save money, save all that we possibly can. We should also learn Dutch."

"And English."

"Still, what man would marry a prostitute? Who could love us? The Dutch tolerate prostitutes, but what Dutchman would marry one? And our foreign clients aren't looking for wives. Many already have one."

"I don't think we should even think about marrying. Not now."

"What then?"

"Save our guilders," said Raluca, "so we can go home again. But not poor. Return with money – and memories that we can try to bury. And there, maybe, we can become honorable wives and mothers who can see into our own children's souls."

The two horses were kicking up wet sand. Prancing hoofs were splashing surf against their bellies.

"So, Mrs. Bliss, what did you and your dad talk about?"

"Mostly you, Mr. Bliss."

"Really?"

"Very really."

After helping with the post-picnic cleanup, Meredith had suggested to Joshua that they rent horses at nearby stables and ride the beaches.

"How did I fare with his parsing?"

Meredith chuckled. "No parsing, silly fellow. He wanted to know if you felt any passion for your job. He's worried that maybe you don't, and you're not saying as much to avoid offending him. Put simply, Dad wants you – and us – to be happy."

"That's very considerate of him."

"There's more to my dad than a hard-nosed banker."

They rode silently eastward for the next two minutes. Their horses clearly were enjoying the beach romp. Joshua pulled back on his mount's reins, slowing the canter to a walk. Meredith did likewise.

She looked expectantly at her husband. "So, are you? Passionate about the job?"

"Your dad has been very helpful. I wouldn't want to hurt his feelings, and I feel loyal to him."

Meredith nodded and patted her horse's neck. "That doesn't sound much like passion."

Joshua shook his head in resignation. "The truth is I'm bored. I'm not saying the job itself is boring or unimportant. It's just that I'm not cut out to be a desk jockey. I go to work, park at my desk and ride a chair. Hour after hour except for a restroom break and lunch. On these beautiful summer days I'm stuck inside. That, Mrs. Bliss, ain't like farming."

"Or," added Meredith, "playing football and riding the hills above Stanford."

Joshua chuckled softly. "You know what kind of job I could be passionate about?"

"Is that a rhetorical question?" she asked saucily.

"I guess it is."

"You need to be unshackled from your desk. On or near the water would be better. Of course," Meredith said pensively, "in almost any job you'd have to sit at a desk at least some of the time."

"Agreed."

"I have an idea," said Meredith.

"Well, what is it?"

"Let me think it through a little bit more."

"And how long will that take?"

"About as long as it would take these horses to cover half a mile if we gave them their heads."

"Uh, you've never ridden a horse all out," Joshua said concernedly.

"First time for everything."

The newlyweds peered at each other, small grins barely creasing their faces, eyes signaling intent.

"Let's race, " Joshua said, and Meredith grinned her agreement. She shouted delightedly as they kicked their canvas shoes against the horses' flanks and flicked their reins. Within seconds their mounts, manes and tails streaming wildly, went thundering down the beach. Pounding hoofs were kicking up clumps of wet sand. After a minute Joshua and Meredith looked at each other and pulled back forcefully on the reins, bringing the horses to a skidding stop. Both animals snorted and Joshua's reared up on its hind legs.

"We should write to our families again," said Alicia. "Let them know we have arrived safely in Amsterdam. But what should we tell them?"

"That we have found jobs in sales."

"Is that enough?"

"For now, I think so," said Raluca.

"Will you write mine for me again?"

"Of course." A pause. "We should get some sleep."

"Raluca, we are sinning."

Raluca lowered her knees until her feet touched the bare wood floor and stood. She began pacing slowly to the room's opposite end. She stopped, paused, pivoted, returned to her chair and sat facing Alicia. "There are ten commandments. Are we breaking one of them?"

"I am not sure."

"If we are sinning...If God loves us, I think he understands our situation."

"I hope so – and forgives us."

"If we are sinning."

"Okay," said Joshua, "so what's your idea?"

"It starts with something I heard Dad say."

"Go ahead."

"Chemical Bank owns a shipping company. It's called Red Star."

"Yes, he mentioned that to me."

"It operates out of Holland – The Netherlands."

"And?"

"And think about it. You left Shelby for California. Now you've moved back across the country. You like the water."

"Are you suggesting what I think you are?"

"Probably," she grinned.

"It would be an adventure, wouldn't it?"

"How many farm boys have picked up and crossed the Atlantic?"

"Another rhetorical question."

"You're catching on, farm boy."

"There is one other thing, though," Joshua said.

"That being?"

"If we're going to do this, it wouldn't be with Red Star."

"Right, you wouldn't want Dad getting you another job."

Joshua smiled. "Come on, let's head back."

They jerked the reins to the right, and the horses wheeled and began cantering back west toward Montauk Point.

"You are thinking about what?" Victoria spluttered. "Why on earth?"

"Dear," Russell said evenly, "let's let them explain."

Which is what Meredith and Joshua did. When they had finished, Russell's visage was projecting admiration, Victoria's dismay and distress.

"What if you can't find a job?" Victoria asked. "What if you become pregnant? What if one of you becomes ill?"

"Mother," Meredith said patiently, "Holland isn't a prison. It's a prosperous country. I'm sure it has fine doctors. If things don't work out, we can leave."

Victoria was about to continue protesting when Russell spoke. "I admire your spirit of adventure. Makes me wish I'd had more of it in my youth. Even if you don't like Holland and come back here in the next year or two, it seems to me you'll still benefit from the experience. You will grow intellectually. You'll see the world differently. Have a broader and deeper understanding of events, of politics and the world economy. And," Russell added brightly, "we could come visit you!"

Victoria knew further questioning would be futile and merely said, almost plaintively, "You will write often, won't you?"

"Of course, Mother," Meredith smiled.

"And," Russell added, "they could even phone us." Which was true. Transatlantic telephone service had been introduced in 1927, the same year talking movies had debuted. Initially transatlantic phone calls had been transmitted not through undersea cables but by radio signals. That first year such calls were obscenely expensive - $75 for the first three minutes – and seldom made. Subsequently, charges had come down.

"Mother," Meredith said lightly, "if you're not careful, we will overwhelm you with letters, postcards, telegrams and phone calls."

Meredith, Joshua and Russell all laughed, and Victoria managed a smile that simultaneously conveyed defeat and doubt.

"This calls for a feast," Russell said. "And cigars. Would you join me in a smoke, Josh? Macanudos?"

"Gladly, sir."

In the garden behind the brownstone, Russell said, "You're sure about me not finding something for you with Red Star?"

"Yes, sir."

"If you're not comfortable calling me Dad, I'd prefer Russell to sir or mister."

"All right, Russell."

"Good. Now, even though you'll be finding yourself a job, I am going to ask you to let me do one thing for you and Meredith."

"And that would be…"

"Buying a house or apartment in Holland. Before you say no, hear me out."

"Go ahead."

"Fathers worry about daughters more than sons. If you have one, you'll learn that. When Clarisse was born, one of my first thoughts was, I need to buy a shotgun to protect her from all the young studs who will be gunning for her. So to speak." Joshua chuckled. "I remember all too well my own youth. Our daughters probably would find it hard to believe, but my earliest intentions as to Victoria weren't entirely honorable. And Victoria for all her stiffness wasn't exactly opposed to a little pre-marital hankypanky. If you compared our wedding date with Clarisse's birthdate, you'd see we just made it under the nine-month wire."

Joshua smiled. "If we have a daughter, I'll keep all this in mind."

"Right. So anyway I would feel a darned sight better if I knew my youngest daughter could begin life in a different country in a nice home in a nice neighborhood."

Joshua nodded. "I think Meredith should hear this from you."

"Agreed. But I want to be able to tell her truthfully that you are all right with the plan."

"With just one amendment."

"And what's that?"

"We will pay you back. Eventually."

CHAPTER 13

With assistance from a muscular tugboat, the Red Star liner began easing toward a dock on Amsterdam's northern waterfront.

Joshua and Meredith were watching excitedly from the ship's open top deck.

"Such a huge port," Meredith marveled. "I've never seen so many ships."

"Same here," said Joshua, "and I hear it's not nearly as large as Rotterdam's which is the biggest in the world."

"Well, we could hardly say no to crossing on a ship belonging to Dad's line."

"And Rotterdam is not all that far if that's where I find a job. I'll bet I could commute by train."

The liner docked about 1,000 yards east from Amsterdam's waterfront Centraal Train Station. Before disembarking, Joshua and Meredith watched luggage being removed from the ship's cargo hold and their stateroom. Then, with caution, they began descending the gangway. A line of taxis, trucks and vans was waiting on the dock. They selected a black taxi and a small black truck.

In well-rehearsed Dutch, Meredith said, "Please drive us to Prinsengracht." Then she pointed to the truck and its driver and gestured for it to follow.

The taxi driver smiled knowingly. "I speak English a little."

Meredith brightened. "Very good!"

The driver opened the passenger side rear door, and Josh and Meredith eased in and sat. The driver closed the door behind them.

"Well, Bliss," she said cheerily, "say hello to our new hometown."

"Hello, Amsterdam."

The driver placed two bags in the taxi's trunk, opened his door and situated himself. "We go now."

Almost immediately the taxi, with the truck following, was driving south and crossing a canal – the Dijksgracht. A right turn to the west and the taxi was soon passing over more canals.

"You wanted water, Mr. Bliss. I think we've found the right place."

The canals were busy, sometimes congested, waterways of commerce – and more.

"Take a look over there," Joshua said, pointing to the left. "Houseboats. Permanently anchored by their looks."

"That is right," the driver confirmed.

"Oh, my!" Meredith exclaimed.

"What?"

"Red lights."

The route west from the dock to Prinsengracht was passing through the center of the red light district. Oude Kerk loomed ahead on the left.

"There's no hiding it here," Joshua observed. "And the women, I don't think I've ever seen so many blonds in one place."

"Hey, Bliss," Meredith teased, poking him in the ribs with her right elbow, "you've got all the blond you need right here."

"Or want," Joshua grinned.

As the driver eased his taxi slowly along narrow Brugsteeg, Meredith was looking to the right and saw her first window whore. She turned away, blushing deep crimson. "I suppose you're still looking."

"Sorry. Can't help it."

"Yes, you can."

Joshua laughed. "Okay, if I force myself."

"They're not all blond," Meredith said, looking ahead and to her left.

Joshua shifted his gaze.

Slowly strolling toward them were two young women. Both were dark-haired with olive-tinged complexions.

"Still pretty though," he said.

"They don't look like…Do you think they are?"

"Can't be sure. And," he grinned, "it's not likely I ever will be."

"You'd better not be, buster."

Prinsengracht was the name of both the street where their new home stood and the canal that paralleled it. Street and canal originated at the waterfront on the western edge of the city center. For about three miles they looped south, gently curving southeast and northeast until ending at the Plantage Muidergracht, a canal that formed the southern edge of a neighborhood populated by many of the Jewish families who had made their way to Amsterdam during the last 800 years. Documented Jewish presence in the city dated to the 1100s. But it was the expulsion of Jews from Spain and Portugal during the 1580s that generated a torrent of refugees.

Joshua and Meredith's home typified others on Prinsengracht. Brown brick, the house rose three full floors and was topped by a triangular gable behind which hid an attic. At the gable's peak hung a large hoist. Its purpose: Lift furniture too bulky for narrow, winding staircases up and through windows.

The house measured only three windows wide but ran long with a small garden at its rear.

"I'm smitten," said Meredith. "The entire setting just oozes with charm. Our house, the canal only a few steps away, the trees. I think we are going to like it here, Bliss."

That same day, about 37 miles southwest in Rotterdam, another young couple was embarking on marriage. Stefaan and Anneke were smiling widely as they exited the small church to the applause of family and friends.

Standing by was an open, white carriage hitched to a pair of handsome brown horses. The carriage would carry the bride and groom to the home of Anneke's parents on Vergeeetmijnstraat. They planned to reside there for the foreseeable future. They didn't have sufficient guilders to afford their own home. Rents were expensive and Mr. and Mrs. Azijn had pointed out the generous space available to them in their home.

After quickly changing from their wedding apparel, Stefaan and Anneke were back in the carriage with their luggage – a pair of sturdy brown leather suitcases – and on their way to Rotterdam's train station. Destination: Brussels where they would honeymoon for five days.

Little more than two hours later, their train was pulling into Brussels' Centraal Station, a vast, architecturally uninspiring gray stone hulk. The station sat where the city's Upper Town met Lower Town which contained the city's historic heart with buildings dating to the early 1400s.

Stepping down from the train onto the platform, burly Stefaan easily hefted both bags. "Better for balance," he smiled. Then groom and bride began climbing a wide, high flight of marble-clad steps to the station's marble-floored ticket lobby.

On the plaza in front of Centraal Station, they paused and looked around. "This way, I think," said Anneke. "This plaza slopes down, and our hotel is in Lower Town."

"You lead," said Stefaan.

Lower Town, in fact, sat on decidedly lower ground than Upper Town. Anneke and Stefaan walked about 50 paces on gradually downward sloping pavement. Then they stopped and gaped. They found themselves standing at the precipice of a street that dropped sharply.

"I think we could sit on our suitcases and slide down," Stefaan said, laughing heartily. "Be careful on those heels."

They began descending slowly. At the hill's base was a small plaza surrounded by hotels, cafes and shops.

Anneke pointed to their right. "That one is ours," she said, "the Hotel Grand Place. It's not really in the Grand Place, but I understand it's only a short distance away."

"It seems like a nice neighborhood," Stefaan said. With a sober expression, he added, "There is but one thing wrong with it."

"Oh?"

"No water. No canal, no lake, no river, no sea. Not at all like our Rotterdam." He chortled at his own small joke.

"That is precisely why we are here," Anneke said brightly. "The only water is the water we will drink and bathe in."

"I hope the tub is large," said Stefaan, again unsmiling.

"Ha," Anneke said, right forefinger pointing at his chest in understanding. "I know your game."

"Really?"

"You want a tub big enough to hold both of us."

Stefaan nodded his concession. "You are the brains of this marriage. I am but the brawn."

Anneke smiled lovingly. "In a big bathtub together, we wouldn't need brains or brawn."

Later that afternoon, they exited the hotel. Strolling hand-in-hand, they walked west about 100 paces to an ancient, narrow street, paved with cobblestones worn smooth. Another 100 paces and they were standing at the northeast corner of the Grand Place – Brussels' renowned central plaza where the city originated as a fortress about 580.

Stefaan and Anneke's feet seemed frozen in place. They shook their heads in wonderment.

"It is – it is stunning," Anneke murmured. "I think I could stand here forever."

"You know I'm not much for words," Stefaan said quietly, "and I cannot think of any now."

What was mesmerizing them were structures framing a cobblestone-paved plaza about 200 yards long and some 75 yards wide. Anchoring the Grand Place on its southwest side was the magnificent City Hall with its stone spire that soared 315 feet. It was begun in 1401 and completed in 1459. Its gray stone façade rose three floors. Above them four levels of small gables punctuated a steeply pitched roof. Across the building's front, above each of 40 tall windows, stood sculptures depicting famed warriors, saints and royalty.

Opposite City Hall stood handsome Maison du Roi, built in 1536 and once the residence of a ruling Spanish king. By 1935 it was housing an art museum. Numerous merchant and craft guild houses – ornately gabled, rising four and five floors, and built through the 1600s – reflected that era's trading power and wealth.

In 1935 the ground floors of the guild houses were serving as restaurants, cafes and shops purveying a range of products including Belgian lace and chocolates.

"Do you know what amazes me most?" Anneke asked. "Even more

than the fabulous architecture? It is the condition of the buildings. They are old – hundreds of years old – and I can't see any blemishes."

In fact, Grand Place structures, most with gold-leaf ornamenting their facades, were lovingly maintained. A government fiat forbidding motorized vehicles from entering the plaza except for making deliveries meant no smudging from belching exhausts.

"Let's walk around the perimeter," Stefaan suggested. "Very slowly."

"Yes," said Anneke, "soak it all in."

They began edging south along the plaza's east side. They gazed in shop windows, but mostly their eyes were drawn to the enchanting architecture.

Outside several cafes, visitors sat at tables, lingering over wine, coffee, jenever and assorted other beverages.

"Look at all these people," Stefaan observed. "They are in no hurry to leave. This place is like a giant magnet. It pulls people in – like us – and won't let go."

When at last Anneke and Stefaan reached Grand Place's northwest corner, they found themselves in front of La Rose Blanche. The restaurant exuded charm befitting its location.

"It is early," said Anneke, "but let's go inside. We will order some food and something to drink. But we must get a window table in that loft." She pointed up toward second floor windows from which diners could leisurely take in the plaza's grandeur.

By the end of their fifth and last day in Brussels, Anneke and Stefaan had strolled through Grand Place at least a dozen times.

"You know something?" Stefaan asked. "I think I could stay here and never miss the waters of Rotterdam. This was the perfect place for our honeymoon. I am glad you picked it."

"Me too. Do you know what's incredible?" She didn't wait for Stefaan to guess. "Think of all the wars that have been fought in Europe. Who can count them? But the Grand Place has been untouched. Not a single scar. Miraculous. I am so glad it was here to give us memories that will last a lifetime."

Stefaan's head shook in admiration. "The plaza isn't the only thing that's incredible and wonderful."

They hugged and fell silent, gazing a final time at the plaza's wonders. Stefaan ended their reverie. "Do you know what is going to be harder than leaving here?" Anneke hunched her shoulders questioningly. "Going back to work on the docks."

Joshua was walking along a dock to a job interview. His destination was the offices of the Royal Netherlands Steamship Company. The firm had been founded in 1856, and in the 1930s its ports of call ranged widely – Dover, New York, Madeira, Paramaribo, Trinidad, Curacao and Port au Prince among others. The company's headquarters were located in Scheepvaarthuis (Dutch for Ship Towards Home). The 1913 structure housed six shipping companies at 108-114 Prins Hendrikkade. The street paralleled the waterfront across a shipping channel from Centraal Railroad Station.

When Scheepvaarthuis came into his view, Joshua paused to take in the long, massive structure. Wow, he marveled, the architect wanted to leave no doubt about who occupied that building. It rose six floors and was designed to resemble a ship with its "point" suggesting a prow. The red brick façade – the "hull" – was crowned with white gables – the "sails."

At the building's entrance, Joshua whispered to himself, "Well, nothing ventured, nothing gained." Would this company have any use for an English-speaking economics major from Stanford? He pushed open the door and ogled the lobby. The marble floor and high ceiling conveyed seriousness and substance. He surveyed the spacious main lobby. He then eyed a building directory mounted in the far wall. He saw that, conveniently, the Royal Netherlands Steamship Company offices were located on the ground floor. He looked to his left and saw the company's name etched boldly in rich wood above handsome wood double doors. He advanced and pushed one open. Sitting primly at the reception desk was a white-haired woman. The nameplate read L. Reidel.

Joshua approached and smiled. "My-name-is-Joshua Bliss."

The woman smiled warmly and replied, eyes twinkling merrily, "And-my-name-is Laura Reidel."

"Good morning, Miss Reidel. I am-"

"My English is quite good, Mr. Bliss. Don't you think?" She was smiling but her voice hinted at the salt of displeasure. Joshua reddened. "There is really no need to speak slowly."

"Excuse me, please."

"You are excused. And I know why you are here. At the end of each day I am fully briefed on guests with appointments the next day."

Joshua nodded, blood draining from his face as his embarrassment began receding. "I am very pleased to make your acquaintance, Miss Reidel." He stepped closer, tentatively extending his right hand.

She leaned forward, half rising from her black leather swivel chair, and took his hand. "It is Mrs. Reidel. Laura Reidel. And I am pleased to meet you."

Laura Reidel, he could see, was a striking woman and, he concluded quickly, an excellent representative of the Royal Netherlands Steamship Company.

Three and a half hours later Joshua exited Scheepvaarthuis. He looked across the gray water of the shipping channel at the equally gray Centraal Railroad Station. He rubbed his bald head and smiled wryly. Of all things, he thought amusingly. Another of life's lessons learned: Expect the unexpected. After three interviews Joshua was offered – and accepted – an entry level accounting position. Thank you, Stanford. If not expected, he had been hoping he would impress management enough to receive an offer. The unexpected arrived during the third interview. Conducting it was president Ernst Heldring, a courtly leader then age 66.

Heldring told Joshua that company executives also wanted him to begin learning sales. Their thinking: His degree from a leading United States university and his English might help win more American customers.

That unexpected development struck Joshua as decidedly serendipitous. Working in sales meant that he would not be enslaved full-time by a desk. He foresaw sales providing opportunities to squire prospects and customers to the company's ships and port facilities. He envisioned sales requiring voyages to the company's far flung ports of call. His love of water – especially open seas – would be requited.

On the walk back to Prinsengracht, he reflected, I'll have to buy flowers for Meredith. After all, coming here was her idea. I am one lucky guy.

CHAPTER 14

Three orange kites were soaring in contrast against a rich blue sky. They seemed to be waging war. They were bumping each other and jockeying for higher altitude. Strips of multicolored cloth formed the kites' flapping tails.

Controlling the aerial combatants were the Looten siblings – Luc 16, Karin 14 and Catherina 12. Their glee barely masked heated rivalry.

"Ha!" Luc shouted boastfully, "my kite is flying higher than yours."

Karin dubiously eyed her brother's hands, then followed upward the course of his string. She spotted a small knot. "Ha yourself!" she cried derisively. "You have added extra string to your spool."

"You," Luc retorted, "are too short and weak to control more string."

"Cheater!" screamed Catherina. "That is what big brothers do. They cheat!"

This children's war was being contested along the north bank of the Rhine River that flowed past Rhenen, a quiet Dutch town of 6,500 people. The Rhine's northwesterly course bent due west near Arnhem, about 20 miles east of Rhenen.

Luc, Karin and Catherina resided with parents Bert, a postal clerk, and Dora, a housewife and seamstress, in a modest home on the southwestern edge of Rhenen. Blond hair and blue eyes marked all five Lootens.

Rhenen had been designated a city in 1258. In central Holland, the town occupied rare high ground – as much as 160 feet above sea level. Residents jokingly called this modest bulge in the earth's surface "the mountain."

Rhenen's serpentine main street, Herenstraat (Dutch for Gentlemen's Street) wound on a slight upward grade from west to east. Straddling the street were charming houses, shops and the handsome, two-story, 40-foot long red brick post office. Topping it were twin gables. Bert Looten, a modest man, was proud to work there. He also savored the feeling that went with directing mail to intended recipients eagerly awaiting its arrival.

Anchoring Herenstraat was the town's inspiring tribute to God; construction of the church had begun in 1492 and was completed in 1531 when its soaring stone-clad bell tower was capped with a crucifix.

Rhenen lay only 23 miles west of the German border, barely over the horizon as seen from the church tower's pinnacle. The city also centered the Grebbe Line, a north-south defensive ribbon fortified with guns, bunkers and trenches. Ironically, only 75 of Rhenen's citizens owned firearms, and most of those were shotguns or single-shot, small-bore hunting rifles.

The nearby Rhine buzzed with shipping activity. River traffic flowed north and west to Rotterdam and Amsterdam and south and east into Germany.

"Look," Catherina called to Luc and Karin, "here comes Father."

Bert waved gaily to his three offspring as he went walking across a grassy expanse bordering the river. "Time to come home for supper."

"Right away, Father," Catherina replied.

She and Luc and Karin began reeling in their kites that descended slowly, fluttering in the afternoon breeze.

Bert was watching contentedly. I am grateful, he reflected, to be living in such a small, peaceful town. We have everything we need or want here. We even have a small zoo. I wouldn't want to live anywhere else. Certainly not in the big cities. When I am handling mail going to addresses in Amsterdam or Rotterdam or The Hague, I almost feel sorry for people living there. So big, so crowded, so noisy. And the crime and prostitution. Thankfully we have almost no crime in Rhenen and no prostitution at all. His children now had their kites in hand and were walking toward him, chattering happily. Rhenen, he mused, might just be a little heaven on earth.

CHAPTER 15

As 1937 was drawing to a close, Rhenen and the rest of The Netherlands were bathed in peace. But much of the remainder of Europe was restive – in large part because of changes wrought by the Treaty of Versailles. Continuing to prove particularly upsetting to millions of Europeans were the arbitrary – even capricious – national boundaries the treaty had created.

An example was the Sudeten province of Czechoslovakia, a nation formed and granted independence in 1919. Spearheading the effort in Paris had been two leading Czech nationalists, Tomas Masaryk and Eduard Benes. Masaryk became president of the newly forged democratic republic. He served in that capacity until 1935 when Benes succeeded him.

One aspect of the new nation had proven nettlesome from its inception.

Czechs comprised only 51 percent of the population but controlled the government and dominated the economy. A minority group particularly aggrieved were German-speaking citizens in the Sudeten province. Only the low Sudetes Mountains separated them from fatherland Germany. Given the Czechs' lingering ill-will against Germany, Benes' government wasn't proving overly solicitous of Sudetens of Teutonic ancestry.

Adolf Hitler didn't feel compelled to stoke unrest there. The Sudetens were showing themselves deft troublemakers. Their elected representatives, fuming at slights perceived and real, went storming out of Czechoslovakia's parliament in Prague. Then German-speaking Sudetens began rioting throughout the province. Hitler thrilled at these developments. President Benes appeared powerless to quell the turmoil. Hitler saw opportunity unfolding.

Father Titus Brandsma saw what Hitler saw, and it worried him. But because Hitler had taken no active role in Czechoslovakia, hadn't even hinted at doing so, Father Brandsma could do little more than pray that Benes and the Czech government could cool tempers and bring stability to the infant nation. After pondering and praying for guidance, Father Brandsma chose not to write a newspaper opinion column voicing his concerns. He concluded that doing so might provoke Hitler to again mobilize his military forces as he had done when re-taking the Rhineland.

In Amsterdam, Joshua was mindful of world events. As an employee of an international shipping company, he recognized the imperative of remaining knowledgeable of global political and economic forces and changes. But he was deriving so much satisfaction from learning his new job and acclimating himself as an American ex-patriot that goings-on in Czechoslovakia were occupying few of his thoughts and little of his time. Moreover he was working assiduously to learn Dutch.

In addition, his home on Prinsengracht was turning out to be considerably more than a quiet cocoon for him and Meredith. Chief reason: She had begun tutoring children of Netherlands Royal Steamship Company employees in English. Nine youngsters, ages 10 to 15, were coming to their home for private language lessons. Meredith didn't try to hide her pleasure at this intrusion into tranquility. She welcomed the challenge as stimulating, satisfying and fun.

"I am learning Dutch as I teach them English," she told Joshua. "And I am learning something else. I think English and Dutch must be two of the most difficult languages to master," she observed. "English seems to have as many exceptions as rules, and Dutch bears virtually no resemblance to the Romance languages."

"Do you enjoy tutoring as much as you did teaching at Xavier?" Joshua asked.

"Even more. I love tutoring. I can actually see each of my students making progress."

Joshua was taking additional enjoyment from getting to know their neighbors. On many mornings as he set out for work he exchanged greetings with Otto Frank whose business was only a few doors away at 263 Prinsengracht.

Business at the Netherlands Royal Steamship Company was flourishing. Joshua saw the need for extra secretarial staff. After mentioning the shortage to his supervisor, he found himself taking on hiring responsibility. His recommendation: Employ temporary staff only when workloads required more help.

A day later Joshua's black desk phone rang. "Hello," he answered, "Josh Bliss."

"Mr. Bliss." The voice was a familiar one. "You have a Miss Isala Van Dyck here to see you. She tells me you are expecting her. You didn't let me know yesterday."

"That's right, Mrs. Reidel, and I apologize. It won't happen again. Please tell Miss Van Dyck that I will be right out to see her."

"Very good, Mr. Bliss."

Joshua replaced the receiver in its cradle. Before standing he entertained a thought. I am tempted to ask Mrs. Reidel to call me Josh. But not yet. In due time. The Dutch wouldn't abide the informality of California. Protocol here is even stiffer than it was at Chemical Bank. Those people took money and themselves way too seriously.

At his desk, Joshua asked Isala Van Dyck to be seated in a guest chair he had borrowed from his supervisor. Miss Van Dyck owned a temporary staffing agency. Her employees were mostly women who worked as secretaries and typists. Her staff did include three men who regarded themselves as professional secretaries between full-time jobs.

She was a striking woman. In her mid-40s, she stood five feet four inches with blond hair and blue eyes. Her lipstick was fiery red. She was trim, almost bony, Joshua observed. He also realized within moments that she possessed a keen business mind. Their negotiations over staffing requirements and compensation were settled quickly.

"I think I have the perfect solution for your needs," she said. "Her name is Edith Wessel. She is young but mature, and she possesses excellent organizing and typing skills. I recommend her with absolute confidence. Would you like to interview her before she starts?"

"That won't be necessary," Joshua replied. "Your recommendation seems like a guarantee and is sufficient."

She nodded her concurrence. "But if for any reason you find her work unsatisfactory, please do let me know promptly."

"I will."

"Good." A pause. "Your Dutch is quite good, but I detect a foreign accent. I hope you are not offended by my comment."

Joshua smiled at this example of frequent Dutch bluntness. "Not at all. You're a good listener. I'm American."

Miss Van Dyck smiled congenially. "You are the first American I have met. It is my pleasure."

"Mine as well."

She began rising and paused. "Meeting you causes me to think of something that comes to mind whenever I read or hear about America. Do you mind?"

"Go ahead," Joshua smiled, sensing that Dutch forthrightness would be coming his way again.

"I have friends in Germany. Good friends. I think it is too bad that Americans fought Germany in the First World War. You have so much in common. Great universities, brilliant scientists, big and successful manufacturing companies. And look at all the Germans who emigrated to America during the last hundred years."

Joshua's mind was processing her words with remarkable speed. He knew in an instant that he had a choice: Debate Miss Van Dyck or let her observations pass unquestioned. He chose the latter option. "We have taken in immigrants from many nations. We are better for it." With that saccharine reply he stood and offered his right hand. Miss Van Dyck accepted it and they shook firmly. "Let me see you out," said Joshua.

Moments later they passed Laura Reidel's reception desk, and Joshua pushed open the door for Isala Van Dyck. After she exited he turned and smiled at Mrs. Reidel. As he was passing her desk, she said meditatively, "There is something about that woman."

Joshua stopped and looked down at the perceptive receptionist. "What do you mean?"

"I am not sure. I guess it is just my womanly intuition." She smiled self-deprecatingly.

Joshua nodded and moved on. But he couldn't help thinking that soon he just might ask Laura Reidel to call him Josh. Meanwhile he hoped only that Edith Wessel would work out as Miss Van Dyck had all but promised.

As Miss Van Dyck was walking briskly back to her agency, she saw two young olive-tinged young women standing and chatting on one of the canal bridges. Jews or gypsies, she thought dismissively. I would hire neither of them. No doubt they are lazy and unskilled. Crafty, probably, and untrustworthy. She continued apace.

"I never imagined there were so many bicycles in the entire world," Raluca marveled. "There must be thousands and thousands of them here."

"Our beautiful Romania has too many hills and mountains for bikes. We saw a few in Cluj but not many. Paris is nearly flat, except for Montmarte, but we didn't see many bikes there either."

Raluca laughed. "Parisians mounting bikes. They probably would think it undignified. Here in Amsterdam people seem to use them for everything – going to work and school, carrying groceries, visiting friends, going riding in the countryside. And the Dutch have bicycle races."

"It would be nice to have one," said Alicia. "On a bike I think I would feel free. I can almost feel the wind in my face. Do you think we could buy one and share it? Maybe an old one?"

"We are trying to save money," Raluca replied. Then she saw and studied the longing look in her friend's eyes. "But if we shop carefully for an old one – in good condition – we could consider buying it."

Alicia squealed delightedly and clapped her hands. "Let's begin shopping right away."

"Is tomorrow soon enough?" Raluca teased.

CHAPTER 16

"Now is the time," Hitler said confidently. "Give the order."

It was March 12, 1938. The next day Wehrmacht troops went marching into neighboring Austria. Not a shot was fired in defense or protest. The most visible reaction among Austrians was unrestrained glee. In Hitler they saw a man who acted boldly, promised a return to prosperity and instilled pride among German-speaking peoples.

None of this surprised Hitler. After the First World War, many Austrians were longing to make their land part of Germany. Treaties forbade such a merger. In 1920 Austria adopted a constitution built on democracy. But the country's two combative main political parties formed their own armies – that often clashed. By 1938 Austria had joined much of the rest of the world in sinking into deep economic depression. Both inflation and bank loan interest rates were hovering around a choking 25 percent. Austrians were hungering for the relief they were hoping Hitler could provide.

"Conquest," Hitler told Germans, "is not only a right but a duty." He was winning millions of believers. He was silencing critics – through intimidation, incarceration, torture and execution. To Goebbels after the walkover in Austria he said, "That went smoothly, don't you think? I must visit Vienna."

A month later, in April, Hitler celebrated his bloodless conquest in Vienna which he had first visited when he was 19 – and where he had stayed for four years. Multitudes of Austrians greeted him with virtually unbridled hysteria. Hitler was euphoric.

"How is Miss Wessel doing?" Isala Van Dyck asked Joshua. She had phoned ahead, requesting an appointment. Miss Van Dyck was a shrewd businesswoman who recognized fully the value of staying close to customers, of demonstrating her interest in their welfare.

"Very satisfactory," Joshua answered. "She does everything we ask and does it well. She frequently asks if there is more she can do."

"Very good. I am pleased to hear that." A pause. "You seem happy here. Do you mind telling me your background?"

"Not at all. I am from the heartland of America – Ohio. I was raised on a farm."

"Are there Dutch in Ohio?"

"Not many. Most families in my hometown are descendants of immigrants from England, Ireland and Germany."

"Oh," her eyes brightened, "what do they think of what is happening in Germany?"

"I'm not sure but probably they are disappointed with Hitler. During the First World War, many German descendants were embarrassed by Germany's aggression. A town called New Berlin changed its name to North Canton."

"I see. Well, I think Herr Hitler is good for Germany and its people." Joshua again chose not to respond to Isala's bluntly stated opinion. "He is almost like God bringing Lazarus back from death. Germany was close to death, was on its knees economically and now it is standing proudly."

Joshua recognized truth in her last comment and curiosity caused him to venture a question. "Do you have ties to Germany? Family? Friends?"

"No. I simply admire Hitler as a great leader. He knows how to inspire. I respect his boldness."

Coming from you, Joshua thought wryly, that is hardly surprising.

Another strong-minded, blunt-speaking Dutch woman was reacting quite differently to Hitler's brazenness. Queen Wilhelmina was pacing in her Noordeinde Palace in The Hague.

"Hitler wants war," she said agitatedly to her prime minister, Dirk Jan de Geer. "I can sense it. He is just itching for a fight. To test his Wehrmacht and Luftwaffe."

"Perhaps you are reading too much into his moves. To me they seem inspired more by political goals than military gains."

De Geer's apologetic words and tone distressed the queen. If we are faced with war, she was thinking, are you the prime minister who should be at my side? She put that troubling thought aside and said, "He has sent troops marching into the Rhineland and Austria. He might not have wanted to fight then, but eventually he will."

"I hope you are mistaken."

"So do I. But if I am right, answer me this: We stayed neutral in the First World War. Do you think we could again in a new war? One Hitler starts?"

"We can only hope."

"We must do more than hope," she responded emphatically. "I want you to see to it that we strengthen our armed forces. They have grown weak and complacent. I want this done immediately and openly. I want it reported in newspapers. Perhaps Hitler will think twice before marching into our little country."

"Your plan could anger Hitler."

Wilhelmina's lips pursed tightly. She inhaled and blew out the breath forcefully. "I seriously doubt if Hitler appreciates subtlety. He is the arch enemy of mankind."

In Wilhelmina's youth, as a 15-year-old queen, she scarcely appeared regal. Nonetheless she earned high marks from another royal not known for gushing flattery. In 1895 Wilhelmina visited Queen Victoria in London. Afterward the woman who had been occupying the British throne since 1837 penned this assessment in her diary: *The young queen still has hair hanging loose. She is slender and graceful, and makes an impression as a very intelligent and very cute girl. She speaks good English and knows how to behave with charming manners.*

By 1937 the slender, gray-eyed girl had grown into a stout woman of inarguably regal bearing. She had won widespread respect and affection from her subjects. Her life, however, had not evaded adversity. Wilhelmina suffered a miscarriage in 1901, gave birth to a stillborn son in 1902 and suffered a second miscarriage in 1906. In 1909, after eight years of childless marriage, she gave birth to Juliana. She then suffered two more miscarriages in 1912. Adversity struck again in 1934 when her husband, Prince Hendrik, died. He had been duke of Mecklenburg-Schwerin, a region in northeastern Germany.

During their marriage, Wilhelmina was the unquestioned leader. She showed her mettle at age 20 when standing up to powerful Great Britain. She ordered a Dutch warship to South Africa to rescue Paul Kruger. Since 1883 he had been serving as president of independent Transvaal which Britain had forcibly annexed during the 1899-1902 Boer War. That conflict was sparked by a lust for gold by British settlers in South Africa. The Boers were descendants of early Dutch farmer-colonists with whom Wilhelmina felt a close kinship. Wilhelmina's teenage fondness for Great Britain had given way to a strong dislike. Defeated Transvaal was reduced to a British colony.

On the eve of the First World War she again demonstrated her nerve – and her wit. She was visiting the powerful German Emperor Wilhelm II who had been ruling since 1888. He boasted to the queen of small Holland: "My guards are seven feet tall and yours are only shoulder-high to them."

Wilhelmina smiled politely and replied, "Quite true, your majesty, your guards are seven feet tall. But when we open our dikes, the water is ten feet deep."

"Hitler does worry me," Joshua said to Meredith. "With his troops in the Rhineland, he could invade and crush us – Holland – before anyone – France or England – could help us. Even if they were so inclined – and they might not be, not after the bloodbath of the world war – I'm not sure they are powerful enough to evict Hitler. I hope we didn't make a mistake coming here. We might have been better off staying in New York or settling in California."

The pair was walking slowly along the Prinsengracht near their home.

"No, you would have been bored silly. And," Meredith smiled affectionately, "made my life miserable."

"Boredom can have its merits," he said without conviction.

"But not for you, Bliss." She playfully punched his left shoulder. "If you go more than ten minutes sitting still, you get antsy."

Samuel Folleck was half-wishing he had been a bit more antsy when he fled with his family from Germany and settled in Amsterdam. He and Guillermo Sevel were standing outside Guillermo's tobacco shop on Merwede Square. Guillermo was puffing his favorite black briar pipe.

"First the Rhineland, now Austria," Samuel fretted. "Perhaps we shouldn't have stopped here in Holland. Maybe I should have moved my family farther west. To America. To put an ocean between Hitler and my family. His hunting ground for Jews could stretch from Moscow to London."

"Do you really think that is a possibility?"

"I don't know. But I have seen Hitler and heard him speak. I think his ambition respects no boundaries."

Guillermo puffed and richly scented smoke curled from his pipe's bowl. "I hope you are wrong, my friend."

"What about you and your family? What if Hitler invades Holland?"

"We would be facing a dilemma. We couldn't chance returning to Spain. We were supporters of our lawful government." Guillermo was referring to Spain's center-left republican government led by President Manuel Azana. "Generalissimo Franco would probably kill us – as he has murdered thousands of loyalists. Maybe we could try escaping to America. Or England. At least we would have the English Channel between Hitler and us. Or maybe we would go into hiding here."

"But where?"

"I don't know. I confess I haven't thought about it seriously." He struck a match and re-lit his pipe. "Perhaps I should – before it is too late"

CHAPTER 17

Hitler could feel his temper – and blood pressure – rising. He had been joined in his office by Goebbels and Goering. It was March 21, 1938.

"The Rhineland. We merely reclaimed what was rightfully ours. Austria. The world has seen that our German-speaking brothers and sisters there wanted to be part of the Reich. Now is the time to recover Danzig." Angrily, he pounded the desk with his right fist. "The world calls it part of the Polish Corridor. Poland!" He spat the word. "That slice of land was ours. Giving it to Poland was another travesty of Versailles."

The port of Danzig had given Poland access to the Baltic Sea. The Poles saw it as a commercial blessing. Hitler saw it as a key to naval power.

That afternoon tensions in Europe rose more when Hitler issued a statement demanding return of the Polish Corridor and Danzig. Poland thumbed its national nose at the mustachioed dictator.

In Freiburg, Karl Kramer tiredly placed a textbook on a round lamp table in the sitting room of the apartment near the Augustinerplatz. He plopped onto a chair.

Hannah walked to him, bent down and kissed his forehead. "You look worried, dear." She straightened and stepped back.

"Hitler is egging on Poland. Nothing good can come of it. He either wants the Poles to capitulate and give him Danzig or refuse and invite an attack. So far they are ignoring our so-called fuhrer." Karl, now pursuing his Ph. D. in history, looked up at his young wife. "I hope Hitler keeps in mind one historical fact: The Poles are fighters. They showed their resolve during the First World War. Ask the Russians. The Poles humiliated them."

"Do you think Hitler would attack Poland?" Hannah asked.

"A virtual certainty. If not this month, then next. If not this year, then next."

"How would that affect us?"

"It could mean that I delay donning a professor's black robe for a gray Wehrmacht uniform. Military service is now compulsory again, and I expect to be drafted."

"What if we moved?" Hannah asked meditatively.

Karl's surprise was obvious. "Leave Germany?" She nodded. "To where?"

"France is but a few kilometers away. Many people in Alsace speak German. Or America. Millions of Germans have emigrated to America."

Karl smiled warmly. "You are right, of course. And perhaps someday we will. But I feel I must complete my studies here. Maybe," he smiled dubiously, "the fuhrer will see value in adding a degreed historian to his staff."

Hannah wasn't smiling. "Hitler," she observed perceptively, "has his own view of history. Mein Kampf."

"His is a rather slightly skewed view."

"True enough. Mein Kampf is drivel. But Hitler seems skewed in every other respect, so why should history be an exception?"

"I think," Karl said appreciatively, "that Hitler would do well to add a certain winstub waitress to his senior staff."

Hannah laughed – and so did Karl.

Hitler's name – and speculation on his aims – was on the lips of millions of Europeans.

"Madame Clarbout is worried that Hitler will seek revenge on her France," said Raluca. She and Alicia had returned from the brothel, and Alicia was heating water for tea. "Everyone knows Hitler despises the Treaty of Versailles," Raluca added. "Madame Clarbout believes he holds hatred for all things French."

"What about our homeland?" Alicia asked, tipping their inexpensive metal teapot and pouring the fragrant liquid into a pair of small, flowered china cups. "Do you think Hitler will invade Romania? Germany did invade us during The Great War."

"Very possibly. Hitler might need our oil. We have lots of it. And Ploesti has many oil refineries. I have seen pictures of them. England and France wouldn't want Hitler to control our oil, but they are so far from Romania – like we are – that I do not think they could stop him."

"Russia?"

"I don't know." Raluca's eyes closed in thought. "I do know that we must keep working and saving our money."

"I just wish," Alicia replied wearily, "that we didn't need to keep spreading our legs."

Raluca smiled at her friend. "Let's finish our tea and get some sleep. I heard that a ship from the United States docked early this morning. Perhaps we will have American clients tonight."

"If Hitler invades Romania, maybe America could come to our rescue," Alicia said wistfully.

"America is even farther away than England or France."

"Have you ever had an American client?" Alicia asked.

"I have never even met one."

CHAPTER 18

"I'm happy, Bliss."

"Me too, Meredith."

"The Netherlands is really feeling like my home. Our home. I love it."

"Same here. The people have been warm and welcoming."

"I can picture us raising our family here."

Joshua and Meredith were riding a pair of rented horses in the countryside south of Amsterdam. Meredith had proposed the outing. Low clouds, promising autumn rain and scudding from the northwest, hadn't curbed her enthusiasm.

"As much as I like living in Amsterdam, it's good to be in the country and on a horse. But," he laughed, "there aren't any hills to climb like at Stanford. And," he said, eyeing the clouds, "the climate here is just a tad wetter than in sunny California. Of course, there are plenty of cows and sheep. Reminds me of the farms around Shelby."

"It's the pull of your farm boy roots," Meredith said wryly.

"Speaking of which," Joshua said, winking his left eye, "if we are going to raise a family here, we must do more farming – of the conjugal variety."

"It could lead to a winter crop."

"Well-seeded, don't you agree?"

"From blue-ribbon stock, Mr.Bliss."

The first drops of cold rain began falling on their hatless heads. They laughed and wheeled their horses north, back toward Amsterdam.

Adolf Hitler was gloating. It was September 29 in Munich, and moments earlier he had signed a pact that would become known infamously as the Munich Agreement. It handed him precisely what he coveted – more land at a cheap price. British Prime Minister Neville Chamberlain and French Premier Edouard Daladier had penned their signatures to the agreement that awarded Hitler Czechoslovakia's Sudeten province with its 3.5 million German speakers. The "price" to Hitler: his promise to seek no further expansion of his Reich.

Chamberlain trumpeted the pact as a guarantee of "peace in our time." Yet privately he was hardly blind to Hitler and his aims. Back in London Chamberlain confided to staff that the fuhrer was "the blackest devil I've ever met."

First Lord of the Admiralty Winston Churchill, not predisposed to silence or renowned for reticence, voiced a different assessment of the agreement. His verdict to Chamberlain: "You have gained shame and you will get war."

Equally outspoken Queen Wilhelmina castigated the agreement as "an empty promise. Just like all of Hitler's. The man is a serial liar."

Two days after the signing, on October 1, Gemany officially annexed Sudetenland.

The coal-fired locomotive had the train steaming from Nijmegen northwest toward Amsterdam. After arriving, black-robed Father Brandsma went walking purposefully to Oude Kerk. He mounted its steps and began renewing his condemnation of Nazism and Adolf Hitler. His audience included Joshua and Meredith. Standing nearby were Raluca and Alicia.

"Our church is not without its flaws," the Carmelite priest acknowledged, earning additional respect with his candor. "The good Lord knows that. Our history has too many black marks. The Lord knows that too. But our church has done good, good that has benefited millions. Not only here in Europe but across the seas. Adolf Hitler and Nazism are different. He is evil personified. His perverse ideology is an affront to God. It is very possible that Hitler is an incarnation of the devil. He visits suffering – torture, murder – on innocents and knows no remorse. Let us pray that leaders of other nations can – will – stand strong against his future aggression that must be regarded as a certainty."

After Father Brandsma finished speaking, he extended both arms in an embrace of his audience. Many crowded closer. Joshua took Meredith's right hand in his left and began edging forward through the throng.

Father Brandsma was smiling engagingly, greeting and shaking hands with all who reached out. Moments later, Joshua and Meredith were standing before him. Joshua extended his right hand and Father Brandsma accepted it. "I've heard so much about you. I've tried reading your newspaper columns, but my ability to read Dutch isn't what it should be."

Father Brandsma chuckled. "But you speak it well. What is your first language?"

"English."

"British?"

"American."

"Ah. Wonderful. I hope someday to visit your homeland."

"I hope you do, Father. Let me introduce you to my wife, Meredith."

Father Brandsma reached for Meredith's right hand and shook it gently. "My pleasure."

Meredith smiled and reddened. "Father, it is my privilege to meet you. Your words are important, and they are being heard."

"Thank you. Your names?"

"I am Meredith Bliss and this is Joshua."

Raluca and Alicia were watching this exchange with envy. *If I wasn't a prostitute,* Raluca was reflecting sadly, *I would be there with the others. Shaking hands with God's messenger.*

Another man, six feet tall, husky and handsome, offered his hand to Father Brandsma. "As you can see, Father," he began, pointing to his yarmulke, "I am a Jew."

Father Brandsma took his hand. "Ah, one of God's chosen people. So good to meet you."

"Thank you, sir." They released each other's hand. "I brought my family here from Frankfurt after Hitler took power. I admire your work. It is important. Please continue."

"I will, I assure you, Mr.-"

"Folleck. Samuel Folleck."

"Where do you and your family live?"

"Merewede Square. I have a clothing shop there."

"Very good. My apparel needs are few and simple, but if I have a need for any, I will visit your shop."

"Please do, sir. It would be my distinct pleasure."

Joshua tapped Samuel Folleck's left shoulder. He pivoted and saw Joshua's smile and outstretched right hand. He took it and they shook firmly. Father Brandsma smiled at this unexpected connection – a bald American and a yarmulke-topped German Jew grasping hands in Amsterdam.

CHAPTER 19

Kristallnacht. Gestapo Sergeant Walter Baemer was holding a long-handled axe. He was standing at the head of a group of police in front of a Berlin shoe shop. His men were armed with axes, clubs and sledgehammers. All were wearing civilian clothes. It was 10:30 p.m. on November 9, 1938. Smirking, Baemer hefted the axe and swung. The shop's window glass shattered. Baemer stepped aside and one of the policemen tossed a burning torch onto the display of shoes. Eli Wasserman, a Jew, owned the shop. Kristallnacht (Crystal Night) was underway.

While Baemer and his henchmen watched the leaping flames, Wasserman and his wife and three children emerged from their apartment above the shop onto the street. When Wasserman raised his hands in protest, Baemer thrust the axe handle into Wasserman's abdomen. He grunted, his knees buckled and he slumped to the pavement. At a signal from Baemer the police moved forward and began kicking the fallen shop owner. His wife covered her face, contorted in anguish, and his children began screaming their horror. The kicking continued until blood was dripping from wounds to the man's face and he lay motionless. Eli Wasserman was Kristallnacht's first fatality.

Triggering the onslaught was an assassination that had occurred two days earlier – in Paris. Seventeen-year-old Herschel Grynszpan, German born, was deeply angered by the treatment of Jews, including his sister Berta, whom Hitler had ordered expelled from Germany. At the Germany-Poland border, Berta and other deportees were going hungry and being beaten by German guards. In desperation Berta sent Herschel a postcard on which she wrote, "We haven't a penny. Could you send us something?"

On Monday morning, November 7, Herschel bought a revolver and ammunition. He walked to Germany's embassy and asked to see an official. Wearing a suit, white shirt and necktie beneath a gray trench coat, he was escorted to the office of Ernst von Roth. Herschel pulled the revolver from his coat pocket and shot von Roth three times in the abdomen. Ironically, von Roth had expressed anti-Nazi sentiments, based largely on anti-Semitic measures, and was under Gestapo investigation for being politically unreliable. He died two days later.

Word of his death reached Hitler that evening at a dinner. In short order he and Goebbels had hatched the pogrom. By the time Goebbels called a halt to the violence on November 11, throughout Germany Kristallnacht atrocities had damaged or destroyed some 200 synagogues, many Jewish cemeteries, more than 7,000 Jewish-owned shops and 29 department stores. A reported 91 Jews were killed. Like the Wassermans, families of some victims were forced to watch the beatings. More than 30,000 Jewish men were arrested and dispatched to concentration camps – Dachau, Buchenwald, Sachsenhausen – where they were brutalized. Three months later, when released, more than 2,000 had been killed.

Kristallnacht in neighboring Austria was no less horrific. Most of Vienna's 94 synagogues and prayer houses were damaged or destroyed. Jews were beaten and otherwise humiliated. Some 100,000 Jews were arrested and 815 Jewish businesses ruined.

In one respect Hitler erred. Because foreign journalists still enjoyed free rein in Germany, Kristallnacht was widely reported – and condemned. Hugh Carleton Greene of London's *Daily Telegraph* wrote: *Mob law ruled in Berlin throughout the afternoon and evening and hordes of hooligans indulged in an orgy of destruction. I have seen several anti-Jewish outbreaks in Germany during the last five years, but never anything as nauseating as this. Racial hatred and hysteria seemed to have taken complete hold of otherwise decent people. I saw fashionably dressed women clapping their hands and screaming with glee, while respectable middle-class mothers held up their babies to see the "fun."*

During the following 10 months, Jewish emigration from Germany surged. More than 115,000 exited the Reich, most to other European countries, the United States and Palestine, but some 14,000 to Shanghai, the most "European" of Asian cities.

In a press release, Goebbels ascribed Kristallnacht to the "healthy instincts" of fellow countrymen. "The German people," Goebbels proclaimed, "are anti-Semitic. It has no desire to have its rights restricted or to be provoked in the future by parasites of the Jewish races."

Outside Germany the pogrom shredded Nazi pretenses at integrity and respectability. Father Brandsma was thinking, but restrained himself from uttering the words Joshua Bliss had grumbled to Meredith: "Heartless bastards. They are criminals who deserve only to be lined up and shot. I would regard it as a privilege to pull the trigger."

CHAPTER 20

Christmas season, 1938. Joshua pulled open and held the door to Folleck's Fine Clothing while Meredith stepped inside.

"Mr. Bliss, Mrs. Bliss!" Samuel greeted them. "Welcome to my shop." He approached the couple, and Joshua reached forward to shake hands.

"With winter coming on, there are a few things we wanted, and we thought we'd check out your store."

"That is very nice of you. How may I help?"

"For one thing," said Joshua, "we are looking for wool stocking caps."

"Wonderful. I have quite a selection. Sailors snap them up."

"Well," Joshua smiled, "I'm not exactly a sailor but I do work for the Netherlands Royal Steamship Company."

"Close enough," Samuel Folleck chuckled. "This way, please."

Joshua spotted a dark brown cap that appealed to him. He tried it on and it fit snugly. "It's simple and I like simple. I'll take this one."

"I like that one," Meredith said. She picked up a navy blue cap with a matching, floppy tassel.

"Very good," Samuel said. "Anything else?"

"Yes," said Meredith, "we would like to see your scarves."

"Of course. Right over here."

On a rack containing more than a dozen scarves Joshua immediately eyed a bright orange, wide wool creation. "That's the one for me," he smiled.

Meredith's head shook. "Talk about clashing. Brown cap and an orange scarf, and your coat is blue."

"Hey," Joshua said, eyes twinkling, "I like clashing. Besides, orange is Holland's national color. I'll fit right in."

Meredith rolled her eyes upward, and Samuel's glistened with mirth.

"Mr. Folleck," she said, "I would like one that matches my new blue cap."

Samuel accepted payment for their purchases and wrapped them in plain white paper secured with white string. "I would like you to meet my wife. She is in the back room, working on our books."

"We would love to meet her," said Meredith.

Moments later she and Joshua were shaking hands with petite Miriam Folleck, nearly a foot shorter than her husband.

A thought popped into Meredith's mind. She tugged Joshua's left arm, led him to the shop's door and whispered. Joshua replied, smiling and whispering his concurrence. They then returned to the sales counter.

"Mr. and Mrs. Folleck," Meredith began, "would you please accept our invitation to join us at our home for dinner? And bring your children?"

Samuel and Miriam looked at each other in obvious surprise. After a moment's hesitation, Miriam replied, "Yes. We would love to." Samuel was beaming.

"Wonderful!" said Meredith. "I can cook kosher, if you prefer."

Miriam's answer came quickly. "That's very thoughtful, dear, but not necessary."

In Rhenen on the afternoon of December 5 the Looten family members were savoring anticipation. The next day they would be celebrating the coming of Sinterklaas. Leading up to the occasion, family members had been buying small gifts, composing poems and penning jokes. The night before the arrival of Sinterklaas, Luc, Karin and Catherina followed age-old tradition; they left bulky wooden shoes near the living room fireplace. They filled the shoes with hay for Sinterklaas's gift-bearing donkey. After the children had gone to bed, Sinterklaas's helpers – Bert and Dora – removed the hay and left little gifts, mostly sweets. Larger gifts were placed in a white cloth sack and left beside the fireplace.

On the morning of December 6 gifts were removed from the wooden shoes and the sack, and the poems and jokes were read aloud.

The children, now ages 17, 15 and 13, did not deem themselves too old to continue the tradition.

"It is too much fun to not believe in Sinterklaas," Luc grinned.

"You are still a child at heart," Catherina teased him.

"I hope I shall always remain so," Luc sniffed with faux haughtiness.

"I do too," Karin said with perfected mock snobbishness.

All three children – and their parents – broke into joyous laughter.

On Christmas morning Joshua and Meredith were strolling from Prinsengracht to Oude Kerk for a 10 a.m. service. Joshua was wearing a blue suit and matching necktie. His brown stocking cap was covering his bald head, and his orange scarf peeked out from above the collar of his blue top coat.

After the service, instead of returning west to their home, they began strolling east on Molensteeg.

"We're far from home but it still feels like Christmas," Meredith said.

"Maybe because we are feeling more and more at home here."

"Home or not, that scarf still clashes with everything," Meredith scolded mildly.

"That's why I keep wearing it, wife. To annoy you. So get used to it." He was grinning wickedly. She punched his arm. "But I also wear it as a sign of my respect for the Dutch."

They crossed a bridge spanning a canal and were approaching a second. Standing on it, chatting, were Raluca Johnescu and Alicia Domian. Anna Clarbout had closed the brothel for Christmas Eve and Day.

As Meredith and Joshua passed the two young women, he nodded politely and smiled. Raluca and Alicia watched them moving along.

"They look familiar," Raluca said quietly. "I am sure we have seen them before."

"I think I know where," Alicia said. "When Father Brandsma was speaking at Oude Kerk."

"Yes, you are right. Interesting. He is wearing an orange scarf, but I don't think he is Dutch."

"How can you tell?"

"His size. He is both tall and broad. And his walk, his smile. Not Dutch, not French."

"Then what?"

"I am not sure. Perhaps American." A pause. "I have seen only a few Americans, but they seem to walk with a certain swagger. They seem blessed with confidence."

"I noticed his wife," said Alicia. "She is blond and beautiful."

"And serene. I think she must love him deeply."

"Let us hope they have a long life together," Alicia said. "That can be one of our Christmas wishes."

The Lootens marked Christmas day as a purely religious holiday. No exchange of gifts, no feast. All five walked to the magnificent Rhenen church, then 446 years old. Afterward Luc, Karin and Catherina went skating with Sonja and Bernard Depauw on the ice of a large pond located just west of Rhenen and close to the Rhine.

"I think we are so lucky to live in Holland," Sonja said dreamily. "Everything is so beautiful. The flowers, the windmills, the farms with their animals. I don't think I would want to live anywhere else."

"I think I would like to stay in Rhenen," said Karin. "It is small and we all are friends."

"Maybe," Sonja said, eyes crinkling in mirth, "I could marry Luc, and you could marry Bernard and we could all stay best friends forever."

Karin did something she rarely did: giggled. "I wonder how Luc and Bernard would feel about that."

"Let's race!" Luc cried. "And then go to our house for hot chocolate."

Sonja and Karin looked at each other and both giggled. Then the five ebullient skaters went flashing across the pond.

Christmas morning in Freiburg was proving particularly happy for Karl and Hannah Kramer. Their apartment was decorated gaily with sprigs of evergreen and lighted candles. They could hear church bells peeling.

Hannah stood barefoot and toe-to-toe with Karl and wrapped her arms around his waist. "I love you."

"I love you too."

"Do you have enough love left over for someone else?" she asked coquettishly.

Karl's eyes widened. "What do you mean?"

Hannah's eyes were glistening. "I think I am pregnant."

"You are? I mean, are you certain?"

"I haven't seen a doctor, but I haven't bled in two months."

"Why didn't you tell me earlier?"

"I wanted to make telling you my special Christmas gift." Karl squeezed and kissed Hannah. "If our baby is a boy," she cooed dreamily, "I think he will be as intelligent, kind and handsome as you."

"If it is a girl," Karl replied softly, "I am sure she will be as beautiful and smart as you are." A pause. "Girl or boy, my Christmas wish is that our child will always live in peace."

CHAPTER 21

In early 1939 tensions were rising in Europe, and Adolf Hitler was the proximate cause. He was enjoying himself hugely. His ambition and reach were again demonstrated when he annexed the rest of Czechoslovakia on March 15.

"The Ides of March were Julius Caesar's downfall," he crowed to Joseph Goebbels. "But for me they are promising – promising more living space for Germany, more riches and pride for the people of our expanding Reich."

"Your vision is unparalleled," replied Goebbels, "as is your mastery of the bold stroke."

Soon after, Hitler arrived in Prague to celebrate his latest, bloodless triumph. As at Vienna, in the Czech capital he was hailed with the wild enthusiasm of a Roman emperor, in his white chariot, drawn by a foursome of proud white stallions, basking in public adulation after a victorious campaign against nettlesome barbarians. In Prague, Hitler was standing on the floor beside the front seat of an open car. The applause cascading over him was thunderous.

Poland possessed a friendship treaty with Germany, but it was fraying, a reality not lost on the Poles. As a result, Poland reached out to Great Britain, and the two governments crafted and signed a mutual assistance pact on April 6.

When news of the pact was broadcast over Dutch radio, Raluca's reaction was one shared by many thoughtful people around the globe. "The pact is useless," Raluca told Alicia. "Even I know that Britain could not come to Poland's aid in a war. Certainly not with men and weapons. The distance is too great and the routes too dangerous. The pact has nice words, but nice words will count for little if Hitler has designs on Poland."

On April 28 Hitler again demanded the return of Danzig and the Polish Corridor. Simultaneously he erased any remaining doubt about his determination by renouncing Germany's friendship treaty with Poland.

Karl Kramer slumped into a chair. Hanna, now visibly pregnant, had handed him an official looking envelope postmarked Berlin. He reached into his pocket for a small, folding knife and sliced open the envelope. He unfolded the single-sheet letter. "I am being conscripted."

Calmly he placed letter, envelope and knife on the lamp table. Then he reached up and pulled Hannah onto his lap.

"How long?" she asked sadly. "How long must you serve?"

"The letter doesn't say. It only tells me when to report." His right arm squeezed her gently while his left rubbed her bulging abdomen. "However long it is, I will have but one goal – survival. I will do what I must to survive. For you and the baby."

In Rhenen a postal carrier delivered the same kind of envelope to Luc Looten. He used his mother's paring knife to slice it open. He unfolded the letter and began reading. Dora saw color draining from her son's face. After he finished reading, Luc sucked in a deep breath and let it out slowly. "This will be a very special birthday, my eighteenth."

Dora reached for the letter, took it from Luc's hands and read. Within moments she was blinking back tears. She was thinking that Bert already probably knew about the conscription notice. At the post office he likely had handled several such envelopes addressed to Rhenen's young men. He would have deduced their content.

"I will bake you a special cake," Dora said lovingly. "What would you like?"

"Chocolate with chocolate icing," Luc smiled, knowing that was Karin and Catherina's favorite. "But first I think I will see if the girls would like to go kite flying. It might be our last chance to fly them for a long time."

In The Hague in her Noordeinde Palace office, Queen Wilhelmina was huddled with Prime Minister de Geer.

"Events are moving swiftly," she observed. "Too swiftly. What are you doing to strengthen our nation's defense?"

"I am trying my best to persuade Parliament to increase defense spending."

Wilhelmina sighed disgustedly. "Sometimes trying one's best isn't good enough. I am sure you understand."

The young man was wearing heavy cotton work clothes – a blue long-sleeve shirt and green trousers. He was squatting, fastening a brown cable to a small brown metal box with a knob that would be used to select channels.

Standing over him and watching curiously was Russell Forbes. In the spring of 1939 he had surprised Victoria by purchasing a television. It was one of only 20,000 in New York.

The installer stood and adjusted a small antenna that was fastened to the television's rear. "All right, sir, let's see what we get." He turned a small knob beneath the picture tube, and the dark screen flickered to life. Four masked horsemen, riding hard and shooting revolvers, were pursuing a stagecoach bouncing across a dusty desertscape behind a straining six-horse team.

The small screen measured only five inches diagonally. It was housed in a wooden cabinet that also contained a phonograph and storage compartment designed to accommodate 78 rpm records. "A console television," the salesman had told Russell. "It's a handsome piece of furniture for any living room." He was describing General Electric Model HM-171 that retailed for $795.

"I could have bought another car for that!" Russell later confided to Victoria. "Well, okay, a used car."

Although in its commercial infancy in 1939, television technology had already compiled more than half a century of multi-national history. Paul Nipkow, a 23-year-old German university student, patented the first electromechanical television system in 1884. Constantin Perskyi coined the word television in 1900, and the abbreviation TV soon followed. Georges Rignoux and A. Fournier conducted the first TV demonstration in 1909 in Paris.

In New York City regularly scheduled programming had begun on August 14, 1928. That same year in Schenectady, New York General Electric was broadcasting programming four nights a week.

After the installer left, Russell dimmed the living room lights, sat on a sofa and called Victoria who was arranging flowers in a dining room vase.

She entered the living room and squinted at the cowboy movie showing on the tiny screen.

Russell patted the sofa and said, "Sit." As Victoria eased herself down, she reached for her bottom to smooth her dress.

"Well," said Russell, "what do you think?"

"Of that?" He nodded. "I might need glasses to see what's on the screen."

His eyes rolled upward. "Don't you see the future?"

"Future? That's an old western movie."

"That's now. I can see the day when television will be reporting news. World news."

"The Times does a good job of keeping up with events," she replied.

"Agreed," said Russell. "But television could be faster. Just imagine showing images from the most distant places on earth – right into our living room. Maybe one day we could see Meredith and Josh walking along a canal in Amsterdam."

"That's utter foolishness," Victoria replied dismissively. "Even radio can't do that."

Russell knew that pushing his vision of future television technology would be greeted only by more of Victoria's skepticism. He decided to shift direction – to the past. "Do you know what this evening reminds me of?"

"No, what?"

"We're watching a movie in a darkened room."

"Yes?"

"That's a clue."

"I don't get it."

"Think back to when we were dating. We were sitting in a movie theater balcony. Over on Lexington Avenue. It was the first time you let me put my hand between your thighs."

"Oh my," Victoria giggled, "one of my weaker moments."

"Yes, dear, but even weaker ones followed. I wonder if our daughters could imagine us in pre-marital clinches."

"I hope not," Victoria laughed. "Actually, even though they're married themselves they might not be able to imagine their parents doing the deed today."

"Or tonight," Russell said, grinning. His left hand reached for the hem of Victoria's dress, then began sliding toward her crotch. She didn't resist.

Unexpectedly, romance intruded Joshua's thoughts. He was at his desk in Scheepvaarthuis. He heard a tugboat horn and looked up. From his office window, he found himself watching the S.S. Simon Bolivar docking when an epiphany struck. The passenger liner owned by his employer had been commissioned in 1927. It displaced 7,906 tons, stretched to 440 feet and cruised at 16 miles per hour. Captain H. Voorspuiy commanded the ship.

"We haven't had a proper honeymoon," he said to Meredith at home that evening. "What would you think about sailing our company's Simon Bolivar to England and taking in the sites in London?" Meredith gazed lovingly and silently. "Well?" he asked.

"Joshua Bliss, I heartily endorse your idea. It's positively splendid! When do we go?"

"It'll be a while, I'm afraid. Between my work and the ship's schedule, it looks like November."

"Book us, Josh. It will be great fun anticipating the trip. I can't wait to write Mom and Dad. And Clarisse and Christine too." A pause. "November. We could do our Christmas shopping in London. At Harrod's. I've heard so much about it. Oh, this is so exciting."

CHAPTER 22

The arrival of warmer weather in 1939 saw the ongoing construction of a wall of military steel in Europe. On May 22 Adolf Hitler and Benito Mussolini shocked many of planet earth's inhabitants by signing an agreement they grandiosely dubbed the Rome-Berlin Axis. The most obvious consequence: The pact put Hitler closer to controlling a slice of Europe running north-south from the Baltic Sea to the Mediterranean. In addition it gave the fuhrer another jumping off point for conquest in Africa.

Amsterdam long had been regarded as Holland's capital and was the site of the Royal Palace, hard by Oude Kerk and the red light district. But the actual seat of national government was The Hague (Den Haag in Dutch). The seaside city was founded in 1230. Its official name: Des Graven Hage (Dutch, literally, "the count's wood" and less literally "the count's hedge or private enclosure"). It was where Queen Wilhelmina spent the majority of her days. By the time she had ascended the throne in 1890, The Hague was the nation's administrative, legislative, judicial and diplomatic hub. Along with the queen's Noordeinde Palace all foreign embassies were located there. So was the Binnenhof, the sprawling home of the nation's parliamentary buildings that encircled a spacious courtyard and its ornate fountain. Binnenhof translated literally as binnen, meaning "inner," and hof, meaning "court." But the Dutch used Binnenhof more as a shorthand way of referring to the complex of parliamentary buildings. Distinguishing them were handsome stone facades, steeply pitched roofs and soaring pinnacles. Fronting the Binnenhof was the Hofvijver, a placid lake that in summer saw ducks swimming and in winter people skating on its frozen surface.

Queen Wilhelmina was in her Noordeinde Palace office when Prime Minister de Geer brought word of the announcement of the Rome-Berlin Axis. Her clear, gray eyes peered past de Geer and out her office window. "This so-called axis puts every other nation in Europe in jeopardy."

"But certainly not The Netherlands," de Geer protested. "We were neutral in the First World War, and we will make it abundantly clear to any and all that we will remain neutral in any future conflict."

Wilhelmina couldn't yet bring herself to calling her prime minister naive, but that's what she was thinking. "This axis is a partnership in name only, not in fact. Hitler will dominate and call the shots. The military shots. Mussolini sees pairing with Hitler as an opportunity for more self-aggrandizement. Mussolini's ego is a match for Hitler's. His hubris might exceed Hitler's. But his intellect, his political savvy and Italy's resources and manufacturing base are no match for the fuhrer and Germany."

"We have had our enemies," de Geer conceded. "Spain for one. But not Germany."

"Since at least the 1400s," Wilhelmina mused, "The Hague's symbol as been the stork – the bird that brings new life. I fear this odious axis will bring only death."

In Freiburg, Hannah Kramer was worrying about both life and death. Her contractions were coming at ever briefer intervals. Compounding her anxiety was Karl's absence; he was away at a Wehrmacht training camp and unreachable.

A few minutes after 9 p.m. on July 29, Hannah's water broke and she was verging on panic. She shuffled to a nearby apartment and asked the matronly woman for help. Minutes later Dr. Robert Kreiter, the neighbor woman at his heels, entered Hannah's apartment. His first priority was calming the frightened young mother to be.

An hour later he was slapping the bottom of a boy. He examined the crying infant and smiled. "All fingers and toes accounted for. He appears to be perfect in every respect." He handed the newborn to the neighbor woman. "Please clean him."

Tears of joy were streaming down Hannah's cheeks and moistening her pillow. "Thank you, Doctor. Thank you so much for coming."

"A new life," Dr. Kreiter marveled. "Is there any greater miracle? Any greater joy?"

Hitler's scheming was proceeding apace. On August 23 he and Joseph Stalin signed a non-aggression pact that secretly sanctioned the partition of Poland between Germany and Russia.

In her Noordeinde office, Wilhelmina was reading headlines of newspapers delivered by de Geer.

"Mr. Stalin might be relaxing, even feeling complacent. But if I were him," the queen opined, "I would now expect Hitler to attempt what Napoleon tried but failed to do – take Moscow."

"I fear you are becoming too pessimistic," said de Geer. "Forgive me for saying so, but you are being quite cynical."

Wilhelmina sighed, her exasperation evident. "Prime Minister, I am being quite realistic."

Eight days later, September 1, at 4:45 a.m., Germany invaded Poland. Some 250,000 Wehrmacht infantry went sweeping across the border. They were organized into 60 divisions, nine of them armored. Battalions of tanks rumbled along with the infantry. Providing air cover were 1,600 of Hermann Goering's stuka dive bombers with their terrifying wing-mounted whistles.

Poland's armed forces were numerous and courageous but outmoded and ill-prepared. Providing the first line of defense were 10,000 Polish lancers. Those mounted warriors were holding seven-foot-long lances. They all had rifles strapped to their backs. They would avoid assaulting tanks, seeing that as suicidal. But they would charge German infantry and inflict as many casualties as possible before wheeling their warhorses and withdrawing. Some would die but many would escape to fight another day – in Poland and later in France, Italy, Belgium and The Netherlands.

Superior German forces were squeezing the defenders, closing in on Warsaw from the west, north and south. Only the Vistula River to Warsaw's east prevented a complete encirclement.

Two days later, September 3, Britain and France made good on their assistance agreement with Poland by declaring war on Germany. To Winston Churchill's chagrin, his post-Munich Agreement prediction had proved all too accurate.

Britain's declaration caused Hitler to convene a meeting with Admiral Karl Donitz, chief of submarine or U-boat operations. "England should be suing for peace, not declaring war," the fuhrer lectured Donitz. "Well, you must begin taking necessary measures – precautionary measures – to persuade England and France that it would be foolhardy to try helping Poland with men, weapons or supplies of any kind."

To Donitz, Hitler's message was as clear as water gushing from a spring originating deep beneath the surface. Donitz's naval forces would begin launching U-boat attacks and sowing British shipping lanes with mines.

Radio Berlin was reporting these world-shaking developments. In Freiburg the Kramers were listening with dismay. Karl had returned home on leave and had been cherishing his time with Hannah and Thierry. Germany's invasion of Poland had cast a black cloud of anxiety over their joyous reunion.

"My future is now sealed as tightly as an envelope with wax. I will be fighting as part of history, not teaching it. There is only one question: Will I be fighting in the East or here in the West?"

"But," Hannah observed bleakly, "there is no war here in the West. Only a declaration."

"It is only a matter of time. I have no doubt about Hitler's designs. He has plans to conquer all of Europe."

"He is mad."

"Oh yes. If not mad then unstable and wrong-headed. He holds himself out as a student of history. If that is true, he must have received a failing grade."

"Can't someone reason with him?"

"Few dare that course of action. Some have tried and they have disappeared."

Distressing events continued unfolding. On September 6 the Polish government correctly viewed its situation as untenable and fled Warsaw for Lublin, Poland's largest city east of the Vistula and dating to the 10th century.

On September 17 the government fled farther east and south into Romania. On that same day Stalin, acting on his secret pact with Hitler, ordered his Red Army into Poland. Stalin claimed that Russia merely was "protecting our own frontiers." He did view Russia's invasion serving as a cushion against Hitler's unsatiated ambition. But he also was seizing an opportunity to exact revenge for Russia's humiliation by the Poles during The Great War.

Eventually, Poland's leaders would escape to the West, first establishing a government-in-exile in Paris and later in London. In the interim, Poles in Warsaw, soldiers and civilians alike, kept on fighting bravely. With ammunition and foodstocks depleted and casualties mounting swiftly, Warsaw at last surrendered on September 28.

CHAPTER 23

During the next seven months Hitler attempted no more territorial gains. Many in the West took to calling the lull the "phony war." Defenses relaxed.

But as early as October 9, a mere 11 days after Poland's surrender, Hitler was readying Germany to flex its military muscle in another direction – west. He had issued an order to his senior staff: *Preparations should be made for offensive action on the northern flank of the Western Front, crossing the area of Luxembourg, Belgium and The Netherlands. This attack must be carried out as soon and as forcefully as possible.*

He also ordered the capture of Dutch Army uniforms to outfit spies who would infiltrate Holland and report on Dutch defensive capabilities. Dutch sympathizers of Nazism gladly procured the uniforms.

November 10. The weather in Amsterdam was cooling. In their third floor walkup on Molensteeg, Raluca and Alicia were contentedly knitting sweaters.

"Thank goodness there are so many sheep in the countryside," Alicia observed. "Wool is cheap."

"Let's knit an extra sweater – for Madame Clarbout."

"Wonderful idea!" Alicia replied. "She likes fancy things. Perhaps we should add a little lace to the neckline."

"Good thinking."

November 10. "Guess what?" Joshua asked excitedly when Meredith greeted him that afternoon as he returned from work to their home on Prinsengracht.

"Pray, tell your fair maiden. I take it the answer to your question must be good news."

"Better than good," Joshua exulted. "I have us booked on the Simon Bolivar to England."

"Oh, Josh! When?"

"November 18 we sail," he said gleefully.

"Only a short voyage and we'll be there."

"It's about a hundred miles to the port of Southampton. Then we take a train up to London."

"I can barely wait!" Meredith was feeling as though she might erupt with excitement.

"London awaits us," said Joshua. "The British Museum, the Tower of London, Westminster Abbey, St. Paul's."

"Do you know where else I'd like to visit?" Meredith asked. "Ye Olde Cheshire Cheese."

"What's that?"

"It was Samuel Johnson's favorite pub. I've looked it up, and it's just up an alley north of Fleet Street. It actually has a Fleet Street address, 145. The pub displays some of Johnson's early dictionaries. I would love to see them."

"Consider it done," Joshua said decisively.

Johnson (1709-1784) was a gifted and versatile writer, authoring magazine articles, a biography, essays, a play, a preface to a collection of Shakespeare's works, and more.

From 1747 to 1755 Johnson compiled his Dictionary of the English Language, a massive work noted for its comprehensiveness and its author's occasionally humorous definitions. He lived just around the corner from Ye Olde Cheshire Cheese.

"It should be a fun place to visit," Meredith enthused. "I read that it has plain plank tables and sawdust on the floor. Right out of the Middle Ages. And it has a fireplace that should make it really cozy in late November."

November 17. "You are remarkable," Alicia told Raluca. "You are already getting started."

Alicia was sitting on one of their two violet living room chairs. She was alluding to the materials Raluca had assembled to begin making lace. On their settee Raluca was sitting with a small pillow on her lap. She was drawing a design on a sheaf of parchment that she had fastened to the pillow. Beside her were small pegs she would be inserting into the pillow along the lines of her design. Next to the pegs were many small bobbins of white linen thread that she would work around the pegs. The result would be what the Dutch often called pillow lace.

"If I become good enough," Raluca said without looking up, "I can sell lace to local shops and increase our income – and savings."

"Can I help?"

"Watch closely. If we both learn to make good lace, maybe we could open our own lace shop."

"The new life we have dreamed about," Alicia murmured wistfully.

"Exactly."

"We will make it happen," Alicia said with conviction.

"We should write another letter to our families," Raluca said.

"You will write mine for me again?"

"Of course."

Alicia rose from the chair and stepped in front of Raluca. She bent forward, reached out and gently hugged Raluca around her neck. "We are sisters," Alicia murmured happily. "I love you."

November 17. Army training for Luc Looten was proving strenuous. Hiking long distances with full packs. Learning to fire and clean a rifle, throw a grenade, thrust a bayonet, crawl through muck beneath live fire. Weather was adding to training's misery. Cold, wet, wind-driven rain was blowing in daily from the North Sea. Shivering was becoming nearly as regular as breathing.

On completing training, Luc learned that he would be assigned to the 22nd Infantry Regiment that was based at the center of the Grebbe Line at Rhenen.

"I am grateful," Luc told an army friend. "I will be stationed close to my family."

November 18. At 6 a.m. Captain Voorspuiy gave the order and the Simon Bolivar began inching away from the Amsterdam dock. After a first stop at Southampton, the vessel would continue to its final destination in the West Indies.

On the top deck Meredith and Joshua were among the throng waving gaily in the dim light to friends come to say farewell. The manifest showed the ship was carrying 400 passengers, including 34 children, in three classes and crew. Joshua and Meredith were occupying a first-class cabin, courtesy of the line's chief executive, Ernst Heldring. Most of the passengers were Dutch (111), English (77) and German (47). Meredith and Joshua were among a small American contingent.

Weather was raw, typical of the North Sea in late autumn. A stiff westerly wind passing over the North Sea's cold waters was reddening Joshua and Meredith's faces.

Soon after reaching the open sea, Joshua and Meredith joined other first-class passengers in going below to a spacious dining room where they consumed a hearty breakfast of eggs, bacon, toast and strong coffee.

"Did black coffee ever taste better?" Joshua asked.

"That's one of your rhetorical questions," Meredith teased. "First one I've heard in a while."

After eating Joshua and Meredith braved the bracing wind and returned to the open, top deck. "I should have worn slacks instead of a dress," Meredith said. "Next time I go below I'll change."

Soon Captain Voorspuiy began making the rounds, shaking hands with adults and patting children's heads. Joshua and Meredith were wearing the stocking caps purchased at Samuel Folleck's shop. When Captain Voorspuiy greeted the young couple and heard Joshua's name, he beamed.

"I understand you are one of our company's men. If you or your wife need anything at all, just let me know."

"Thank you, sir," said Joshua, "we will."

After the captain moved on, Meredith said softly, "He seems like a nice man."

"Highly regarded," Joshua replied, "by Mr. Heldring."

Slicing through swells, the Simon Bolivar was heading southwest across the lower reaches of the North Sea. The ship was on course to pass through the Strait of Dover and into the English Channel. After steaming past historic Hastings (site of William The Conqueror's 1066 victory over King Harold), Brighton and Portsmouth, the ship would make its Southampton stop.

Nearing lunch hour, Meredith shivered and said, "I'm going below to our cabin. I need to pee."

Joshua chortled. "All that coffee and this cold wind does have a certain effect on kidneys."

"Very funny, Bliss."

"Do you want me to come with you?"

"Not unless you have to pee too. I'll be back in a few minutes."

Joshua, smiling his love, watched his bride pull open a door to begin descending steel stairs. Standing at the starboard rail he returned his gaze to the west. The Simon Bolivar was nearing the estuary of the Thames River on England's east coast. Joshua was smiling with anticipation. He looked at his watch. 12:30 p.m. I might as well go below too, he was thinking. Pee and wash my hands before lunch.

The ship's crow's nest was attached to the front mast, a little more than halfway to the top. The officer on watch duty shivered and rubbed his chilled hands together. Another thirty minutes before my shift ends. He put his powerful binoculars against his eyes and scanned the water for hazards. Can't be too careful in busy shipping lanes, he thought. Just ahead and slightly to starboard he saw a shadow in the water. He gulped, blinked and looked again. He reached to pull the lanyard to ring the warning bell. Too late.

Before Joshua could move away from the rail, a thunderous explosion shattered the tranquility. Joshua's hands lost their grip on the rail, and he rocked backward as flames and sharp shards of steel and other objects rocketed up and beyond the starboard side. Dazed, Joshua was surprised to find himself in a sitting position. Then shrieking voices began raggedly piercing the sea air. He looked around. Several adults and three children were lying still. Others were bloodied and groaning. He shook his head to clear his mind and bellowed, "Meredith!"

In their cabin the explosion had knocked Meredith off the toilet seat. What in the world? she thought. This can't be good. I've got to get to Joshua. She struggled to her feet and hurriedly pulled up her panties and stockings. She forgot about changing into slacks and ran for the cabin door. She pulled it open and looked down the passageway toward the stairs. She could see flames beginning to erupt.

Joshua regained his footing and began stumbling over and around fallen passengers toward the door. He heard a voice calling and turned. It was Captain Voorspuiy. Blood was coursing down his face from a gash above his left ear. "Are you all right, Mr. Bliss?"

"I think so. You?"

The captain's left hand felt for the wound. It came away blood-covered. "I think I'll be all right. I need to get my crew to seeing after passengers. Your wife?"

"She went below."

"Go to her."

Joshua pulled open the door and immediately felt heat. In the next instant flames were climbing the stairs. "Meredith!" he called. "Meredith, can you hear me?"

"Josh. The fire." She choked on black, gaseous smoke. "I can't get up the stairs."

"Meredith, don't wait for the crew to get the fire under control. Head to the stern and the stairs there."

"Okay. Josh, how are you?"

"I'm fine."

"What happened?"

"I don't know. Go. Go now."

"Okay."

"Meredith. I love you."

"Me too for you, Bliss."

She backed away from the flames and began retreating down the passageway. At the door to their cabin, Meredith hesitated. She pulled it open. I need to get my stocking cap and coat. Quickly she pulled them on and returned to the passageway. She looked to her left, toward the stern.

On the top deck Captain Voorspuiy's crewmen were beginning to combat the flames with extinguishers and calm passengers. Within minutes they were helping children and adults into lifeboats. Before crew could begin lowering them, a second explosion, on the port side and as violent as the first blast, rocked the ship. Another round of screams erupted from terrified passengers, and more flames were shooting skyward. A nine-inch glass shard bored into Captain Voorspuiy's upper left chest and he fell.

The watch officer in the crow's nest looked down and was sickened by the carnage. Then he felt the mast begin toppling. He screamed primally.

Joshua began stepping toward the captain when a hunk of flying steel shot upward and hammered his head just behind his left temple. He could feel himself falling. The impact seemed to jar loose every bone in his skull, but he felt no pain. He did feel consciousness slipping away. A strange and strangely peaceful sensation. He saw himself in a small, high-ceilinged room. It was dimly lit. The walls were black. Faint light filtered through the lone window, a tiny aperture near the ceiling. Then an unseen hand reached up and slowly pulled down an opaque shade. Impenetrable blackness.

Heat and smoke were stinging Meredith's eyes and throat. She coughed. Twice. As she was nearing the rear stairs, she felt the ship tilting toward its stern. She looked down and spread her arms, struggling to maintain balance. When she looked up, new danger greeted her. A curtain of flames was blocking the stairs.

In the radio room, the operator muttered, "Bloody fucking time not to work." The explosions had rendered his radio set useless.

The tilting Meredith experienced was the Simon Bolivar settling into the sea by its stern. A combination of damage from the explosions, spreading fire and in-rushing sea water was complicating and slowing the lowering of life boats.

To escape billowing smoke, Meredith went scurrying back toward the center of the long passageway. There, coughing, she dropped to her hands and knees to stay below the rising smoke. "Dear Lord," she whispered, "please spare me." She coughed twice more and rested her forehead against the deck, trying to focus on finding a way out.

Though the Simon Bolivar's disabled radio was unable to transmit an S.O.S., a measure of luck worked to its advantage. Almost immediately, other vessels in the busy Thames estuary shipping lanes went steaming toward the stricken, blazing liner. They were ignoring the threat of more torpedoes or mines. Soon they were taking on survivors, raising some from lifeboats and plucking others from the sea.

CHAPTER 24

The two explosions had blown down both of the Simon Bolivar's masts, and she had foundered quickly, sinking to the depths of the English Channel.

Joshua awakened slowly on the deck of a rescue vessel. He found himself wrapped in a heavy, blue wool blanket. Fellow passengers in a lifeboat had snatched him from the cold water.

"You are quite the lucky fellow," a British businessman told him. "You weren't wearing a life jacket. We saw you falling and grabbed you as soon as you struck the water."

Joshua nodded groggily. "My wife, I need to find her."

"That could take a while, sir. Many boats helped in the rescue."

Some survivors were taken to nearby, coastal Harwich. Others including Joshua were among those transported to London's St. Thomas Hospital, located just across Westminster Bridge from the House of Commons. The hospital was one of London's most renowned. In 1856 a grateful British public gave nurse Florence Nightingale, of Crimean War fame, a gift of $150,000. She used it to fund the Nightingale Home For Nurses at St. Thomas.

Of the 400 aboard the Simon Bolivar when it left Amsterdam, 84 died. Among them were Captain Voorspuiy and Meredith Bliss.

In The Netherlands news of the sinking shocked and angered virtually every resident. Ernst Heldring was distraught. He and his staff worked quickly to identify casualties, mourning the dead and pledging assistance to the wounded. He also phoned Prime Minister de Geer.

"You will lodge a formal complaint to Germany's ambassador to The Hague and seek compensation," Heldring said forcefully, his temper barely held in check.

"We have no proof it was Germany's doing," de Geer replied bureaucratically.

Heldring exploded. "Who else on earth would mine the English Channel? Do you require Adolf Hitler to phone you and say, 'My fault?'"

"I am sorry," said de Geer, "but my hands are tied, unless we can establish that the mines were of German origin."

"Mr. Prime Minister," Heldring said acidly, "may I remind you that remnants of those mines are lying at the bottom of the sea with my ship and the innocent souls who went down with her?"

"I do understand your distress," de Geer said, trying to placate Heldring.

"No, sir, you most clearly do not."

Something unusual was prevailing at the Folleck supper table: silence. The radio report of the sinking left the Folleck family with heavy hearts. "I pray that Mr. and Mrs. Bliss survived," Samuel whispered, ending the quietude. "I know Mr. Bliss was very excited about the voyage. So was Meredith, he told me."

"May God be with all who were on that ship," Miriam murmured. "The living and the dead."

"The radio report said torpedoes or mines are suspected," said Aaron, 13. "Who do you suppose would do something like that?"

Adolf Hitler summoned Admiral Donitz. The naval commander smartly strode the long walk from the far end of Hitler's office to his desk. The admiral was wondering how Hitler was reacting to the news, including the heavy loss of life.

The fuhrer rose and Donitz saluted. "Sit down, Admiral." Hitler's face was offering no clues. His words, however, did that and more. Without preamble, Hitler began. "That should be a clear message to the Dutch and every nation with people on that ship." Hitler, Donitz was thinking, must be forgetting that Germans were among the casualties. "Especially the British and that blowhard Churchill. His Royal Navy and the Dutch shipping companies will be more cautious. They will think twice before trying to aid our enemies."

Not a word about the people onboard the Bolivar, Donitz was musing. Callous. That is the word that seems to best fit Herr Hitler. His eyes seem unseeing, like those of a dead man. "You no doubt are correct," Donitz replied obsequiously. "Britain has declared war on us, and it should realize that bears consequences."

"Very good," said Hitler, lowering his dark eyes to papers on his desk. "That will be all."

The next afternoon Joshua was discharged from St. Thomas. Dutch embassy staff were there to greet and look after survivors.

"Are you certain you are ready to leave?" Joshua was asked.

"Yes, thank you."

"We have booked rooms for all survivors at hotels here in the West End. May we drive you to one? The Dorchester perhaps? It will be a few days before we can get you and the others back to Amsterdam."

"That's all right," Joshua said quietly. "But first, could you hail a taxi to take me to the United States Embassy?"

"Of course, sir. But we will happily drive you."

The ride from St. Thomas to the American embassy was a fast one. Only 10 minutes was needed to cross Westminster Bridge and drive northwest about a mile and a half to the hulking, gray embassy at large, leafy Grosvenor Square. The embassy sat a mere three blocks east from spacious Hyde Park. As the Dutch embassy car passed famed Hyde Park Corner, Joshua saw a shabbily dressed man standing atop a wooden box. He was voicing his beliefs and frustrations – as fellow citizens did there virtually daily. Perhaps, Joshua mused, I'll have to take my turn on that box. Let London and the world know what I think of that cowardly son of a bitch in Berlin. If I had the chance, I'd force his head into a bucket of piss and hold it down until he fucking drowned. And even that would be too good for him. He wouldn't burn like some of the Bolivar people.

The Dutch embassy staffer had phoned ahead to the U.S. embassy. After Joshua exited the car, he passed through open, wrought iron gates. As he approached the entrance, two Marine guards snapped off crisp salutes, never mind that Joshua was a civilian. Between them, attired immaculately in a black suit with black necktie and wearing black horn-rimmed glasses stood young embassy official Kenneth Hixon. "Welcome, Mr. Bliss," he said solemnly, extending his right hand. Joshua took it and shook wearily. "Let me offer you my sincerest condolences on the loss of your wife. We are all deeply sorry."

"Thank you," Joshua said hoarsely, lips barely parting.

"How might we assist you? We are at your complete and immediate service."

"A telephone. I need to make calls to Amsterdam and the States."

"Right away," said Hixon. "Please follow me."

"And could I borrow a watch? Mine was ruined, and my cash is water soaked and likely worthless."

Without hesitation, Hixon removed his watch. "It's yours."

"I'll return it after I make the calls."

"Please keep it," Hixon said. "And if you'll hand me your wallet, we'll see that your cash is replaced."

"They are guilders."

"Not to worry."

Joshua nodded his gratitude. "After I make my calls-"

Hixon cut him off. "We have a guest room prepared for you here. Or we can drive you to the hotel of your choice. Just let me know."

"I think I would prefer a room here to a hotel. At least for tonight."

"Very good. Now, this way."

"Mr. Hixon."

"Yes?"

"There were a few other Americans onboard. The survivors..." Joshua's throat thickened.

"We are doing everything we can for them as well. When we learned you were coming here, we dispatched staff to St. Thomas. You probably passed them on your way here."

"Thank you."

Joshua was given privacy in Kenneth Hixon's office. He sat at the desk and stared at the black phone. Right hand trembling, he picked up the receiver and asked the embassy operator to place a call. Moments later a voice answered the ringing. "Hello."

"Mr. Forbes?"

"Yes."

Joshua drew in a breath. "Mr. Forbes – Russell – this is Joshua." He looked again at the watch. "I'm sorry if I've called at a bad time." He was alluding to the five-hour time difference between London and New York.

Excruciating conversation ensued. Long, poignant pauses slowed the dialogue. Both men were weeping. Joshua was half-choking on his words.

"There won't be a funeral," Joshua said, barely able to get the words off his tongue. "Meredith's body wasn't recovered. She was below so…"

"I understand," Russell said, swallowing hard and trying to hold back the first, overwhelming wave of grief.

"But there will be a memorial service. I'm not sure exactly when. It will be after I return to Amsterdam. That was our home and…and it's where I feel it should be held."

"We will be there."

"Thank you."

"I need to figure out how to break the news to Victoria. She's not home yet from a fundraiser. And Clarisse and Christine." Russell sniffled.

"I wish I could do more. But if you'll excuse me, I need to call my parents and brother."

"Joshua."

"Yes."

"If it will help, I will pay your family's way to Amsterdam."

"You're not coming home?" Paul asked. Noah and Goldie, in tears, with arms around each other, were standing behind their elder son.

"Not yet," said Joshua, coughing to clear his constricted throat. "I feel a need to stay in Amsterdam. At least for a while. I hope you and Mom and Dad understand."

"I think we do." Paul looked up and back over his left shoulder, and Noah nodded his understanding. "Can you hold on a minute, Josh? Mom and Dad want to talk with me."

"No problem. The embassy said to take as much time as I need."

Paul cupped his right hand over the speaker and conferred with his parents. Then he resumed speaking to his brother. "We all can't come together, Josh. We can't let the farm go untended. Friends would probably pitch in to help, but we agree that would be asking a lot, considering how long we'd be gone. Probably close to a month, maybe more, to make the crossing, visit with you and get back home. Mom and Dad want me to come now. After I get back here, they will come visit you."

"That sounds like a good plan."

"I guess I'd better get myself a passport."

"Get to the post office right away. Tell them why you need it fast. If it looks like there will be a delay, phone our congressman."

"It could be dangerous," Victoria said worriedly, hands pressing together. When hearing the news from Russell, her eyes closed, her skin became clammy, her head drooped forward and she began collapsing. He had been gripping her shoulders so was able to steady and ease her to a sofa. "There might be more mines or German submarines."

"We should go anyway," Clarisse said, grimly determined.

"I agree," said Christine.

Their husbands, George Morgan and Donald Halston, had remained politely mute, but both were supportive and ready to accompany their young wives.

Russell was grateful that his daughters had spoken so quickly and unequivocally. It absolved him from having to persuade Victoria to make the trip that, he acknowledged silently, could be hazardous.

"Joshua said he will let us know as soon as he returns to Amsterdam and schedules the service. Meanwhile, I think we should begin making arrangements. I'll tell my colleagues at the bank."

"I'll inform my employer that I'll need a couple weeks off," George said.

"I'll do the same," said Donald. "I'm sure they'll be understanding."

On November 25 Joshua and the other Simon Bolivar survivors were put in a caravan of rented buses and driven to Southampton. There they boarded the Oranje Nassau, the liner dispatched by the Netherlands Royal Steamship Company to bring them back to Amsterdam.

Cold and raw though the temperature was, Joshua chose to remain on the open top deck. The ship headed northeast through the English Channel and across the North Sea. Tears welled in Joshua's eyes as the vessel went steaming over the site of Meredith's watery grave.

Hitler had quickly put aside thoughts of the Simon Bolivar's sinking and was moving ahead with other plans. Simultaneously, Joseph Stalin decided to flex his military muscle in a way that would prove threatening to northern European nations, including The Netherlands.

On August 24, 1939, Hitler and Stalin had signed the Molotov-Ribbentrop Pact. A secret clause made neighboring Finland part of Russia's sphere of influence. Stalin decided quickly to convert that technicality to reality. On November 26 he falsely accused Finland of shelling the border village of Mainila. Four days later Russia attacked adjacent Finland. Russia enjoyed virtually total air supremacy, and invading Russian infantry outnumbered Finnish defenders by more than two to one. Stalin was expecting the hostilities to end within days or weeks. Instead, stubborn and creative Finns united and resisted fiercely. Accustomed to wearing white in Finland's snowy winters and adept on skis, they consistently outmaneuvered Russian troops. The plucky Finns held on for more than three months. In March 1940, with both sides exhausted from the arduous winter campaigning and Stalin suffering acute international embarrassment, Finland and Russia reluctantly agreed to a peace.

Russia's fiasco in Finland underscored to paranoid Stalin his folly in having previously purged the Red Army of its most experienced and talented senior officers. He subsequently recalled some – the ones he hadn't had executed.

In The Hague, Queen Wilhelmina was seeing developments with her usual flinty assessment. "Germany has invaded Poland. Russia has invaded Poland and Finland. Japan has invaded China. This is looking very much like the early stages of a second world war."

CHAPTER 25

Joshua pulled on his brown stocking cap, wrapped his orange scarf around his neck and slipped on his blue woolen jacket. He then went walking from Prinsengracht to Merwede Square.

Once there he pulled open the door to Folleck's Fine Clothing. He stood still, stone-faced, no trace of a smile.

A single glance by Samuel Folleck from a customer to Joshua told Samuel everything. He accepted payment from the customer and made change while Joshua waited just inside the front door.

The customer picked up his package from the sales counter and turned to leave. Samuel hesitated a few seconds and then began following.

Joshua held open the door for the departing customer. Then he and Samuel, equals in height, shook hands and embraced.

"Do you mind if I call Miriam?" Samuel asked gently.

"Go ahead," Joshua murmured. "I think she should hear it from me."

"Our children are still at school," Samuel said. "If it's all right with you, we will tell them after they get home."

"That's fine."

"Joshua, when you feel like it, would you join us here for supper?"

"Yes. Thank you. And I have a favor to ask."

"Anything."

It was nearing noon on December 12 when Raluca and Alicia awakened. They had returned late to their apartment after servicing clients the night before.

Raluca stretched her arms wide and yawned.

Alicia threw aside their blanket, swung her legs off the bed and stood. She pulled apart the window curtains. Her reaction was visceral. Her eyes widened and blinked – twice – and her head snapped back. "Raluca!" she cried. "Look outside!"

Raluca's look was quizzical. "What has you so excited, sister? You sound like a school girl."

"I am feeling like one."

Raluca rose slowly, yawning again. She stepped around the bed and stood next to her friend. "Snow!" she squealed in delight. "Let's get dressed."

Within minutes they had slipped into dresses and shoes and pulled on hats and coats. They went racing down the stairs and outside onto Molensteeg. Snow was accumulating on barren tree limbs and the pavement below. They eyed each other and grinned mischievously. They weren't wearing gloves, but that didn't deter them from bending, scooping handfuls from the wintry blanket and quickly making two snowballs. They jogged a few paces from each other, whirled and threw large snowballs. Raluca missed but Alicia's ball was on target and struck her friend's right shoulder. They shrieked their joy and bent to make and throw more round missiles.

In nearby buildings other residents, including whores, heard the commotion. Soon Molensteeg was the site of a giant snowball battle. Cries of the merry contestants were being heard up and down the street and, like a contagion, glee was spreading as more adults – young and not so young – joined in the frolic.

"This is almost like home," Alicia exulted.

"Almost," Raluca replied poignantly, "almost."

Some 30 feet behind Alicia a solitary man paused to watch the wintry revelry. He smiled, turned away and continued his journey.

Raluca packed another snowball, straightened and let fly. Her throw was errant. The white ball sailed wide of Alicia and smacked the back of the man. He was attired in black from his fedora to his shoes. He was heading west, slowly toward Oude Kerk.

The ball's splat startled him, causing him to flinch. As he whirled to see the ball's source, Raluca caught a glimpse of a white collar. A priest! she realized. Her face reddened. Mortification set in immediately. Timidly Raluca waved at the priest, then pointed abjectly at herself and mouthed, "I am sorry."

But the priest was laughing. He waved off her apology. Then he stooped, used his gloveless hands to form his own ball and returned Raluca's throw. She stood motionless and let the ball strike her upper left chest. The priest laughed again. So did Raluca, her embarrassment ebbing.

The priest waved gaily, turned and continued toward Oude Kerk.

Three days later at 9:30 in the morning, Joshua left his office and walked outside Scheevaarthuis to the waterfront. He stood motionless, staring out to sea. Moments later he heard a soft "Joshua." He turned and it was the Folleck family – all five of them.

Joshua smiled warmly. "Thank you so much for coming. I know it was asking a lot for both of you to come and close your shop."

"Pishtosh," Samuel replied. "We would have been disappointed if you hadn't asked."

"Your children…" Joshua smiled at Aaron, Mariah and Julia. "They are missing a day of school."

"This is much more important," said Miriam. "The children would have it no other way."

"My family should be here any minute," Joshua said, "and so will my colleagues here at the company. Plus many others. But I also wanted special friends with me today, so I really appreciate you being here."

Miriam felt her eyes moistening and reached for Samuel's left arm.

Joshua took in the waterfront scene. The United States and Dutch flags were flying at half-staff on 20-foot poles erected for the occasion. That was Ernst Heldring's idea. Bouquets of flowers abounded. Sixteen boulders sat covered with heavy black cloth. Fifteen were similar in size. One was substantially larger. On the ground in front of each boulder were votive candles, not yet lit.

Others began arriving. Paul Bliss. The Forbes clan – Russell, Victoria, Clarisse and George, Christine and Donald. Families and friends of other victims. Hundreds in all. Ernst Heldring, receptionist Laura Reidel at his side, and the entire headquarters staff of the Netherlands Royal Steamship Company. Joshua was surprised – and touched – to see the nine children of employees Meredith had been tutoring in English. Most of them were weeping, brushing away tears in the December cold.

Heldring approached Joshua and they shook hands.

"Thank you all for joining us," Heldring said, projecting his voice in English, then Dutch. "Members of Joshua Bliss's family are here from America, and we are so glad they have made the long journey. It is cold and windy and we won't keep you outside overly long. After this memorial service, please come inside Scheepvaarthuis where we have hot food and beverages."

True to his word, Heldring kept his comments brief. "These people, the eighty-four who lost their lives, were the most innocent of victims. And every one of them was special in his or her own unique way. They all were loved and they will be missed for many years to come. They should all be honored and in a very visible or public way." He pointed toward the shrouded boulders lining the waterfront. Heldring had not sought municipal approval for his plan, and he expected no bureaucratic complaints. He then nodded to a pair of young employees. Each was dressed smartly in sharply pressed black suits, and both had shunned wearing topcoats and hats. They moved to the boulder nearest Heldring. At his subtle signal, they solemnly removed the black cloak. They waited until attendees at the front of the throng had time to take in the memorial. Then slowly the men began removing the black veils. Beneath each of the first 14 was mounted a bronze plaque, two feet by two feet, on the boulder. Each bore the name and birth and death dates of a company employee – Captain Voorspuiy, the watch officer who had plunged to his death with the collapsing mast and crow's nest, and the others, most of whom had been working in the engine room. The 15th read:

Meredith Bliss, born March 10, 1915
Died November 18, 1939
Wife of Joshua Bliss

Laura Reidel, weeping softly, dabbed at tears. She had to suppress an urge to walk to Joshua and embrace him. Not appropriate, she was thinking, not now, not here. Poor young man.

Affixed to a much larger boulder was a plaque, four feet by four feet, that bore the names of the other 69 victims.

"Life can be fleeting," said Heldring, eyes misting, "and often is. We believe with all our hearts that these eighty-four men, women and children deserve this more permanent memorial. May these boulders and plaques remain in place long after our company ceases to exist." He sniffled. Then he motioned to 16 other company employees, also dressed in black. They moved forward, genuflected and lit the votive candles. Heldring waited patiently until all the candles were sending their small flames skyward. "Thank you all for coming. Now, please come inside."

As the crowd began shuffling toward the entrance to ship-shaped Scheepvaarthuis, Russell whispered to Joshua, "Please stay behind for a moment." Then to Victoria and his daughters and their husbands, he added, "Go ahead. We'll be along shortly."

Russell took Joshua's left arm and led him to the memorial to Meredith. Russell inhaled deeply and slowly exhaled. Then, beneath his topcoat he reached for an inside suit jacket pocket. He removed an unsealed envelope and handed it to Joshua who looked at it mutely. It was thick with cash - $5,000 in $50 bills.

"Sir, Russell, I can't take this."

"Look, I know you've got a job. But maybe something will come up. Something special you might want to do or buy."

"You've already bought our house. You said it was a gift, but I am determined to pay you back."

"Of course," Russell said agreeably, not wanting a debate, "and you will. But this" – taking the envelope from Joshua's hands and tucking it inside his suit jacket – "is a special gift. Part of the memorial to my youngest daughter. I've been a very lucky man, and I want to share my luck."

That night Paul stayed at Joshua's house. The Forbes family had taken rooms at the Grand Krasnapolsky Hotel that was built in 1866. It held 468 rooms and stood only a block east of Dam Square and the Royal Palace. Laura Reidel had made the reservations.

"So, you are leaving day after tomorrow with the Forbes."

"Yes, and if it's still all right with you, as soon as I get back to the farm, Mom and Dad will begin making plans to visit."

The brothers, wearing coats and gloves but hatless, were strolling east from Prinsengracht. Ahead loomed Oude Kerk.

"That's perfect. Tell them I will meet their ship, and they can stay with me."

"Will do."

"I wish there was more I could say, Josh. The right words just don't seem to want to come out."

"Don't worry."

"Some day they will."

"Some day will be soon enough."

They walked past Oude Kerk. Dusk was lowering its curtain.

"Want to head back to your home?" Paul asked. "Get something to eat?"

"Not yet. Let's keep walking for a while."

"Any place in particular?"

Joshua looked up. The sky was clear and darkening quickly. "Not really. I'm just not ready to go back yet."

Approaching from the opposite direction were two young women. Joshua didn't take note of them but Paul did. He made brief eye contact as they passed. They are both pretty, he thought, very pretty. Especially the taller one.

Raluca and Alicia were making their way to the brothel for a night's work.

"We've seen one of them," Raluca said, looking back at the two men. "The bald one."

"Yes."

"When Father Brandsma was speaking at Oude Kerk."

"You are right."

"The one with hair," Alicia said, "I wonder who he is."

"He is a big man. Perhaps another American."

"I think they resemble each other," Alicia said. "Do you suppose they might be brothers?"

"If they are," said Raluca, "I wonder why they are out walking this evening. It's cold, and they didn't seem to be in a hurry."

"I hope their night will be better than ours."

CHAPTER 26

Laura Reidel was returning from the women's restroom to the reception desk. She regarded it as both a welcoming station and the company's first line of defense. Strangely, she acknowledged to herself, she also viewed the desk as sort of a personal sanctuary. There she experienced daily doses of happiness. Widowed and childless, Laura sometimes seemed more at home at work than in her apartment.

She had been observing Joshua for the last six weeks. He wasn't his usual ebullient self and that, she knew from the experience of personal loss, was understandable. His parents, Noah and Goldie, had come and gone, and Laura found herself worrying. Was he taking good care of himself? Eating properly? Spending too much time alone when he had grown accustomed to steady companionship?

One Friday afternoon in early February 1940 employees were leaving Scheepvaartuis. Singly, they were filing past Laura's desk. She was organizing items and preparing to leave. She reached for her purse and began rising. She saw Joshua entering the lobby. A thought, then another, struck her and she hesitated. In the next instant she shook off indecision and chose to do something unprecedented for her.

"Good night, Mrs. Reidel," Joshua said somberly.

"Good night, Mr. Bliss." A brief pause. "Joshua."

Hearing his first name from Laura Reidel's lips surprised and stopped him. He turned. "Yes?"

She struggled to find words she deemed suitable. "Joshua, I hope you will forgive the informality." Joshua shrugged and smiled slightly. "I like to cook and most days I cook only for myself." Actually, virtually every day, she was thinking. "I wonder if you might like a home-cooked meal." I am just about old enough to be his mother, she thought, and perhaps motherly instincts I have kept buried are coming to the surface. She felt crimson – in sharp contrast to her prematurely white hair - staining her face at what he might regard as impertinence, an invasion of his privacy.

"That sounds nice," he said politely if unenthusiastically. "Thank you. My own skills in the kitchen are limited. Severely, one might say." He sensed immediately that the unexpected invitation had resulted from lingering sympathy but wasn't uncomfortable with the prospect of dining with the smart and smartly appearing receptionist.

She nodded. "Tomorrow evening then? Seven o'clock?"

"Very good."

"Thank you for accepting," Laura said stiffly. "My address is 135 Herengracht. Second floor."

Herengracht, like Prinsengracht, the name of a street and the canal it paralleled, was only two blocks – or only a five-minute stroll – east of Joshua's home. At Laura's door he tapped twice, and the door opened nearly instantly.

"Welcome to my home, Joshua. Let me take your coat and scarf."

"Thank you, Mrs. Reidel."

"Mrs. Reidel is appropriate at work. If you don't mind, though, I would prefer Laura here."

"All right, Laura." While she hung his things on a wooden coat tree, Joshua quickly surveyed her living room. Spacious, he saw, with subtly patterned beige wallpaper and earth-toned, upholstered chairs and sofa. "Your apartment looks very nice."

"Thank you. May I get you something to drink? Wine, perhaps?"

"I'd like that. Thank you."

"Good. I will be right back." She moved quickly toward the kitchen.

Joshua looked more closely around the living room. A handsome, dark bookcase stood against the far wall. Atop the bookcase stood a model of a three-masted sailing ship. I'm not surprised, he mused, given her many years at the company. Flanking a chair upholstered in green with tiny red and yellow tulips was an end table topped by a lamp and a photo. He stepped closer. The photo showed a girl, about age six he guessed, sitting on her father's lap and next to her mother. Joshua looked hard. Laura Reidel as a youngster, he surmised. He looked around the room. Only that one photo. *I wonder if she has more in other rooms. She's never mentioned a husband or children. Now,* Joshua mused, smiling inwardly, *I'm more curious than ever about her. I wonder how much I'll learn tonight.*

Not much as it turned out. Over wine in Laura's living room and dinner followed by Dutch chocolate cake and jenever in her small dining room, she revealed little about her personal history. Just that she was an only child and that her parents were deceased. Her strategy for the evening rested on querying Joshua about his background, providing ample opportunity to talk and possibly lighten the burden he had been shouldering. It didn't occur to Laura that Joshua would be interested in learning her background. Joshua talked willingly about his past. He described for Laura life on a farm near a small Ohio town, attending university in a California that sounded exotic to Laura, and working and living in bustling New York.

"You know," she disclosed, "despite all the years I have worked at the company I have never sailed abroad."

I wonder, Joshua mused, *if that's because you couldn't afford to or because you possessed neither the desire nor a traveling companion.* Instead of questioning her, he said only, "Someday, maybe, you will. Maybe visit America. And our farm."

Laura chuckled. "Not likely, Joshua."

"But not beyond imagining and possibility."

"Perhaps."

"Don't rule it out."

"All right," she smiled warmly, "I won't."

Joshua glanced at the watch given him by Kenneth Hixon in London. 10:30. "It's getting late," he said softly. "Let me help you clean up before I leave."

Laura began to decline his offer but reconsidered. "That would be nice. Thank you."

Clearing the table and washing and drying glasses and tableware, they said little. The silence didn't discomfit either of them. In fact Laura was happily thanking herself for inviting Joshua. She was feeling a sense of satisfaction and warmth that she had seldom experienced since being widowed.

Afterward in the living room, Joshua slipped on his coat and wrapped the orange scarf around his neck. There is still much more I'd like to know about you, he was reflecting. Maybe some other time. "Thank you very much for having me over, Laura. I certainly enjoyed your home cooking. And, our conversation."

"This evening was a treat for me," she said. Laura held out her right hand.

Josh was feeling an impulse. He wanted to hug Laura. Instead he took her hand and they shook gently.

In their new home in Rotterdam, Stefaan and Anneke were enjoying the privacy that resulted from moving away from her parents' house. The young couple had just finished washing and drying dishes. She wiped her hands on a small, blue towel, and he hung the white drying towel on a wooden peg over the sink. Stefaan looked lovingly at his wife and embraced her. His hug was strong and long.

"What brought that on?" Anneke asked teasingly. "Is that a sign? You are ready for a tumble? In bed? Or perhaps right here in the kitchen on the floor? Well?"

Stefaan didn't laugh, and his smile was forced. "Let's go to bed – and talk."

"What's wrong?"

Stefaan hesitated. "Nothing."

"I do not believe you. Not for an instant, Stefaan Janssen. Talk to me. Right here and now."

He sucked in a breath, his chest heaving. "What do you see in me?"

"What?" Her question sounded more like a demand.

"What do you really see in me? I am only a dockworker. A simple dockworker. I load cargo. Unload. It is dirty, sweaty work. At Holland-America you work with powerful people. No one sweats. No one stinks."

Incredulously, Anneke peered deeply into her husband's eyes. "Why are you even thinking such thoughts? Where did they come from?" Stefaan shrugged. "Listen to me, Stefaan. You are the man of my dreams."

His eyes began glistening with misty film. "I am very fortunate you dream of an ordinary man."

"You are wrong," Anneke said passionately. "An ordinary man would not entertain such foolish thoughts. He certainly would not know how to speak them."

"We will never have riches."

"I have you. We have each other. Do we need more?" she asked rhetorically.

"Well, I want more for you."

"Nonsense," Anneke said spunkily. "Enough of that. Understood?"

"I suppose so."

Anneke felt an immediate need to change the direction and tone of the conversation. "We are going to take a tumble. Right this very minute. Right here." She pulled Stefaan toward her and backed against the kitchen table. She hoisted herself onto the tabletop and leaned back on her elbows and spread her legs. Her eyes were glistening coquettishly. "Must I say more?"

CHAPTER 27

Bert Sas was simultaneously feeling grateful and apprehensive. The handsome, blond Dutch Army major was serving as The Netherlands' military attaché in Berlin. The assignment required analytic skill, savvy, tact and courage. A key aspect of his mission was forging a productive relationship with Colonel Hans Oster, a senior officer in the Abwehr, the Nazi's intelligence gathering agency that was established in 1921.

The word abwehr is German for defense and was used as a concession to Allied demands that Germany's intelligence work after the First World War be limited to defense purposes only. Abwehr headquarters in Berlin were at 76/78 Tirpitzafer, conveniently adjacent to offices of the High Command of the Armed Forces.

Major Sas was succeeding faster and more profoundly than he had anticipated. His candor and absence of hubris were contributing factors. Colonel Oster had come to respect and like Sas, and he harbored abiding disrespect and dislike for Hitler.

Sas's gratitude resulted from a whispered conversation with Oster on a snowy street corner in early 1940. That same brief exchange was fueling Sas's apprehension.

"Hitler means to take your country – by force," Oster murmured, lips barely moving. The falling snow was obscuring the view of anyone watching them. The nature of Oster's job virtually dictated communication with Sas. It did not extend to divulging Nazi secrets. "I don't know precisely the timing or location yet, but I think soon after the spring thaws when roads become more firm and passable."

Sas blew out a breath that crystallized in the sub-freezing air. "This is very kind of you," he replied in a whispered mumble. "I appreciate the risk you are taking. We are a small country, and our military forces sorely lack modern equipment and weapons. Our queen is resolute but not blind to our vulnerability."

"If I hear more I will contact you."

Sas nodded his gratitude and the two men parted, snow accumulating on their hats and coats. Returning to The Netherlands embassy, Sas used a coded cable to send his findings to The Hague. The cable was delivered to Prime Minister de Geer. He pooh-poohed the missive. "Sas needs to learn not to believe everything the Abwehr tells him," de Geer said to Queen Wilhelmina. "Passing along false, misleading information is the Abwehr's stock in trade."

"Still," said Wilhelmina, "you must continue to pressure Parliament to provide the funds to modernize our nation's defense capabilities."

"I am working on that, your majesty. But we must treat cables like this with suspicion. Healthy suspicion. We have seen what Hitler has done to try to goad other nations into giving him flimsy excuses to invade. We must seriously consider all risks and avoid provocations that could prove disastrous."

Wilhelmina refused to meekly accept her prime minister's advice. He was timid, she believed, and prone to sugarcoating harsh realities. "Get word to Major Sas that he is doing excellent work. Tell him that message comes directly from me. Instruct him to keep reporting promptly what he learns."

Sitzkrieg. That's what many Germans were calling the quiet months following the seismic, four-week campaign in Poland. Elsewhere in Europe the lull had acquired another sobriquet – the Phony War.

"Yes, your majesty."

"Hitler's expansion plans," she continued, "they are not done. He is merely giving his forces time to rest and regroup. And to build more tanks and airplanes. I envy Germany's manufacturing expertise and capacity. If there is to be a fight, I am determined to stand and preserve the House of Orange." Her eyes narrowed flintily. "I still have a white fur coat somewhere" – an allusion to her army's camouflaged winter combat uniforms. "Hitler's Third Reich is an immoral system. Those bandits will stop at nothing to gain their ill-gotten ends."

In Berlin, Hermann Goering was reporting to Hitler.

"How is our airborne training proceeding?" Hitler asked.

"Superbly. General Student is a most able leader, one of my best men."

"Have you told him his first mission?"

"Yes. But I have sworn him to secrecy until I instruct him to brief his senior officers."

"How does he assess his chances of success?"

"He is very confident," Goering said, beaming. His own confidence more than equaled that of General Student. "Student believes in his planes, equipment and weapons. With good reason. They are superb. Most of all, he is supremely confident in his airborne troops. Their training has been professional and thorough. They don't yet know their first mission, but General Student has informed them it is crucial to our success. Morale is higher than their parachutes when they snap open during practice jumps."

"Does Student plan to jump with his men?"

"He would have it no other way."

Kurt Student, born in 1890, was a pleasant-looking if not handsome officer. He was trim and rather slightly built. He seemingly was created to fit snugly in the cramped cockpits of early 20th century airplanes. During the First World War he had served as a fighter pilot. His skill and courage were beyond question. On the Eastern Front over Galicia, a region straddling Poland and Ukraine's border, he downed a French plane, quickly re-equipped it with a German machine gun and flew it in combat. Later he switched to the Western Front and won six dogfights against French fighters before being wounded.

After the war Student was assigned to a position in military research and development. He specialized in troop carrying gliders which, unlike bombers and fighters, were not forbidden by the Treaty of Versailles. After Hitler's rise to power and the secret establishment of the Luftwaffe, Goering appointed Student to head its training programs.

Three years later, in July 1938, Goering summoned Student. "I have been giving considerable thought to the merits of parachute troops as quick-strike forces."

"An intriguing concept," Student mused aloud. "I can see how it would confuse an enemy and disrupt movement of its troops and supplies."

"How would you like to form a parachute unit and organize the training?"

"A most welcome prospect," Student smiled enthusiastically. "I believe I shall call it the Fallschirmjagen Division." A pause while more creative ideas began percolating. "I will have special wings insignia designed and awarded to each man who successfully completes the training."

CHAPTER 28

"I am not feeling well," Alicia said. "I think I have a fever." She was semi-reclining on the violet settee in their apartment.

Raluca reached out and placed her right palm against Alicia's forehead. "Yes, you do. I think you should go to bed. Let me help you up. I will bring you a pitcher of water and a glass. Drink every drop. That is what your mother would tell you, right?" Raluca smiled affectionately. "I will tell Madame Clarbout you are sick."

Late that afternoon on March 7, Raluca left the apartment and began striding toward a food shop farther east on Molensteeg. She had proceeded only a few steps when she saw a figure leaning contemplatively over the concrete railing of a canal bridge. He was wearing a dark suit and necktie and an unbuttoned topcoat. He was hatless and bald.

Recognition dawned and Raluca slowed her pace. The man raised his head slightly but neither smiled nor acknowledged her presence with even a subtle gesture. You look sad, Raluca was thinking, very sad. She was tempted to utter a small greeting but refrained, at first not knowing why. Then she reconsidered. Well, yes, I do know why. It is my occupation. It shames me. I have seen you before. At least twice. Once at Oude Kerk you were with a woman. Your wife? Or a girlfriend? I haven't seen her since then. Where is she now? I saw you a second time with a man. Who was he? Where is he now? Why are you alone and why do you look so sad? You are a mystery man, she smiled inwardly. Her curiosity seemed to be intensifying with each passing moment. Her musing continued. Perhaps I should follow you – but not too closely. Oh, stop it, Raluca, she scolded herself. You are a stranger, she silently told the man, and should remain a stranger to me. Perhaps it would be best if I never saw you again.

Three days later, on Friday, Raluca saw the bald young man standing on the same bridge at the same time of day. He still looked sad. If anything, even sadder. The gloomy weather, she thought, might be depressing you. It does that to many people.

Rain was falling lightly, and a cold northwest wind was blowing briskly. Raluca was carrying a black umbrella. The man, about 40 paces from her, was wearing a brown stocking cap that seemed out of place with his dark suit, necktie and topcoat.

Raluca felt compelled to stop, as though an unforeseen force was blocking her way. The man directed his eyes toward her, but his gaze showed no sign of interest in Raluca or anything else. The force impeding Raluca from the man gave way, and she found herself stepping onto the bridge. Like a thunderclap a thought seemed to explode inside her mind. I am not sure about this. Not sure at all. It makes me feel like a cheap streetwalker, and I am not that. She was nearing Joshua. Why am I doing this?

Joshua straightened and stepped back from the railing. His somber face now showed a glimpse of curiosity.

Raluca closed to within three feet and stopped. The edge of her large umbrella was within inches of Joshua's face. He didn't seem to mind.

"You look sad," she murmured, "very sad. Why?"

Joshua's eyes locked on Raluca's but he said nothing. To Raluca's surprise her right hand reached for his left. Joshua looked down at her hand gripping his.

"Hello," he said softly. "Who are you?"

"Hello." She looked up at the underside of her umbrella, then returned her gaze to Joshua. "My name is Raluca. It is cold and wet. Your head must be soaked. Come with me, please."

Joshua hesitated, then looked down at Raluca's hand, still holding his. She tugged slightly and he began following her.

"Step under my umbrella," she said. Moments later they were approaching the entrance to Raluca's apartment house. She thought of Alicia upstairs, still recovering from flu symptoms. She continued walking west on Molensteeg, Joshua still beneath her umbrella and looking steadily down at her.

Why am I walking with this stranger? he wondered. Raluca, that's not a Dutch name. And she doesn't look Dutch. But her eyes are kind. She seems nice. But...

A few steps more and they were at the brothel's entrance. "I work here," Raluca said quietly. She realized that, for the moment anyway, her shame had given way to compassion. "Would you come inside with me, please?"

Joshua looked up from beneath the umbrella and saw the red light bulb. Well, should I go inside? What do you think, Meredith? He looked into Raluca's eyes, still saw kindness and nodded. Soft chimes sounded as they entered. Madame Clarbout was emerging from her living quarters onto the rose-colored carpet. Before she could say anything, Raluca raised her right hand, forefinger extended, and placed it against her lips. Anna Clarbout nodded and turned away.

Water was dripping from the umbrella. Raluca closed it and inserted it into a high-sided container with a half-dozen other umbrellas. "Let me take your coat and cap," Raluca said. Joshua removed his topcoat and pulled off the soggy stocking cap. Raluca hung the coat on a peg extending from a wooden coat tree and perched the cap on top. "Please follow me." She led Joshua to a staircase, and they began ascending. Soon they were on the third floor and standing at the door to Raluca's small chamber. She pushed open the door. "Come."

Joshua followed her inside and she closed the door behind them. "This is the first time I've been in one of these," he said quietly as if, ironically he mused, in a church.

"This is strange for me," Raluca said softly.

"What do you mean?"

"I don't bring men here. They come on their own."

"Why me?"

"I saw you a few days ago, and you looked very sad. Today you still looked sad. You still do. I saw you once with a beautiful woman. Perhaps she has left you. I saw you with a young man once too. But not since. Maybe you miss them."

"You are very perceptive."

"It is something I have learned." A pause. "You must be cold."

"I'm chilled to the bone."

"Yes. If you remove your clothes, I will also, and we can lie down and be warm."

Joshua smiled wryly and shook his head slightly.

"Is something wrong?" Raluca asked.

"I'm not sure."

Slowly he slipped out of his suit jacket. Raluca took it from him.

"Go ahead," she said.

Joshua unknotted his necktie and pulled it away from his shirt. Raluca took it. During the next couple minutes he removed his remaining clothes except for his boxer-style shorts. He hesitated, then stepped out of those. He pulled off the watch Kenneth Hixon had given him in London and handed it to Raluca.

"Pull the covers back and lie down," Raluca instructed as she carefully arranged Joshua's clothing atop the chest of drawers.

Lighting in the room was dim but sufficient for Joshua to see Raluca unhurriedly removing her clothing. If she's self-conscious, Joshua mused, it doesn't show. Naked, she eased herself onto the bed, pulled the covers over them and lay still. Joshua was lying supine, arms crossed on his chest. A minute later Raluca edged closer and Joshua felt arousal, his penis stiffening quickly. It was, he realized, his first erection since losing Meredith. Still, his arms remained crossed.

"I do not understand," Raluca whispered. "You do not want me?"

"Yes, I do." Joshua's erection evidenced his desire. "You are very pretty and seem very nice."

"Then why don't you take me?"

A long pause. "I'm not sure. Just put your head on my shoulder. Please."

Raluca placed her head on his left shoulder. "Like this?"

"Yes." With his left hand beneath her, he began lightly stroking the small of Raluca's back. Her skin was smooth and cool to his touch. His erection began shrinking.

Raluca was savoring the petting. She sensed, correctly, that Joshua's affection was genuine. It touched her. Never before had she lay with a man who was content to hold and caress her. You are different, she was thinking, buy why? "I will stay awake with you," she murmured. "If you want me later tonight, I will be ready."

"All right. Maybe I will." Joshua was sorting his thoughts. Do I feel guilty for being with this woman? I don't think so. Am I embarrassed to be with a prostitute? Well, I wouldn't want my friends and family to know. But I don't feel embarrassed right now. Am I worried I'll get the clap? Not really. Even if I should be. He turned his head toward Raluca. Her eyes, wide open, were mere inches from his. She smiled. For the first time Joshua returned her smile. With his right hand he reached across his chest and brushed her cheek. Then he removed his hand and his head rolled away. He lay staring at the ceiling.

This is all very strange, Raluca was reflecting. A mystery. But I like it.

Within about 30 minutes Joshua dozed off. Raluca's left hand, resting on his chest, felt the even breathing of deepening sleep. She smiled and lightly kissed Joshua's neck. Soon she also closed her eyes, with sleep arriving soon after.

Hours later the small room's lone window was beginning to admit the new dawn.

Joshua stirred and groaned lowly. His head turned toward Raluca. She was awake and eyeing him intently. They both smiled. Then her left hand slid lower and felt a new erection.

"Now?" she asked.

"Yes."

Joshua eased from the bed, stood and began dressing. He looked down. Raluca was staring up, contemplatively.

"How much do I owe you?" he asked.

She had been anticipating the question. "No charge."

"Why?"

"It was good for both of us. The benefits, they were equal."

Joshua smiled. "Thank you, but I don't want you having trouble with your madame."

"I don't think there will be a problem. Don't worry."

"I won't." Joshua removed his wallet from his trousers. He placed 10 guilders on the chest of drawers.

"That is too much," Raluca protested mildly.

He smiled thinly. "Seems just right to me. It will keep me from worrying." He slipped the watch over his left hand.

"You would worry about me? A whore?"

"I might."

"It is Saturday," Raluca said. "Do you have to work?"

"No. But you do, right?"

She shrugged. "Always on Saturday."

"Goodbye." He turned to exit the small chamber.

"Your name?"

Joshua looked back over his right shoulder. "Josh. Joshua Bliss."

"American?"

"Yes. You?"

"Romanian."

Joshua blinked his surprise. In yesterday's dusk and the room's low light, he hadn't taken note of her slightly olive complexion. Several questions, one immediately after another, came speeding to mind. Instead of asking them, he said merely, "Raluca is a very pretty name." He was thinking he would like to see her again but checked the impulse to suggest a second night together. *This was good for me. I should let it go at that.* He nodded, stepped through the door and departed.

The following Wednesday, the Ides of March, Joshua was straightening his desk at the close of the work day. As he entered the lobby, Laura Reidel was putting on her coat. "If you don't mind," she said, "I will walk out with you."

"Sure thing."

They exited Scheepvaarthuis into the gloom of a North Sea winter that still had not released its grip on Amsterdam.

"You seem more like your old self, Joshua. I am glad."

"Your wonderful cooking was good for my body and my spirits."

"Perhaps you'd like to join me again."

"I would love to, Mrs. Reidel."

"We are outside the offices," she chided him good naturedly.

With mock imperiousness, Joshua said, "Let me amend my previous reply. I would love to, Laura."

They both laughed and began walking west on Prins Hendrickkade. They remained together, chatting about company happenings until reaching Laura's home on Herengracht.

"Tomorrow at the office let's look at our calendars," Laura suggested, "and pick a date."

"That sounds fine," Joshua said. He offered his right hand and Laura took it. "Good night."

"Good night, Joshua."

He turned left or south until arriving at the next canal bridge. He turned right or west to cross the span and complete the short walk to his home on Prinsengracht. Half way across the bridge, he was startled. "Raluca."

She had been leaning, her back against the railing. "Hello."

"I wasn't expecting to…"

"See me again so soon?"

"Yes. It's quite a coincidence."

She shook her head slightly. "Not really."

"What do you mean?"

"You told me you lived on Prinsengracht. I was curious. I – There were things I wanted to ask you. I decided to wait on one of the bridges in this area each evening." She looked down, feeling sheepish. "I hope you don't mind."

Joshua smiled. "Not at all." He stepped closer. "There are things I would like to ask you too."

"Would you like to come with me?"

With his right thumb and forefinger, Joshua rubbed his chin. "Actually, I would like you to come with me."

He could see his invitation had startled Raluca. "Where?"

"My home. It is very close to here." Now Joshua was sensing that uncertainty – perhaps anxiety – was adding to her surprise. "Don't be afraid."

She smiled thinly. "I am not afraid of you. But no man has ever asked me to his home. It is not the custom."

"Maybe it's time to begin a new custom. We have more questions to ask each other," Joshua grinned. "Come on."

She nodded and they began walking west off the bridge.

In his kitchen Joshua prepared a modest repast – frying potatoes and ham slices, scrambling eggs and browning bread. He made coffee and they both drank it black. "This is good," said Raluca. During the meal they said little, confining comments to the weather and briefly relating each other's upbringing on their Ohio and Romanian farms.

When they finished eating, Joshua said, "The dishes can wait. Come with me."

In his bedroom Joshua turned on a floor lamp. Immediately Raluca saw a photo. Joshua was pictured with the beautiful young woman she had seen with him at Oude Kerk when Father Brandsma had spoken there. Joshua began to undress and Raluca did likewise. Then he surprised her. He grasped her shoulders, pulled her closer and gently kissed her forehead. Her eyes remained open, his closed.

Opening his eyes, he smiled and motioned her to the bed. They lay down and Joshua initiated lovemaking. Not raw sex, Raluca realized, but warm, slow lovemaking. Joshua was caressing her, from forehead to knees.

Afterward, in shared whispers, the questioning began. In their answers, neither felt a need to be evasive.

The next morning Joshua awoke early. He shaved, bathed and dressed. He returned to the bedroom and looked in. Raluca still was sleeping. He reached down with his right hand and jostled her left shoulder. Her eyes sprang open.

"I need to leave for work," Joshua said. "Take your time. Find something to eat. Leave when you want."

"You trust me?"

"Have you given me any reason not to?" Her reply to his rhetorical question – the kind Meredith used to appreciate hearing from him – was a smile. He pointed to the chest of drawers. "I have left guilders for you. But," he hastened to add, "not as payment for services. They are for you and your friend Alicia to save for that lace shop you want to have."

CHAPTER 29

Hitler's next lie shocked the world on April 10, 1940. His earlier pledge to seek no additional territory crumbled ignobly when his forces – Wehrmacht and Luftwaffe – simultaneously attacked little Denmark, Germany's neighbor to its immediate north, and sparsely populated Norway across the North Sea.

Norway's King Haakon VII immediately fled to London. On hearing that news, Queen Wilhelmina said dryly to her daughter, Princess Juliana, "Perhaps we too should inquire about lodgings in London." By now the queen had concluded that nothing less than divine intervention would ward off a German attack on her Holland.

Hitler's assault on Norway reflected his respect for Britain's military might. He wanted to deprive England of any northern air bases.

When Wehrmacht troops went marching across Denmark's border, the Danes mounted no opposition, and Hitler didn't bother himself with the nicety of a declaration of war. He did voice his rationale to Goering, still his second-in-command: "These pesky Danes are Aryan and with them on our northern border it only makes sense to be certain their land and port facilities don't fall into anyone else's hands."

"You make perfect sense – as always," said Goering who, like virtually all in Hitler's inner circle, had mastered toadyism.

Hitler was hardly alone in his grand ambitions. One fellow Nazi-in-spirit if not in name was a Dutchman. Anton Adriaan Mussert was born in 1894 in Werkendam, a northern Netherlands town. He showed an early interest in technology and later studied civil engineering at Delft University of Technology. He married Maria Witlam. Ironically Mussert, his most prominent feature sagging bulldog-like jowls, bore a resemblance to a leader he would eventually come to loathe – Winston Churchill.

After university, Mussert's chief interest shifted from engineering to politics – of the extreme right wing variety. On December 14, 1931, he and 11 others founded the National-Socialisticshe Beweging (Dutch for National Socialist Movement or NSB). From its inception, Mussert viewed his NSB as a counterpart to Hitler's Nazis. The two parties differed, however, in a central respect. In the NSB's early years, Mussert boasted that its membership included Jews. To him they provided proof of the NSB's supposedly widespread support. That thinking would change after Hitler's anti-Semitic measures in Germany gave Mussert cause to reconsider.

The NSB gained political traction but slowly. In 1933 in Utrecht a demonstration against Queen Wilhelmina's monarchy attracted only 600 protesters. Mussert and his cronies weren't deterred. They kept preaching their ideology. A year later in Amsterdam an NSB rally pulled in 25,000 demonstrators. The movement kept growing. In the 1935 Dutch parliamentary elections, NSB candidates received 300,000 votes.

That outpouring of support jolted Queen Wilhelmina. She recognized that the NSB's surging popularity was jeopardizing the House of Orange and commissioned a campaign to undermine Mussert's credibility. It succeeded. In the 1937 balloting for parliamentary seats, votes going to NSB candidates fell to nearly half as many as they had won two years earlier.

Two years later Mussert was considering war as a virtual certainty. In early 1940 in The Hague he met with his NSB co-founder, Cornelis van Geelkerken. "I think we should assume Germany will attack Holland."

"When?" van Geelkerken asked.

"Soon. Hitler's patience must be thinning."

"What do you have in mind?"

"I want Hitler to see clearly and quickly that our NSB is an ally. A strong one. Holland should become integral to Herr Hitler's Reich. We would be assured a bright future. Resisting Hitler would be folly. We should do anything we can to head off Dutch resistance to a Wehrmacht invasion."

"Plant false information in the press?" asked van Geelkerken. "Sabotage our railway system? All of that would take considerable time and resources."

"You are correct," Mussert said. "I have in mind something that would weaken any resistance and do so much faster."

In a park in Berlin, Dutch Major Bert Sas and Abwehr Colonel Hans Oster were sitting on a wooden bench.

"Invasion now is a certainty," Oster murmured.

"No way to avoid it?"

"None that I know of."

"Do you per chance know the date?"

Oster sighed shallowly. "I can't be certain, but my best information leads me to believe our forces will attack yours on May 10."

Sas returned to The Netherlands embassy and wasted no time in sending a coded cable to The Hague. Prime Minister de Geer gave Sas's cable the same cynical reception accorded his earlier missives. Merely another false alarm, de Geer concluded. Nothing to warrant rushing to her majesty. I will inform her at our next briefing.

"Your plan is fraught with risk," van Geelkerken told Mussert. "Too much so in my view. Need I spell out the consequences of failure? We are talking treason."

"I concede it's not for the faint-of-heart. But bold action is required if what I am hearing is accurate."

"And that would be?"

"Germany's invasion is imminent."

Prime Minister de Geer arrived at Noordeinde Palace. He paused to take in the queen's favored residence. The palace and the street it occupied bore the same name. The palace address was 68-76. As European palaces went, Noordeinde's origins were decidedly uncharacteristic. It had originated as a medieval farmhouse. In 1533 it was enlarged, becoming a spacious residence. In 1940 by royal standards Noordeinde still appeared a paragon of modesty. Its whitish stone façade rose only two floors. Windows were typical of medieval times – high with little space separating them. Flanking the structure's main section were wings that jutted to both the front and rear, creating an H form. Behind the palace were sprawling gardens and handsome stables.

The prime minister was agitated but not by the latest rumored report of a German invasion. On entering Queen Wilhelmina's office, a stranger was following him.

"Good morning, Prime Minister," she greeted him.

De Geer bowed slightly. "Your majesty."

"Your guest?" she asked.

"Of course. Let me introduce you to Vladimir Poliakov."

The queen's eyes brightened. "A familiar name. It is my pleasure to connect a face with that name." She stepped closer to the stranger and extended her hand. Poliakov accepted it and they shook firmly.

"The pleasure is mine," Poliakov said. He was a *New York Times* foreign correspondent and his was an oft-seen byline. "I have long admired you."

"You have had more than ample time to do so," Wilhelmina chortled, "considering how long I have occupied the throne. Of course, I would not have been surprised if you had acquired a different assessment. Many no doubt have."

Poliakov chuckled slightly. De Geer remained silent.

"Your majesty," said Poliakov, "I wish the circumstance of our meeting was more pleasant than it promises to be."

"We have some disturbing news," de Geer said grimly.

"I see."

De Geer motioned to Poliakov to proceed. "I have it on good authority that the NSB is plotting a coup." Wilhelmina's eyes widened. "They would launch the coup by storming this palace and kidnapping you."

Wilhelmina blew out a breath between barely parted lips. "Your source?"

"I regard it as impeccable. He is one of Mussert's inner circle. The informant doesn't deny wanting to have The Netherlands as part of Hitler's Reich. But he opposes a coup and most certainly cannot abide seeing you come to harm."

"Well, Mr. Poliakov, it seems that I am in your debt. You certainly have my gratitude."

"Thank you, but I assure you it isn't necessary," he smiled. "Generally my first priority is informing my editors. In this case, though, it seemed only proper that you not learn of this plot from a *Times* article."

"Again, I thank you. Most thoughtful."

"Prime Minister, I trust you will move quickly to take pre-emptive measures."

"Yes, your majesty. I have already issued orders to strengthen defenses around Noordeinde and to seek out and arrest Mussert and his plotters."

"Good. See that it is done with dispatch"

"In view of learning about this plot, I feel obliged to report more information." De Geer gulped. "There might not be enough time to locate the plotters."

"Oh?"

"I hope what I am about to tell you turns out to be another baseless rumor."

"Hitler?"

"I am afraid so. Our military attaché in Berlin – Major Sas – cabled that Germany plans to invade on May 10."

Wilhelmina grimaced. "Neutrality. Is it still possible?"

"It doesn't seem so."

"No, I suppose not."

CHAPTER 30

May 7, Tuesday. Luc Looten was enjoying a leave with family members at their Rhenen home. He was wearing civilian clothes and relishing the company of his parents and sisters. It felt luxurious to be clean, warm, dry and well fed.

Adding to his pleasure was a visit from Sonja Depauw. She and Karin were best friends, and she both admired and liked Luc. "Please be careful, Luc," Sonja said. "If there is war, don't take any unnecessary chances. Promise?"

"That is an easy promise to make," Luc smiled.

"Good," said Sonja, "now be sure to keep the promise for as long as you are in uniform. We must have another ice skating race next winter."

"But why?" Luc laughed. "You know I will win."

Late that afternoon before supper preparations had begun, Dora Looten turned on the living room radio for the five o'clock news. It was shocking. "All military leaves," the announcer reported, "are cancelled immediately. Soldiers must return to their units without delay."

Luc didn't have far to travel. His unit was responsible for manning the Grebbe Line's center, just to the east of Rhenen's town center. "I need to change and get going," Luc said, rising from a chair.

"You can't stay for dinner?" Dora asked plaintively.

"You heard the announcement, Mother. Without delay." Luc rushed up the stairs to his room.

"Bert," Dora asked, "what do you think?"

He looked at Luc's 19th century carbine, in a corner, leaning against a wall. "I think our government has not prepared our Dutch Army to fight a modern war. If German troops invade, I think our men will have no chance to stop them. None at all."

"Oh my," Dora gasped.

"Retreat and surrender," Bert continued, "would seem the wisest – safest – option."

Karin and Catherina were sitting silently on the sofa, frowns signaling their worry. Sonja clasped her hands and bowed her head.

"Actually," Bert added, "I believe our Army's only chance to avoid catastrophic casualties would be to surrender immediately."

"Do you think that is what would happen?" Dora asked.

"No. We are Dutch."

Bert Looten's thinking accurately depicted the distressing status of Holland's military preparedness. Only 20 battalions were operational for the nation's defense, and most were ill-prepared for combat. Soldiers' small arms were obsolete. So was most of the Army's artillery. The Dutch Army also possessed little armor, and its Air Force could boast of only a handful of reasonably modern planes. Dutch military transport capability hadn't advanced appreciably in centuries. Ponderous horse-drawn wagons were plentiful; motorized vehicles were few. None of those shortcomings could be rectified quickly, and the nation lacked the industrial infrastructure to wage prolonged combat.

In a Europe that had borne witness to seemingly endless warfare, why was The Netherlands so unready to defend itself?

One reason was the military decay that ate away muscle during the long lapse of time since Dutch forces last saw combat in 1903. That year saw the conclusion of the Aceh War in the Dutch East Indies. Aceh was a region at the northern tip of Sumatra, a 1,000-mile long north-south island that spanned 250 miles at its widest point. Ironically, triggering the conflict was Dutch belief that the United States might be plotting a takeover of Aceh, a major pepper-producing area also rich with oil deposits. Fighting pitting the Dutch and native Acehs was on-off-on again warfare that persisted for 30 years. It hardly qualified as an experience base for 1940 Dutch armed forces.

A second reason was the mass psychological effect of widespread pacifism during the 1920s and 1930s.

A third was governmental budget cuts imposed during the Great Depression.

A fourth was the misguided belief by some Dutch officials that membership in the League of Nations would provide sufficient protection against foreign aggression.

Finally, and devastatingly, compulsory military service was reduced from 24 months to six – scarcely enough for training and not nearly long enough to create and sustain unit cohesiveness.

By 1940 The Netherlands had begun increasing military budgets but with little effect. Chief reason: Other European nations had begun re-arming years earlier, and their orders had manufacturing plants operating at or near full capacity. Dutch orders went largely unfilled. Luc Looten was bearing witness to the regrettable consequences of inaction and underfunding. Grebbe Line trenches were long and wide enough but lined with wood and vulnerable to fire from incendiary artillery bursts. Grebbe Line bunkers also were largely constructed from wood and hardly able to withstand punishing modern artillery. Large stands of forest to the east would deny Dutch defenders clear fields of fire – and provide protection for German artillery batteries.

Dutch generals were expecting German artillery to be followed by hard-charging tanks supported by well-equipped infantry. They did not anticipate the disruption and confusion that would ensue following drops by Kurt Student's airborne troops.

May 8, Wednesday. "Mr. Bliss," Joshua heard Laura Reidel's voice on his desk phone, "your guests are here."

"I'll be right there." It was early afternoon. Joshua was receiving an opportunity to do what Ernst Heldring had told him was intended as his future role at the company – working in sales. In the lobby he greeted two customers. He shook hands with Richard McCarthy of General Electric and Ralph Connolly of Caterpillar. McCarthy's GE division in Erie, Pennsylvania made electric motors for pumps. Connolly's unit of Caterpillar produced excavating equipment. Joshua's mission: Discuss shipping arrangements and rates and persuade the two companies to increase their business with Netherlands Royal Steamship Company.

Joshua, wearing a new blue pinstriped suit with a solid red necktie, was feeling confident and jaunty. His attitudinal shift toward the positive wasn't going unnoticed by Laura. She smiled, pleased to see Joshua apparently recovering from his grief. For Joshua the prospect of winning more business for the company and continuing liaisons with Raluca were, in fact, lifting his morale to heights nearing those of his early months in Amsterdam.

His itinerary with McCarthy and Connolly began with showing them around the company's headquarters offices and nearby port facilities. Joshua was proving himself an able company emissary. The two customers were impressed by the firm's operations and Joshua's knowledgeable observations.

"You know your business," McCarthy said admiringly. "And to be honest it would be nice to have an American sales liaison onsite here in Amsterdam. It should make for good communications."

After dinner McCarthy and Connolly spent the night in the Grand Krasnapolsky Hotel. Neither man visited the nearby red light district.

May 9, Thursday. Joshua met the two men for breakfast at the hotel. Afterward they taxied to Centraal Station where they boarded a train bound for The Hague. Joshua wanted McCarthy and Connolly to see

Holland's seat of government, rich with history and where regulatory policies affecting business were set.

May 9, Thursday. At airfields in western Germany, General Kurt Student reviewed his airborne forces – their planes and gliders, troops, weapons, radios and other equipment. He then gave a final briefing to his assembled senior officers who would then disclose to their men the next day's missions. Chief among them: Capture Queen Wilhelmina. "She's in The Hague at her Noordeinde Palace. Once our troops are on the ground, we must move quickly from our landing zones near The Hague airfields. We can expect resistance, but our intelligence believes it will be light and easily overcome by our speed and aggressiveness."

Student's airborne troops also would be landing at airfields around Rotterdam and near Wageningen, a village only about three miles east of Rhenen. The airborne assault on Rotterdam was intended to swiftly seize the city's sprawling port facilities, including those of the Holland-America Line. Wageningen was targeted because troops landing there would be expected to close quickly on the center of the Grebbe Line.

May 9, Thursday. "It is a certainty. Tomorrow my country attacks yours," Colonel Hans Oster told Major Bert Sas. They were standing, arms and hands resting against their backs, in front of the park bench on which they had sat for their most recent exchange. This morning there was no need to sit; their meeting required only brief moments. "Did you receive a reply to your last cable to The Hague?"

"None."

"Too bad."

"Yes."

"I am sorry."

"I know."

May 10, Friday. **3:55 a.m.** Germany launched its attack on The Netherlands, Belgium, Luxembourg and northern France. Tiny Luxembourg's

fate was sealed expressly because of geography; it lay between Germany
and parts of The Netherlands and Belgium to its immediate south. German
artillery batteries commenced firing and armored units began advancing
westward.

Luc Looten tensed when thundering reports from the first artillery
blasts sounded far to the east. He knew it wouldn't be long before Grebbe
Line bunkers and trenches were targeted. "My Lord," he mumbled intensely,
"please spare us from bodily harm. And please, show mercy on my family
and our town."

5:30 a.m. Junker Ju-52 transports began descending to 800 feet just
east of Wageningen. Red "ready" light bulbs switched to green "go lights,"
side doors opened and Kurt Student's paratroops began jumping into the
first glimpses of the new dawn.

6:00 a.m. More Ju-52s were approaching Dutch airfields around The
Hague and Rotterdam. One after another starboard side doors began
opening and troopers began jumping, their detached static lines streaming
from the opened doorways. White silk chutes were snapping open, swaying
gently as they ferried their lethal loads to earth.

6:00 a.m. Queen Wilhelmina went striding briskly to the small
radio studio near her palace office. With jaws clenched and gray
eyes radiating defiance, she stepped to the microphone: "My people.
Although our country with conscientiousness during these past
months had taken a punctilious stand of neutrality, and we had no
other intention than to hold this position strictly, did the German
Wehrmacht during this night launch a sudden attack on our territory,
without any warning. This notwithstanding the serious promise that
neutrality would be respected as long as we maintain it ourselves. I
hereby send a flaming protest against this desecration of good faith
between civilized countries. My government and I now shall do our
duty. Do yours, everywhere and in all circumstances, everyone in
the place you are fond of, with severe watchfulness and with inner
fortitude and passion, what you can do with a clear conscience."

As the queen left the studio and began walking back to her office, she
could hear small arms fire crackling. She thought of her daughter Juliana
who had turned 31 on April 30. Above all, she thought resolutely, I must
keep her safe from marauding Wehrmacht.

7:45 a.m. In Rhenen the telegraph operator came rushing into the
mayor's office. The message was from the regional government in Utrecht,
24 miles to the northwest. The terse telegram instructed the mayor to begin
evacuating the entire population of 6,500 as soon as possible.

London. On hearing the news of Germany's newest blitzkrieg, Neville

Chamberlain resigned in humiliation. Parliament moved immediately to replace the disgraced prime minister with First Lord of the Admiralty Winston Churchill, now age 66.

Berlin. Adolf Hitler also stepped before a microphone. He proceeded to broadcast a monumental lie concocted in collaboration with Joseph Goebbels. "Our Wehrmacht troops have begun advancing west into The Netherlands, Belgium and Luxembourg. This action is not meant to be merely rightful conquest of needed territory for the Third Reich. Instead it is meant to protect those countries from imminent invasion by England and possibly France."

That his announcement lacked any shred of credibility anywhere else in Europe or beyond mattered not at all to Hitler. What did matter was acceptance by German citizens – and possibly by German-speaking peoples already under Hitler's black-booted heels.

In occupied Norway that morning, a collaborationist newspaper, *Arbeiderbladet,* trumpeted this elongated headline:

GERMAN TROOPS HAVE MOVED INTO NETHERLANDS, BELGIUM AND LUXEMBOURG THIS MORNING TO PROTECT THE NEUTRALITY OF THESE COUNTRIES AGAINST IMMINENT BRITISH-FRENCH ATTACK

In truth Hitler moved against those countries so that Wehrmacht forces could skirt France's heavily fortified Maginot Line to its north and use the newly conquered lands as launch points in Hitler's campaign of revenge against the French he so vilified. It was at their treasured Versailles where the treaty that crippled Germany had been crafted and signed. In addition, by occupying The Netherlands and Belgium, his forces could preclude any British efforts to rescue France from the north.

May 10, Friday. Word of the evacuation order spread quickly among Rhenen's 6,500 residents. Bert Looten went running from the post office on Herenstraat to his family's home on the southwest edge of town.

Pushing open the front door, Bert was sweating and winded. "We have little time," he told Dora, Karin and Catherina. "If what I heard is true, the Germans plan to begin bombing our town."

"But why?" Dora asked.

"We are in the way of the German advance," Bert said. "But I also think the Germans want to show how easily they can destroy a town. We are to be their example to Western Europe."

"How much should we take?" Karin asked.

"As much as we can carry," Bert replied. "It's impossible to say when we can return home."

"If we ever can," Karin said somberly, accurately divining her father's troubling thought. "Our home might not exist."

Within the hour the Lootens were lugging suitcases and cloth bags toward the nearby Rhine River. Joining them was a trudging parade of fellow citizens including the Depauw family. Most of the evacuees were experiencing difficulty coming to grips with an unsavory reality: They were wartime pawns and refugees. Anger and denial were gradually surrendering to debilitating sadness.

The few residents who owned cars were loading them and planning to drive west to Rotterdam. It was a decision many would regret.

Awaiting the evacuees were nine coal-hauling vessels. They were painted black, low-sided and ranged in length from about 240 to 300 feet. Crews lowered gangways and townspeople slowly began boarding.

Karin Looten and Sonja Depauw stood together, looking forlornly at the town they were abandoning. "Rhenen is such a happy place to live," Sonja said wistfully. "I think I am already missing it."

Karin patted her lifelong best friend's left shoulder. "We must keep hope. And we must stay together."

"Forever and always," Sonja added. "That must be our pact."

A blast followed by soaring orange-blue flames startled the refugees. The Lootens and Depauws stopped and turned to look back. The first of many German artillery shells had detonated in the town's center. With additional urgency the evacuees completed ascending the gangways.

As the nine vessels started easing away from the shoreline and steaming west toward Rotterdam, incoming shells began leveling Rhenen's center. Evacuees were aghast at the destruction unfolding only a few hundred yards to the south. Explosions, flying chunks of homes and shops, shooting flames, billowing smoke. Their town was disappearing before their disbelieving eyes.

Sonja didn't try to stem the flow of tears trickling down her cheeks. Karin draped her right arm across Sonja's shoulders and pulled her close.

German artillery wasn't confining its shells to Rhenen's homes, shops, town hall and other structures. Its gunners also were zeroing in on Grebbe Line defense works. Shells were detonating ever closer to the bunkers and trenches. Hell on earth, Luc was thinking, I am witnessing it now.

Farther to the east German tanks and infantry were meeting little

Dutch opposition. If I am lucky, Lieutenant Karl Kramer told himself, I will survive this day and live to see my wife and son again.

May 10, Friday. Kurt Student was standing, unbuckling his parachute harness straps. His descent from a Ju-52 transport had gone swiftly and smoothly. He began surveying the action at an airfield just east of The Hague. He was grim-faced but satisfied with what his eyes were taking in. With practiced dispatch his airborne troops were overrunning three airfields on The Hague's outskirts, and they already had seized key bridges in Rotterdam. We have struck quickly, forcefully and successfully, Student concluded. Hitler's vision of airborne forces is proving accurate and wise. We should have all of Holland within a day or two.

That's what Hitler had been predicting to Goering and Goebbels – Queen Wilhelmina's routed army disintegrating and surrendering in no more than two days. "And that irritating queen," Hitler sneered, "she will be our prisoner for as long as I wish – and perhaps only as long as it takes the world to forget her and the Dutch to despise her."

In her Noordeinde Palace office, Queen Wilhelmina was listening to a plea from Prime Minister de Geer. "Please consider evacuating, your majesty. For the sake of Princess Juliana and Prince Bernhard and your own. The Germans must be planning to abduct you. That must be why they have dropped thousands of parachutists around The Hague."

"You might be right. But I have no intention of deserting my people. The war is young. Let's see how things go."

"We cannot hope to hold off the Germans. The Poles couldn't and they had far more troops than we do."

"True enough," Wilhelmina conceded. "But I am not running. Not yet."

Joshua Bliss, Richard McCarthy and Ralph Connolly were standing near the waterfront, admiring The Hague's port facilities which, though much smaller that those at Rotterdam and Amsterdam, were nonetheless the product of Dutch engineering expertise. In awe they also were watching hundreds of billowing parachutes and listening to gunfire.

"Gentlemen," said Connolly, "as a Marine veteran of the First World War, I think we can conclude that we are not witnessing a Dutch Army exercise. It would seem that Hitler has made Holland his next objective."

"I defer to your expertise, Mr. Connolly," Joshua said with respect. "I'm very sorry you are caught up in this mess."

"Not your fault," Connolly said reassuringly. "Besides, unless I miss my guess, The Hague isn't Hitler's only target. He probably has troops moving against other Dutch cities, and I'd bet anything he has mobilized troops and tanks that are crossing the Dutch border as we stand here."

"What now?" said McCarthy.

"Our hotel might be the safest place," Connolly said. "It has guests from many nations not at war with Germany. Including America. If the Dutch can't hold, non-belligerents will probably be allowed to leave."

"Let's get started," Joshua said, and the three men loosened their neckties and began jogging back to The House of Orange, located across the street from the Binnenhof and only some 1,000 feet from Noordeinde Palace. Minutes later they were standing, panting, at the hotel entrance.

"Whew," said Connolly, sweat staining his shirt beneath his suit jacket. "I haven't run that far since basic training at Parris Island."

Connolly's words barely registered with Joshua. His thoughts had turned to Meredith and her slow, terrifying death from the heartlessness of Germany's war machine. In the street fronting the hotel civilians and soldiers alike were scurrying in both directions, some seemingly toward the danger posed by the airborne troops, others toward any structure affording a haven, no matter how tenuous. In the next moment three Luftwaffe fighters came speeding from the east, their machine gun shells ricocheting off cobblestones, scarring buildings, shattering windows and ripping into flesh.

In another two seconds they had disappeared from sight over the nearby North Sea. In their wakes: Carnage. Motionless corpses lay silent. Screams and moans from torn and broken bodies were signaling the first horrors of war in The Hague. Some of those not hit were running to the wounded, offering comfort but able to offer little else. They included Joshua, Richard McCarthy and Ralph Connolly. The latter was kneeling beside an elderly woman, in shock, her left arm shattered. He uttered soothing words and then ripped off his necktie and used it as a tourniquet to staunch her bleeding. He looked around. "Richard," he shouted, "over here." McCarthy came running from the corpse he had been delicately inspecting. "Help me get her inside and onto a bed."

Joshua, kneeling, was tending to a groaning soldier who had been shot in his right buttocks. Two spreading stains told Joshua the bullet had passed through. "I'm no expert," he said, "but I think you will survive this."

The soldier looked up gratefully. "Thank you."

To Joshua he looked like a boy. Can't be more than eighteen or nineteen. He eyed the soldier's carbine. "I don't think you'll be needing this for a while. Mind if I borrow it?"

"Please. Take it." Joshua nodded. "And my extra rounds," the young soldier added, pointing to a pair of ammunition pouches.

Joshua saw Connolly and McCarthy carrying the wounded woman. "Mr. Connolly," he shouted. "I'll try to get back to you later."

"Do what you can," Connolly called back. "And don't worry about us. If we get through this, I can assure you that you'll have all my business."

Joshua waved a silent thank you. Now what? he thought. He examined the carbine.

"Here," said the wounded soldier, "let me show you." With Joshua's help, he maneuvered, grimacing, to a sitting position. "It is really quite simple." First he showed Joshua how to fire the carbine. Then he removed his ammunition pouches and showed Joshua how to reload.

"Thanks." Joshua stood. "Your name?"

"Vandervoort."

Joshua looked at the carbine in his right hand, pouches in his left. Am I being foolish? Downright stupid? This isn't my country. America isn't at war. No, the Germans killed Meredith, and Holland is where I've chosen to live. To make my living. And I have friends here. Dear friends. I can't just run or stand aside while Germans slaughter more innocents. There's probably not much I can do, but anything sounds better than nothing. Joshua knew his time for deliberating was growing perilously short. Gunfire was becoming louder and more insistent by the minute. Those parachutists are moving in. I think my best bet is staying close to Dutch soldiers.

Hitler had miscalculated Dutch resolve. In barracks in and around The Hague, shocked Dutch officers were recovering their poise and rallying their men. Stunningly to General Student, Dutch troops began counterattacking – fearsomely. Within hours they were taking back the three airfields. In the bloody process they were killing, wounding and taking prisoner large numbers of airborne soldiers whose first taste of combat was proving brief and frequently fatal. The Dutch also were destroying numerous Ju-52s that had landed on the airfields. Their crews had believed they could safely refuel before returning to Germany – if they had to return any time soon. After all, they had been told unequivocally that Holland would be part of the Third Reich in only one or two days. Anticipated celebration, they could see, was being supplanted by catastrophe.

Prince Bernhard was pacing in his palace office. Long proud of his German ancestry, he now found himself appalled by Hitler's treachery. That the fuhrer was Austrian by birth did nothing to salve Bernhard's boiling emotions. Late that morning of May 10, he secured a carbine, courtesy of a palace guard who was dubious of loaning Bernhard a gun but couldn't deny a request from the prince.

As the guard was departing, Princess Juliana entered. At the sight of her husband holding the carbine, her eyes narrowed. "What are you doing?'

"My job."

"Your job?"

He turned away from Juliana and stepped to an office window. He used the muzzle to smash the glass. He loaded and shouldered the weapon. Bernhard didn't have to wait long. "Get down behind the desk," he ordered Juliana.

About two minutes later another three German fighters came sweeping in low. Bernhard knew his chances of success were slim but nonetheless took aim. At the instant the pilot of the lead plane squeezed the trigger on his machine gun Bernhard fired two shots. Rounds from the plane thudded into the palace wall. Bernhard's shots struck the oncoming fighter but with little effect. Still, Bernhard was experiencing a small measure of welcome catharsis.

Juliana stood. She was experiencing relief and dismay. In the next moment, Wilhelmina appeared in the doorway. She watched as Bernhard stepped away from the window.

"What were you doing?" Juliana cried in disbelief. "You could have been killed. You don't need to prove you are brave."

"He is being protective and loyal," the queen said proudly.

Juliana spun and shot an angry glance at her mother. Both she and the queen knew the words – He is my husband, please leave this matter to us – aching to escape Juliana's mouth and assault her mother's ears. She swallowed that retort and instead turned back to her husband. "Promise me you will not do anything like that again."

"I am sorry, dear, but I can't do that."

"Cannot or will not?"

"Actually, both."

Joshua spent the night of May 10 in a furniture store on the eastern edge of The Hague. He slumped, exhausted, in a chair. With him were Dutch soldiers Johan Smit, Piet DeVries, Tom de Bruin and Klaas van de Berg.

They had participated in re-taking one of the airfields. Joshua had fired at several German paratroopers, hitting three and killing one of them with a bullet that had crashed through the soldier's right eye. He had cringed at the sight.

On the store's hardwood floor lay Joshua's borrowed carbine and ammunition pouches. He had refilled them with rounds collected from dead Dutch soldiers. Gone was his necktie. He couldn't remember the moment when he yanked it off. His suit jacket and trousers would never be worn again for business. The high quality wool trousers were torn in several places, and the jacket's elbows were shredded from his having dived to the ground several times in taking cover and shooting from the prone position. His bald head was smudged in several spots.

"Tomorrow," Joshua said quietly, "I am heading back toward the center of town. I want to check on my customers at the hotel. And maybe with a phone I can reach my company in Amsterdam and learn the situation there."

"I will go with you," Tom de Bruin said tiredly.

"Same here," Johan Smit and Klaas van de Berg chimed in.

"Me too," Piet DeVries echoed.

May 11, Saturday. The Dutch were showing no appetite for capitulating. They had stymied the German assault on both The Hague and Rotterdam. Hitler was fuming. He called Goering to his office. "I want your Luftwaffe to attack Rotterdam. Not with merely a few sorties. And not with additional airborne troops. The ones on the ground now are either lost or barely holding on."

"You want me to send in heavy bombers?"

"Waves of them," Hitler growled. "I want Rotterdam leveled. I want to teach those stubborn Dutch a lesson that won't be lost on even the most pig-headed. If they fail to surrender, we will level another city – Utrecht."

"Yes, fuhrer."

"How long before you can mount the attack?"

"Two days. Maximum."

"Do not leave the house," Stefaan instructed Anneke.

"I must go to work."

Stefaan smiled, love tempering exasperation. "My dear, do you seriously think Holland-America is doing any business today? No ships will be leaving port. It would be suicidal. German planes would no doubt attack them. And the line's ships at sea, you know better than I that those ships will not try to enter the port."

"Even so," Anneke said defiantly, "I need to check and phone lines are down."

"It is simply too dangerous to be on the streets. I am insisting that you stay inside."

"What about you?"

"I will stay with you."

The last place Queen Wilhelmina wanted to stay was inside.

"Mother," Juliana protested, "please be sensible. Here you have thick walls and guards. I have enough to worry about with Bernhard determined" – she was tempted to say crazy – "to join the fighting. And he is a young man."

"So," Wilhelmina said tempestuously, "you think I am too old."

"I think you are too valuable. That is precisely why Hitler wants to capture you."

"I will not be cowed. The Grebbe Line is where I should be. I intend to die as the last man in the last trench."

"Mother! Please! For the sake of our nation and our people, restrain yourself."

May 12, Sunday. The world was watching Holland. A lull was prevailing. No one expected it to last long. The Dutch were caring for the wounded – theirs and the enemy's – and impounding German prisoners. Juliana kept entreating Wilhelmina to flee. She continued refusing.

In Rotterdam Stefaan Janssen believed danger had ebbed. He brushed aside Anneke's protests and decided to go walking toward the docks. She, he kept insisting, must remain at home.

"If you are going to the docks, why can't I go to my company? The fighting has stopped."

Stefaan drew in a breath. "There are still German soldiers about. Snipers. You could be shot."

"So could you."

Stefaan gritted his teeth, hesitant to articulate his chief concern. He rubbed his eyes. "You could be raped."

May 13, Monday. Luc Looten watched the first explosion. The detonating shell sprouted flames and hurled chunks of ground skyward. Then like relentlessly advancing soldiers, the ensuing explosions came marching closer to the Grebbe Line bunkers and trenches.

No direct hit, Luc thought, that's what I have to hope for. Within minutes his uniform was blackened, his face smudged and eyes reddened. This could be my last day on earth, he knew. I don't know where my family is but, God, please spare them.

The artillery storm began slackening, and Luc knew what that portended. Minutes later he saw the first German tank nosing though battlefield smoke Then a second emerged followed by a third. Next he expected to see Wehrmacht infantry.

Lieutenant Karl Kramer, Corporal Klaus Bohnenblust and Private Max Thiessen were advancing with mixed emotions – ones they shared but only privately. They were confident in Wehrmacht weapon superiority. Buoying them was their training that included mock attacks. They also were apprehensive. They knew casualties would be thinning their ranks.

"Commence firing!" came the shouted command.

Luc and fellow soldiers began shooting at the advancing Wehrmacht. They could see the effects of their rounds. Germans were staggering and collapsing. Red was staining gray uniforms. Helmets were separating from heads. Dutch small artillery pieces were targeting German tanks, and machine gun rounds were shattering Wehrmacht bones and ripping flesh.

The German attack ground to a halt. Tanks and troops began backing away.

Luc removed his right hand from the carbine's trigger. He rubbed his eyes and shook his head. They will come back, he was thinking. We Dutch might be stubborn but the Germans are relentless.

Lieutenant Kramer, Corporal Bohnenblust and Private Thiessen were among soldiers resting beneath trees. The respite was welcome, but they knew it would be brief.

Kramer leaned back against a tree trunk and removed his helmet. He rubbed his irritated eyes. I was lucky, he thought, pure and simple. How much longer can my luck hold? His thoughts turned to Hannah and Thierry. He reached behind for his wallet. He opened it and removed a small photo of Thierry perched on Hannah's lap. She was smiling beatifically, and wide-eyed Thierry was staring intently.

"May I see it?" Bohnenblust asked.

"Of course." Kramer handed the snapshot to his corporal.

"Your wife is beautiful and your son, I am sure you must be a proud father."

Kramer smiled. "I am."

"You will be all right, sir," Bohnenblust said comfortingly. "I am sure of it."

A Wehrmacht captain was moving slowly among his men. "Everyone up," he ordered quietly. "We have our orders. We are going forward again, and this time we will succeed."

Minutes later German artillery again unleashed its ear-shattering fury on the Grebbe Line defenders. Amidst the man-made thunder, Luc heard a soldier weeping. He looked to his left. About 15 feet away a Dutch soldier was crouching, hands covering his eyes. When the first artillery shell burst above the trench, the weeping gave way to uncontrolled sobbing. Farther to Luc's left, perhaps 50 yards, a shell scored a direct hit. Luc could hear the resulting screams, and a moment later felt the blast wave, mercifully lessened by the trench's zigzag design.

The barrage continued for another 10 minutes and, as it was tapering off, Luc could hear the first, faint rumbling of the oncoming tanks. He gritted his teeth and blew out a breath. The rumbling was growing louder and more menacing. In the next few seconds the tanks' long barrels poked through the smoke. Another few moments and Luc realized that Dutch artillery batteries were running low on ammunition; the oncoming tanks were taking no hits. Then came the infantry. Germans armed with fast-firing machine pistols, grenades and rifles were jogging forward, shooting as they advanced.

Luc took a step up from the trench bottom, leaned against its forward wall, positioned his carbine, aimed and fired. He saw a soldier fall and felt fleeting satisfaction.

Luc's next shot struck the left arm of Karl Kramer. The young lieutenant dropped his machine pistol. He fell to his knees, his right hand reaching instinctively for the wound.

In that same sliver of time, the sobbing Dutch soldier threw his carbine down, vaulted the trench's rear wall, scrambled to his feet and began running. Luc whirled to watch.

Private Thiessen saw the panicked soldier running. He squeezed his machine pistol's trigger and a hail of bullets went whizzing above Luc's head and tore into the soldier's back, buttocks and thighs. He fell, his uniform reddening in several spots.

Luc, lips pursed tightly, turned back toward the advancing Wehrmacht troops. He saw a corporal helping the officer he'd shot to his feet. Luc took aim again, but a ricocheting bullet grazed his trigger hand. Luc yelped, blood beginning to cascade off the back of his hand. Grimacing, he shook the hand and mumbled, "Close call."

The coal-hauling fleet carrying Rhenen's citizenry, including the Lootens and the Depauws, was making steady progress west toward Rotterdam. At the moment passengers could hear no gunfire.

"Father," said Karin, "do you think the war is over?"

"If it is," he said, "we have lost."

After shaking blood from his hand, Luc returned his gaze to the front. A second later he found himself looking up at the snout of a luger. Gripping it was injured Karl Kramer. The lieutenant saw Luc's bloodied hand, and Luc saw the stain from the wound he had inflicted on the young officer. Luc jerked his carbine up, barrel pointing at Kramer's chest. Both men squeezed triggers but not quite simultaneously. Kramer's point-blank round thudded into Luc's chest a split instant before his carbine round nicked the top of Kramer's shoulder.

"Ungh" was the only sound to escape Luc's mouth before he fell backward against the trench's rear wall. Slowly he slumped to its muddy bottom.

Kramer watched impassively as the eyes of his young adversary glazed over. He felt no emotion. There wasn't time. He and the other men in his platoon were leaping into the trench, firing to their left and right against outflanked defenders. The Grebbe Line was crumbling.

CHAPTER 31

May 13, Monday. Rotterdam was a proud city, proud of its history and proud of its pre-eminent place in the worldwide shipping industry. The city straddled the Nieuwe Maas (a continuation of the Rhine River) near the mouth of the Lek River. A 17-mile canal connected Rotterdam's center and port to the North Sea. The city was incorporated in 1299 although it was settled centuries earlier. In addition to shipbuilding and its vast port facilities, Rotterdam had earned renown as a titan in the manufacture of chemicals, paints, alcoholic beverages, cigars and sugar. Destinations for its exports spanned the globe.

On the morning of the 13th, a three-day stalemate was keeping opposing forces stuck. Dutch forces under Colonel Pieter Wilhelmus Scharroo continued holding the north bank of the Nieuwe Maas. German airborne forces under General Student and newly arrived forces led by General Rudolf Schmidt, a tank unit commander, held the south bank. Schmidt's units included the motorized Adolf Hitler Regiment and the 9th Panzer Division. Despite overwhelming firepower and superior mobility, the Germans had proved unable to oust the gritty Dutch defenders. This situation, along with the Germans' failure at The Hague, had Hitler in high dudgeon.

May 14, Tuesday. That morning Hitler took to the airwaves with an unexpected and uncharacteristic concession: "The resistance capability of the Dutch Army has proved to be stronger than expected. Political as well as military reasons dictate that this resistance is broken as soon as possible. It is the task of the Army to capture Fortress Holland by committing enough forces from the south, combined with an attack from the east front. In addition to that the Air Force must, while weakening the forces that up until now have supported the 6th Army, facilitate the rapid fall of Fortress Holland."

On hearing Hitler's declaration, Queen Wilhelmina couldn't resist smirking, at least briefly. Speaking to de Geer, Juliana and Bernhard, she said, "That despicable Hitler at first believed his Wehrmacht and Luftwaffe would have us begging for a truce within a day or two. Now he compliments our stand by referring to our small nation as Fortress Holland. History will long remember this day."

Stefaan Janssen was walking through the sprawling port with its array of docks, dry docks, warehouses, oil and petrochemical storage tanks, and office buildings. He saw few signs of fighting or damage. An exception was the Holland-America Line ship SS Statendam. Three days earlier German troops had boarded the vessel and set up machine gun emplacements. Almost immediately Dutch defenders took aim with their own machine guns and mortars. Shooting commenced and fires broke out on the ship. The Germans hastily evacuated. On the 14th the Statendam still was burning.

Anneke was chafing at her forced confinement. I need to get out, she told herself. I hear the shooting. It has died down. I need to see for myself what is happening. But I will stay away from Holland-America. She smiled inwardly. If I get too close, Stefaan might see me and wouldn't that cause a ruckus. She left their home.

On learning of Hitler's directive to bomb Rotterdam, General Schmidt decided to take an initiative. He was a First World War veteran, having served on both the western and eastern fronts. He had seen more than enough devastation. Quickly he wrote a letter that was translated into Dutch. It was an ultimatum for the Dutch to stand down. He instructed that it be delivered to Colonel Scharroo.

Three German soldiers, under a white truce banner, went forward with the ultimatum. They were stopped at a bridge. Dutch troops seized their weapons and threw them into the river. The Germans were blindfolded and guided to Colonel Scharroo's command post in the city center. Watching this scenario unfold was Anneke. She began walking toward the bridge, hoping to learn what was transpiring.

Scharroo read the letter. It told him that if the Dutch didn't cease resisting, the Germans would begin destroying Rotterdam from the air. The colonel phoned his boss, General Henri Winkelman, commander-in-chief of the Dutch Army. After listening to Scharroo read the letter, the stuffy Winkelman chose to stand on protocol. He told Scharroo the ultimatum must be returned to Schmidt to be properly signed – full name plus rank.

Although skeptical of the wisdom of Winkelman's reaction, Scharroo followed the order. He sent the letter back with his adjutant, Captain J.D. Backer, with Winkelman's demand.

Hermann Goering was following orders too. He had ordered 90 Heinkel HE111 bombers to take off from three bases near Bremen in northwestern Germany. Distance from the bases to Rotterdam was about 240 air miles. Sixty of the bombers would attack the city from the northeast, the others from the south.

Anneke could scarcely believe what she was hearing. The Dutch were willing to surrender to avoid a mass bombing, but only if the German commander rewrote his letter with a proper military signature. Stupidity and arrogance, she was thinking, a terrible time for them to rule over common sense. How many of my fellow citizens might suffer needlessly because of this foolishness? I am not eager to see Germans occupying my city, but I do not want my beautiful hometown blown to smithereens.

General Schmidt exercised remarkable restraint. Instead of losing patience and letting his temper boil over, he quickly had his interpreter write the new letter. It included a deadline: The Dutch must comply by 4:20 p.m. It was now a few minutes after 1 p.m. Schmidt signed the letter as Winkelman had dictated and handed it to Captain Backer. While Backer was being escorted to the bridge, Schmidt was standing outside with General Student. They saw the first 30 German bombers approaching from the south. "My God," Schmidt cried, "this is going to be a catastrophe!"

Two quick-thinking German officers acted with dispatch. Kurt Student tried radioing flight commander Walter Lackner, but his aircraft already had reeled in its aerials. Near the bridge Dietrich von Choltitz, concerned that his men could become friendly fire victims, ordered red flares launched. Up they went – too late to be seen by the three lead bombers that dropped their loads. But the 27 trailing bombers in the southern formation saw the spreading red, closed their bomb hatches and began turning homeward to the east.

1:25 p.m. The bombs dropped by the lead planes had sparked fires that were spewing thick billowing smoke that obscured the red flares from the 60 bombers flying from the northeast. Escorting them were Messerschmidt fighters.

Anneke saw the air fleet coming and began running for home on Jacob Catsstraat. Her foremost thought: I hope Stefaan is taking shelter.

During the next few minutes bombs ranging from 110 to 550 pounds began raining down on virtually defenseless Rotterdam. Precious few anti-aircraft batteries were positioned to protect the city. Over the next 20 minutes more than 1,300 bombs fell, most exploding in Rotterdam's one square mile heart.

Seeing bombs dropping from the bellies of planes that had descended to 2,300 feet to increase accuracy, Stefaan entertained only one thought: Get home to Anneke. Moments later the trailing bombers descended even lower – to 2,000 feet – to improve vision through spreading smoke.

Stefaan's way home was proving hazardous in the extreme. Around him, dogging every step, central Rotterdam was being obliterated. Buildings were exploding. Stones, bricks and glass shards were rocketing through the heated air. People were screaming, trying to escape, and dying.

Winded, Anneke paused. She leaned forward, hands resting on knees. Then she straightened and looked around. If there is a hell, she thought grimly, it is right here today in my Rotterdam. Her home was close – and never seemed so distant.

As Stefaan went running by a three-story home, a bomb plowed through its roof and detonated. The fierce explosion sent thousands of red bricks and countless glass shards cascading down on him.

Only two hundred more meters, Anneke was thinking, and I'll be home. Will it still be there? Three paces later an exploding bomb sent a small piece of cobblestone shooting toward her. The stone missile struck her left eye and she crumpled, blacking out before falling to the street. Blood began streaming from her fractured eye socket.

Almost immediately word reached Queen Wilhelmina of the devastation being visited on Rotterdam. She also was told of Hitler's threat: "Fail to surrender and tomorrow Utrecht will meet Rotterdam's fate." Her head shook slowly. "This is one time I believe Hitler is not lying," she told de Geer. "We have no choice but to capitulate or see our small nation erased from the map of Europe."

Before Rotterdam's Armageddon ended, many non-Dutch including some Americans were buying tickets and boarding any vessels in the ports of Amsterdam, The Hague and Rotterdam that were heading to sea and safety. Holland-America Line already was beginning to move its headquarters to Curacao in the Dutch West Indies. At the time Holland-America was operating 22 ships. Sixteen were at sea, away from Rotterdam's flaming port. Germans captured the remainder intact except for the Statendam that by now was reduced to a smoldering hulk. Patriotic shipbuilders worked furiously to scuttle other vessels under construction.

Rotterdam's toll was staggering. Nearly 1,000 people were killed, horrific but miraculously low considering the overall devastation. Thousands more were injured. Among the dead were 185 Dutch military personnel – soldiers, sailors, airmen. Only a few buildings in the city center were left standing. The German onslaught leveled 24,978 homes – leaving 800,000 homeless – and destroyed 24 churches, 2,320 stores and shops, 775 warehouses and 62 schools.

Before the afternoon ended Colonel Scharroo decided to capitulate. He walked to the bridge where earlier communication exchanges had proved fruitless. General Schmidt arrived to receive the colonel.

Scharroo saw no need to feign politeness. "I resent you, a senior Wehrmacht officer, for breaking your word."

Schmidt, chagrined by his inability to ward off the air attack, chose not to try deflecting blame. Instead he said merely, "Herr Oberst, ich verstehe wann Sie bitter sind." (Translation: "Colonel, I fully appreciate your bitterness.")

That afternoon in The Hague, Dutch soldiers – some surprised – found a few civilians still fighting with them. Joshua Bliss still was carrying the Dutch carbine, extra ammunition in his suit jacket pockets and his brown satchel. The papers inside, he mused wryly, now have limited value. He had heard of the queen's surrender announcement. Understandable, Joshua sympathized, but deeply disappointing. This beautiful country with its peace-loving people to be under the heel of that bastard in Berlin.

Amidst the fighting Joshua had jerked the helmet from a dead German to cover his own bald head. Would Paul believe this? Meredith? It's surreal. Snipers – Dutch and German – seemingly occupied the top floors and roofs of every building in The Hague.

A block from the Binnenhof, Joshua and Privates Smit, DeVries, de Bruin and van de Berg were edging around a corner. They startled a patrol of eight Germans. Joshua and his comrades opened fire as did two Germans. The others spun and went running for shelter. De Bruin's shot downed one of the two Germans who had stayed to fight. The other, seeing his friend fall, threw down his bayonet-fixed rifle and raised his hands. Joshua, holding the carbine's barrel in his left hand, blinked and used his right hand to rub his irritated eyes. Then he returned his right hand to the trigger. He stepped ahead of his comrades, moved closer to the surrendering German and stopped. About eight feet were separating the two men. Just a kid, Joshua thought, probably eighteen or nineteen. Neither spoke a word. The German was puzzling over the strange sight: a civilian in a ruined business suit and wearing a Wehrmacht helmet. He thought he detected a distant look in the civilian's eyes. He was right. At that moment Joshua's thoughts again had shifted to Meredith. He was visualizing her below deck, choking on smoke, engulfed in flames in a sinking ship. Joshua blinked and shook his head to free himself from the ghastly vision. He didn't aim. He simply squeezed the carbine's trigger. The bullet tore into the young German who screamed and fell. Joshua stepped closer. The German was clasping a left thigh wound with both hands. Blood was seeping from between his fingers. Joshua pointed the carbine muzzle at the soldier's midsection.

Private de Bruin, scarcely older than the German, hesitated briefly, then went rushing forward. He reached out with his right hand, grasping Joshua's left shoulder. "No," de Bruin murmured urgently. "It would be murder."

Joshua grimaced and shook his shoulders.

De Bruin removed his hand.

The wounded German looked up, uncertain whether his life was about to be extinguished. He forced himself to cease groaning.

"Many have committed murder today," de Bruin said softly. "One more would be one too many."

Joshua sighed deeply. He had confided nothing about Meredith to his new comrades. He delayed another moment, then removed his right forefinger from the carbine's trigger and let the barrel's muzzle point to the pavement.

CHAPTER 32

May 15, Wednesday. Early that morning in London, Winston Churchill decided to take a precautionary measure. He ordered a fast British destroyer, the Hereward, to The Hague.

That afternoon in a school in Rijsoord, a village southeast of Rotterdam, General Winkelman officially surrendered the nation.

In Rotterdam, virtually surrounded by water – salt and fresh – and sliced into sections by rivers and canals, a pressing problem materialized almost immediately: Potable water was scarce. Numerous Rotterdammers thought of the same solution. They began trekking east from the city center to the Rotte River – from which the city derived its name. There they crossed a bridge to the Heineken Brewery with its huge vats of clean water.

The thousands of homeless were quickly finding refuge outside the bomb zone with family members and friends. Most were forced to sleep sitting in chairs or lying on floors.

Anneke found her home, just east of the city center, slightly scarred. Inside she went to the kitchen and turned a faucet handle. Clean water poured out. Gently she cleansed her bloodied face. She could feel her damaged left eyeball but did not need a mirror or physician to tell her sight in the eye was gone. Her face was badly bruised, streaked with black, purple and yellow. She moved to the bedroom she shared with Stefaan. With scizzors she cut a pillowcase into a long strip. She positioned it across her left eye and forehead and looped it around her head where she tied it off. I must look like a graven pirate, she thought briefly.

Next she moved to the living room and sat at one end of the sofa. She pivoted, raising her legs onto the sofa and semi-reclining. Finding a comfortable position proved futile. She waited an hour. With no sign of Stefaan, she stood and stepped outside. Then she began heading west toward her parents' home on Veemarkt. The house sat near a café for livestock traders. Or did. As with the rest of the neighborhood the house and café both had been reduced to smoking rubble.

Dreading what she might see next, Anneke proceeded gingerly, sidestepping debris. At what had been her parents' home, she saw a corpse. She recognized her mother's bright yellow dress – a sign of spring now singed and smudged. Anneke forewent decorum, raising the hem of her dress to dab at tears. She walked farther along the silent street to where her father's shop had stood. She stepped onto a pile of bricks and saw her father's body, lying supine, eyes frozen open. She began edging her way toward him. At his side she knelt. Using her right fore and middle fingers, she closed his eyelids.

That same afternoon Prime Minister de Geer, Juliana and Bernhard finally persuaded Queen Wilhelmina to evacuate. German troops, superior in number to defenders and better weaponed, were closing in on Noordeinde.

Outside the palace, three black Packards awaited the queen and a small entourage including de Geer, Juliana and Bernhard. The odor of burnt gunpowder was permeating the air. Wilhelmina sniffed twice.

Joshua and Privates Smit, DeVries, de Bruin and de Berg saw the evacuation getting underway.

"Gentlemen," Joshua said grimly, "I believe that might be your queen."

Piet Devries confirmed the observation. "I can tell from newspaper photographs that that is the queen – and her daughter."

The three cars began making their way west toward the waterfront where the destroyer Hereward was docked. Debris clogging the street was slowing progress to little more than an automotive crawl.

"If you've nothing better to do," Joshua said, a narrow grin creasing his smudged face, "I suggest we provide an escort."

At that moment an open Dutch Army truck, carrying 10 soldiers, began following the cars.

"It seems she has one now," Joshua said, "but it follows and offers little protection. I say we flank the cars."

"Good thinking, Mr. Bliss," said Tom de Bruin. "Perhaps we are making you a good Dutch soldier."

"I accept that as a major compliment. But I do have a request."

"Yes?" Tom asked.

"Could you please call me Josh? I believe I am older than you gentlemen but not by much."

The four young soldiers chuckled.

"I was thinking we should address you as uncle," Johan teased.

More chuckling, heartier this time.

"You must return the favor," Piet grinned. "First names only."

"Gladly," said Joshua. "Now let's go. Tom and Johan, if you don't mind, take the right side of the street. Piet, Klaus and I will take the left."

The men divided and began flanking the Packards and the trailing truck. Joshua half-waved to the truck-borne soldiers and one returned the gesture.

The slow-moving motorcade traveled another 200 yards when gunfire erupted. Several rounds struck the lead car, shattering its windshield, right headlamp and front passenger side window. More shots targeted soldiers in the open truck. Two fell to the truck bed before they could return fire. The others let loose a volley at upper floor windows and roofs on both sides of the street. They leaped from the truck to the street as the motorcade stalled.

Joshua and his four companions, not in the line of fire, crouched and began scanning. "Look for muzzle flashes," Piet shouted above the din.

Inside the middle Packard, its driver cried to the occupants, "Get on the floor. Now!" The queen, her daughter and son-in-law obeyed the command.

Tom and Johan saw a muzzle flash from a half-open fourth floor window. Both secured their carbine stocks against their right shoulders before taking careful aim. They squeezed their triggers simultaneously. Two rounds shattered the window glass. No further sign of movement.

For brief moments silence prevailed eerily. Queen Wilhelmina raised her head and peered upward through a rear window. More shots from above rang out from the right side of the street. She heard bullets pinging off the car's top and trunk hood.

Joshua didn't see the muzzle flash, but thought he spotted movement on top of the roof. For the next five seconds, nothing. Then he saw a form rise above the roof's low retaining wall. The form was gray-uniformed and holding a machine pistol. Joshua aimed and fired. The machine pistol began plummeting. The uniform disappeared behind the wall.

More silence ensued. Joshua and his companions again scanned the upper floors and roofs. No signs of menace. Then he, Piet and Klaas began running toward the cars. From the opposite side of the street, Tom and Johan did likewise. The soldiers from the truck began running forward and formed a protective ring around the Packards.

Drivers of the middle and third cars pushed open their doors and pulled open rear doors. The lead car's driver was dead.

From the middle car's rear driver side door, Juliana stepped out. She was ashen. From the passenger side, Bernhard emerged. Following Juliana came Wilhelmina.

"Your majesty," Piet said, "are you all right?"

She nodded. "Thank you." Then she spotted the young civilian, head still covered by the German helmet, she had seen shoot the rooftop sniper. With her right hand she beckoned him.

Before Joshua could respond, a voice from the direction of the lead car semi-croaked, "Your majesty, my God. You are alive." The voice belonged to de Geer.

"Very much so," she replied, "thanks to these men." She motioned toward Joshua, Piet, Johan, Tom and Klaas. Again she beckoned Joshua.

He stepped forward, removed the helmet and bowed slightly. "Glad to be of service, your majesty."

Wilhelmina scrutinized his dusty, torn suit and shirt, barely recognizable as one that once had been white. "You are not Dutch."

Joshua grinned, white teeth contrasting against smudged face. "American."

"I think we will need more of you. Many more."

"There are many more of us. Maybe President Roosevelt will see fit to send some."

"I shall have to cable him to that effect."

"Your majesty," de Geer cut in, "my driver is dead and we must get to the docks."

"I can drive that thing," Joshua said, gesturing with his extended right hand toward the Packard. "Do you mind?"

De Geer hesitated, but Wilhelmina didn't. "Not at all. Please do. After all, it's an American car."

"Just one thing," Joshua smiled.

"Yes?" Wilhelmina replied.

"My four companions…your soldiers. I would like to keep them with us."

"I too." She eyed them. "Thank you. I thank each of you."

The four young privates flushed crimson and shifted awkwardly from foot to foot.

"If it's okay-"

"Okay? A good English word?"

"A good American word," Joshua smiled. "If it's okay with you, majesty, I would like Piet" – Joshua motioned toward his new friend-in-arms – "in the car with me. I think it would be good if Tom, Johan and Klaas rode in the truck."

"By all means." A pause. "Were you ever a soldier, Mr.?"

"Bliss, majesty. Josh Bliss. I grew up on a farm and came here to work. I'm with the Netherlands Royal Steamship Company."

"Well, Josh Bliss, if President Roosevelt does send us American soldiers, I hope many of them are farm boys."

"No doubt they would be."

Four of the Dutch soldiers ran forward to the lead car, hurriedly removed the dead driver and carried his body to the truck. Respectfully they lifted and placed him on the truck bed along with the two soldiers – one dead, the other wounded in his left upper arm – who were hit in the snipers' initial volley.

Joshua slid behind the steering wheel, re-started the powerful engine and shifted gears.

Dockside, the gray-painted Hereward was waiting. Queen Wilhelmina and her group were preparing to board the destroyer for the voyage to England where in London she would establish The Netherlands' government-in-exile. She stepped away from Juliana, Bernhard and de Geer and toward Joshua, Piet, Tom, Klaas and Johan. "Once again, gentlemen, I thank you."

"You are assuredly most welcome," Joshua replied.

"It won't be easy for the time being," Wilhelmina said, "but if ever I can do anything for you, please get word to me."

"Actually," Joshua said quietly, "I have a favor to ask now."

"Of course. You have fought for my country. And perhaps saved our lives. What is the favor?"

"I would appreciate it if you could get a message to my family in the States."

"You are not leaving? You could go with me on this ship."

"Thank you, but not yet."

"Why, if I may ask"

"Friends in Amsterdam. I need to check on them."

Wilhelmina nodded thoughtfully. "Getting to Amsterdam could be a problem. The rail line probably has been bombed. Perhaps bridges. Roads too."

"You could be right."

"But you are going to try anyway."

"I am."

Piet, Johan, Klaas and Tom were looking on proudly. Their growing respect for their American comrade was rising once again.

"Yes, you will." A pause. "Do you ride, Josh Bliss? Horses?"

"Yes, I do."

"There are stables behind my palace. We own some fine horses. Please feel free to take your pick – if you deem that the best transportation to Amsterdam."

"That's very kind of you. Thank you."

"The Germans no doubt will be confiscating my horses. Heaven knows what use they would make of them. Well," said the queen, "we must board."

"Ma'am, your majesty?"

"Yes?"

"I seem to have lost my satchel. I could use a piece of paper and a pencil for that message to my family."

"Of course." She eyed de Geer with his briefcase. Impatient though he was, de Geer laid the briefcase on the dock, stooped, opened it and removed a lined pad and a pencil. He handed them to Joshua.

"I'll keep it brief."

The queen turned her gaze to the four young soldiers. "Will you be evacuating with us?"

Piet glanced at each of his comrades. "I think we will stay with Joshua."

CHAPTER 33

May 15, Wednesday. After the fall of Poland, Norway and Denmark, Great Britain decided to continue adhering to a policy that limited bombing to only military targets and infrastructure components such as ports, railroad yards and refineries. Civilian population areas would remain off limits. The leveling of Rotterdam jettisoned that policy – in a hurry. The night after that bombing the Royal Air Force launched a raid on the industrial Ruhr area in western Germany. British bombers surprised the Luftwaffe by targeting civilian manufacturing facilities seen as aiding Germany's war effort. They included steel plants with blast furnaces that, at night, were helpfully illuminating targets. Close by most such facilities lived large civilian populations. That night they – as well as workers inside the plants – bore the RAF's wrath and suffered numerous casualties.

The raid shocked and enraged Hitler. He had told the German people that they would be safe from Allied air attacks.

A mere five days of warfare in The Netherlands produced heavy casualties. More than 2,300 Dutch soldiers were killed. Some 7,000 were wounded. About 3,000 civilians perished, and countless more were injured.

Unexpectedly, Germany's losses were more numerous. Some 2,200 soldiers and airmen were killed. Another 700 were missing – all those Dutch rivers and canals swallowed many corpses – and presumed dead. Some 7,000 German military personnel were wounded. One was General Student. He was shot in the head by a Dutch sniper but survived – thanks to the skill of a Dutch surgeon. In addition the plucky Dutch captured more than 1,500 enemy troops. Those captives immediately were forced aboard vessels heading to England where they would remain prisoners for the war's duration.

Less disturbing to Hitler than the loss of men was the loss of German aircraft. He summoned his pompous Luftwaffe commander to his office and was unsparing in the upbraiding that ensued. "I am holding your report," Hitler began, eyes blazing disdain. "I can hardly believe my eyes." Hitler did not invite Goering to sit. "Incredibly we lost two hundred eighty Ju-52 transports. Two hundred eighty JU-52s shot down or destroyed on

Dutch airfields to those supposedly ill-trained, outmanned Dutch. The Luftwaffe – your Luftwaffe – lost five hundred and twenty bombers and fighters in all. Do you call that good planning?"

"No, fuhrer." Goering could feel perspiration popping out on his forehead and leaking from his armpits. "Not by any means."

"Do you know what this means? How it forces me to alter strategy?" Goering knew the answer but feared replying in any way. "Those aircraft – more than five hundred of them – will not be available for the quick and decisive invasion of England that I had planned. And the English, they now have bombed our factories. Your poor planning has disrupted my timetable."

Unbeknown to the determined Dutch defenders, they had spared England from having to hastily defend against a German onslaught and, thus, changed the course of the war – and history.

Goering at last summoned the courage to utter a few words. "It will not happen again, fuhrer. You have my solemn pledge."

CHAPTER 34

May 15, Wednesday. Josh, Piet, Johan, Tom and Klaas remained dockside long enough to watch the Hereward begin pulling away. They waved and Wilhelmina, Juliana and Bernhard returned the time-honored farewell gesture.

"Let's hope they have a safe crossing," Piet said.

"Yes," Joshua murmured, "let's."

"Do you suppose we will ever see her again?" Tom asked. "Do you think she will ever return home?"

Joshua forced a small smile. "If her will sees a way, I have no doubt she'll be back."

"Now what?" Klaas asked. "We are soldiers of a defeated army."

"I think," said Piet, "that a prisoner of war camp will be next for us. But," he added, "not necessarily for you, Josh. Not if you rid yourself of that carbine and helmet and stay away from us. Or anyone in a Dutch uniform."

Joshua nodded. "I would like to remain in your company, gentlemen. I have not had the privilege of knowing finer men. But I confess that imprisonment lacks appeal." His soldier friends chuckled. "So I think I'll take the queen up on her invitation."

"Her stables?" Piet asked. Joshua nodded. "We will go with you."

Thirty minutes later the five men were admiring the queen's mounts. Twenty of them, geldings and mares. On their walk to the stables, Joshua had found his satchel.

"I have an idea," said Joshua. "You are foot soldiers, not cavalry. But I am thinking that you could lead these wonderful animals from here. Perhaps get them some place where they would stay free from Wehrmacht hands. I hate the idea of these noble beasts pulling heavy wagons or artillery pieces."

"An excellent idea," Piet said enthusiastically. "Choose one and we will lead the rest. Perhaps we can get them to sympathetic farmers before we surrender."

Joshua began walking by the stalls, examining each animal. "Endurance should be more important than speed." He chose a tall brown gelding with a vaguely orangeish tint. He patted the horse's snout. "I think I have a new name for you," he grinned. "From now on, you are Orange."

The four soldiers chuckled. "I believe you have made an excellent choice," Piet said, "of horse and name."

Joshua pulled open the stall's gate for a closer look. "Let's get you saddled and get going." Then he stepped back outside and closed the gate. "I'll be back in a minute." He and the soldiers went walking to a tack room at the far end of the stables. They returned to Orange's stall with a blanket, saddle and bridle. Piet positioned the blanket and Joshua followed with the saddle and bridle. "I think I'll keep the carbine," he said. "At least for now. If need be I can get rid of it." With a short length of rope he secured the weapon to the pommel. Then he turned to face his friends. His throat was thickening. He breathed deeply and forced a swallow. He blinked, trying to hold back tears. He could see his friends making the same effort. "I... uh...I don't know if we'll see each other again. Believe me, your friendship means more to me than you can imagine."

"No," Piet said, "I do think we can imagine, and I think I can speak for all of us. You are the first American we have met. We also hope you are the next one we see."

Joshua nodded and extended his right hand. Four other right hands, in turn, grasped his and shook firmly. Then he turned and inserted his left shoe in a stirrup and swung onto the saddle. "Farewell, my friends." He tapped Orange's flanks and the horse responded with a strong, proud gait.

As Orange exited the stables, Piet murmured hoarsely, "Safe travels, Josh Bliss."

"Well, Orange, if we aren't forced into taking detours, we've got about thirty-five miles to Amsterdam. That should take a good six hours, so let's not push it. Okay?"

Horse and rider began heading northeast from The Hague. "Holland is a beautiful land, boy, isn't it? Fields of flowers, fragrances that don't need to be bottled as perfume."

They hadn't traveled far when a series of artillery blasts startled the horse. Orange reared back, forelegs thrashing the air and neighing nervously.

"Easy, boy." Joshua's words were softly spoken and comforting. He patted Orange's strong neck. "This is strange and plenty scary, but you'll be okay."

A few miles farther north Joshua pulled back on the reins. He studied the situation, looking left and right. "Well, this will be a challenge. Are you up for it?" He was talking to Orange about a canal bridge that had been blown. The canal bank sloped steeply. Joshua eased Orange down as slowly as possible and then into the cold water. "Okay, boy, let's see how good a swimmer you are. Here we go."

Orange completed the crossing easily. At the bottom of the bank, Joshua dismounted. "I think this will be better. I wouldn't want you slipping. Both of us would wind up taking another dip." He took Orange's reins and began leading him up the muddy bank. Joshua's right foot slipped and he dropped to a knee. "Oops. Just a little more dirt." Joshua looked at his suit and laughed. "I'm not sure it will be good even for rags. Looks like I'll be visiting Mr. Folleck's clothing shop." Then he eyed his shoes. "By the time the leather dries, they will probably be at least a size too small. What would Laura Reidel say if she saw me like this? Or smelled me. Nothing like wet wool to wrinkle noses."

The rest of the ride proved less eventful. Dusk was lowering its nightly curtain when Joshua and Orange reached the southern neighborhoods of Amsterdam. "Almost home, boy. Let's keep going. I wonder if we'll see any Nazis. I'm going to untie the carbine in case I have to dump it in a hurry. Aren't you glad to have such a brilliant new master?" Joshua asked, laughing at the self-deprecation.

Amsterdam's streets were eerily quiet. Most residents were reluctant to chance encountering enemy soldiers. Joshua and Orange were drawing stares from the few people who were curious – or brave – enough to venture outside homes, shops and cafes. Hotel guests were cocooning inside rooms, lobbies and bars.

"It looks like Amsterdam has fared better than The Hague or Rotterdam," Joshua said to Orange. "Let's head for my company's offices first. I doubt if anyone is still there, but let's check. And then there's you. Not sure what I'm going to do. I've got to think about that."

Joshua's route was taking him through the city's center. Ahead he could see looming Oude Kerk's tower with its clock. "I don't pray much, Orange. But tomorrow maybe I'll pay a visit to the church. Couldn't hurt, right?"

As Joshua and Orange were nearing Oude Kerk, a woman was peering intently at them. She shook her head slightly in incredulity. Joshua grinned and with his right hand tossed off a small wave.

In the dimming light, the woman asked, "Joshua, is that you?"

"It is indeed," he chuckled.

"Are you all right? You look-"

"Like the loser of a cat fight?"

Raluca laughed. "I think many cats must have clawed you."

Joshua chuckled. "This suit is headed for the trash bin. I can hardly wait to get out of it. Maybe instead of taking a nice, warm bath, I will simply jump into the Prinsengracht."

Joshua dismounted. He was holding the carbine in his right hand.

"Where-" Raluca stopped herself. "I am curious but my questions can wait."

"I would hug you, but I know I smell as bad as I look. What are you doing outside?"

Raluca's head drooped forlornly. "I do not think God has much use for me and my kind. But I felt a need to enter his house." She gestured toward Oude Kerk.

"You might be underestimating God."

"Perhaps." She looked up and smiled. "Just one question for now. Where will you keep the horse?"

Joshua directed his reply to Orange. "Sorry, boy, but my house doesn't have a stable. Neither does our shipping company. I think I should take you to the stable where Meredith and I rented. I think the owner will be happy to add you to his line. Especially when I tell him you belonged to the queen."

"The queen?" Raluca blurted.

"The one and only," Joshua grinned. "If the stable owner believes me, he will probably expect me to ask for a queen's ransom."

"Will you?"

"No. He will love my asking price. It simply will be: Don't ask questions." He and Raluca both laughed. "Well, I guess I'd better mount and get moving before it's too dark to find the stables."

Joshua swung onto Orange, and Raluca stepped closer and patted the horse's neck.

"Things are changing fast," Raluca said somberly. "Will we see each other again?"

Joshua, unsmiling, looked down. "Do you want us to?"

"Yes."

"Good."

"Joshua, please be careful tonight." She pointed to the carbine. "I would feel better if you tossed that in the canal."

"I might. But it's you I'm worried about. German soldiers soon will be everywhere – including the red light district." His lips pursed thoughtfully. "There's no telling how they will treat you." A pause. "Would you like to come stay with me?"

"Tonight?"

"Not just tonight."

"You mean all the time?"

"That is exactly what I mean."

A welter of visions began crowding Raluca's thoughts. "Alicia. She needs me. Let's see. I will talk with her. Not yet, but soon."

CHAPTER 35

Joshua smelled. After finding a new home for Orange at the stables, he returned to his home on Prinsengracht. He began peeling off his sodden clothes that he had worn for more than a week. He had sweated in them, slept in them and doused them in canal water. "Phew," he muttered, nose wrinkling. "They smell worse than a crowded pigpen." He dropped them into a pile and stood scrutinizing them. Burn was the first and only thought he gave them. Tomorrow I'll arrange to have the whole kit and caboodle torched.

Naked, he filled his bathtub with warm water. Slowly he eased himself down. God, he thought, I can't remember a bath ever feeling this good. He sat soaking, nearly motionless, for half an hour. I have no idea what the future is bringing my way, he mused, but I hope it doesn't include more shooting and killing. I've seen and done more than enough of it. More than I could have imagined – until actually facing the situations.

After toweling off, he shuffled to his bedroom and flopped gracelessly onto the bed. I don't think I've ever been this tired. Not even after two football practices on a steamy August day. I am flat-ass exhausted.

On awakening he shaved, dressed in a suit and necktie and went striding to Scheepvaarthuis. In the company's lobby, Laura Reidel was sitting at her desk, a telephone receiver held against her left ear.

Joshua looked at the lobby clock. 10:05. He stood still, waiting for her conversation to end. It didn't take long.

"Sorry I'm late," Joshua said. "Several days late, actually. I take it that things are not business as usual."

"If you call no business not business as usual," Laura replied with uncharacteristic acidity, "you are correct."

"So the company is closing down."

Laura shrugged. "No choice, really. I will stay today to answer queries from customers worried about the status of their shipments. I can't really blame them. They have much money at stake. Anyway I am afraid my job is done until after the war ends."

"And no telling when that will be."

"Probably not until you Americans decide Hitler is a serious threat to your country's interests," Laura said bluntly. "I do not mean to be cynical, but that is the sad truth of the matter."

"I can't disagree."

"It was only twenty-two years ago that America rescued Europe from German depredation. We can't expect your country to come running to our rescue again. Although heaven knows I wish it would."

"Don't give up hope."

"I will try not to."

"I came back to Amsterdam alone. Have you heard from my customers?"

"Yes," Laura said, her visage brightening. "Mr. Connolly telephoned from The Hague. He and Mr. McCarthy will be departing soon with other foreign nationals."

"Good. I'm glad they are all right."

"Mr. Connolly sang your praises, Mr. Bliss. It would seem our queen is indebted to you."

"No more. She agreed to see that a note I wrote gets to my family. And she gave me the use of one of her horses. That's the only reason I'm back here so soon."

"Nevertheless, you must have made quite an impression. I am proud of you."

"Thank you. Are many other staff here?"

"Most came in but they have already gone. Nothing much to do."

"Right. Well I guess I'll clean out my desk and say farewell to anyone still around."

"Mr. Heldring would like to see you. He is still in his office. Shall I alert him?"

"Okay, thanks. Do you think you'll still be here when I leave?"

"Yes, unless the phone stops ringing."

Members of Amsterdam's Jewish community were feeling stomach-tightening anxiety, and the Folleck and Sevel families were no exceptions. The first German soldiers were entering their Merwede Square neighborhood. The conquerors had not yet said or done anything untoward. They seemed content to stroll nonchalantly in pairs, chatting and taking little notice of Amsterdammers. But their mere presence raised tensions among Jews who had fled Germany after Hitler's takeover.

Adding to the concerns of Samuel and Miriam was the absence of any communication from Joshua since before the invasion commenced. They didn't know his whereabouts and were praying that he had been spared Meredith's fate.

It was nearing noon. Joshua had spoken at length with Ernst Heldring who expressed curiosity about – and gratitude for – Joshua's civilian-martial exploits.

"After the war ends and I have to believe it will, if there is still a Netherlands Royal Steamship Company, you will have a job – if you want it."

"I appreciate that, sir. Above all, I hope that all of our colleagues here survive."

"A noble sentiment," Heldring said appreciatively. "I share it." A pause. "I have something for you. I should have seen to it that you had it sooner."

He opened a desk drawer, removed a photo and handed it to Joshua. It had been taken at the dedication of the memorial, a moment after the black shroud had been removed.

Joshua held the photo. With his right forefinger and thumb he rubbed his eyes. "Thank you."

In the lobby Laura Reidel again was answering a customer's phone inquiry. "I wish I had more certain news," she was saying sympathetically. "If I learn more later today, I will let you know promptly."

Ever the caring, diligent employee, Joshua was thinking.

Laura placed the receiver in its cradle. "I forgot to mention you had a visitor early this morning. Isala Van Dyck came to check on the company and whether we will still be needing Miss Wessel."

"And?"

"I told her it didn't seem likely."

Joshua chortled. "Did she take it badly?"

"Actually she seemed quite chipper. I sensed that she wasn't altogether distressed by the turn of events."

"You probably are right. We both know she's fond of Hitler."

"Loathsome," Laura said scornfully. Her head shook. "So, Mr. Bliss, you are off."

"To where I'm not sure," Joshua shrugged.

"You know you have my very best wishes."

"I do."

"Mr. Bliss – Joshua – I do hope we don't lose touch." She rose suddenly, stepped toward Joshua and with no hesitation or sign of self-consciousness embraced him.

Joshua wrapped his arms around her. "So, now it's Joshua inside Scheepvaarthuis," he gently teased. "It would seem certain that it is no longer business as usual."

"I dare say not," Laura murmured.

They pulled slightly away from each other, hands still grasping each other's forearms. Joshua bent forward and lightly kissed Laura's forehead. She didn't redden.

"We will stay in touch," Joshua said softly. "Wherever I wind up on the planet. You have my word."

Outside, Joshua made a decision that, under normal circumstances, he knew would be unwise. He walked to his bank and withdrew his entire account balance. Even if the banks remained open – as in fact they would – Joshua concluded that the Germans could confiscate funds at will and with no notice. What he had in mind with regard to safeguarding his money carried risks but he was guessing no greater than the risk of leaving his deposits with a bank in an occupied nation.

Raluca and Alicia had no such decision to make. They had never opened a bank account. Indeed, they had never stepped inside a bank. They had been hoarding their modest but increasing savings behind a bedroom baseboard. With the black curtain of Nazism descending on Amsterdam, they were glad not to have to worry about bank deposits.

After returning home, Joshua began looking for a hiding place. In the event of a fire, he concluded, lower would be better than higher. Flames and heat tend to rise. *I need to do some shopping.* He left the house and returned within the hour with a collection of hand tools and a small metal box. In his living room he slid the sofa away from the wall. Next, working carefully he loosened two floorboards. The resulting fit was tight, but it accommodated the small box containing his cash.

He put the sofa back in place and smiled at his handiwork. *I should hang onto these tools. Never know. They might come in handy again.*

The Dutch were reeling at the rapidity with which their nation had shifted from peace and pride to occupation, shame and fear. Within the next 24 hours both Wehrmacht and Gestapo men began appearing on virtually every Amsterdam street. A day later the Nazis announced the first restrictions. They ordered window shades lowered and shutters closed at night to make identifying targets more difficult for anticipated Allied air raiders. The occupiers also imposed a midnight to 4 a.m. curfew. Any Amsterdammer caught disobeying these restrictions, the announcement promised, would be subjected to severe punishment.

"Early signs of more sanctions certain to come," Samuel Folleck told Guillermo Sevel. "How long will it be before the Nazis begin persecuting Jews? It is happening in Germany, Austria and Poland. Why should it be different here?"

"Maybe you should stop wearing your yarmulke," Guillermo said, trying to be helpful. He had ceased wearing one while still in Spain.

Samuel's eyes glinted resentment at his friend's suggestion – but only briefly. "Perhaps you are right. I will consider taking it off."

"Your son?"

"Yes, it might be best if Aaron stopped wearing his."

"You have told me about the police beating Jews in Germany," said Guillermo.

"Yes, there is no need to call extra attention to our Jewishness."

I could still get out of Holland if I wanted to. Joshua was strolling beside the Prinsengracht's slowly moving water. Not for the first time during the past two days he was ruminating. To sharpen his concentration, he was doing something he hadn't done since leaving New York: Smoking a cigar. He found puffing it therapeutic. Watching gray smoke curling upward in tight circles seemed to free his mind of distractions. I could skedaddle with other Americans. Or not. I have money saved from my job plus the money Russell gave me. But my company is out of commission, and who's to say how long the Nazis will be in charge? Or how repressive they will be. I have my family to think about but also my friends here. Paul is perfectly capable of doing the heavy lifting on the farm. Joshua flicked lengthening gray cigar ash into the canal. If I stay here, I'd better find something – anything – that brings in some guilders. Wouldn't have to be much. But I don't want to run through my savings if I can avoid it. I think I'll walk over to Meredith's memorial. The picture Mr. Heldring gave me is very nice, but I'm feeling a need to stand close to it again. So much has happened. She should know about it all. A smile creased Joshua's face. He pivoted, drew deeply on the cigar, and began striding toward the waterfront memorial to the Simon Bolivar victims.

Anneke Janssen was grieving and pondering. The man of my dreams is only a memory. I feel like I've lost everything. Stefaan. My mother and father. My job. Most of my town. Anneke fingered the beige patch she had fashioned to cover her sightless left eye and the still visible bruising. She was walking on the fringe of Rotterdam's demolished center. Strolling near the waterfront she gazed at the headquarters of the Holland-America Line. Sitting south of the Nieuwe Maas, it had survived the bomb blasts and the ensuing inferno. Is there any future for me here? Maybe I should try starting over again some place else. Perhaps Amsterdam. My grandparents live there, and I am sure they would want me to stay with them. I need to visit them anyway. Tell them about Stefaan and Mother and Father. They will be heartbroken. Perhaps they will need me to stay with them. At least for a while. Thinking she might be needed lightened Anneke's leaden spirits. She returned to her home, packed a suitcase and began walking south.

The next morning Joshua arose early. After breakfasting and shaving, including the fringe around his bald pate, he walked to his bedroom. No need for a suit and tie, he decided quickly. He pulled on a pair of brown corduroy pants and a plain blue shirt. He sat on the edge of his bed and slipped on argyle socks and brown loafers. I almost feel like I'm back on campus at Stanford.

At his home's front door he stepped outside and sucked in the morning air. Cool and damp. Pretty much the norm here in Holland, he smiled inwardly. But no need for a jacket. The walk will warm me up.

His destination: Merewede Square and Folleck's Fine Clothing. Joshua hadn't walked far when he began seeing occupation troops. Their uniforms were clean, he observed. Perhaps they were support personnel who hadn't seen combat. Many were standing idly, chatting and smoking cigarettes. Several were sitting in cafes, sipping coffee or expresso. None acknowledged his presence, and only a few so much as shot him a passing glance. Only a few days here, he reflected, and they already seem bored.

Gestapo Sergeant Walter Baemer was anything but bored. His mission was to detect and eradicate signs of dissent and resistance. Both were anathema to Hitler. Sergeant Baemer wasn't averse to fabricating charges to satisfy his easily aroused sadistic urges. He had demonstrated his willingness – eagerness – to dish out abuse to innocents on Kristallnacht. He foresaw his new duty post in Amsterdam offering ample opportunities to further strengthen his solid reputation with senior Gestapo officers. He was itching for action. With Germany's swift but costly victory still fresh, Baemer's blood was up.

No anti-Semitic measures had yet been announced in Holland, but Baemer knew they were coming. He drove his black Mercedes into Merwede Square, pulled to the curb, braked, exited and stood. Dreadful weather here, he reflected glumly. If it's not raining it's threatening to. Eventually it must be depressing. Small wonder the Dutch are so fond of flowers. Anything to brighten their drab country. And shit. Baemer's nose wrinkled. The Dutch need fewer horses and more motorcars. Well, that will have to wait. We probably will confiscate most of their automobiles and trucks. After all, our men will need adequate transportation, and our German factories are busy making military equipment, planes, tanks and weapons.

Baemer saw a bald man enter a nearby shop. He looked awfully young to be bald, Baemer mused curiously. Then the sergeant saw the shop's name. Sounds Jewish, he thought. I think I'll check it out.

When Baemer pulled open the door to Folleck's Fine Clothing, Joshua and Samuel were standing at the sales counter. Joshua was briefing Samuel on his recent experiences, albeit omitting gory details.

Samuel eyed the Gestapo sergeant and nodded. Joshua looked back over his shoulder.

"How may I help you?" Samuel asked.

"By telling me if you are Jewish," Baemer said breezily.

"Are you interested in religion?" Samuel replied.

"Clever man," Baemer said without rancor. "But I think you've answered my question. How about you?" he asked, motioning with his right hand to Joshua.

"Why are you asking?"

"It's part of my job."

Joshua could feel temper heating. "What else is part of your job?"

"Cheeky fellow. I can tell you my job does not require me to accept insults without consequence."

"Do you find questions about your job insulting?" Joshua asked.

Samuel was wishing, more fervently by the second, that Joshua would cease this oral sparring match. He could foresee it escalating to violence.

"I find them impertinent."

"Do you see a difference?"

"What I see is that you are not Jewish. Yes, I can see that very clearly. You are one of those Aryan pigheaded Dutch that our fuhrer believes should be eager to become citizens of our Reich. I am wondering if the fuhrer has misjudged the worthiness of the Dutch."

"He might be misjudging that and more," Joshua said dryly.

Baemer smiled wryly. "Time will tell us much."

"It usually does."

"Well," Baemer said not unpleasantly, "this has been most interesting. I shall not forget."

"Nor will we."

After Baemer exited, Samuel said quietly, "Be careful, Joshua, please. For your sake and everyone else's."

CHAPTER 36

"We must establish control over the Dutch population quickly," Hitler told Goebbels. "They are Aryan – except of course for their Jews – and could become significant contributors to the Reich. They have a very developed economy that could help us. That is my hope and goal. But the Dutch are notoriously stubborn and resilient, and they need to learn quickly that we will deal pitilessly with opposition. I need able administrators in The Netherlands, and I need to appoint them without delay."

Wehrmacht and Gestapo officers and men already in Amsterdam as members of the occupation force were beginning, not surprisingly, to explore the city's red light district.

Anna Clarbout convened a meeting of her 19 prostitutes. "Please sit down," she said. "This is a very difficult situation for all of us. I think you know I hate the Germans. They attacked my homeland – France – in the First World War, and at this very moment they are attacking again. I am praying that French soldiers can stop the Huns, but I am not confident that God is paying attention. If he isn't, I can't explain why. The Huns are devils. We can expect German clients any time now. One could walk in while we are meeting. I would prefer to turn them away. All of them. That would be after spitting in their faces. But if I do that, I have no doubt our house would close. The Germans would see to that. Without German soldiers, we would have very few clients. The shipping companies are shutting down. We will have very few, if any, businessmen from other countries coming to Amsterdam. They would be stupid to risk it. Now, each of you has a choice to make. You are not forced to be here now, and no one will stop you if you choose to leave. I would not blame you, not in the slightest."

Raluca and Alicia turned to each other and shrugged. They surveyed the other women. None made a move to leave. Each needed income and what other source of money was available?

"If you stay tonight and have a German for a client and can't stand the thought of servicing another and change your mind and leave, I will wish you well." Anna paused while a thought formed. She smiled wryly. "I think we should have new pricing. Perhaps we will try charging Germans twenty-five percent more. Maybe fifty percent." Anna laughed and the women laughed with her. "I think our meeting is adjourned."

Afterward the prostitutes took to talking among themselves.

"So," Alicia said quietly to Raluca, "we will stay and service the conquerors."

"For now, yes, I think that is best. But, we do not need to show Germans affection. No kissing. No foreplay. Just lie down, spread our legs and move as little as possible."

"Yes," Alicia murmured grimly, "let the Nazis do all the work."

One thought Raluca chose not to share with Alicia, not yet. That was Joshua's invitation to live with him. I would really like to, Raluca admitted to herself. No more whoring. Being with a man who actually likes me. But I can't abandon Alicia. Not when so much is uncertain. Not when we do not have enough money saved to stop whoring and start our own business. Our own lace shop. Our dream. She has journeyed so very far with me. From our little farms in our beautiful Romania to Paris to here. Whoring alone in a city full of Nazi masters. Or monsters. That cannot be her destiny. The long journey to our destiny. I do not know when it will end. Or where or how.

CHAPTER 37

The major Dutch passenger lines – Holland-America, Netherlands Royal Dutch Steamship, Red Star – weren't the only oceangoing fleets with ships at sea. The Dutch Navy had vessels on maneuvers as well as ones in homeports. It managed to get virtually all of those underway before the Germans could seize them and safely to England. One warship, the light cruiser Jacob van Heemskerk, was not yet completed. Remarkably, fast-thinking and fast-acting Dutch naval officers arranged to get it towed to England.

Some Dutch soldiers managed to board the fleeing ships, and in England formed the Princess Irene Brigade. Among them were Piet, Tom, Johan and Klaas. They had found refuge for the queen's horses on farms and then, instead of surrendering, went hustling back to the waterfront.

Then there was Holland's large merchant marine. Captains of commercial ships at sea when Germany invaded their homeland directed vessels to England. During the next five years they would contribute substantially to the Allied war effort.

Others who managed to escape the Germans included Dutch aircraft pilots. Just two months after Holland's fall they formed two all-Dutch squadrons in England. Still other flyers were transported to the United States. The Royal Netherlands Military Flying School was established at Hawkins Field in Jackson, Mississippi. In 1943 an all-Dutch fighter squadron was formed in England.

After Holland's surrender the Nazis contemplated certain practicalities. One, crucial, was providing an adequate food supply. A result was permitting Dutch fishing trawlers to continue their work. Nazi occupation officials did, however, impose certain requirements. Before going to sea trawler captains had to register their vessel names. They also had to pledge to return to port before dark – after which the Nazis anticipated that patriotic seafarers might be tempted to participate in clandestine resistance efforts. The trawlers also were required to stay within three miles of shore or risk attack by a converted tugboat equipped with anti-aircraft cannon and manned by Wehrmacht troops armed with machine guns.

On land as well the Nazis were quickly taking control of transportation. Before the invasion few Dutch drove cars. Nevertheless, to strengthen Wehrmacht transportation and limit civilian mobility – and thwart attempts to include themselves in any resistance work – the Nazis confiscated most cars. Bribes did succeed in keeping a few cars in private hands. Horse-drawn vehicles continued to ply streets and roads, and trams and trains kept operating. But the Dutch simply kept relying on their most commonly used transportation modes – their feet and bikes.

Hitler selected a crony, albeit an appropriately experienced one, to be his top cop in The Netherlands. Johann Baptist Albin Rauter first met Hitler in 1929. From his youth in his native Austria the new occupation police chief preferred to be known as Hanns Albin Rauter.

Born in 1895 Rauter graduated from high school in 1912 and then majored in engineering at the Technical University in Graz. At the outbreak of the First World War he volunteered for the Austro-Hungarian Army.

Later, Rauter moved to Germany to be closer to Hitler. In 1935 he joined the feared Waffen SS and in 1940 was heading one of its departments.

Rauter's forehead was high, his eyes penetrating and his jaw square. He enjoyed Hitler's confidence.

"You will have wide discretion in The Netherlands," Hitler told Rauter mere days after Holland's surrender. "You may do whatever you deem necessary to suppress dissent and maintain order. At the same time, you must keep in mind that I am hoping that most Dutch will see the wisdom of integrating with the Third Reich and willingly accept our rule."

"You can rely on me," Rauter replied. "I will begin by balancing firmness with tact. We will hope that approach proves effective. If the Dutch behave belligerently, I shall respond with appropriate force."

Rauter moved with dispatch to establish his office in The Hague in the Binnenhof.

Hitler's next major occupation appointment established Arthur Seyss-Inquart as Reichs Kommissar or civilian governor. "You will report directly to me," Hitler instructed him, "and I will expect frequent reports."

Born in 1892 in Moravia to an ethnic Czech school principal and his German-speaking wife, Seyss-Inquart showed himself to be patriotic, ambitious and energetic. After completing secondary school he went on to study law at the University of Vienna. At the outbreak of the First World War he, like Rauter, enlisted in the Austro-Hungarian Army. He served with distinction in Russia, Romania and Italy, was decorated several times for bravery and was wounded. During his recovery, Seyss-Inquart completed his law degree.

Seyss-Inquart married Gertrude Maschka, and the couple had three children. In 1921 he opened his own law practice. Tall and big-boned with dark hair, he presented the look of an imposing statesman. In 1933 he was invited to join Austria's government as a state counselor. He was not a member of the ruling National Socialist Party. He was, however, attuned to many of the party's views. By 1938, with Hitler making clear his intentions, Seyss-Inquart joined the party.

In February Austrian Chancellor Kurt von Schuschnigg appointed Seyss-Inquart minister of the interior. In short order he became central to helping Hitler fulfill his ambition. On March 11, with the Wehrmacht poised to invade Austria to prevent a national vote on maintaining independence from Germany, Schuschnigg resigned. President Wilhelm Miklas summarily appointed a reluctant Seyss-Inquart to succeed Schuschnigg.

The next day Wehrmacht troops began marching toward the Austrian border. Thinking quickly and decisively, Seyss-Inquart telegraphed Hitler an invitation to peaceably enter Austria. Although transparently insincere, the invitation pleased Hitler as it publicly, if falsely, justified the takeover of his smaller neighbor.

The following day, March 13, Seyss-Inquart sealed Hitler's esteem by joining the Nazi Party. That same day the lawyerly Seyss-Inquart drafted and signed into law the act reducing Austria to a province of Germany.

Hitler continued demonstrating his respect for the accomplished Seyss-Inquart. The fuhrer made him an honorary Waffen SS officer and in May 1939 appointed him minister without portfolio in his Berlin cabinet. Soon after the September 1 invasion of Poland, Hitler named Seyss-Inquart chief administrator for southern Poland. In Hitler's eyes Seyss-Inquart possessed another attractive attribute; he was virulently anti-Semitic.

Soon after his appointment as civilian governor of The Netherlands, Seyss-Inquart joined Hanns Albin Rauter in setting up his office in the Binnenhof.

One man disappointed by Seyss-Inquart's ascension was Anton Mussert. The latter, still heading Holland's National Socialist Movement or NSB Party, had hoped Hitler would recognize his support of the fuhrer's views and invite him to lead the occupation government. After all, Hitler knew about Mussert's plan to abduct Queen Wilhelmina. Although the plot failed, Mussert felt confident that Hitler had found favor with his bold endeavor. But Hitler favored another role for Mussert. He directed him to work closely with Rauter and Seyss-Inquart in controlling any uncooperative Dutch countrymen.

"There must be no organized resistance in The Netherlands," Hitler told Mussert. "Work closely with the Gestapo to prevent – or quash – resistance."

Mussert also took office space in the Binnenhof. He soon made the acquaintance of Sergeant Walter Baemer who would become a trusted operative.

CHAPTER 38

After the nine coal ships evacuated Rhenen residents on May 10, the vessels had headed southwest toward Rotterdam. Because of bomb damage in and around its port, the ships were forced to tie up east of the city. Passengers including the Lootens and Depauws took refuge in towns and villages throughout Holland's southwest. Sympathetic strangers made them feel welcome in their homes. Some Rhenen refugees, however, were reduced to taking shelter in livestock sheds, forcing the evacuation of the animals.

"Father," Karin Looten said to Bert on May 17, "the fighting has ended. We all are hearing it is safe to return to Rhenen. I would like to go ahead."

"Karin-"

"Father, Sonja would go with me, and new friends here have told us we can borrow their bikes. Let me ride ahead with Sonja. I promise to start back after we've seen our town. It might be easier on our friends if they hear a report before seeing all the damage."

"Let me speak with your mother."

"I already have," Karin smiled only half apologetically. "She said I should talk to you. And Sonja's father said it is all right with him if it is all right with you."

Bert smiled the understanding smile of a wizened parent and shook his head. "You are still playing the same game you learned as a small child." His observation seemed more a sign of affection than an accusation.

"That's because I keep winning it."

Daughter and father stepped toward each other and embraced.

"If you run into problems, see German troops on the way-"

"We will turn around."

From a farm near the village of Geldermalsen, about 12 miles southwest of Rhenen, Karin and Sonja, both 17, began pedaling toward their hometown.

Light precipitation didn't deter them. With the rain keeping most people inside, Karin and Sonja were feeling as though the road was theirs alone.

Two hours later they dismounted the bikes. The wetness on their faces was no longer rain alone. Tears were mingling with raindrops. Rhenen now resembled a small-scale Rotterdam. The center of the small town was virtually obliterated. Rubble abounded. Deep piles of bricks, stones and wood beams now ranked among the town's tallest structures. Only a few buildings remained standing. Remarkably one was the post office which looked hardly touched by the storm of explosions. *Father will be happy,* Karin told herself. *He can return to work.* She used her right sleeve to dry her face.

With trepidation the girls began pedaling to the southwest side of town. They had proceeded fewer than 100 yards when Karin and Sonja abruptly braked. A girl, perhaps six years old, lay supine and lifeless, on the cobblestone sidewalk in front of the one remaining wall of what had been a stationery shop. A bullet had ripped into her face between her eyes. The sight and stench of her decomposing body caused Karin and Sonja's stomachs to heave. They turned aside and retched. The bitter aftertaste of vomit lingered. They turned back toward the small body and tentatively began walking the bikes toward the corpse. Neither recognized the girl. "I don't know so many of the younger children," Karin said sadly.

Moments later, still distracted by the horror they had witnessed, Karin didn't see a loosened cobblestone. Her bike's front tire twisted sharply to the left and Karin plunged to the pavement.

Sonja hopped off her bike, lowered it to the pavement and rushed to Karin. "Are you hurt badly?"

Karin lay still, stunned. "I don't think so." Sonja reached for Karin's right hand and helped her rise slowly. Her dress now was sodden and smudged. Her tangled blond hair looked more like the dark, woven twigs of a bird's nest. They remounted the bikes. Two minutes later they stopped again. More tears began trickling from Karin's eyes, but these were resulting from a wave of relief and gratitude. A living room window was cracked, but the walls of the Looten family home were intact. The roof appeared damaged but only slightly. Karin and Sonja lowered the bikes' kickstands and walked to the front door. Karin pulled it open and they stepped inside.

"It is ghostly," Karin said. "That's what it feels like. Our family once lived here, but now it seems ancient and foreign. Everything is just like we left it. No fire damage. Not even water stains on the ceiling. Only that one cracked window. Thank you, God. Mother and Father will be so relieved."

"I feel very happy for you," Sonja said. A few minutes later she learned her family's luck was good too. Their home was barely scathed. She and Karin both were fortunate that their homes were far from the ruined town center.

The two girls weren't alone in Rhenen. As they rode back toward the town's main street, Herenstraat, they heard the unmistakable sound of the blacksmith pounding rhythmically against his anvil. Why? Karin and Sonja thought. What could you possibly be doing? Approaching his shop, they could see him laboring. The front wall of his shop had been blown away. He saw the girls but didn't interrupt his sweaty work with so much as a cursory nod. Briefly Karin closed her eyes in contemplation. Is he trying to work his way past anger? Or through grief? Later, after everyone has returned, I must talk with him.

Karin and Sonja kept on riding and saw more death – the corpses of two horses and three cows. Scavenging birds were making meals of them.

A minute later on Herenstraat an even bigger surprise greeted the Karin and Sonja. Two girls, appearing to be about ages eight and ten, were pushing an infant sister in a black baby buggy through the rubble.

Karin and Sonja braked their bikes and hopped forward off the seats, their brown shoes resting against the wet pavement. "Where are your parents?" Karin asked.

"At home," the older girl replied.

Home alive or home dead? Karin wondered. "Are they all right?"

"Yes. Our house is a mess, and they are putting things back in place."

Karin smiled and nodded. "Be careful."

"We will," the girl said cheerily.

Two days later large numbers of Rhenenites began returning. Most came by borrowed horse-drawn wagons and carts. A few returned in trucks driven by newly found friends. Initial emotional reactions ran a gamut: Shock. Rage. Disbelief. Sadness. Relief. Determination.

A policeman cautioned adults and children alike not to wander off streets or nearby country roads. The advancing Wehrmacht had left gardens and fields sown with mines. Clearing them would begin soon, he said, but that project wouldn't assure one hundred percent removal.

Immediately another project found numerous Rhenen residents digging. The bodies of the 276 Dutch soldiers killed defending the Grebbe

Line's center were still lying where they fell. With trepidation, Rhenen families went walking up a grade toward the battlefield crest of their local "mountain." They were carrying shovels and hope. Hope that their sons, brothers, nephews and cousins had been wounded or captured.

The stench of rotting flesh was permeating the mid-May air. Dora Looten thought she had braced herself for the worst. She hadn't. When she stood looking down on Luc's corpse, her knees buckled. A heaving sob slowly built and erupted from her twisted face. Bert slumped, letting his right hand rest on Dora's left shoulder. Karin, weeping, stepped forward and placed a hand on her mother's other shoulder. Catherina stayed two paces to their rear; she couldn't bring herself to look at her beloved brother's remains. Her first thought: I will never again fly my orange kite. It would be too sad to fly it without Luc.

A few minutes later townspeople who were spared the trauma of finding their own among the dead began offering solace. The Depauws, Carl and Eefie and their children Sonja and Bernard, approached the Lootens. They extended their arms toward Dora, and Bert and Karin stepped away. Carl and Eefie then helped Dora to her feet, gently grasping her upper arms to steady her.

About 15 minutes later commenced the sight and sound of steel shovels slicing into moist earth. The townspeople, including Bert and Carl, began digging a long burial trench. Permanent graves with headstones would have to wait.

CHAPTER 39

It began with a knock at their door. Dora Looten, preparing supper in the kitchen, wiped her hands on a plain white apron and walked to the front door. A second knock followed before she pulled the door open.

"Yes?" Dora said, puzzled by the sight.

"Hello, ma'am," Lieutenant Karl Kramer said, half-smiling through his embarrassment. "I am sorry to inform you that you must quarter us." He reddened at the imposition he was announcing. Then he semi-turned and gestured toward Corporal Klaus Bohnenblust and Private Max Thiessen.

Dora blinked. "Quarter you? I am sorry, but I am not sure I understand."

"We are members of the unit that will be occupying Rhenen. There are eighteen of us. I command the unit. We need places to live and have been ordered to seek quarters in homes until other arrangements can be made. For the moment there are very few structures that can accommodate my men. Your home is one of them. Your town has no hotel standing."

"I see. Yes, well, how long do you expect to need lodging here?"

"I cannot say. I know this is an inconvenience, and I apologize."

Dora nodded. "We lost our son in the fighting," she said, eyes misting. "So we do have one spare room."

"I am sorry about your loss. Yes, I think we three can share his room."

"It will be cramped."

"We are soldiers," Kramer said kindly. "We can make do. Even a floor will seem a luxury compared to the open ground. The rest of your family?"

"My husband Bert is working at the post office. We have two daughters. They are helping the less fortunate – townspeople who lost everything or had homes severely damaged." She could see that Kramer had been wounded but expressed no sympathy.

Kramer nodded. "Well, if you don't mind, we will take our few belongings up to your son's room. We have a little money – marks – so we will pay you for the food we need."

Dora watched them go clomping up the stairs in their boots, holding machine pistols in their right hands and field packs in their left. She was surprised not to be seething with anger or resentment. Perhaps that is behind me, she thought, or will come later.

In Luc's room the men placed their packs and weapons in the corners and beneath the bed.

"Corporal, Private, a word. Our Wehrmacht has defeated the Dutch, but they fought with valor and honor. We owe these people – this family – respect. They have lost a son. Probably about your age. We must comport ourselves correctly. At all times. Any questions?"

"None, sir," Bohnenblust replied. "But I hope our stay here is short. I am feeling very awkward in the room of a soldier who might have fought us. One we might have killed. The woman must realize that. So will her family."

"I quite agree," said Kramer. "As I understand the situation, our engineers soon will be building a barracks for us. I have no idea what kind or where it will be located. But presumably it will be large enough to house the eighteen of us."

Food was scarce. Each day Dora, Karin and Catherina took marks from the soldiers along with their own guilders to area farms, hoping to buy fresh or canned food. Other townspeople were making the same treks, some – those also quartering enemy soldiers – with the same two currencies. Some townspeople turned to fishing in the Rhine – chancing death or maiming by mines possibly hidden in the open space between the town and the riverbank. Daily caloric intake was barely adequate to keep pounds from dropping from frames.

The first public building repaired was a local school. That returned a sense of normalcy to Rhenen's children. What was upsetting to students but was quickly becoming part of daily routines was watching or listening to dogfights between Luftwaffe and Allied aircraft. More than once Karin, Catherina, Sonja, Bernard and other students sitting near school windows craned their necks trying to catch glimpses of the lethal aerial combat. Once they saw a wounded Messerschmidt spiraling toward earth across the river on the south side of the Rhine. The crash sent a fireball skyward, and the explosion rattled school windows. I hope it was a German plane, Karin thought.

Nights brought scary sounds and frequent nightmares. Karin and Catherina, still sharing a bed, heard the drone of Allied bombers heading east to bomb German targets. The girls prayed for successful raids and the safety of pilots and crews.

Seldom were all three occupation soldiers in Luc's room at night. Lieutenant Kramer had divided each 24 hours into two-man shifts of two and three hours. He included himself on the patrols. One night Karin – she thought the time must be a little after midnight – heard an unusual sound. She sat up in bed. The sound seemed to be coming from Luc's room. Should I stay here or investigate? she asked herself. She looked at Catherina who was sleeping soundly. Karin pulled the lone blanket off her legs and slowly swung them over the side of the bed. She tiptoed to the door and eased it open. No sign of light beneath the door of Luc's room. Carefully, Karin went inching her way to the door. She put her right ear against it. Whimpering. Is that what I am hearing? Then a voice. It belonged to Private Thiessen, and he was trying to stem the weeping.

Her lips pursed tightly, Karin sucked in a deep breath through her nose and held it while she pondered. Slowly she let the breath escape. Then she gently turned the knob and inched open the door. No creaking. She listened as Thiessen began softly praying. "Dear Lord," she heard him petitioning, "the big bombers come every night. I know you can't make them stop. I am afraid that Allied soldiers will come some day. I think they will be seeking revenge. I ask you for my life. Please spare it."

Karin stepped back, carefully closing the door. Her first thought wasn't of Thiesssen. It was of her brother. Did Luc pray for his life? she asked herself. If he did his prayer wasn't heard. Or was it heard and ignored? What kind of God – if there is a God and I am not sure anymore – would permit so much death and suffering? We know the Nazis are evil, but they keep winning battles and conquering countries. Why would a loving God permit that? It cannot be God's will. Not a loving God's will. What use is praying? Does it really make any difference at all? There is one thing I am learning; war makes you think. Many of the thoughts are not so nice. But maybe it is good to begin thinking seriously about God and prayer and death and what happens afterward. I am not sleepy, but I will go back to bed – and think.

Just as for centuries the Dutch had been demonstrating ingenuity, pluck, hard work and perseverance, so in early June were the residents again displaying those attributes. Not on the scale of the miles long canals the Dutch had dug, the dikes they had built and the huge windmills they had designed and manufactured to reliably pump water into canals, rivers and ultimately the North Sea. But nonetheless impressive, especially as a demonstration of heart and neighborly compassion.

Upon returning to Rhenen, townspeople not forced to quarter German occupation soldiers opened their homes to the homeless. Simultaneously, using only readily available materials, residents began building temporary shelters for families who couldn't be squeezed into houses still standing. Soon all residents of the battered town were under cover from summer rains.

CHAPTER 40

On June 5, 26 days after German forces first had struck from the east, the Wehrmacht began advancing south from Belgium and Luxembourg. France found itself caught between the jaws of a powerful military pincer. Bravery by isolated French Army units and individuals wasn't sufficient to compensate for abysmal French leadership. In fact, early the morning of May 15, just five days after Germans began cutting across northern France, The Netherlands, Belgium and Luxembourg, French Premier Paul Reynaud had telephoned Winston Churchill and bleated in English, "We have been defeated."

Churchill, predictably, was aghast. The very next day, May 16, he put aside risks and ordered a Royal Air Force pilot to fly him to Paris. He was determined to check circumstances for himself, and he would attempt to brace up the defeatist Reynaud. Churchill would fly to Paris twice more before the French capitulation. What galled Churchill was knowing that France's Army outnumbered Germany's. What French forces lacked more than manpower and weaponry was leadership with spine. Any sense of soldierly gallantry was being undermined by pathetic government officials. Leaders they are not, Churchill concluded.

Now, with British and French troops – along with Poles who courageously had served as a rearguard – having been evacuated at Dunkirk, little stood in the way of Hitler's most prized conquest.

On June 14 Raluca and Alicia arrived at the brothel to the sound of heart-rending sobs. They scurried to the door of Anna Clarbout's apartment. They knocked once, waited futilely for a reply and pushed open the door. Their boss was distraught.

"Paris," she wailed, "my beautiful city of light has fallen to the Huns."

For the next 20 minutes Anna remained inconsolable. Raluca and Alicia flanked her on a sofa, one with her arm around Anna's shoulders, the other covering her clasped hands with her own.

Eight days later, June 22, France officially surrendered to Germany. Anna was despondent. For the following three days Raluca and Alicia took it upon themselves to serve as de facto nurses. They made sure Anna ate well, bathed and helped apply fresh makeup.

On June 28 thousands of Parisians were spilling tears. That day Adolf Hitler arrived triumphantly. In pre-dawn hours, he had flown from a village in northern France to Paris' Le Bourget Airport – where in 1927 thousands of deliriously happy Parisians had thronged to greet Charles Lindbergh after his unprecedented transatlantic flight in his Spirit of St. Louis. Hitler arrived at 5:30 a.m.

In a Mercedes he entered the city he had all but idolized. To Hitler, Paris stood as the mecca of art and architecture and richly deserved its reputation as the city of light.

The fuhrer's first stop was the ornate Paris Opera in central Paris. Then he ordered his driver farther west and across the Seine to the Eiffel Tower. There he was photographed, raptly admiring Gustav Eiffel's magnificent design and engineering achievement. Standing beside Hitler was Albert Speer, the fuhrer's chief architect.

From the tower Hitler turned his gaze to the northeast and Montmarte, the highest point of land in Paris. Crowning the hill was Sacre Couer, the white church of the Sacred Heart. Hitler directed his driver to re-cross the Seine and take him up to the church from where he could savor a commanding view of his newly conquered citadel of intellect and art.

Incredibly, by 8:30 a.m., Hitler's Mercedes was returning him to Le Bourget. Later, after the war, Speer quoted Hitler as having said, "It was the dream of my life to be permitted to see Paris. I cannot say how happy I am to have that dream fulfilled today."

Speer thought it sad that Hitler saw fit to spend fewer than three hours touring the city of his dreams.

On hearing the news of Hitler's visit to Paris on her office radio, Isala Van Dyck scrunched her shoulders and clapped her hands in elation. That Parisians and Anna Clarbout were distraught was of no concern to Isala. She regarded the French as haughty to the point of being insufferable. Her antipathy toward France combined with her adulation of Hitler produced a glee that put her squarely among a Dutch minority. Whatever I can do to further the fuhrer's interests, she told herself, I will do gladly and without compunction. He is the leader who can restore the greatness that my Holland enjoyed in the sixteenth century.

Although in a minority, Van Dyck was far from alone in her pro-Nazi sympathies. One of the noisiest minority members was Anton Mussert. He was taking to heart his charge from Hitler to control his country's patriotic fervor, and he was intent on going a step further. In late June, Mussert – with the endorsement of Seyss-Inquart – gave a speech in Lunteren, a small town only nine miles north of Rhenen with a similar population. Mussert urged fellow Dutch to embrace Nazism and renounce the Dutch monarchy. Queen Wilhelmina, Mussert thundered, had abandoned the Dutch in their hour of need and fled to England.

Most Dutch recoiled in disgust at Mussert's rantings. His credibility, not strong heretofore, now was irreparably weakened. But not universally ruined. In The Hague Mussert found an unlikely believer in Hendrik Seyffardt. At age 68 he had risen to lieutenant general and had headed the Dutch Army General Staff. Incredibly to most Dutch, Seyffardt began trying to recruit countrymen for the Waffen SS and its occupation role in Poland. His initiative earned him instant and widespread enmity. But Seyffardt did succeed in persuading several thousand Dutch to turn their backs on Holland by joining the SS. One reason for their doing so: They believed that serving in the SS would lead to senior positions in Hitler's self-proclaimed New World Order.

Seyffardt's recruits were sent to Hamburg for basic training and then to East Prussia for additional training. Eventually they would see combat in Russia near Leningrad.

If I were a man, Isala Van Dyck convinced herself, I would join them. Unless I was offered and accepted an equal or more important role with the Nazis here in Amsterdam. I will see that my views are known in the right places.

During the same week in late June, Joshua was taking an afternoon stroll. He was proceeding leisurely east on Barndestaag near the Nieumarkt plaza. He glanced casually at a window sign, looked away and then his head snapped back. The hand-lettered sign read: Help Wanted. The shop, Joshua could see, sold and serviced bicycles. Why not? He thought. Nothing ventured, nothing gained. If the job is still available and I get it, it could be just what I need – something to occupy my time and give me a little steady income. The job probably doesn't pay much, but I don't need much.

Joshua pulled open the shop door and stepped inside.

The shopkeeper was checking the rear spokes on an obviously much-used bike. He looked up. "May I help you?"

"Actually," Joshua replied, "I saw your help wanted sign. Is the job still open?"

"It is – for a man with the right qualifications. What are yours?"

Joshua smiled at his bluntness. He had long grown accustomed to this

Dutch tendency. He decided to reply with a question. "Why do you need help?"

The shopkeeper's left eye narrowed at what he regarded as cheekiness. Still, there was something appealing about this bald-headed stranger with a bent toward curiosity. I am curious myself about his age. How old – or young – is he? "I had a young assistant. He was killed."

"How? Where?"

"By Germans. At Rhenen."

"I am sorry. You have my condolences."

"Thank you."

"Where is Rhenen?"

More curiosity, thought the shop owner. I almost feel like I am the one being interviewed. "It's a small town to the east near the Rhine. It was the first town the Germans destroyed."

"I see. Well, you asked for my qualifications, and it would be impolite to expect you to ask again." Joshua smiled wryly as did the shopkeeper. "I rode bikes a lot while growing up and at university. But more important, I grew up on a farm. We had lots of machinery and it needed frequent repairs. I learned how to use tools. The right tools for each job."

"That is a very good answer." The shopkeeper smiled appreciatively. "I might even call it the right answer."

"So," Joshua ventured, head bowing slightly to his left, "is the job mine?"

"It is." The shopkeeper extended his right hand. Joshua took it and the men shook firmly. "I am Karel Veeder."

"Thank you, Mr. Veeder. It is very nice to make your acquaintance. My name is Josh Bliss."

"Not a Dutch name."

"No. And since I am going to be working for you, I will eventually satisfy your curiosity and save you from asking questions. I am sure you will have much to teach me about bicycle sales and repairs, and I will listen and try to be a good student."

On June 26 Germany again unleashed terror on the seas. A pack of U-boats ganged up on the Maasdam, a Holland-America liner the company had made available for service to the Allies. The U-boats launched a series of torpedoes, and the Maasdam went down. Among the dead were American nurses on their way to England. For Joshua the sinking presented an all too grim reminder of Meredith's fate. I'm not sure if or when, Joshua thought, but if given another chance to strike back at the Germans, I wouldn't hesitate to take it.

Joshua's first two days working at Karel Veeder's bicycle shop were more rewarding than he had anticipated. The labor had Joshua recalling the pleasure he had derived from using tools during his years on the farm. It felt good to put his hands to work, to identify a problem and achieve a solution. The job seldom called for him to step outside the shop, but it didn't chain him to a desk. Joshua judged himself an apt student of bicycle construction and repairs, and he soon realized – and appreciated – that Karel was an enthusiastic and able teacher.

Karel proved able in another regard. He had so far shown himself able to harness his curiosity. He hadn't probed Joshua for details on his background. Joshua had told Karel that in due time he would reveal his story, and "eventually" seemingly satisfied Karel.

In the early afternoon of Joshua's third day on the job he left the shop to buy a piece of fruit that would serve as his lunch. An apple or a plum, Joshua told himself, either will tide me over nicely until I get home and fix supper.

Across the nearest canal to the west, Joshua saw a small food shop. Outside the shop, the grocer had arrayed an attractive variety of fruits and vegetables.

As Joshua was crossing the bridge that spanned the canal, one of Amsterdam's narrower channels, he saw a woman examining the fresh produce. He continued walking toward the shop when the woman, her selections in hand, turned to enter the shop to pay. In profile something caused Joshua to pause. Yes, he was sure, that woman is wearing an eye patch. A tan one. Or as Meredith would correct me, Joshua smiled lovingly, a beige one. Tan or beige, I would have teased her, what's the big diff?

Joshua slowed his pace. Moments later the one-eyed woman exited the shop. She was carrying her purchases in a black cloth bag. She paused to place the bag in her left hand while retaining her purse in her right. Joshua had stopped and was watching her from about 30 feet.

She looked up and toward the near end of the bridge where Joshua was standing, right hand resting on a railing.

Boldly, the woman stepped toward Joshua, closing the gap. "You are staring at me," the woman declared accusingly.

Joshua nodded. Curiosity was compelling him to walk closer. "Guilty as charged," he smiled, "and I apologize."

The woman slowly appraised him – his choice of words and his attitude. "Your Dutch is quite good – for someone not a Netherlander."

Joshua rubbed his right thumb and forefinger together, pondering his reply. "What if I told you I am from a remote – and tiny – village in the north of Holland?"

"Ha," the woman laughed gaily, "we have no villages that remote. So I would say you are lying."

Joshua laughed at her bluntness. "Then I will have to keep improving my Dutch."

"Bravo! Your willingness to learn is commendable. But I must tell you," she said, pointing to three occupation soldiers who were loitering down the street, "I think you could fool those Germans now."

"Perhaps," Joshua said dryly, "someday I might need to. But right now I need to buy a piece of fruit and get back to work."

"Where do you work?"

Joshua half-pivoted and pointed back across the canal. "In that bicycle shop."

The woman smiled and paused before replying. "I think we will meet again. My eye patch, your bald head. It should be difficult to miss each other."

CHAPTER 41

August 1940 proved another memorable month for the Dutch. It began with surprise action by the regional government in Utrecht. Incredibly, only three months after the bombing, it was making available funds to begin rebuilding Rhenen's town center. The process for acquiring those funds, however, wasn't lacking bureaucratic requirements. First, residents and business owners whose homes and shops had been destroyed or damaged were forced to complete a form that asked for an assessment of the extent of structural damage and a list of lost items along with how much they had cost and when and where they had been purchased. Housewives took to keeping notepads and pencils handy so they could jot down facts as they popped into their minds.

Completed forms were sent to the Damage Enquete Committee in nearby Wageningen. The committee staff included two appraisers who knew well the market value of Rhenen homes and shops. Following a detailed review of submissions, applicants were directed to a bank that informed them of the amount of credit now available and the uses to which it could be applied. The credit was regarded as a loan, to be repaid with interest.

The daunting process notwithstanding, Rhenen's determined citizenry plunged ahead. They even decided to take advantage of the rebuilding program in an unforeseen way. After clearing away rubble, they decided to significantly widen the town's medieval streets. This bustle of activity was taking place under the watchful eyes of Lieutentant Karl Kramer and his 17 occupation troops.

Berlin not only didn't interfere with Rhenen's reconstruction but endorsed it. The Nazis thought it would strengthen their efforts to win the cooperation, if not the hearts, of the Dutch.

That foresight did not extend to matters of the sea. German submarines continued preying on oceangoing vessels without regard to purpose or national flags. During that same August, U-boats attacked another Holland-America liner. The Volendam was carrying 900 passengers and crew toward England when the torpedoes struck. As the wounded ship listed, the captain ordered the liner abandoned. Miraculously, only one life was lost during the transfer to lifeboats and rescue vessels. Remarkably if not miraculously, the Volendam stayed afloat and was towed to a Scottish harbor.

Back on land in another area of Holland, the Nazis were demonstrating their seemingly bottomless capacity for heavy handedness. Leyden University, founded in 1575 and the nation's oldest, was located in the city whose name it bore. The campus lay 12 miles northeast of The Hague and 21 miles southwest of Rotterdam.

With the new school year getting underway, the Nazis ordered university administrators to dismiss Professor E.J. Meyers. Not because of any real or perceived academic deficiencies but because he was Jewish.

The move quickly generated unforeseen consequences. Leyden students who respected and liked Professor Meyers began protesting. Word of their demonstrations reached Nazi civilian governor Seyss-Inquart. "Students must cease protesting immediately," he declared. They refused. Seyss-Inquart, charged by Hitler with trying to win the hearts and minds of the Dutch, nevertheless initially permitted pique to outweigh measured response and ordered the university closed.

Soon he reconsidered the rashness of his action and offered to re-open the university – on one condition: All Jewish students must re-register as such. The students – virtually all of them, Jew and Gentile – refused and the university remained closed.

I am not sure I should do this, Anneke Janssen was ruminating. She was standing alongside the narrow canal that marked the western end of Barndestaag. At the far end of the short street ran a wider canal. In between resided Karel Veeder's bicycle shop.

The time was nearing noon. If I stay here, Anneke mused, perhaps he will leave the shop to buy his lunch. Or maybe not. Maybe some days he brings his lunch. She became exasperated with her indecision. This is stupid. I am a widow. I now know exactly how fragile and fleeting life can be. She breathed deeply and began walking – a bit nervously, she admitted to herself – toward the shop. At the door she hesitated briefly before pulling it open.

She saw a middle-aged man, Karel Veeder, standing at the sales counter. He was flipping through some papers. Anneke felt a rush of disappointment.

"Yes, ma'am," Karel asked, looking up, "how may I help you?"

Before Anneke could reply, a bald head emerged through a doorway from behind the sales counter. Joshua saw the beige eye patch and said, "Mr. Veeder, you needn't interrupt your paperwork. I'll wait on this customer."

Joshua then moved around the counter and stepped toward Anneke. "What brings you here? Are you interested in buying a new bike? Or perhaps a used one? I don't see a bike outside the door," Joshua said, right eyebrow elevated in doubt, "so may I conclude that you don't have a broken bike in need of repair?"

Anneke blushed. "I was planning to say I need a used bike."

"But?"

"But that is not true."

"Sooo…"

"So I thought it might be nice if we saw each other again. Talked a bit. Perhaps learn a little about each other." Her redness, receding, returned anew in a blaze of crimson.

Joshua didn't try to refrain from teasing gently. "So, you were planning a subterfuge."

"Guilty," Anneke replied, eyes downcast.

"But you thought I would see through it. I am not sure I would have." He laughed. "No need to be embarrassed. Really."

She lifted her head. "I have never," she stammered softly, "done anything like this."

"And I never sold or repaired bikes until a couple days before we met. And I wouldn't be doing it now if not for the war."

Karel Veeder, overhearing their exchange, smiled without looking up.

Anneke realized Joshua was trying to help ease her past awkwardness, and she was beginning to feel a trifle more comfortable. "Yes, the war has forced many changes."

"For you personally?"

"Yes." A pause. "And for you?"

He nodded and Anneke could almost see a cloud of regret descend and envelope Joshua.

"Well," she said, "we don't know each other's name. Perhaps exchanging names could be a start."

"I think it could be. My name is Joshua. Joshua Bliss. People call me Josh which is what I prefer."

"Mine is Anneke Janssen. I don't have a short name."

"Then Anneke it is." He held out his right hand and Anneke accepted it.

Two days later subterfuge of a more serious nature was occupying Joshua's thoughts. Karel Veeder had left the shop and ascended to his apartment, climbing the stairs in the back room where repairs were performed. He had gone up to retrieve parts order forms he had forgotten to bring down in the morning.

Joshua was in the back room, sitting on a low stool, replacing broken spokes in a front wheel. Daily he was growing more proficient with repair work. A few feet away, just past the entrance to the front display room, two men were murmuring furtively. At first Joshua paid no attention to their hushed tones. But when he heard the words Nazis and resistance in the same sentence, his mind shifted instantly from bike repairs to riveting curiosity. Listening closely, he heard several references to a particular street, one not familiar to him.

Joshua carefully laid his tools on the wooden floor and straightened. Casually, not wanting to startle the men, he stepped through the doorway. "May I help you?" he said pleasantly.

"No, I mean we, uh, are interested in new bikes."

Joshua stepped closer. "Come with me. I think you might like two of our new models at the front of the room." He extended his right arm behind the man nearest him and all but shepherded the pair to the shop's front. "There," he said, pointing exuberantly at a new, blue model with orange trim, "isn't that a beautiful machine?"

"Uh, yes," said the second man.

Before either could say more, Joshua whispered, "Is there something special about Corellistraat?"

Both men's eyes widened in alarm. They looked at each other. "Perhaps you misunderstood," said the first man.

Joshua chanced placing a calming right hand on the first man's left shoulder. "Don't be afraid. Let me assure you, I am not an informer for the Nazis." The two men eyed Joshua dubiously and then turned to each other, looking for a sign. Should they answer the young man's danger-laden question? Or should they simply exit the shop without hearing another word? Joshua sensed that if he was going to learn anything he needed to offer a stronger assurance of his sympathies. "My wife – her name was Meredith – was lost on the Simon Bolivar," he said, lips taut. "That should tell you all you need to know about my feelings for the Nazis."

The following Sunday Joshua arose early. After shaving, bathing and breakfasting, he pulled on brown corduroy pants, a blue short-sleeve collarless shirt and a light brown jacket. He slipped into his most comfortable shoes for walking. He had consulted a map of Amsterdam and began walking unhurriedly southeast from his home on Prinsengracht.

Corellistraat lay a little south of the city's central district. It was a street so short that casual passersby could easily miss it. Soon Joshua crossed the wide Amstel Canal and knew he was getting close.

198

It could just about pass for an alley, Joshua mused as he stood at the street's north end. It sure ain't Main Street in Shelby or University Avenue in Stanford. Unless you are very local or have a particular reason for being here, you could live a lifetime and never step foot on Corellistraat. I'm certainly not local but I do have a particular reason, so I think I'll have a look-see. Now Josh Bliss, he questioned himself, can I do that without looking too obvious? Or maybe that's what I want. To appear obvious and have someone ask what the hell am I doing here. I guess I'd better have an answer that sounds believable. How about the truth? I'm looking for someone – some people – who might be willing to take a chance on me. To help me do my bit to make the occupation something more than a daily walk in the park for the Nazis. Well, self, nothing ventured, nothing gained. Let's put one foot in front of the other and see what happens. If anything.

CHAPTER 42

The first week of September was feeling more like Dutch summer than looming autumn. Sunshine, 70 degrees and westerly sea breezes comprised the weather's daily rhythm. It was intoxicating, and on the month's first Saturday Karin Looten and Sonja Depauw were drinking it in with large, gay gulps of teenage laughter.

The two 17-year-olds had decided to take a bike hike. They were wearing colorful, knee-length skirts, white blouses and white socks and brown leather shoes. Together at nine o'clock that morning they started from the Lootens' house.

"Which way should we go?" Karin asked.

"Let's not really plan a route," Sonja said brightly. "Let's just begin riding west of town along the Rhine. We will follow the river only as long as we feel like it. If we see a country road that looks interesting, we will simply follow it for a while."

"That sounds good," Karin said. "Sort of a plan that isn't a plan."

"Precisely," chirped Sonja. "It is our no-plan plan."

Both girls threw their heads back and laughed. As they began pedaling west, two tresses of blond hair were streaming behind them, untamed on the wind. They rode parallel to the river for about three miles. Ahead and to their right they saw the entrance to an unpaved road that ran north.

"Let's try it," Karin said.

"Exploration in the finest tradition of our early Dutch seafarers," Sonja said with mock solemnity.

"They roamed the world!" cried Karin. "This morning we are roaming our own little world around Rhenen."

"It's so peaceful out here, isn't it?" said Sonja. "No traffic. No farmers in their fields. No German soldiers. It's like there is no war and nothing to worry about."

"The only sounds are our own voices," Karin said, "and our bike tires rolling on this dirt road."

"Look," said Sonja, pointing upward and to the right or northeast across an unused pasture. "A stork's nest on top of that old barn. I think I see a baby stork poking its head up."

The barn was dilapidated from lack of use and upkeep. In earlier times a farmer had built a stork's nest platform on the barn's roof. Doing so was commonly practiced in The Netherlands, Belgium and France. Throughout the region storks were seen as symbols of new life. This nest was indeed home to an as yet unfledged stork and its parents with their magnificently wide white wingspans. Storks also were valued for practical reasons as consumers of insects, reptiles and small vermin.

"Let's get a closer look," Sonja said cheerily. Abruptly she angled her bike off the road and began pedaling across the pasture. A few seconds later a violent explosion shattered the rural stillness and hurled Sonja and her bike high into the comfortably mild September air.

Still on the road, Karin felt the blast's shock wave blowing against and past her. She closed her eyes and looked down and away. Her balance began to falter. But she managed to steady herself.

When Karin's eyes opened, the country quiet had returned. She looked at the field and saw shredded pieces of the bike and ragged parts of a body. She stepped away from the bike, released her grip on the handlebars and let it fall to the road. In the fog of shock Karin stepped unsteadily off the road and began edging, one halting step after another, toward her friend's sundered body. Severed legs. Bones and blood. A barely recognizable face. Blond hair fanned away from the head. Shredded skirt and blouse. Karin dropped gracelessly to her knees. She brought her hands up and covered her eyes. No tears were falling. They would come later. She knelt for several minutes, then stood. She looked around helplessly for anything she could use to cover Sonja's remains. Nothing. Her head rocked back and she heaved a sigh. Then she turned and began trudging back toward the road. Never had her feet felt so leaden. On the road she righted her bike, turned it around, mounted and began pedaling back toward Rhenen.

Hundreds of miles to the east another violent explosion was shaking a nation. This detonation was political. Among the millions feeling the tremors were Raluca's parents, Gheorghe and Magdalena Johnescu, and Alicia's, Ion and Livia Domian.

Early in the morning in Romania inside his Peles Castle, King Carol heard footsteps. Many of them. Loud ones. Boots running noisily on the castle's hard floors. Rapidly climbing stairs. The king grasped his wife Elena's shoulder and jostled it. She groaned, shook sleep from her eyes and sat up. The footsteps were nearing their chamber. Both were fearing what so often befell royalty – a coup ending in death. They held each other tightly.

The door to their chamber burst open. Twenty soldiers armed with rifles and submachine guns entered the room and surrounded the couple's bed.

Elena couldn't control her trembling. She struggled to suppress an urge to urinate.

The last to enter the chamber was General Ion Antonescu. Summarily the general – an ardent fan of Hitler – announced that the king and queen were under arrest for being anti-German.

On their farms near Apahida, the Johnescus and Domians were grateful the coup had been bloodless. Still, they were deeply concerned for their nation's future. "Antonescu is ruthless and could lead us to ruin," Gheorghe said to Ion after the two farmers had completed a day's work. "If war comes to Romania, I am glad our daughters will not be here. Yes, the Germans occupied Holland, but I have heard nothing about more combat after the surrender. And nothing about atrocities. I do wish we were receiving more letters from our daughters."

"They are intelligent girls," Ion said, trying to convince himself of their well-being. "I think they will manage to stay away from trouble."

"They have shown they can be headstrong," Gheorghe said, unconvinced.

"Yes, but thoughtful as well," replied his friend.

"I know Magdalena won't stop worrying."

"Mothers never do."

King Carol and Elena were driven from their castle near Sinaia south to Bucharest and held in an apartment where guards were posted outside the door around the clock.

Antonescu wasted no time imposing his will. In a matter of hours he began paving the way toward an absolute dictatorship – his own. He ordered the constitution suspended and dissolved Parliament. He installed Michael, Carol and Elena's son, as king but forbade him from taking the oath of office. Antonescu pointedly told Michael what was becoming blindingly obvious: The young king would serve as a mere figurehead, sitting – surviving – only at Antonescu's pleasure. He saw Germany, Italy, Austria and now Romania combining to defeat the progenitor of communism – Russia. With Western Europe, save England, already under Hitler's boots, Antonescu wanted to partner with a seemingly inevitable winner. He viewed Carol as a self-important dawdler. Immediately after seeing Michael crowned as his lackey king, Antonescu suggested strongly to the young monarch that he advise his parents to go into exile. They soon did, journeying first to neutral Switzerland, then south to Marseille and across the Mediterranean and the Atlantic to Mexico. A central reason for the hasty departure was Elena's being part Jewish. Carol foresaw her possible fate under the virulently anti-Semitic Antonescu. But the royal pair didn't depart Bucharest empty handed. In a secretive move that soured most Romanians and deeply distressed Michael, Carol managed to arrange to leave in a nine-car train filled with much of Romania's gold reserves and many of its art treasures.

In Amsterdam the news of Antonescu's coup unsettled Raluca and Alicia. After work at the brothel, in the early morning hours they had returned to their Molensteeg apartment. Before dropping into bed, they were chewing meditatively on bread and sipping tea.

"It is time, you know," said Raluca, "that we write letters home again."

"Yes," Alicia sighed. "I don't know if home ever has felt so far away. We are under the Germans here, and the same could happen in Romania. It would be nice if we could go home. Do you think we have enough money?"

Raluca closed her eyes. "What would we go back to? You know the answer as well as I do. It would be the same as when we left. Poverty with no hope of a future." Her eyes opened and looked sympathetically at her friend.

"But at least," Alicia murmured plaintively, "we could be with our families."

As much as the vision of seeing her family appealed to Raluca and as much as Alicia's departure would free Raluca to move in with Joshua, she chose to speak words of cold reality. "I don't think we could return even if we tried."

"Why not?"

"Because we are trapped. The Nazis control every nation on our way. Holland, Belgium, France, Germany, Austria. How safe do you think it would be for two young women? We could be stopped. Locked up in a concentration camp. Or worse."

"If we stay here-"

"If we stay here," Raluca gently interrupted Alicia, "at least we can keep hoping."

CHAPTER 43

Anneke and Joshua were sipping steaming coffee inside a small café on Prinsengracht. They were seated at a window table for two. Trees were changing to their colorful autumn costumes and dropping leaves onto the streets and into the canals. The pair had shared their life stories in an earlier such café conversation.

"General Seyffardt is having some success with his recruiting campaign," Joshua observed. "I hear about nine thousand Dutch have answered his call and begun training to join the SS."

Anneke's serious mien stiffened. Through clenched jaws, she hissed, "They – and he – are to be vilified. Traitors to our nation." This was the first time Joshua had seen Anneke flash hot anger. It surprised but didn't distress him. He regarded it as long overdue. "How could those men...How could Seyffardt, a former chief of staff, side with the man who slaughtered innocents? Including Stefaan. They are far beyond the pale."

Joshua peered into his friend's blazing blue eyes. Part of him was tempted to reach across the small table and cover her hands with his. Attempt to calm and comfort the young widow. The other part felt he should hold back. Not be seen as patronizing. The second part prevailed. Joshua said simply, "It might be a long time coming, but let's hope justice is served."

Anneke unclenched her teeth and blinked. "If it is, I want to serve as an eyewitness. No pun intended."

"None taken," Joshua replied somberly.

Outside the café, Anneke and Joshua were strolling slowly north along the Prinsengracht. Anneke saw one of Seyffardt's recruiting posters affixed to the side of a fire station. The large, colorful poster showed a helmeted, grim-visaged Waffen SS soldier towering over east-pointing heavy artillery gun barrels. The text read:

Nederlanders – For your honor and conscience, Rise up against Bolshevism. The Waffen SS calls you!

Anneke accelerated, striding rapidly ahead of Joshua. He watched with growing curiosity. At the fire station wall, Anneke hesitated only an instant. Then she reached forward, grasped the poster's top edge and ripped it down. She ground her heels into the poster and spat. Then she turned back toward Joshua and, incongruously, shrugged as if saying, I couldn't help myself.

Joshua smiled understandingly and tossed off a casual right-handed salute.

Anneke waited patiently until he caught up with her. "I know," she acknowledged semi-sheepishly, "I was rash."

"Just be careful where and when you are rash."

"You are right."

Observing the incident from across the canal was Lieutenant Julius Dettman of the Gestapo. Who is she? he wondered. And who is he? He is bald but otherwise appears an ordinary fellow. She appears anything but. A one-eyed tempest. She bears watching more closely. I will have to assign someone to keep an eye on her.

"There is something I feel I need to tell you," Raluca said somberly.

"Are you all right?" Alicia asked, eyeing her friend worriedly.

"I am not sick, if that is what you mean."

"Good. But you look and sound like something is bothering you. Is it?"

"Something, yes...I...You have seen Joshua Bliss, and I have told you about him."

"Did he tell you he doesn't want to take you anymore?" Alicia asked. "Is that it? I know you like him."

"No, no," Raluca sighed. "He has asked me to live with him."

Alicia's eyes widened. "Really? Well, of course, you would not joke about something like that. So, what is wrong? You will accept his invitation, won't you?" Now, Alicia's words were coming in a rush. "That is wonderful! You would be silly not to say yes. Even if it is not permanent, it's still wonderful."

"More like a miracle," Raluca said self-deprecatingly.

"It might restore my faith in God," Alicia said with a hint of whimsy. "So why your long face and sad voice?"

"I don't want to leave you alone."

"What? Why would you give even a minute of thought to staying here when you could put the brothel behind you? I never, ever thought you to be foolish, but that would be foolish. I won't stand for it."

Raluca couldn't refrain from chuckling lowly. "You are the best, Alicia. Absolutely the best."

"When you go to live with him, it wouldn't mean we wouldn't see each other. Just not at the brothel."

"Our dream. The lace shop. I don't want to let go of that dream." Raluca's voice was gaining strength. "Also I do not want you working alone and living alone here. If I lived with Joshua, I wouldn't have money to help you with the rent. Or food."

"I would manage. I could tell Madame Clarbout I would like to work more. More days, longer hours."

Raluca's head shook slightly. "I do not like that idea, not at all."

"So what did you tell Joshua?"

"That I needed time to think about it. I am telling you now in case someday I do accept his invitation. If it is still open."

"I love you, Raluca, but that was foolish."

Adolf Hitler didn't trouble himself waiting for a formal invitation from Ion Antonescu to begin sending Wehrmacht troops into Romania. The fuhrer issued the order on October 8 and his legions, poised near the Romanian border, began moving forward immediately.

Hitler lusted for control of Romania's rich oil fields and its sprawling complex of a dozen oil refineries around Ploesti, the nation's most prosperous city, in the country's southeast. Those refineries annually produced 10 million tons of oil including 90-octane fuel, the highest quality in Europe. Hitler and Goering saw that rich fuel as crucial to meeting the Luftwaffe's needs.

German troops in Romania soon numbered more than half a million and were well-equipped and trained. And Antonescu? Ambivalent about their arrival, he didn't openly object to their presence or even openly question it. Doing so, he sensed, would prove counterproductive to his determined effort to forge strong bonds with the fuhrer and his expanding Reich.

"We are only twenty years old," Raluca said to Alicia," but the situation in our homeland seems to be getting worse."

Passing by a newsstand on the way from their apartment to the brothel, Raluca had noticed a newspaper headline – sanctioned by Nazi censors – trumpeting the Wehrmacht's unopposed move into Romania. Raluca bought a copy. She and Alicia read the account in the brothel's sitting room while waiting for customers – who more often than not these days were occupying Germans. For them, Raluca and Alicia had adhered to their strategy: No kissing or foreplay, lie as still as pond water and make the encounter as joyless as possible.

Now, while walking home after work, they were discussing the latest development in Romania. "I think it is time," said Alicia, "that we write to our families again and let them know we are all right."

"Agreed."

"And," Alicia said, eyes brightening, "this time I would like to try writing my own letter."

Raluca's head turned toward her friend, eyes beaming. "Wonderful! I know you can do it."

Hours later Raluca and Alicia awakened to learn more unsettling news. This news, though, wasn't reaching them from far off Romania. Instead it was emanating from Nazi occupation headquarters in the Binnenhof in The Hague.

Nazi civilian governor Seyss-Inquart issued the first anti-Jewish measures.

"Starting today," Seyss-Inquart's proclamation declared, "all civil servants throughout The Netherlands are ordered to complete a form on which they describe in detail their family lines. There will be no exceptions. The information must be complete and accurate. Any civil servant not complying will forfeit his job. This procedure will help maintain order throughout The Netherlands."

The ploy was transparent to all Dutch and infuriating to most, including resident aliens such as Joshua, Raluca and Alicia. The forms would ease the Nazis' chore of identifying Jews. In Germany the Nazis had imposed such a registration on civil servants soon after Kristallnacht.

At the same time, Nazi occupiers barred Jews from positions in the air raid defense service. Hermann Goering in particular applauded this restriction. It precluded any need to worry that disgruntled Jews might divulge Luftwaffe flight plans or defense capabilities.

Seyss-Inquart had not as yet ordered any deportations of Jews, but they had ample reason for worrying. Seyss-Inquart did begin threatening Amsterdam's newly jobless shipyard workers with forced labor in Germany. Many promptly went into hiding, with friends and extended family providing secretive shelter.

In London Queen Wilhelmina, Juliana and Bernhard took up shelter in a house at 77 Chester Square, just behind its stately neighbor, Buckingham Palace. Behind the house was a spacious garden, and the queen regarded it as her private sanctuary, a daily reminder of the rhythms of life, death and renewal.

Once settled in her new home, she quickly made it her practice to greet every Netherlander who escaped to England. "My people are paramount," she said to anyone who dared question the practice as productive use of her time as leader of the government-in-exile. "I must do all within my power to keep up morale and hope."

Arthur Seyss-Inquart decided to take on himself the task that Anton Mussert and collaborationist Dutch General Hendrik Seyffardt had failed to achieve: Persuade the Dutch of the wisdom of forging closer economic ties with Germany. Seyss-Inquart used both Nazi-controlled radio stations and newspapers to communicate his message. "The strong and visionary leadership of Adolf Hitler has lifted Germany and her people from the ash heap of poverty and despair to new heights of prosperity and confidence. In the new Germany, good jobs are plentiful and prospects bright for enduring success. This can be a future in which the people of The Netherlands can share and share equally. You need only heed and cooperate with the informed policies and practices of the Third Reich."

Apart from collaborationists and those men whom Seyffardt had recruited for the SS, most Dutch sniffed derisively at Seyss-Inquart's urgings. They saw him for what he was – an interloper in a position of power granted him by the dictator who had ordered the invasion of their country, destruction of Rhenen and Rotterdam and rapidly implemented restrictions on Jewish neighbors and friends.

Seyss-Inquart's entreaties having failed to win converts, he was desperate to avoid giving Hitler reason to doubt his competence. He authorized Anton Mussert's NSB to create a paramilitary organization. Named the Landwacht, it would act as an auxiliary police force. "Your mission," Mussert instructed Landwacht members, "is to defend the interests of the Reich."

In Rhenen Bert Looten voiced the sentiments of millions of Netherlanders when he said to Dora, Karin and Catherina, "Our beloved nation is disappearing under Hitler's heels."

While most Dutch were taking care to vent frustration and anger to family and close friends or not at all, Father Titus Brandsma refused to be silenced. Friends urged the priest to muzzle himself. He acknowledged – and thanked them for – their concerns, but continued speaking out against Nazism and its anti-Jewish bias. "Adolf Hitler's promises are as empty as the cargo holds of a freighter after unloading at the port. The difference is, the holds soon will be filled with new cargo, whereas Hitler's promises will remain forever barren of truth."

Father Brandsma was speaking from one of his favorite outdoor "pulpits" – the steps of Oude Kerk. "The weight of Hitler's lies eventually will come crashing down on him. History tells us that rule built on terror and lies often meets an early and inglorious end."

In Berlin Joseph Goebbels reported Father Brandsma's words to Hitler.

In short order, Goebbels was cabling top cop Hanns Albin Rauter in The Hague. "Brandsma's words are powerful, and he speaks them well. He must be silenced. Watch for an opportunity to remove him from his pulpits and keep him from them."

Still another political earthquake – one with coming, widespread ramifications – shook Romania on November 23. Ion Antonescu, after exchanging cables with Berlin, announced with his customary bombast that Romania had joined the Axis Powers. His hubris – characterizing militarily weak Romania as a partner with Germany – didn't go unnoticed far from Bucharest. On their farms near Apahida, the Johnescus and Domians questioned Antonescu's sanity. "The man must be crazy as well as stupid," Gheorghe said to Magdalena while scrubbing his hands before sitting down to supper. "Does he really think for a minute that Hitler will pay him any heed in making decisions that affect our country's future?"

"I think we are lucky in one way," Magdalena said thoughtfully.

"Oh? In what way?"

"We are living very far from not only Bucharest but also from Ploesti. I don't think Hitler will pay much attention to our little corner of Romania. I think our lives will go on mostly as they have been."

"I suppose you are right," Gheorghe replied respectfully. "Now you have me wondering – again – if that is still true for our daughter."

"I don't think so, dear. A mother knows her daughter, and Raluca's letters say so little that I feel certain she is not telling us everything."

"So she won't worry us?"

"Precisely."

"Now I will probably worry even more."

Magdalena laughed despite the seriousness of their dialogue. "You, my wonderful husband, will be worrying about your daughter until you draw your final breath."

"Would you have it any other way?"

"I wouldn't have *you* any other way."

Four days later, November 27, before Romanian influentials – former government officials, professors, artists – could mount any semblance of meaningful protest, Antonescu ordered arrests. Some of the 64 rounded up were Jews. All were men of principle and loyal to a constitutional government and an elected parliament that had worked in concert with deposed King Carol and his son, powerless King Michael.

Later that day the 64 were ordered from their cells and herded into the courtyard of Jilava Prison in Bucharest. Awaiting them were 50 members of the Iron Guard. They were armed with submachine guns. No final speech was made. A command was given to fire, and shots echoed through the courtyard. The 64 were slaughtered, with some executed after being wounded and pleading for mercy.

CHAPTER 44

On the Sunday afternoon before Christmas, Joshua was feeling pangs of loneliness. Warm memories of Meredith and preparations for holiday seasons past with his family were tormenting him. He was experiencing an unwelcome lassitude. This house, he reflected listlessly, has never seemed so big and so empty. Meredith. The children she was tutoring. They filled this house with sounds. Happy sounds. I still miss them. Maybe more now than ever – especially at this time of year. I wonder what Anneke is doing. I hope she and her grandparents are enjoying their time together. I have to get outside. I need to breathe fresh, cold air.

Early that evening Joshua pulled on a sweater, jacket, his brown stocking cap, orange scarf and fur-lined gloves he had purchased at Folleck's Fine Clothing. Stepping outside he looked up at a clear sky. The stars, he mused, I couldn't begin to count them. Each one a sun burning brightly. Or burning itself into cold, dark oblivion.

Joshua set out, his feet carrying him south on Prinsengracht. But mentally he was feeling directionless. After a couple minutes, he scolded himself. Snap out of this, Bliss. This stupor. Meredith wouldn't tolerate it. She would tell me in no uncertain words to quit feeling sorry for myself. To quit wallowing in self-pity. The words he imagined her saying scornfully caused a slight crease in his face – a small smile.

Joshua turned east on Raadhuisstraat. Minutes later, with a more purposeful gait, he was passing by the Grand Krasnapolsky. He looked at the entrance and smiled. He was remembering Meredith's family staying there while in Amsterdam for her memorial service and dedication of the waterfront plaque bearing her name. A few more paces and Joshua lengthened his stride as he turned left or north and headed toward Molensteeg. He paused at the entrance to the brothel and then pulled open the door.

Raluca was chatting casually with Alicia and a dozen other prostitutes. She saw Joshua and rose. Unsmiling, he beckoned tactfully with his right hand, and she came walking toward him.

"Upstairs?" she murmured so lowly her word barely registered.

His head shook slightly. "I would rather not." His lips pursed tautly before they parted for his next, whispered words. "I want to be with you but not here. Can you come to my home? It's the holiday season" – Joshua's words weren't coming easily – "and I would like my home to feel more like it."

Raluca looked into his eyes appraisingly. Do you really want me? she was thinking. Or do you want a substitute – a one-night substitute – for your wife? If it is that, I don't resent you. My job is to satisfy, not question motives. But I don't see you as part of my job, and I do wish you would want me for me. That might be too much for a prostitute to wish for. Stop it, Raluca, she commanded herself; just answer his question. "Yes, I think I could go with you," she whispered. Alicia and the other prostitutes were watching curiously. "Give me a minute while I go speak with Madame Clarbout."

Joshua nodded and watched Raluca turn away and go walking gracefully toward the door to Anna Clarbout's apartment. While waiting, his weight shifted from foot to foot.

Raluca tapped on Anna's door and moments later it opened. Another minute and Raluca emerged.

In the bed that Joshua had shared with Meredith he made love with Raluca Johnescu. They kissed, tentatively at first, then with mounting intensity and pleasure. Their hands began caressing continuously and gently, from foreheads to rounded bottoms.

I hope, Raluca was telling herself, that his thoughts are only of me. That is selfish, I know, but at least I am being honest with myself.

Joshua surprised Raluca by rolling her on top of him, her knees straddling his hips. That position was forbidden by Anna Clarbout who deemed it more intimate than paying customers deserved. But Joshua was in his own bed and not paying, and Raluca loved looking down into his open, smiling eyes.

Afterward, lying side by side and breathing heavily, Raluca spoke first. "Thank you for asking me to come here again. It will be the best Christmas present I receive. I will remember it always." The other thought she was thinking she held in check: *If I am not already falling in love with you, I think I could.*

She would have been pleased to know that, during their lovemaking, no vision of Meredith occupied Joshua's mind. He had cherished looking at Raluca and was feeling grateful she was lying with him and giving him an undiluted dose of badly needed affection. He thought seriously of asking her again to move in with him but refrained. *I don't want her believing I invited her here merely as a tool to get her to leave the brothel and her apartment and Alicia.* He did decide to voice a question: "Can you stay all night? Will you?"

The next morning they were sitting in his kitchen, sipping coffee. Steam from their cups was curling enticingly upward.

"Umm, this is so good," Raluca said, virtually purring. "It is hot and rich. I think I could drink two or three cups." Between sips she pressed her hands against the cup's hot sides.

"Then," Joshua chuckled, "that's exactly what you'll do. And," he added cheerily, "I will match you cup for cup."

Raluca laughed. "All this coffee and we haven't eaten yet. We might be matching each other pee for pee."

Joshua laughed, harder and longer than he had since Meredith's death. It was every bit as potent a catharsis as their lovemaking.

Eventually, Joshua fried eggs and browned bread and they ate ravenously. After finishing they sat back, sated. Then Joshua watched as Raluca's mien turned pensive. "What is it?" he asked.

"Well," she said, "it is the holiday season, and I always think of my family. It has been so long since I have seen them. I do miss them. Very much. I can't help wondering if I will ever see them again."

Joshua sighed. "Part of me wants to say, 'Of course you will.' But that would be stupid because I just don't know."

"Thank you," Raluca smiled. Then her head shook sadly. "Hitler seems to have an iron grip on almost all of Europe. From Holland to Romania he has control. I wish there was something I could do to help change things."

Joshua paused before replying. "There is something I've heard about."

"What?"

"Let me check. I don't want to say now. Not yet. Not until I'm sure. But we have that much in common – a desire to strike back at Hitler." She nodded. "If I learn something – anything – that I believe you would want to know, I will tell you. Trust me."

"Trust you?" Raluca replied, smiling thoughtfully. "That might be the easiest thing anyone has asked me to do."

The next morning Joshua began walking south, again headed for Corellistraat. This time, though, instead of a mere look-see and perhaps a chance encounter, he would attempt a discreet inquiry. If no one approached him, a stranger walking slowly and apparently curious, he would try making a connection inside one of the short street's small shops.

That tactic turned out to be unnecessary. He entered Corellitstraat and walked no more than 40 deliberate paces when he felt a tap behind his right shoulder. Joshua stopped, a surge of adrenalin-fueled anxiety heating his face. He turned and found himself looking into the ice blue eyes of a striking man his equal in height but older – maybe in his forties – cleanshaven and with a full head of light brown hair.

"Looking for something in particular?" the man asked not unpleasantly. "I saw you here before."

Joshua had rehearsed his answer that morning in the kitchen. "I seem to have lost my way – from America – and I am looking for a new way."

"America?"

Joshua had known he would be taking a risk in disclosing his national origin. But he had concluded that doing so would reduce any suspicion that he might be a Nazi informant. "I have been here for about three years. I was working for the Netherlands Royal Steamship Company."

The man's face remained stoic, eyes still narrowed. "Why are you looking for a new way?"

"My wife went down with the Simon Bolivar."

"Were you onboard?"

"Yes."

"Anything else?"

Joshua pondered that question for several moments. "Last May, in The Hague, I was there on company business. A wounded Dutch soldier gave me his carbine."

"You used it?"

"Several times."

The man's visage remained inscrutable. "Would you care to come with me?"

Joshua had been sensing strongly that the man's questions had been asked out of more than mere curiosity. "I think so."

"This way," the man said, turning back in the direction from which he had come. He led Joshua a few paces to a doorway on their left. As he pulled open the door, Joshua glanced up at the address: 6.

Inside, the man led Joshua about 25 feet through a narrow, high-ceilinged corridor. Then he stopped and pushed open a plain brown door that bore neither lettering nor a number.

After Joshua followed him inside, the man closed the door. He shed his brown leather jacket and black stocking cap and hung them on a wooden coat tree. Joshua did likewise with his jacket and cap.

The man walked to a small wooden desk, its top paperless, and sat. He gestured toward two bare wooden chairs opposite, and Joshua sat.

"Your name?" he asked. "I would prefer your real one."

"Joshua Bliss."

"Where do you live?"

"Prinsengracht. I also work in a bicycle shop on Barndestaag."

The man had not yet offered to shake hands, and his voice remained cool if not cold. "Mine is Kees de Heer."

Joshua decided not to ask if that was his real name. "Thank you for inviting me in."

The man remained silent for long moments before speaking carefully measured words. "You have suffered a great loss. You have my sympathy. Revenge is an understandable motive. But to be effective it must be controlled. We want our country to be free again, and we would like to live to see it that way ourselves. Some of us might become martyrs, but that is not our goal. That means any risks we take must be calculated. Carefully."

"A wise approach."

"Frankly, Mr. Bliss, at the moment I have no particular mission for you. But since we know how to locate you, I or one of our people will contact you if we believe you can help."

"I understand."

"I brought you here which is something I rarely do."

"You needn't worry."

"If I had thought otherwise, you wouldn't be sitting here."

De Heer turned away from his desk, bent down and opened a low cabinet. Straightening and turning to face Joshua he said, "You might need this sometime." He handed Joshua a .22 caliber pistol outfitted with a silencer.

"I've never seen one of these," said Joshua.

"There is nothing new about them." De Heer was right. An American inventor, Hiram Maxim, trademarked the Maxim Silencer in 1902. Years later Office of Strategic Services William "Wild Bill" Donovan demonstrated a silencer for President Franklin Roosevelt in the White House Oval Office. While Roosevelt was writing a letter, Donovan fired 10 silenced shots into a sandbag he had brought for the demonstration. Roosevelt didn't hear the shots and was astonished at seeing the smoking gun.

"Where did you get this one?" Joshua asked.

"It was not a problem," said de Heer. "Through our Dutch friends in England and they from your OSS."

"OSS?"

"Office of Strategic Services. Sort of a cousin to our resistance."

The day after Christmas, about midmorning, Joshua began walking toward Molensteeg. This time he did not enter the brothel but continued past it to the entrance to the building where Raluca and Alicia shared their apartment. He stepped inside and nimbly climbed the stairs to the third floor. He tapped the apartment door lightly. No answer. His knuckles were poised to tap again when the door opened.

"Mr. Bliss!" Alicia's surprise was evident.

"Hello, Alicia. Will you kindly do me a holiday season favor?"

Were this the brothel or the street and not their apartment, Alicia's response to a request for a favor would have had her going on guard immediately. But everything Raluca had told her about Joshua precluded even the first inkling of suspicion. "What is it?"

"Mr. Bliss. Don't call me that."

Alicia blushed. "Of course. I know you like Josh. Raluca told me. Please, come in."

"Thank you."

"You are here to see Raluca."

"Yes."

"Sit. Please. She just finished in the bathroom down the hall. She is dressing in our bedroom. I will let her know you are here."

The pair began walking south. Both were bundled against a raw, penetrating cold.

"I hope you managed to enjoy Christmas," Joshua said.

"I did. We didn't have to work, and we both wrote letters to our families."

"Good."

"Your Christmas?"

"Lots of memories. I tried to remember only the good ones. Like our night – and breakfast – together a few days ago."

Raluca reddened and smiled. "But memories, that is not why you came to see me."

"No. I promised to let you know if I found anything of interest." She looked questioningly at him but said nothing. "Do you know Corellistraat?"

"No."

"I'm not surprised. It's very short. Not much more than an alley. I want to show you where it is. It's not far south of the Amstel Canal. After I show you, I will tell you what I learned."

"And I am not to tell anyone." Joshua nodded his affirmation. "Not even Alicia?"

"Let me think about that."

"You can trust her. I trust her."

"It's not trust. If I become involved, if you become involved, we might become privy to sensitive information. Do you remember when I first mentioned a possible way of getting back at the Nazis? I said there could be risk. The more a person knows the greater the risk."

"And," Raluca added, "the less a person knows the smaller the risk."

"So like I said, let me think about it. Right now, we have no involvement – except knowing the location of Corellistraat."

"Any particular street number?"

Joshua hesitated. His lips pursed, then his teeth bared in a tight-faced grimace. "Number six."

CHAPTER 45

"This was a good idea," said Joshua.

Anneke shrugged off the compliment. "It is the first week of January and still early enough to celebrate the start of a new year," she said. "I think we agree that we hope this year will be happier than last year."

"I couldn't agree more."

Anneke and Joshua were gliding on steel blades atop the frozen surface of the Prinsengracht. She had come to the bicycle shop the previous day to propose the outing.

The next day Anneke met Joshua at the shop when he was finishing work. She was carrying her skates, long laces tied together, over her right shoulder. On the way to Joshua's home to get his skates, they stopped at a café for gouda sandwiches and coffee. Afterward they strolled to his home. He dashed inside to get his skates. Outside, they walked to a canalside bench where they removed shoes and pulled on skates. Darkness had fallen and the Nazi blackout was in effect. But the moon and stars were providing sufficient illumination.

"We are not alone," Anneke said. A pair of skaters was approaching from the south.

"No wind, no sleet, it's a perfect night for skating."

It was that. Anneke and Joshua went gliding south, then east and northeast for more than two miles until the looping Prinsengracht ended at the Plantage Muidergracht. Mostly they skated in silence, each comfortably wrapped in private thoughts. They were oblivious to the sound of their skates cutting narrow grooves in the hardened surface. Along the way they encountered numerous skaters. Some were gliding alone, others in pairs or small groups. Those in groups were noisy, chattering and laughing.

At the Plantage Muidergracht, Joshua said, "Do you want to rest before we head back?"

Anneke drew in a breath and blew it out. She smiled at the sight of her exhalation rising and disappearing into the night air. "I don't think so."

"Not tired?"

"Not at all. The exercise has been a tonic."

Joshua nodded. "All right, let's go."

A few strides to begin propelling them and again they were gliding smoothly. When about a half mile from the bench in front of Joshua's home, Anneke said, "Do you want to race?"

Joshua grinned, white teeth contrasting with the darkness. "I suppose you want a head start."

"I have been skating since I could walk," Anneke replied spunkily. "Perhaps I should give you a head start."

"Ooh," Joshua teased, "that sounds very much like a boast."

Anneke's left forefinger felt to be sure her beige eye patch was properly positioned. "You could call it that. I prefer to consider it a challenge."

"Or a dare."

"If you like," she said with faux smugness.

"Still," Joshua rejoined with mock derision, "the gentleman that I am demands that you push off first. I will give you to a count of five. Finish line is my house."

"Very well, gentleman Joshua Bliss."

And with that, Anneke dug the toe of her right skate blade into the ice and lunged forward.

Joshua counted aloud. "One. Two. Three. Four. Five." Then he pushed off.

His pursuit was strong, but he quickly realized the mettle of Anneke's boast. She's backing it up, Joshua mused. This is going to be close.

As the distance to his house closed to within approximately 60 feet, Joshua had just about drawn even with the flying Anneke. Then, to his surprise, she found a reserve of strength and accelerated. Joshua tried but couldn't match her burst of speed.

In front of his house they skidded to a sharp stop that sent ice chips flying. Anneke's laughter came as fast and as strong as her final surge on the skates. Joshua bent forward, hands on knees and gasping. When he straightened, he caught the contagion that was Anneke's mirth. Within seconds he was laughing – as hard as when he and Raluca had convulsed themselves over her joke that matching each other's cups of coffee on empty stomachs would have them matching pees.

After laughing to the point of tears, they made their way canalside, plopped down on the bench and removed their skates. Then they pulled on their shoes, cold at first touch to their warmed socks and feet.

"I haven't had so much fun…I don't think I can remember," Anneke said. "This was grand."

"We'll have to do it again."

They stood, no more than a foot separating them. Anneke found herself hoping for intimacy – a long, strong hug, a tender kiss, a slow parting hinting at the promise of more closeness. Joshua leaned forward, his left cheek brushing her left just below the eye patch. Then he stepped back. Anneke felt the pang of disappointment.

"Let me walk you home," Joshua said politely.

"Thank you, but there is no need. My grandparents' house on Gravenstraat is but a five-minute walk – if that long."

"Are you sure?"

"Yes."

"Good night, Anneke."

"Good night."

Joshua watched as Anneke rounded the corner from Prinsengracht east onto Leliestraat. Just ahead stood imposing Nieuwe Kerk and just to its rear, Gravenstraat. In the dim glow from the moon and stars, Anneke saw three German soldiers, clustered and smoking cigarettes. She pulled her stocking cap lower until its front edge met the eye patch. The soldiers glanced at her curiously but said nothing, and a few paces beyond she was entering her grandparents' home.

"A one-eyed woman," said a soldier. "I wonder how she lost the other."

"If we see her again," said another soldier, "you can ask her."

"Maybe I will."

While many Netherlanders were enjoying ice skating in January 1941, the nation's Jews were denied a popular form of entertainment.

Arthur Seyss-Inquart, taking his cue from Hitler, announced another restriction meant to further identify, segregate and denigrate Jews. He announced through newspapers and radio that henceforth Jews were forbidden from entering movie theaters.

In London, Queen Wilhelmina was growing increasingly exasperated.

I need more than a short stroll through my garden, she concluded. A long walk to sort my thoughts and reach a decision. That is what I need. And alone. I need to walk alone. I shall have to dress in the plainest, most inconspicuous clothes I own. She laughed aloud. Most of my wardrobe won't pass for London dreary. Let me see what I can find.

After donning a stylish navy blue dress and black heels, Queen Wilhelmina looked out the window of the room she had made her office. A steady, windless rain was falling. Even better, she thought. Who in London will pay the slightest attention to a woman beneath an umbrella? Now, to get outside before anyone notices I have gone and insists that I be accompanied. I do need time alone. She stopped at her desk, bent forward and cheerily scribbled a note: *Juliana, Out for a walk in the rain. Mother.* Moments later the queen, attired smartly in a black trench coat, black gloves and modest black box-style hat was opening her umbrella and taking her first steps toward escape and solitude. Ironic, it occurred to her, that at this moment in a foreign country I once detested for its actions in South Africa I feel freer than I did at home. The English winter gloom notwithstanding, her spirits lifted.

From Grosvenor Place behind the grounds of Buckingham Palace, she began walking north. A few minutes later she was rounding the corner to her right onto Constitution Hill. Ahead on her right she could see the northwest side of the palace. This, she mused contentedly, is almost like walking in a winter rain in my homeland, except that here it is not quite as cold. In front of the palace the queen turned left and began trodding the long, straight street that was The Mall. No one has taken notice of me yet. And unless Juliana has come looking for me I am likely not yet missed at the house. Besides, if anyone sees the note, I would hope the reaction is something short of panic. All right, now let's forget everything around me. Just let the rain pattering on my umbrella close out any distractions. Let me concentrate on the issue that most vexes me. First, our military situation. Militarily, we pose no threat to anyone and might as well not exist. Oh, some of our soldiers, sailors and airmen escaped here to England, but not enough of them to make a major difference and then not for a long time and not without leadership and major assistance from the Allies. And right now there are precious few of them. Politically it is much the same. Our government is in exile and largely invisible on the world stage. Hitler wanted to abduct me, but he probably regards my exile as more politically expedient. I doubt if he has thought a whit about me since I left. And if he has, he has not let it cost him sleep or appetite. What then? Why should I even be consuming minutes much less hours and days worrying myself half to death over my country's future? Its fate? With each soggy step I take in this London excuse for air, the answers seem more and more clear. What I say – what I do – here in London can affect – does affect – the morale of my people. To the degree my words and actions stiffen our national spine, the more likely it becomes that brave Dutch men and women will form a resistance force. Perhaps several such groups. I hear one has been formed in Amsterdam. Maybe in each major city as well as in the countryside. They should know they are resisting for a cause that has hope, that believes ultimately it can and will prevail.

Queen Wilhelmina's gait now lengthened with more spring in each step. She was beginning to feel a spiritual swagger. In the street near the curb, a bicyclist went pedaling by the queen. A woman rider, Wilhelmina smiled. Bless her. She is not letting rain stop her. It's been decades since I last rode a bike. I wonder how Juliana would react if I told her I wanted a bike. Apoplexy. I can see it now.

At Trafalgar Square, she looked up at the statue of Admiral Horatio Nelson atop his 185-foot column, surveying the horizons. "Never mind the pigeon droppings on your coat," the queen murmured. "How far and how clearly do you see from your lofty perch? That is what matters, don't you agree?" She was unable to suppress a smile. "What do you see for my beautiful Netherlands? Even from down here, I will tell you what I see, Admiral." Mindful that she was thinking aloud, Wilhelmina peeked out from beneath her umbrella in all directions. Passersby were doing precisely that – passing her by. If anyone heard me, she laughed inwardly, they probably are regarding me as nothing more than a slightly daft matron.

She turned right or south onto Whitehall. Soon she was passing by the Horse Guards barracks and Number 10 Downing Street, both on her right. She remembered reading that Number 10 Downing Street had been home to British prime ministers since 1732. As the queen went striding by Churchill's official residence, she tipped her umbrella in a respectful salute. You might walk with a slight slouch. Perhaps it is your balls pulling you forward. I think you must be well endowed physically, intellectually and emotionally. If Juliana ever bears a son, I might suggest that she name him Winston.

Now Wilhelmina was turning right again, this time onto Birdcage Walk. As she was doing so, a red double-deck bus passed closely by the curb, spraying her ankles and shoes with puddle water. Sure, I am a Londoner now, the queen reflected whimsically. Ahead she could see at the avenue's end the white façade of Buckingham Palace. I think I see clearly now the action I must take. It is an action that will signal to any and all Dutch men and women that they have my unwavering belief in their goodness and support for any resistance they might organize against Hitler's legion of evil.

Now, walking west, the cool air rushing past the queen's face seemed to be serving as a cleansing agent. Purifying, Wilhelmina thought.

"Mother!" Juliana almost shrieked as Wilhelmina stepped inside their house and closed her umbrella. "Do you know how much you frightened me?"

"I believe so," the queen replied calmly, shedding her gloves, trench coat and hat.

"Do you know how close I was to sending out a search party?"

"Not very? My note stopped you, didn't it?"

"Well, yes," Juliana admitted, her ire deflating.

"Hmmm…My feet are damp. I am going to change my shoes. While I am at it, dear, would you please tell Prime Minister de Geer to come to my office?"

"With staff or alone?"

"Alone would be better."

"Now?"

"Just long enough to change shoes and run a brush through my hair. I think this London pea soup would tighten anyone's curls."

In her desk chair, Queen Wilhelmina straightened her back and laid both hands on her desk. She smoothed the sleeves of her dress. She looked, she believed, suitably regal for the task at hand. She slightly parted her lips and extended her tongue to moisten them.

A knock at the door caused her to look straight ahead. "Come in, please."

Prime Minister Dirk Jan de Geer pushed open the door. "Your majesty wishes to see me?"

"I do. Please sit down." Wilhelmina did not stand to greet him.

"You gave us a fright, leaving the house unescorted."

"I needed to clear my mind."

"Did you?"

"Let me begin answering your question with a question." De Geer shrugged his expected acceptance. "Looking at the current situation, do you still favor the French mode? Of how we should relate to Hitler and his Reich?"

De Geer paused momentarily before replying. "Yes, I do. Like you I have always wanted what is best for our country. Yes, I continue to believe that the French have chosen a wise path. It is a path that bruises national ego but minimizes damage and preserves life. The cost if not preferable is bearable. Hitler is unstoppable. His Reich most probably will not endure for a thousand years as he is fond of declaring. But it does seem destined to outlast us and more likely the next generation. That is the grim reality, and we must live with it."

Queen Wilhelmina nodded. De Geer misinterpreted her signal that she had understood his position for acceptance. "This is difficult but necessary."

"Of course it is. But after all, we always have enjoyed good relations with Germany."

"You mean until they invaded our country and flattened Rhenen and Rotterdam."

"Tragedies, to be sure. But we must look to the future."

"On that point we agree entirely. And that is why I must dismiss you as prime minister."

"You…" De Geer almost blurted, You what? But that would have been superfluous and he knew it immediately.

"You are relieved. As of this very moment." De Geer was struggling to find and voice words that did not seem either self-pitying or petty. None came. "You may if you like," Queen Wilhelmina continued coolly, "issue a press release announcing you are stepping down for any reason or reasons you choose to cite. I will not contradict you publicly in any way."

De Geer blew out a breath through barely parted lips. He mumbled, "Thank you."

"You may quote me as expressing my sincerest gratitude for your long and loyal service."

"When will you announce my successor?"

"Tomorrow. I expect you will want to stay in London. Find lodgings outside this house, and we will pay rent until you find something else."

"May I ask, please, do you have someone in mind?"

Queen Wilhelmina already had decided to whom she would extend the offer to join her cabinet-in-exile. His physical appearance would fail to inspire, but she was confident that his intellect would impress. She also believed him to be made from sterner stuff than de Geer. Her choice was Pieter Gerbrandy. For a man of hardy Dutch stock, Gerbrandy looked comically small. He stood only four feet eight inches. His mustache was long and drooping, causing him to appear even shorter. Over time, though, he would prove the wisdom of his queen's appointment. Later, for example, Gerbrandy would work successfully with Churchill and Roosevelt to smooth the path for America's entry into the war by ceding control of Dutch Aruba and Curacao with their oil riches to the Allies.

By this time Queen Wilhelmina was earning Churchill's respect, no mean feat. He said of her, "She is the only real man among the governments in exile."

Joshua was repairing a bicycle chain in the shop's rear. Karel Veeder stepped into room and said, "Someone is here to see you. A woman."

"All right," Joshua replied, thinking that Anneke was paying a visit. He stood, rotated his back to loosen kinks and crossed into the display room. His eyes widened in pleasant surprise. He began walking toward the woman. "Raluca. Nice to see you."

"Hello, Joshua."

"What brings you here? Have you and Alicia decided to buy a second bike?"

"No. Could you step outside with me?"

"Sure." Joshua's curiosity spiked. An unexpected visit from his prostitute lover and a request for privacy.

In front of the shop, Raluca looked in all directions. No pedestrians were approaching. "Alicia has a client. He is a Gestapo lieutenant," Raluca whispered. "His name is Julius Dettman. Last night he told Alicia something I think you might want to know. Also your contact on Corellistraat, perhaps." Raluca paused. "Should I tell you more?"

"Go ahead."

"You know that Jews live in most sections of Amsterdam." Joshua nodded. "But many live together in a neighborhood south of Oude Kerk."

"I know the neighborhood," Joshua said. "I've heard it referred to as the Jewish quarter." The area lay a little more than half a mile south of Oude Kerk and the red light district. Bordering it on four sides were canals. Bridges provided access and egress.

"Lieutenant Dettman told Alicia that the Gestapo and soldiers plan to surround the neighborhood and trap the Jews inside."

"And then what?"

"I am not certain. Alicia said Dettman said something about a roundup of Jewish men. She didn't ask for more information. She didn't want to seem too curious. She – we – know that we could be mistaken for Jews. Our coloring…"

Joshua nodded. "Do you know when this is supposed to happen?"

Raluca shook her head and shrugged. "Soon, Alicia thinks." A long pause while Joshua absorbed the information. "I hope I did the right thing – by coming here."

"You did precisely the right thing."

"Do you think Alicia did the right thing by telling me?"

Joshua didn't hesitate. "Yes. It's time you tell her what we hope to accomplish. Maybe Dettman will tell her more. Pillow talk might keep his tongue loose."

"I think so," Raluca smiled knowingly. "And Alicia will tell only me what she hears. We can trust her."

"I agree. I know how close you two are. She would do nothing to endanger you."

He and Raluca extended their right hands and shook politely. Then Raluca turned away and began the short walk north along a canal to Molensteeg.

Inside the shop, Karel watched Joshua re-enter, consumed with thoughts obviously unrelated to bicycles. Joshua stood motionless, eyes closed.

"Don't worry," Karel said, "I don't ask about your private matters."

"Thank you."

"But," Karel added teasingly, "it must be very nice to have two pretty young women interested in you."

For the remainder of the afternoon, Joshua forced himself to concentrate on repairing broken bikes. It wasn't easy. Images – of Meredith, the Follecks, Laura Reidel, Paul, Alicia, Raluca – kept trying to disrupt his concentration.

When quitting time arrived, Joshua pulled on his blue jacket, orange scarf, brown stocking cap and gloves. "Good night, Mr. Veeder."

"Good night, Joshua. Will I see you in the morning?"

Joshua stopped and turned toward Karel. "Why do you ask?"

"I could see your mind was elsewhere this afternoon." Karel stopped short of asking questions that had been all but boring holes in his brain.

"I will be here. On time."

Exiting the shop, Joshua turned right and walked east to the end of short Barndestaag. He turned right again, this time to a street paralleling still another canal – the Kloveniers Burquiel. He walked south to the Amstel and crossed it. From there it was but a short walk to Corellistraat.

At No. 6, Joshua tapped lightly and then pulled open the unlocked door. He removed his stocking cap and rubbed his bald head. He proceeded down the hallway and knocked on the door to the room where he had talked with Kees de Heer. No reply. Joshua turned the doorknob and pushed. Locked. Should I wait? he asked himself. Probably not wise to be seen loitering here. He turned to depart when he heard a door open farther down the corridor. Joshua turned back. De Heer was standing there. He silently beckoned Joshua. At the open door de Heer motioned Joshua to enter.

"The locked door," de Heer said, "it is an extra measure of security. Gives us time to see who is outside." De Heer opened an inner door and the two were back in the room de Heer used as his office. He still had not offered his hand to Joshua. "Sit down," he instructed. "Am I right that this is more than a courtesy call?"

Joshua nodded. "I've heard something I thought you would want to know. If I was wrong, just tell me."

"I will."

Joshua proceeded to share the information Raluca had provided. He revealed the original source and the go-between, Alicia. De Heer listened closely.

After Joshua had finished speaking, de Heer closed his eyes, pressed his lips tightly and shook his head. "I can envision the day when we could disrupt the Nazi action. But not yet. Our resistance cell is only now being organized. We don't have the manpower to carry out a large-scale operation. You did make the right choice to come here. Any time you think you have sensitive – and relevant – information, please do bring it here. The women – Alicia and Raluca..."

"I trust them implicitly. To gather good information and be discreet when passing it to me."

"They are whores."

"They are Romanian and they detest Hitler."

On exiting Corellistraat, Joshua took a few steps homeward toward Prinsengracht. Then he decided to take a sightseeing detour.

During the 10 minutes needed to reach the Jewish quarter, darkness had descended. Pedestrian traffic was thinning as most people had returned to their homes for supper. With the area illuminated only by moon and stars, Joshua could see that the neighborhood's architecture differed not at all from others throughout the city. Certainly the Dutch penchant for municipal cleanliness extended to the Jewish quarter; trash on the streets was not to be seen. Some shop windows advertised kosher foods, but otherwise the array of commercial establishments would have appeared normal in any other section of the city. He saw a couple streetwalkers patiently waiting for clients and nodded politely to each as he passed.

I don't know what kind of roundup the Germans have in mind, Joshua mused, but I'm going to let the Follecks and Sevels know what I've heard. If they have friends, maybe they can alert them. Or should I? Perhaps this is a case of not knowing being the better part of knowledge and valor. I'd hate for them to get caught up in something bad because of what I told them. I'm beginning to see more clearly the danger of knowing too much. I have a feeling I'm going to be keeping more secrets here in Amsterdam than I ever kept before. It's a strange and uncomfortable concept – knowledge as a threat. I'm not even sure I should tell Raluca about this bit of reconnaissance. Now that I'm thinking about it, maybe we should avoid seeing each other in public. I wouldn't want the wrong pair of eyes seeing us together. Okay, time to head for home and some chow.

CHAPTER 46

Arthur Seyss-Inquart wasn't blind or tone-deaf to the predictable consequences of what he soon would be ordering. His credibility among the Dutch already was shredded. His next order and the resulting action would dissolve the remaining scraps. His stark reality, though: He had little choice but to bow to directions from Berlin.

Seyss-Inquart sighed, picked up his desk phone and called Anton Mussert to his Binnenhof office in The Hague. It took Mussert only a few minutes to reach Seyss-Inquart's nearby office.

With an air of resignation, Seyss-Inquart motioned to a guest chair in front of his desk and Mussert sat. His posture was ramrod straight, gray paramilitary uniform cleaned and crisply pressed and contrasting with Seyss-Inquart's black civilian suit and matching necktie.

"How may I be of service?" Mussert asked.

"I have instructions from Berlin," Seyss-Inquart replied unenthusiastically.

Mussert listened closely while Seyss-Inquart described the mission. When Seyss-Inquart finished, Mussert replied, "I am confident we will achieve the desired result."

"As you can see, though," the civilian governor emphasized, "the situation has its ambiguities. We can't predict the initial reaction, so you must be prepared to deal with a range of contingencies."

"We will be. In that regard, I should phone Herr Rauter."

"That would be wise," said Seyss-Inquart.

"I will coordinate actions with him."

The next afternoon in Amsterdam, Anton Mussert met Hanns Albin Rauter in the latter's office. With Rauter were two Gestapo – Lieutenant Julius Dettman and Sergeant Walter Baemer.

"Governor Seyss-Inquart has cautioned us to be prepared for contingencies," Mussert was saying. "But we will have the element of surprise, and frankly I doubt if we will meet any semblance of resistance or backlash. It doesn't seem to be in their nature."

"Still," said Rauter, "we should map out the plan carefully and be certain our men have been fully briefed."

Two days later, in early February, Isala Van Dyck was nearing one of the canal bridges that would have her exiting the Jewish quarter. Isala had no particular fondness for Jews, but neither did she harbor any deep-seated resentment. Business was paramount, and she had several good clients in the Jewish quarter. They treated her temporary agency secretaries and typists well, and they paid her invoices promptly. Occasionally a client would question the accuracy of her billings, but that was to be expected from any client, Jewish or Gentile.

As was Isala's custom she was dressed smartly. Her blond hair, as always, nicely framed and highlighted her striking facial contours. On this sunny morning, the hour approaching noon, her mood was upbeat.

As she stepped onto the bridge, she saw approaching a dozen uniformed policemen. Leading was a Gestapo sergeant. Strange, thought Isala, I am not aware of any commotion here in the Jewish quarter. She crossed the bridge and then stepped aside while the police went striding by. Isala had other business to attend to, but curiosity won out; she decided to wait to see what would be transpiring.

Sergeant Baemer's men moved deeper into the neighborhood. They began entering shops and pulling stunned men, mostly middle-aged and older into the streets. When the total reached 20, the abducted were herded together.

Other Jews – pedestrians, residents in their homes and shop owners – were watching with a welter of reactions – curiosity, fear, rage.

Sergeant Baemer spoke briefly and tersely to his captives. "You are under arrest. You will come with us for processing."

"What are the charges?" one of the men asked.

"You are undermining the integrity of the Third Reich," Baemer replied as he had rehearsed.

"Because we are Jewish," the man said, less a question than an accusation.

"Because you threaten to stain Adolf Hitler's New World Order."

"Hitler," the man scoffed. "His only order is to run roughshod over helpless peoples."

Others among the captives were beginning to wish that their outspoken neighbor would cease voicing his derision. They were worrying that it might provoke Baemer to unleash violence.

"Herr Hitler," Baemer retorted, "has a vision that has escaped you

Jews. He sees a Europe of Aryans who will bring prosperity to all, not just to secretive, cheating scoundrels."

"Hah," snorted the man, "I see that your soft brain has soaked up the rantings of the half-mad fuhrer."

"Enough!" barked Baemer. "Escort this collection of scum to the processing center."

Baemer's men began herding the captives. At the bridge Isala watched them approaching. Thank goodness, she was thinking with relief, I don't see any of my clients.

After crossing the bridge, Baemer led the group to the Holland Schouwburg, a Dutch theater that had been built in 1892. For now it was seen as a convenient – situated as it was near the Jewish quarter – and adequately large building for processing arrested Jews. In 1942 it would become Amsterdam's central deportation center for Jews being sent east to death camps in Germany and occupied Poland.

Processing early that afternoon consumed little time. The Gestapo, who later would become renowned for its meticulous record keeping, compiled the names and ages of this first group of rounded-up Amsterdam Jews.

Sergeant Baemer ordered the 20 men into the rear of two canvas-covered trucks. Lieutenant Dettman watched silently.

"You are treating us like cattle," said the man who had been showing spunk.

"And you are no better than that," Baemer spat.

The record showed their destination – Mauthausen Concentration Camp in Austria.

Word of the arrests and deportation spread throughout Amsterdam with the speed of an out-of-control plague. Some Amsterdammers reacted passively. Many, including Gentiles, were outraged. Jews had been integral to Amsterdam's culture for centuries, and in recent years Holland had taken in thousands of Jews fleeing Hitler's anti-Semitic fury. Now, Hitler had brought his manic hatred to a nation known for – and proud of – its tradition of tolerance.

Joshua Bliss was livid. Hitler, you fucking Nazi bastard. You're a liar, a bully, a murderer. You killed my wife and God knows how many others you are killing right now. Joshua was pacing his living room and was finding no relief from his rage within its confines. He pulled on his jacket, scarf and gloves and stepped outside. He crossed the street to the canal's edge and breathed in deeply. He began walking north and east. The winter cold against his bald head reminded Joshua that he had forgotten his brown stocking cap. He thought only briefly about returning to retrieve it. Maybe the cold is what I need. Should I visit the Follecks? Go to Corellistraat? See Raluca? Anneke? He found himself nearing Herengracht and the apartment of Laura Reidel. I wonder if she's home. It's been a long time since I've seen her and I promised to stay in touch. Why not?

Joshua soon found No. 135 and ascended to Laura's apartment. She answered his knock on her door. "Joshua!"

"Hello, Laura."

"Please, come in. This is a surprise. A most wonderful one."

"I'm sorry if I've come at a bad time."

"Not at all. I was just reading. Please, let me take your things."

Joshua shed his jacket, scarf and gloves. "I had a lot on my mind and realized I was near your home and decided to see if you were around."

"I am so glad you did. Please, sit."

Joshua eased himself onto one of the upholstered chairs. "You look wonderful, Laura."

"Hah. With no job to go to, I have little better to do than brush my hair and put on makeup."

Joshua chuckled. "You are doing it as skillfully as ever."

"Thank you, Joshua. I think I can guess what is on your mind. Everyone is talking about it. It is a tragedy. And unless I miss my guess, it is a tragedy that will be compounded many times. Twenty Jews. Hitler won't be satisfied with that."

"I'm thinking the same thing."

"Joshua?"

"Yes?"

"You wouldn't be thinking of doing something rash, would you? No one I know has more cause to take revenge on the Nazis."

"I wouldn't call it rash. But, yes, I am tempted to do something. Just standing by idly while the Nazis ruin more lives doesn't make for a tasty cup of tea."

"No. Knowing you, I am certain it doesn't." A brief pause. "Joshua, speaking of tea, could I tempt you with a cup? Maybe it would help you sort things out. If you would like to use me as a sounding board," she smiled warmly, "I am available."

"A cup of your tea sounds good," Joshua said.

"Join me in the kitchen while I make it."

Joshua rose. "Okay."

"Ah," said Laura without looking back, "there is that fine American word again. I just might have to try using it."

"Okay."

Laura laughed. As she filled a teapot with water, she said, "I am looking for a job."

"Haven't found one to your liking?"

"Not yet. But I must tell you something rather amazing. A few days ago I was walking and heard someone call my name. It was Isala Van Dyck. She asked if I was interested in working for her agency. I think she was actually trying to be nice."

"Or merely trying to add to her cadre of skilled secretaries and typists."

"That too, no doubt."

"What did you tell her?"

"Not what you would expect." Joshua laughed. "Yes, I always found her insufferable. But I didn't tell her that her offer was insulting and of no remote interest. I simply said I wanted to keep exploring other possibilities."

"So, are you changing your mind about her?"

"Oh, not at all. I wouldn't dream of working for that bigot." The teapot began whistling. "Ah, ready to pour. Joshua?"

"Yes."

"This city, my beloved hometown, is changing. Not for the better, I am afraid. There are too many Gestapo. Too many Nazis and Nazi sympathizers. Too many Isala Van Dycks. You cannot evict or eradicate them. Knowing you, I won't be surprised if you do become involved in some sort of resistance. If you do, I hope you can refrain from taking on too much risk."

Joshua sighed. "I'm not sure what I might be doing. But to be honest, if I do get involved, I don't know if risk can be avoided. And honestly, I don't know if risk would be a deterrent. Oh, I don't want to throw my life away. Believe me. But sacrifice might be necessary."

Joshua and Laura repaired to her living room with teacups in hand. They began sipping in silence. Then Joshua spoke. "I'm glad I came here. It's just the kind of therapy I needed."

"Good. Now, I hope you will repeat that promise."

"That being?"

"You will stay in touch."

"You have my solemn word."

Two days later Rauter and Mussert again were conferring, this time in Gestapo offices in Amsterdam.

"What is the mood in the Jewish quarter?" Mussert asked.

"I have men patrolling the streets, and they haven't reported any unrest," Rauter replied. "Nothing visible or vocal, at any rate."

"Have you informants there?"

"None as yet," said Rauter. "But elsewhere we have had a few individuals offer their services."

"For a fee?"

"Some, yes. Others seeking opportunity to curry favor."

"Have you enlisted any of them?"

"Not yet," said Holland's senior cop.

"The twenty we took was a warning sign," said Mussert. "But I think we should move quickly to cow the Jews and any of their sympathizers."

"More arrests? More deportations?"

"That's not what I have in mind," Mussert said grimly. He then went on explaining his next action meant to assure intimidation. "What do you think?"

"It seems rather extreme," Rauter said, "but you have my endorsement."

During the next two days, Mussert selected from the ranks of his NSB 50 men. He interviewed each one. He wanted men who either suffered no qualms over the new mission or persuaded him that they could quell any uncertainty.

The following afternoon the 50 descended on the Jewish quarter. Leading them was Sergeant Baemer. The NSB men were armed with an array of wooden clubs. After crossing the bridge into the quarter, they began fanning out. During the next half hour they assaulted residents indiscriminately. Men, women, teenage children felt the crushing blows of the clubs. Shrieks of pain and screams of terror were piercing the winter air. People were running to their homes and shops, locking doors behind them, lowering blinds and closing shutters. In the Jewish quarter, the nightly blackout was beginning hours earlier than usual. The salty smell of leaking blood was scenting the streets. Some broken bodies lay unconscious. Others were moaning. Still others were struggling to their feet and shuffling painfully toward the nearest haven.

Whistles began blowing, signaling the cessation of the attack. Anton Mussert had positioned himself at the bridge. Sergeant Baemer and the first contingent of Mussert's thugs returned from their exercise in wanton savagery.

"Anyone killed?" Mussert asked.

"I don't think so," Baemer said. The cold notwithstanding, Baemer used his right sleeve to wipe perspiration from his forehead. "The men did a good job of following instructions. Plenty of injuries. Doctors – Jewish and Aryan – will be kept busy all day and night."

February 11 brought an escalation of the violence. This time Mussert, again with Rauter's consent, assembled a force of some 200 NSB members. They pledged their willingness – for some it was eagerness – to inflict pain on the city's Jews.

This time, though, the fighting wouldn't be one-sided. Unbeknown to Rauter, Mussert and Seyss-Inquart, Jewish leaders had been emerging. They were organizing self-defense groups in neighborhoods where Jews lived throughout Amsterdam. As Mussert's thugs entered streets with Jewish residents, they soon found themselves facing determined opposition. Some scuffles escalated into pitched battles. Wooden clubs swung by Jewish men and women were inflicting as many – in some places more – injuries as they were incurring. This time the screams weren't emanating only from the throats of Jews. In Merewede Square Samuel Folleck and Guillermo Sevel were fighting back-to-back. They were swinging clubs with a ferocity that was surprising themselves as much as their attackers. Blood was coursing from a gash above Guillermo's left eye. Half-blinded he went on fighting fearsomely.

Witnesses were aplenty. From their apartment window on Molensteeg, Raluca and Alicia were watching two Jews batter an NSB man. They backed him onto a canal bridge and kept pressing forward until the NSB man turned and fled. At the far end of the bridge a man was waiting patiently for the NSB escapee. The man, garbed in black, stood arms akimbo. When the NSB man shifted to his left to sidestep the man, the latter blocked his path. "You should be utterly ashamed," Father Titus Brandsma said sternly. "You would do well to make haste to Oude Kerk and beg for the Lord's forgiveness."

The man stood speechless, gaping at the Carmelite priest. Father Brandsma stepped aside and the NSB man, blushing deep crimson, went scurrying on.

"Wait here," Raluca said and went dashing from the apartment. Acting on impulse, she ran down the stairs, jumping from the third step to the bottom. From the rear of the hallway she wrestled their bicycle to the front and out the door. Within moments she was pedaling across the canal bridge, a cold breeze whipping against her face and billowing her dark hair. No snowball this time, she smiled inwardly. "Father!" she called out.

The priest stopped and turned. Raluca began braking in time to avoid a tire-screeching stop. She dismounted and lowered the kickstand.

"You must have been in quite a rush," Father Brandsma said. "No coat."

Raluca's heart still was pumping too hard for the cold to penetrate. "Father, I watched what you did from my window. You were brave, and I wanted to thank you for being brave."

"Perhaps if I had given more thought to the situation, I would have been less brave. After all," he smiled wryly, "that fellow had the club."

"I don't think so."

"Well, thank you. But should you be outside now?"

"What do you mean?"

"You can see what those Nazi-sponsored hooligans are doing to Jews."

"Oh, it is my coloring. I am not a Jew."

"You are not Dutch."

"Romanian."

"Orthodox Catholic?"

"Yes. That is how I was raised."

"I understand." Father Brandsma forced the fore and middle fingers of his right hand beneath his white Roman collar. Seconds later they were holding a small, silver crucifix on a silver chain. He used both hands to loop the chain over his head. "Wear this outside your dress – where the Gestapo can see it."

Raluca reddened. "Father, I can't accept this. If you only knew-"

Father Brandsma raised his left hand, palm outward and cut her off. "What I know doesn't matter. Lower your head, my dear." Raluca complied. He slipped the chain over her head and adjusted it so that the cross was centered against Raluca's upper chest. "My mother gave me this crucifix when I went off to seminary. I believe she would be pleased to know you are wearing it."

Despite the cold, Raluca began experiencing a remarkable sense of comfort and warmth. "Thank you, Father. Thank you very much."

"You are most welcome," he said. To Raluca's surprise he raised and lowered his right hand, then shifted it from left to right, completing a wordless blessing. In the next moment he turned and continued striding toward Oude Kerk.

Raluca watched the distance between them widening. I hope, she reflected, that I can possess your courage. She fingered and looked down at the small cross. Acting on a second impulse she remounted the bike and began pedaling south. At Barndestaag she turned left or east. Seconds later she dismounted in front of the familiar bicycle shop. She parked the bike and entered. Joshua was examining a repair order form at the sales counter. He looked up and smiled.

"Joshua," Raluca said, breathless.

Joshua saw the cross and his curiosity was aroused. "What are you doing here? And without a coat."

"I can explain." And Raluca did. She told Joshua about the street skirmish between NSB men and Jews who, she assured him, were giving as well as getting. In her excitement, she almost forgot to mention the gift from Father Brandsma. Only when she began fingering it unconsciously did she remember.

"I'm glad you came to tell me," said Joshua. "This looks bad and I have a feeling it's going to get worse. After work I'm going to visit the Follecks to see how they are doing. But let me remind you that, in the future, we shouldn't be seen together in public. It could be bad for you."

"Bad for us."

"Possibly. I think Father Brandsma gave you good advice. Keep wearing the cross so it can be seen. Even when wearing a coat – which you should be doing now."

"Okay."

"Aha! Either I am being a bad influence on you or you are learning proper American English." He laughed and Raluca laughed with him. Joshua then stepped around the counter, saw no sign of Karel or customers, extended his arms and drew Raluca close to him. She looked up. "This bicycle shop doesn't strike me as the most appropriate setting for what I was going to say. But the timing feels right. I love you."

The next morning, February 12, Rauter and Mussert met to review yesterday's operation.

"I suppose," Mussert began, "that I was wrong about the Jews not fighting back."

"You will not hear me dispute that assessment," Rauter said dryly. "I would say your strategy – striking out against Jews in scattered locations – was badly flawed. In some places, I was told, your NSB men were outnumbered and outfought by ragtag Jews."

"That is regrettably true."

"So if we are to intimidate Amsterdam's Jews, if we are to make further roundups less likely to cause a serious backlash, a different strategy would seem to be in order."

"Do you have one in mind?" Mussert asked, appropriately deferential.

"I do. It is not a matter of police genius. It is a matter of borrowing tried and true military strategy. You chose to divide your force, and defeat was predictable. That, by the way, is my biggest concern regarding our fuhrer's ambition. I worry that he will try to conquer too many nations in different directions from Germany and fatally divide the Wehrmacht. Of course, that is my very private belief. Do you understand?"

"Fully."

"Here in Amsterdam we are going to consolidate our manpower and strike a single target."

"When? Where?"

"The Jewish quarter. And I expect you to begin preparations this afternoon."

Late that afternoon Mussert, riding in a Gestapo staff car, led a caravan of German Army trucks to the Jewish quarter. Mussert's men immediately began unrolling bales of barbed wire. A few hours later they had cordoned off the neighborhood. While the barbed wire was being emplaced, Mussert's carpenters were building checkpoints at each of the bridges that spanned the quarter's surrounding canals. Their work completed, Mussert's troops began manning the checkpoints in shifts around the clock.

The next morning Rauter, with Seyss-Inquart's backing, announced that the quarter was closed to non-Jews. Rauter's thinking: If Jews in the quarter are segregated, non-Jews would be less likely to intervene in their behalf. Arrests of individual Jews or groups of them would be less likely to arouse sympathy, much less armed resistance.

Rauter's encirclement strategy didn't account for Jews living elsewhere in Amsterdam. But once he had emptied out the quarter, he believed that locating and arresting scattered Jews would be a decidedly easier task.

Joshua and Raluca were sitting on the edge of the bed in her chamber at the brothel.

"This is probably the safest place for us to meet," Joshua said softly. "It's virtually public and men are expected to come here. Perhaps we can occasionally take a chance and meet at my home or your apartment."

"But," Raluca added, "we must take great care not to be seen entering or leaving, right?"

"Right," said Joshua. "That will be absolutely necessary if we become actively involved with a resistance movement."

"When do you think that will happen?"

"It's really up to people like Kees de Heer. He has told me that he isn't eager to be a martyr. So I think he will start a resistance movement only after he is satisfied that he is fully prepared. That probably means being organized, armed, trained and briefed."

"So for now, we wait."

"Yes, and that's what you are going to do while I go have a look-see at the Jewish neighborhood."

"You are going to try to sneak in?" Raluca said worriedly.

"No. I don't think I could pass for a Jew and with the checkpoints, I am not keen to swim a canal again. That one time, on Orange's back, was enough. I just want to see for myself the barbed wire and how many soldiers are guarding the perimeter and the checkpoints."

"Joshua, I think this is the right time for me to say what I think you already know."

"I think I do, but I want to hear it, so go ahead."

"I know you loved your wife very much. And she was a better woman than I am or ever will be. Smarter, better educated, prettier – I have seen her picture – and not tainted with a stain like mine. I am more than a little afraid to say it, but I do love you."

Joshua's eyes closed while he nodded. "Those are words I've wanted to hear – since the day I said them to you."

"Good. I am glad that I spoke them."

Joshua opened his eyes and sighed. "Now, Raluca Johnescu, listen very carefully. I do not know when this war will end. I do not know what the world will look like. I do not know if we will survive. But if we do, I want you in my life." Raluca's eyes were beginning to mist. "You are right about Meredith. I did love her as much as any man can love a woman. There will always be a place in my heart for her. But I never again want to hear you disparaging yourself. I think of where you started – on that little farm – and the courage it took to leave and the resourcefulness it has taken to make your own way." Raluca sniffled. "That is my last word on that. I do not want to hear another word from you on that either. Okay?"

"Okay. I will try to honor your wishes. I will try not to compare myself with your wife. But…"

"But what?"

"But it will not be easy, because I am stained."

On February 19 Joshua set out on a bicycle borrowed from Karel Veeder to conduct his reconnaissance of the Jewish quarter. Though only a few minutes pedaling from the shop, Joshua never arrived. A block away from the Jewish neighborhood he saw eight policemen led by Sergeant Baemer approaching the entrance to Koco, a candy and ice cream shop owned by a Jewish couple.

Joshua braked and watched. Moments later Baemer's men were pushing the husband and wife and their teenage son into the street. The police began pummeling the victims. Their assault enraged Joshua – and nine members of a Jewish self-defense group who had been walking toward the Jewish quarter to conduct their own reconnaissance.

Joshua lowered his bike's kickstand and watched as the Jews went running to the aid of their countrymen. Words of caution from Laura Reidel and Raluca leaped to mind. He considered them briefly – and then went dashing forward. In the next instant the surprised police found themselves on the losing side of a brawl. Joshua joined the fray by throwing a right-handed punch to the left jaw of the police leader. The blow stung Joshua's fist, but it also sent Sergeant Baemer staggering backward, his heels striking the curb and toppling him to the seat of his uniform trousers. Baemer shook his head to clear his thoughts. As he began using his arms to push himself up, Joshua reached down and grabbed Baemer by his uniform's lapels. His eyes were blazing with contempt, and Joshua did something unprecedented for him: He spat in Baemer's face. Then he shoved Baemer who fell onto his back.

By now Baemer's men were eager for only one action – retreat and escape. Baemer himself rolled over, rose to a kneeling position and pushed himself to his feet. He looked hard at Joshua who didn't flinch or blink. Baemer shuffled away, trailing the men he had been leading.

The Jews watched the police depart then turned their gaze to Joshua. "Who are you?" one asked.

Joshua paused, catching his breath, before replying. His mind was rapidly processing conflicting thoughts. He answered simply, "A friend."

The Jews nodded and a second man said, "Thank you."

"My privilege," Joshua said. Then he pointed to the shop owners and their son. They were standing, hunched and in pain, next to their shop's entrance. "Let's see about getting them patched up."

Karel Veeder watched closely as Joshua pulled the borrowed bike into the shop. He saw the abrasions on the back of Joshua's right hand. "Not your ordinary bike ride," Karel observed dryly. "As the bike appears undamaged, would I be right in saying that you hurt your hand in some other fashion?"

Joshua grinned wryly. "You might say I stuck it in someone else's business."

"There are times to make such business your own. I think I am glad you did."

Baemer's failed effort at intimidation led Seyss-Inquart, Mussert and Rauter to accelerate their plans to cow Amsterdam's Jewish population.

"We must move more decisively and on a larger scale," Seyss-Inquart said grimly. "These Jewish self-defense groups must be taught a lesson. They must learn that lashing out at our men will be self-defeating."

Seyss-Inquart then dictated to Rauter and Mussert his expectations. "It is an ambitious plan," Seyss-Inquart acknowledged, "but it is necessary, and I expect it to succeed. Rauter, you are in charge. Do not disappoint me."

Rauter quickly convened a meeting with senior officers, including Lieutenant Julius Dettman and Sergeant Baemer.

That night at the brothel, Dettman was lying naked beside Alicia Domian. After a long period of contemplative silence, Dettman, staring up at the ceiling in the dimly lit chamber, whispered, "This is getting out of hand."

"What is?"

Dettman's head turned toward Alicia. "I think it is better you not know."

Alicia knew she had a choice. Remain impassive and probe no further, or gamble. "If you are involved with the treatment of Jews, you probably are right. The less I know the better." After a lengthy pause, she chose to gamble. "But if discussing your concerns with someone would help you feel better, I am a good listener. Besides, by now I think you know you can trust me."

Dettman turned away. He resumed staring at the ceiling, sorting his own mélange of thoughts. "We are planning a bigger roundup of Jews. Much bigger. It is really not a backlash that bothers me. It is knowing that the Jews we round up and deport might never return. When it comes to Jews, some Nazis don't have a conscience. But some of us still do. Some us of are Nazis in name, but not in spirit."

Alicia knew she now was privy to sensitive, important information. I have to decide what to do with it she told herself. Keep it to myself? Tell Raluca? If I tell her, will she act on it? I have a feeling she might, and that could be trouble for both of us. At that moment in sorting her thoughts, she felt a need to be more certain that Dettman would continue feeling kindly toward her. Would continue to choose her as his bed partner. To accomplish that Alicia concluded she needed to violate Anna Clarbout's code of conduct with clients. Alicia turned on her side. With her left hand she felt for Dettman's penis and took hold. Dettman turned to her in obvious surprise. She smiled warmly and began stroking.

At midmorning on February 22 a Nazi staff car braked in front of a shoe store across Merwede Square from Folleck's Fine Clothing. Sergeant Baemer and two Gestapo members exited the car and entered the store.

Miriam Folleck was arranging apparel behind the shop window. She called to her husband. "Samuel, come here. Now."

"What is it," Samuel asked as he walked to join her.

"I just saw three Gestapo enter our friend's shoe store."

"Maybe they are shopping."

"I don't think so. They looked in too much of a hurry to be shopping."

Moments later Baemer emerged from the store. Behind him his two men were half-dragging the store owner, a strapping man of 33, toward the staff car. He was trying, futilely, to free himself from their grip.

The owner's wife exited the store in a frenzy. "Why are you taking him? Where are you taking him? When will you bring him back?"

Baemer turned and snapped, "You will get no answers from us. We don't owe you any explanation."

Baemer's men shoved the store owner through the car's rear passenger side door.

From across Merwede Square, Miriam and Samuel watched the tableau in dismay. We could be next, Samuel was thinking, any one of us.

That day and the next, February 23, the Nazis rounded up 425 Jewish men between the ages of 20 and 35. They were chosen for their youth, strength and ability to perform hard labor. After being processed at the Holland Schouwberg, the men were forced aboard trucks and driven to Kamp Schoorl in eastern Netherlands. From there they would be shipped farther east to Buchenwald and Mauthausen. Of those 425 men only two would survive the war.

Seyss-Inquart and Rauter were congratulating themselves on the afternoon of February 24. They were sipping cognac when Mussert phoned Seyss-Inquart.

"I have news," Mussert began.

"About what?" Seyss-Inquart asked. His mood was expansive, and he was expecting any news to add to his sense of achievement.

"It is about a strike," Mussert said.

"A what?"

"Tram drivers in Amsterdam are striking in protest to yesterday's roundup."

"Are the drivers Jews?" Seyss-Inquart asked, incensed that anything so untoward as striking Jews would disrupt his celebrating. He placed his cognac snifter on his desk.

"No."

That morning in front of Noorder Kerk, slightly more than half a mile northwest of Oude Kerk and the red light district, angry non-Jewish Amsterdammers had held an open air meeting. In short order they had decided to organize a strike to protest the roundup and deportation of Jews to forced labor in Germany. Members of the Communist Party of The Netherlands, already declared illegal by Seyss-Inquart, printed and distributed a flyer that called for a strike to begin throughout the city.

First to respond were Amsterdam's tram drivers. Others, including municipal service workers and schoolteachers, soon followed suit. Then like a virus spread by the droppings of birds in flight, the strike spread to other cities, including Utrecht.

Laura Reidel was among residents who felt a surge of civic – national – pride at the courage of fellow Dutch. She bundled up and left her apartment, walking and smiling with no particular destination in mind.

Courtesy of bedtime whisperings, Alicia Domian knew what was coming next. What she learned from Lieutenant Dettman seemed futile to oppose, so she remained silent, adding to her storehouse of knowledge and building Dettman's trust in her while continuing to grant him additional favors.

What Dettman disclosed to Alicia was word that Seyss-Inquart and Rauter would respond fast and with overwhelming force to suppress the strike. They would hold nothing in reserve.

They did precisely that. By February 27, brutal attacks by the police and Mussert's paramilitary Landwacht had crushed much of the strike. Rauter's police tracked down several of the strike's leaders. Lieutenant Dettman and Sergeant Baemer presided over the firing squad that executed the captives outside the city.

Rauter wasn't finished. He moved swiftly to establish concentration camps in The Netherlands. One was located near the city of Vught and was named Kamp Vught. A second, meant to be a transit camp, was built near Amersfoort and was named Kamp Amersfoort. The third, also designed as a transit station, was called Kamp Westerbork. From there some 110,000 Dutch Jews eventually would be deported to death camps, mainly Auschwitz and Sobibor.

In addition, in the existing Dutch prison at Scheveningen, Rauter ordered built a special block for what he would term political prisoners – a euphemism for resistance fighters and their supporters. Detainees would be held indefinitely, some until war's end. Many were severely mistreated and, by May 1945, 738 men and 21 women would die at Scheveningen or be executed at the nearby killing field – the Waalsdorper Vlakte.

Rauter, again with Seyss-Inquart's endorsement, also initiated a system of retaliation for assaults on Nazi officials and their Dutch collaborators. At first one killed Nazi meant 10 Dutch were lined up and shot. One killed Dutch collaborator would lead to three Dutch executed. By war's end Dutch resistance acts became increasingly frequent and violent, and those retaliation ratios rose.

After the strike Father Brandsma took to his pulpits – inside and outside churches – and again condemned Nazi policy and actions. "Only the godless," he thundered, unconcerned about possible retribution, "would attack and arrest innocents. Only the depraved would arrest and tear away innocent husbands, fathers, sons and brothers and send them to concentration camps for uncertain fates."

During a surgical dissection of Nazis and Nazi policy from the steps of Oude Kerk, Father Brandsma's audience included Joshua and Raluca, standing apart, as well as Lieutenant Dettman and Sergeant Baemer. Joshua recognize Baemer and kept his distance, tugging his brown stocking cap down over his ears.

After Father Brandsma concluded, Joshua sidled to Raluca. "I would really like to talk to him," he whispered. "Not just while shaking hands but have time to sit with him. In private, without Gestapo lurking" – he nodded toward Dettman and Baemer – "and watching his every move. Or seeing us together with him."

"Is it possible?" Raluca asked.

"Perhaps. I think it's time you met someone on Corellistraat. He might be able to arrange such a meeting. But we should arrive separately. Early. Soon after the curfew ends. How about seven?"

"I can be there."

"I'll plan to arrive a few minutes before seven. You'll see me at the entrance to number six. I'll go inside and wait for you. The door will not be locked."

"I am excited, Josh. And afraid."

This time Kees de Heer shook hands with Joshua. He bowed slightly toward Raluca. "I can arrange a meeting with Father Brandsma but not here. Too close to our core, and I don't want to risk having to set up another command center for our group."

The meeting with the priest would take place at Oude Kerk in a small sacristy where clergy donned vestments for services. The room was located just to the right of the church's main altar.

"I am looking forward to seeing him again," Raluca said after the meeting with de Heer. "He is such a kind man. He does not make you feel little."

They were in the Molensteeg apartment with Alicia. Raluca had related to Alicia and Joshua her previous encounters with Father Brandsma – the first resulting from the errant snowball and the second after the priest confronted the escaping NSB thug.

"I will look to you to make the formal introduction," Joshua said to Raluca.

"I don't know," said Raluca. "I am nervous about this meeting."

"Are you afraid the Gestapo will see you with him?"

"It's not that."

"What is it?" Joshua asked.

Raluca hesitated, glancing at Alicia who intuitively understood Raluca's dilemma. "He doesn't know I am a prostitute. Or at least I don't think he does. If he asks me what my job is, I would be ashamed to tell him. But I don't think I could lie to him – a priest."

"I see. Well, do you want to back out of this meeting?"

"Do you?"

"No."

"You wouldn't be ashamed to be with me if he learns – or knows – I am a whore?"

Joshua paused before answering. "If we were back in my little hometown in the States, I probably would be. Yes, I would be. At least under normal circumstances."

"I thank you for your honesty," Raluca said.

"Let me finish," Joshua said. "Circumstances here are not normal. We are caught in a war, and that changes a lot, including the way I see things. Here in Amsterdam, my horizons have lengthened. My perspectives have broadened. Besides," Joshua smiled wryly, "you're not wearing a sign that says prostitute. And you're not wearing a scarlet letter."

"A scarlet letter. What is that?" Raluca asked.

"I'll explain later. Over coffee."

As de Heer had instructed, Raluca arrived first at the seemingly vacant Oude Kerk. It was early morning on the first Saturday in March. She walked down the center aisle, nearly to the front. She entered a pew and slowly made her way to the far right. She sat, closed her eyes and bowed her head. Dear God, she prayed, I hope you can find it possible to forgive me for the life I am living. I am not ready to leave Alicia alone, and that means I will continue living in sin. I hope you understand and someday erase the stain from my soul. I also hope, somehow, that you can protect the people of this city and this nation. I also ask you to look kindly on my family in Romania. I am asking much, I know. I hope it is not too much.

Raluca neither saw nor heard Joshua edging into the pew, two rows behind her.

"Raluca," he whispered, "don't turn around. Let's go."

They both rose and stepped into a side aisle. Joshua looked around and back and saw no one. They stepped into the sanctuary, staying to the far right until they reached the sacristy's open door.

Father Brandsma was standing. His eyes widened brightly. "How wonderful!" he said, making no attempt to hide his pleasure. "I thought I would be meeting two strangers. But I see before me two familiar faces. And," he said teasingly, "one familiar bald head." He stepped forward, offering his hand to Joshua. They shook firmly. Then the priest extended his right hand to Raluca. She gazed at it indecisively for a long moment. Then she reached out, and they shook hands gently.

"I am happy to see you again, Father," Raluca said softly.

"And I am happy to see you wearing the cross. Now, please sit." All three sat on chairs with wooden arms and seats and backs upholstered in gold-colored cloth.

"Thank you for agreeing to see us," said Joshua.

"My pleasure," said Father Brandsma, shrugging modestly. "I was told only that two people in good stead with Mr. de Heer wanted to see me. I admire you for taking on the risk that goes with meeting me. I am being watched almost constantly. Indeed, I am expecting to be arrested and detained at any time. Mr. de Heer has told me it will happen."

"You are not afraid?" Raluca asked meekly.

"I have my moments of fear. It is only natural. I am very human," he chortled. "But I think that I can defeat my fear of the Nazis and what they might do to me. Certainly I hope to see my lovely homeland free from the Nazis' grip. But if that is not to be, at least I will know that I have done all

I could to undermine Hitler. I realize that might sound boastful, but that is my true feeling."

"I do not think you are boasting," Raluca said, shaking her head. "I think you have great courage, and the people of this country must see that and be grateful."

Father Brandsma reddened. "Thank you, child. I don't think I have ever been paid a greater compliment." A brief pause, as the priest looked searchingly at Raluca. "If I remember correctly, you are Romanian." Raluca nodded affirmation. "I think you have shown great courage in leaving your native land and making your way here. I believe you will continue to show courage for as long as you are on this earth."

Joshua was smiling proudly at both Raluca and Father Brandsma. Comforting warmth was spreading through his torso.

A thought entered Raluca's mind, and it caused her to blush. "Father," she murmured tentatively, "I feel I should tell you something."

"No," said Father Brandsma. "You need not tell me anything. I see you for what you fundamentally are – a caring young woman."

"Thank you, Father. Could" – Raluca cleared her thickening throat – "could I ask you a favor?" He nodded. "You know I am Orthodox, not Roman Catholic. But would you mind giving me another blessing?"

"I would be happy to, child."

Raluca rose from the chair, Josh rising with her. "I would feel better if I was kneeling," said Raluca.

"Me too," said Joshua.

"That is not necessary," said Father Brandsma, rising from his chair. "But that is fine if it makes you feel more comfortable."

Raluca and Joshua dropped to their knees and looked up.

"Lord," the priest began, "thank you for this special time together with Raluca and Joshua in your house. May we have the privilege of another meeting like this one." Then as Father Brandsma's right hand moved up, down and left to right, he intoned, "In the name of the Father, the Son and the Holy Spirit."

"Amen," murmured Raluca, eyes welling.

"Amen," echoed Joshua, turning toward Raluca and feeling a rush of affection and admiration.

CHAPTER 47

From a distance of about 100 feet Isala Van Dyck recognized Joshua's bald head and confident stride. Tulips and daffodils soon would be blooming and scenting Amsterdam's spring air. Homeowners, apartment dwellers and shopkeepers watched their window boxes returning to life. Bulbs were sending shoots up through soil, and they were stretching for the sun's rejuvenating warmth. Watering was not a problem; frequent spring rains kept soil well moistened.

It was shortly after 1 p.m. and Isala guessed that Joshua was returning to the bicycle shop after lunching. She was returning to her office after treating a client to lunch in a café on the Niewmarkt plaza that lay just east of the bicycle shop on Barndestaag. As the distance between the two was closing, Isala could see that Joshua was deep in thought, eyes downcast, oblivious to his surroundings. I wouldn't be surprised, Isala was reflecting, if he walked right past his bicycle shop before realizing it. She decided to hail him. "Mr. Bliss," she called.

Joshua looked up. Her smiling visage failed to warm him, but he responded cordially. "Hello, Mrs. Van Dyck."

They now were about 20 feet apart. Joshua stopped. Isala kept striding gaily. When about three feet away, she offered her right hand. Joshua accepted it and they shook hands politely.

"It is a fine spring day, don't you think?" she asked.

"Yes," he replied, "it's very nice."

"How is the bicycle business?"

"Slow," Joshua said truthfully, "but we are glad to be open and operating."

"Not so many Jewish customers anymore?"

"Not as many. But in general all people have less money to spend."

"I lost Jewish customers too when their quarter was closed to non-Jews. But losing Jewish customers is but a necessary consequence on the way to having the greater good."

"The greater good?" Joshua asked coolly.

"Yes," Isala answered forthrightly, "a country that is more Aryan, more pure."

On a previous occasion, Joshua had let pass Isala's anti-Semitic declarations. But not this time. "Not everyone feels as you do."

"I know and I have a feeling that you are one of them."

"You are right. Some of us, as you know, have been willing to protest. To resist. The tram drivers, schoolteachers, Father Brandsma."

"They are simply wrongheaded. I am sorry" – she clearly wasn't – "to offend you, but Jews have done more to damage Aryan ways of life than to benefit them."

"Mrs. Van Dyck, do you have any facts, any facts at all, to support your beliefs?" Joshua could feel his face heating and his blood pressure escalating.

"The facts are plain to see." So far she had refrained from baring her temper. "Have you read Mein Kampf?"

"Yes, I have read Mein Kampf, or tried. It is drivel. Fanciful drivel."

Joshua's intemperate characterization of Hitler's credo splintered Isala's restraint. "It is the bible for Aryanism," she replied hotly.

"A bible for the weak-minded," Joshua said through gritted teeth, "or for warped minds."

Isala ceased her effort at maintaining any semblance of equanimity. "Mr. Bliss, have you listened to Mr. Goebbels broadcasts? He and Herr Hitler have presented all the facts to know that Jews have been a blight on nations and economies wherever they have been permitted to grow in number and control the flow of money."

You are hopeless, Joshua was thinking. "Have you always felt this way?"

"Thanks to Herr Goebbels and Herr Hitler, I now see the big picture more clearly."

"Do you have any Jewish friends? I don't mean Jewish customers but actual friends?"

"I wouldn't want to sully myself," Isala said disdainfully.

"I see. So you disapprove of people who have Jewish friends. Who have protested against Nazi policy and thuggery. Who might resist."

"If," Isala said bitingly, "I knew of anyone resisting Nazi interests, I would be only too happy to report them."

"To the Gestapo?"

"To the proper authority."

"They might be people you know," Joshua said, "perhaps your friends."

"If they were my friends and they were resisting, I would no longer regard them as friends. Because, in fact, they would be traitors to our cause."

Joshua closed his eyes and let his head droop. He let perhaps five seconds pass before he looked up. "Mrs. Van Dyck, I don't know why you have let hatred rule your mind, but I actually feel sorry for you."

"For me?" she bristled. "If either of us needs pity, it is you. You are incapable of seeing the world as it should be. A world that sees clearly the value of racial purity. I have misread you. I thought a man working for an international shipping company would have a better understanding of how the world works. More is the pity."

"Mrs. Van Dyck, I haven't misread you. That, indeed, is a pity."

"She is despicable," Raluca said after hearing Joshua's account of his encounter with Isala. She and Joshua were sitting on the edge of the small bed in her brothel chamber. "But, Joshua, she is something even worse. Even more worrisome."

"I think I know what you mean."

"Of course you do. Isala Van Dyck is now your enemy."

CHAPTER 48

A pair of Wehrmacht occupation soldiers were weaving unsteadily along a street on the outskirts of Rhenen.

Watching from their bikes as they were riding home were Karin and Catherina Looten. It was late afternoon and the girls were returning from a shopping mission to a farm west of Rhenen. Each had a brown cloth bag tied to their bikes' handlebars. The bags contained onions and apples. The farmer had harvested the apples the previous autumn and carefully stored them in his basement. It was amazing, the girls agreed, that apples could be stored so long.

"They look drunk," Karin observed, gesturing toward the soldiers.

"Either that," Catherina said, "or they are acting silly."

"I vote for drunk," Karin chuckled.

"That is my vote too," Catherina laughed. "Too much schnapps. Schnapps and beer. I sometimes think that is all German soldiers drink."

"Come on," said Karin.

The sisters continued pedaling until they were flanking the soldiers.

"A little too much alcohol?" Karin taunted them. She laughed.

One of the soldiers, Private Billheimer, swung his head toward her. "What we drink and how much we drink is none of your affair."

"So very witty. Oh, I think you are quite drunk," Catherina teased. "You smell like fresh manure."

The other soldier, Private Melzer, lunged clumsily at Karin. In his stupor, though, he nearly toppled to the pavement. Laughing, Karin sharply twisted the handlebar to the left, easily evading him.

"You should return to your barracks," Karin continued taunting, "if you can find them." She and Catherina both laughed and rode on.

The barracks to which Karin referred was a newly built, simple structure erected on the southwestern edge of town, not far from the Lootens' home. It quartered the 18 occupation troops. The building was covered in white stucco and roofed with red tiles. Inside the barracks, Lieutenant Kramer occupied a small, private room. He regretted having to abandon the Lootens' home. The other soldiers slept on cots in an open bay.

"We had better sober up before going back," said Private Melzer. "If the lieutenant sees us like this, we will be working extra shifts."

"Agreed," said Billheimer, "or he might withhold some of our pay. He is a stickler for decorum and discipline. I have never seen him drink."

"There is really nothing more to do in this wretched little town except drink," said Melzer. "There aren't even any whores. I wish we could have been assigned to Amsterdam or one of the other big cities."

"Maybe we could persuade those girls to give us a tumble. Young and tender meat."

"You are drunk and dreaming. Everybody in this town knows everybody's business. They wouldn't do it. Besides, they hate us."

May 10 was the first anniversary of Stefaan Janssen's death. Anneke walked to the bicycle shop early that afternoon to ask Joshua if he minded walking with her after work.

"This is a hard day for me," Anneke said, "and also for my grandparents. I was just thinking that walking with someone more my age might help this evening. If you have other plans, I understand."

"I would be happy to walk with you," Joshua smiled. "I'm glad you asked. I should be finished here by six."

Anneke arrived back at the shop a few minutes before Joshua's quitting time. She greeted Karel Veeder who replied with a warm, "Hello, Mrs. Janssen." He turned away from the sales counter and called to Joshua in the repair room. "Joshua, Mrs. Janssen is here."

Minutes later Anneke and Joshua exited the shop to be greeted by cool but dry evening air. Anneke was wearing a powder blue cardigan sweater over her white blouse and Joshua a brown pullover.

"Any particular direction or destination in mind?" Joshua asked.

"Not really. Let's start that way," she replied, pointing to the right or east.

They strolled in silence at an easy pace for about 10 minutes. "I still have dreams about him – us," Anneke said softly. Joshua was wondering whether she might weep. "Some are happy but some are sad. I see buildings exploding. I see lives extinguished. I see pieces of broken bodies."

"I don't know if there is anything I can say that will help," Joshua replied. "I am sorry."

"That's all right. I know you care and that is enough. I feel so empty, Josh. And even when I am with my grandparents or other people, sometimes I feel lonely."

"I understand," Joshua said. "I felt that same way for a long time."

"I am sure you did. Do you…Do you still have dreams about your wife?"

"Yes, but not as often. I will always have a warm spot, a large spot, in my heart for her. I have no doubt about that. So I think I will always dream about her. Not often, but my memories of her will never be forgotten."

They turned left or north and a block later left again. Joshua's hands were stuffed into his brown corduroy pants pockets. Anneke's hands were clasped behind her back.

"I am glad we met, Josh. You are a good listener. I think you understand other people's feelings very well."

He shrugged. "Do you feel like eating?"

"Not yet. Let's walk a little more."

"Okay. Just let me know when you're ready. We'll pick a nice, quiet restaurant."

"Okay," Anneke smiled. "I like that word."

Joshua chuckled lightly. "Who knows? Maybe okay will be one of those words that everyone speaks around the world. Of course some Europeans and Asians probably hate it. See it as a corruption of the King's English."

Oude Kerk's façade was coming into view.

"You know," Anneke revealed, "I have never been a particularly religious woman. But now I feel a need to go to church, to go inside Christ's house. I don't think he will mind, and I think it will help me. What do you think?"

"With just one eye," he smiled, "you can still see Christ clearly."

In the summer of 1941 Europe hadn't seen such dark nights since before the introduction of gas lamps. After sunset the continent was shrouded in blackness that would have seemed familiar to a resident of the Middle Ages. The reason: Nazi mandated blackouts.

Streets and roads were virtually deserted too. Vigorously enforced curfews were keeping millions of Europeans housebound from sunset to sunrise.

Even inside, a strange and unsettling quiet was pervading Dutch homes. Seyss-Inquart announced that occupation troops would be confiscating all radios. The BBC and Radio Orange, broadcasting from London, were providing precisely the kind of programming the Nazis knew could loosen their grip: Information and hope. The voices of Winston Churchill, Queen Wilhelmina, Charles de Gaulle and other respected leaders were giving succor to those needing it most – the jobless, the penniless, Jews and the nascent Dutch resistance.

Assessment of the Nazis' radio roundup could be viewed two ways. The Gestapo, in league with local police, seized about half of all radios in The Netherlands. But that meant that about half of Netherlanders were willing to risk arrest, torture, deportation and execution to continue being able to listen to voices talking of sacrifice, perseverance and, ultimately, freedom from oppression.

The Sevels surrendered their radio. The Follecks hid theirs – in plain sight. Samuel hollowed out an upholstered ottoman that became their radio's hideout. The Lootens decided to keep theirs, hiding it in the closet that was tucked beneath the stairs leading to the second floor. When the radio wasn't in use, Catherina placed it in the closet and slid it beneath the first step leading up to the bedrooms. After shoving the radio into that tight spot, Catherina maneuvered a length of wood, painted black, against the radio. Another who kept his radio was Joshua. On the top floor of his home, inside a closet, he used a thin-bladed saw to remove a section of the ceiling. Then he maneuvered a larger piece of wood through the hole so that he easily could push it aside whenever he wanted to retrieve – or hide – his radio. Not foolproof, he realized, but unlikely to be detected in a crowded closet without a light bulb.

"I am applying for home leaves for all of us," Lieutenant Kramer said to Corporal Klaus Bohnenblust. "We have been on duty here for a year and things are peaceful."

The two soldiers were strolling through Rhenen where townspeople were continuing their rebuilding work.

"I agree," said the corporal. "We all are eager to see our families. And you must terribly miss your wife and son."

Karl Kramer nodded. "I am recommending that four of us go on leave at a time. Two weeks for each of our men and one week for me."

"Only one?"

"I would prefer two, but I think my recommendation will be viewed more favorably if I am to be away for only one week. You would be in charge while I am away, and I will make sure the men know you have my complete confidence. Indeed, I am recommending you for promotion to sergeant."

Bohnenblust looked at his commanding officer in surprise. "Thank you, sir."

"You deserve it."

After supper that evening, Kramer and Bohnenblust were patrolling the eastern half of the town. Kramer was armed with his holstered luger and Bohnenblust with his machine pistol. The men were experiencing buoyed spirits, anticipating their home leaves and the corporal his promotion.

Nearby, Catherina suggested to Karin that they take an evening stroll along the Rhine. That would mean traversing the grassy plain separating town from river. Karin's first reaction was concern. Her memory was dredging up unwanted images of Sonja lying in a farm field in pieces.

"Mines?" Karin said.

"They have been found and cleared. "

"Or so we are told."

"Come on," Catherina urged her older sister. They were now 18 and 16.

"It is a beautiful evening, and the last time we were at the river was when we were boarding the coal ships."

"All right," conceded Karin.

"That is more like it," Catherina exulted. "Come on; let's go." She grabbed Karin's left forearm and pulled vigorously.

The two girls went running toward the river, shouting their joy.

Dusk was lowering and clouds were obscuring the moon and stars.

"Did you hear that?" Corporal Bohnenblust asked. "Doesn't that sound like the Looten sisters?"

"It does," Lieutenant Kramer agreed. "They shouldn't be out this late."

"Curfew violation," said the corporal.

"I am thinking more about safety. Mines. Who can say with certainty that they all have been cleared? Or unexploded shells buried just below the surface? Just walking along a river bank in the dark is not wise."

Bohnenblust chuckled. "You sound like their father."

"After living with them I sometimes feel like an older brother." Bohnenblust chuckled his understanding. "We will give them a little space and time, but then let's go in that direction," the lieutenant said, gesturing toward the river.

"Just in case," Bohnenblust said, "right?"

"Right."

"It is so peaceful here, isn't it?" Catherina said wistfully. "We can hear the water lapping against the shore. We can hear the breeze rustling the leaves. Some birds chirping good night."

"This was a good idea," said Karin. "Here by the river I almost feel free."

"Do you know what I am thinking?" Catherina asked.

Karin smiled indulgently at her younger sister. "I will not even attempt a guess."

"We should fly our kites again. Luc's too. In his memory."

"That is a very good idea, younger sister. Perhaps tomorrow afternoon. Afternoons most often seem to be when the breezes are strongest."

Privates Billheimer and Melzer had consumed nearly half a bottle of jenever. Each was carrying a machine pistol, slung by a strap in front of their chests. "The lieutenant has warned us about drinking too much," said Melzer.

"What else is there to do?" Billheimer said bitterly. "And what is there to fear from Kramer. He is a professor, not a soldier. He has grown soft in this good-for-nothing town. Why are we even still here? Typical of the Wehrmacht. Put some troops in an out-of-the way dump and forget about them. Do the generals seriously expect a revolt in Rhenen?"

"Still," Melzer said soothingly, "I think we have had enough."

"I need to piss," said Billheimer. He squinted, peering into a night lit only dimly by stars and a half moon. "We are closer to the river than the barracks. I have always wanted to piss in the Rhine. We wouldn't be here if Hitler would have been satisfied to stay on the German side. What good can come from occupying this shitpot of a country anyway?"

Billheimer turned and tripped over a tree root. Melzer caught him before he fell. A few moments later they arrived at the riverbank. Darkness was cloaking the ground beneath the trees lining the shore.

"Here," said Billheimer, handing the jenever to Melzer. "Hold it." Billheimer unbuttoned his fly and freed his penis. "Ah," he sighed as a steady stream of urine shot into the Rhine. "Best piss ever."

"What's that?" said Melzer as Billheimer was fastening his fly.

"What's what?"

"Listen." A pause. "Someone is coming. We shouldn't be here. Let's go."

"Wait," said Billheimer, stepping away from the river bank. "Female voices. Only a couple women. Nothing to fear."

As he and Melzer turned to leave, two women appeared from a nearby clump of trees. Just a few steps separated soldiers from women. Recognition came instantly. "Well, well," Billheimer sneered, "look who is violating curfew and come to join us."

The soldiers' unexpected presence startled Karin and Catherina. "Who-"

"No bikes this time," Billheimer caustically interrupted Catherina.

"Oh, it is you two," Catherina said, her heart rate slowing. Then she saw Melzer holding the bottle. "Still drinking, I see."

"Your smart mouth," Billheimer growled, "is the best the Dutch have to offer."

"You are pathetic," Catherina said disdainfully.

"Catherina, please," Karin cautioned her. "Let's just leave."

"Yes, leave them to their drunkenness. This war will end one day, and where will we see you? Drunk on your faces, in a gutter, in your own vomit."

Billheimer swiftly closed the gap between him and Catherina. He swung hard with his open right hand. His blow struck her face and sent her tumbling, dazed and sprawling onto her back.

"Catherina!" Karin cried. "Are you all right?" She turned and knelt at her sister's left side. Looking closely she could see blood trickling from Catherina's left nostril. Karin helped Catherina to a sitting position. Karin looked up at Billheimer. "You are an animal," she snapped, "a drunken animal."

"If I am an animal then I should do what animals do." He bent low and shoved Karin away from her sister and onto her bottom. Billheimer then turned to Melzer. Pointing to Karin, he said, "Grab her and make sure she doesn't interfere."

"Interfere?"

"Just do what I say."

Catherina's mind was clearing and she began struggling to her feet. Billheimer smacked her face again, this time with his left hand. The blow sent Catherina reeling.

Melzer took Karin's left arm and dragged her, still on the ground, away from her sister.

Billheimer again began unfastening his fly. Before Catherina could scoot away, he dropped on top of her, reached forward and pinned her shoulders to the ground. Catherina smelled the alchohol on Billheimer's breath and felt a worm of fear crawling through her stomach.

"Don't," Karin said, more pleading than demanding. "Or I will scream."

Billheimer shot a glance at her. "Scream and I will slit her throat." He proceeded to unsheathe a knife with a four-inch blade. He let its tip touch Catherina's throat. She whimpered and squeezed shut her eyes. "Just one scream from either of you," Billheimer warned, "and her blood will be on your hands."

"I will report you," Karin said, not altogether believably.

"Do that," Billheimer sneered, "and you will be next to feel the knife blade. Then your parents."

"Billheimer-" Melzer started to say.

"Shut up and mind the sister. Put your knife to her throat. They are out after curfew. We could kill them, dump their bodies in the river and that would be the end of it."

Billheimer then rocked back on his haunches and finished unfastening his fly. Again he freed his penis, this time swollen. Then he backed farther away, reached forward and forced Catherina's legs apart. She whimpered again and Billheimer leaned forward and once more touched her throat with the knife point. "You are a virgin, I will wager, and have been for too long."

The grass along the river was spring lush and soft. It made a comfortable, natural mattress. It also rendered approaching footfalls soundless.

Billheimer grasped the hem of Catherina's skirt and pushed it forward past her waist. Then he reached for the top of her panties.

"I wouldn't," the disembodied voice said calmly.

Billheimer looked up, startled and confused. Melzer felt fear surging and shivered.

"Stand up," the voice commanded coolly. "Drop the knife. You too," the voice said, clearly directed at Melzer who complied immediately.

"Who?" Billheimer spluttered, his penis shrinking rapidly.

Lieutenant Kramer stepped from behind a thick tree trunk. Corporal Bohnenblust emerged from the other side.

"Melzer, release the girl." The private obeyed instantly. "On your feet, Billheimer." He rose slowly. "Close your trousers. And drop the knife now."

Billheimer obeyed, fumbling with the fly while he and Melzer were eyeing Kramer's drawn luger and Bohnenblust's menacing machine pistol.

"Corporal," Kramer ordered, "help the girl up." As Catherina rose, her skirt fell. She pressed her palms against it, a habitual smoothing movement.

"Lieutenant Kramer," Karin said, beginning to feel a wave of relief that followed escape from a threat.

"You know these girls?" Billheimer asked incredulously.

"He was quartered with us last year," Karin said before Kramer could answer.

"You two stand together," Kramer ordered. "And remove your weapons and put them on the ground."

"What?" Billheimer said.

"Do as you are told," Kramer said, still carefully modulating his voice.

Billheimer and Melzer pulled the machine pistol straps over their heads and laid the guns on the ground. They then stood shoulder to shoulder.

"Corporal Bohnenblust, escort the girls to their home. Wait for me."

"Sir," said Bohnenblust, "are you arresting them?"

Kramer, jaws clenched, didn't answer. Instead, he said, "Billheimer, Melzer, back to the river's edge."

They looked at each other, feeling uncertainty and the first twinges of anxiety. They obeyed, slowly stepping backward. Lieutenant Kramer leveled his luger at them.

"Sir," said Bohnenblust, "don't."

For Billheimer and Melzer anxiety was surrendering to panic. "Sir," Billheimer croaked, "we made a mistake. We apologize. Never again."

Kramer ignored the plea. To Bohnenblust he repeated, "Take the girls home."

"Sir," said the corporal, his mind still searching for a bloodless exit, "if you shoot them, if their bodies are found, there could be reprisals. We might be ordered to execute these people. Arrest them. Court martial them."

"Corporal, escort the girls. Now."

"Yes, sir." Bohnenblust breathed deeply, then he, Karin and Catherina began edging away. Karin looked back over her shoulder.

Kramer waited nearly a minute before speaking. "You can thank the corporal for sparing you from immediate execution." The two privates felt instant relief. "Now, into the river."

"What?" Billheimer said, puzzled.

"If you can swim the river, you will live."

"Sir," Melzer pleaded, "we can't. The river is too wide. The current… We couldn't make it. Not with our boots on."

"Take them off," Kramer said firmly.

"Sir, please," Melzer wheedled.

"Swim or be shot," Kramer said coldly. "That is your only choice."

Both privates knew further begging would be futile. Billheimer, in particular, realized he had underestimated the lieutenant's toughness. The two men sat on the ground and pulled off their boots. They stood, removed their uniform caps and dropped them.

Kramer motioned with his luger, and the privates turned and began wading into the river. Melzer shivered – from the water's penetrating cold and his abiding terror. They continued wading until the water was chest deep. Melzer looked back over his shoulder but only briefly. Then they leaned forward and began swimming.

Lieutenant Kramer stood impassively. He watched until darkness swallowed the privates and he could no longer hear their stroking. He picked up their boots and caps and tossed them into the river. Then he did likewise with their machine pistols. Lastly he retrieved the half empty jenever bottle and heaved it into the Rhine. Then he turned away and began walking toward the Looten home.

"We need to report them missing, or it could mean trouble for you," Corporal Bohnenblust said concernedly to Lieutenant Kramer. They were standing outside their occupation barracks. Two days had passed and Privates Billheimer and Melzer had not appeared.

"You are right. If you will write the report, I will send it in."

"Very good, sir. Sir?"

"Yes?"

"The girls. When they returned home, they told their parents about the assault. But they left out the worst details. When their parents asked me if the soldier who struck their daughter would be disciplined, I assured them that we would deal with him severely."

"They asked no further questions?"

"None, sir. And the girls said nothing more."

"Very good."

"Sir. Do...Do you think?-"

"I have no idea if they made it across."

CHAPTER 49

Once again, in August 1941, Governor Arthur Seyss-Inquart imposed additional restrictions on Holland's Jews. He ruled that Jewish students could no longer attend public schools. The same restriction had been imposed on Germany's Jewish students after Kristallnacht.

Parents of Jewish students in Amsterdam began enrolling their children in the Jewish Lyceum located in the Jewish quarter now closed to non-Jews.

For the children of Samuel and Miriam Folleck, Guillermo and Juanita Sevel and Otto and Edith Frank, the change meant hiking east each morning to the Lyceum and returning to their homes on Merwede Square.

It was nearing noon on the first Sunday after the Jewish children from Merwede Square had begun making morning treks to the Lyceum. Joshua and Anneke were strolling along the Prinsengracht. She still was living with her grandparents on nearby Gravenstrasse and had asked Joshua if he felt like taking another walk.

"Do you feel like lunch?" Anneke asked.

"I could use some."

"Good." Anneke had spotted a small kiosk on a bridge spanning the canal. "We will eat very Dutch."

"That's what I thought I've been doing," Joshua said, eyes twinkling teasingly.

"You are wrong. You only think you have. Today I will initiate you into classic Dutch cuisine." Anneke was grinning impishly. "You are a man of adventure, right?"

"Hmmm…Maybe."

"No maybe. You are. So today you must try eating local."

"Huh?"

"Come."

She led Joshua onto the slightly arched, stone-paved bridge. They walked to the kiosk at the bridge's crest.

"Two," Anneke said to the vendor.

He handed her two white herring, each lying on a small sheet of plain brown paper. Each fish was about 10 inches long, headless and finless but with tail intact.

Joshua looked at the herring with undisguised misgivings. "Raw?"

"Very. But also very fresh."

"How do we eat them?"

"Watch." Anneke elevated her right arm above her head. She was holding the herring by its tail. Then she tilted her head back. Slowly she began lowering the fish until its first inch passed between her parted lips into her mouth.

"Good aim," Joshua said, "and you do it with one eye."

Then Anneke bit and began chewing. After swallowing she looked at Joshua with her right eye. "Now you."

Joshua let his eyes roll upward in dubiousness, then began duplicating Anneke's technique. After biting, chewing and swallowing, he looked at Anneke. His surprise was evident. "Very good," he proclaimed, "really."

"Yes," she said knowingly. "Raw but slightly pickled. Sometimes they are smoked."

"Do you have a favorite?"

"The flavors are very different, and I like them both."

After consuming the herrings, Joshua and Anneke crumpled the brown paper around the tails and handed the remains to the vendor. They resumed strolling and chatting for another hour until they stood in front of Anneke's grandparents.

"This was terrific," Joshua said. "I'm glad you asked."

"Yes, I enjoyed it very much."

"Well," said Joshua, "let's plan to do it again soon." He extended his hand and Anneke took and clasped it firmly. She didn't shake it, and she didn't release her grip.

"We have become good friends, haven't we?" Anneke asked.

"Of course."

"Quite close."

"Yes, of course."

"Then why," she asked bluntly, "don't you show me affection? Is it my blind eye? Does it turn you away?"

"Not at all. I told you, your eye patch is what I noticed first. It drew me to you."

"Then why? You have not even kissed me."

Joshua's lips pursed. He sighed deeply.

"Oh," Anneke said, "there is another woman." Joshua nodded and Anneke released his hand. "Well, you are faithful to her. That is good."

CHAPTER 50

The telephone in the Franks' home rang. Anne removed the receiver from its cradle and listened. "Father," she called, "it is for you."

Otto took the receiver from his younger daughter and listened intently. He replaced the receiver and immediately left the house. Briskly he walked across Merwede Square to the Follecks. Samuel was in his ground floor clothing shop. He was accepting payment from a customer. He saw Otto beckoning emphatically and excused himself from the customer. "I will be back in a moment with your change." Samuel stepped to where Otto was standing inside the door.

"Is someone using your radio?" Otto whispered.

"Aaron, I think. Maybe the girls."

"Tell him to hide it. Now."

Samuel nodded and Otto turned and departed. Samuel walked to the base of the stairs leading up to their apartment. "Miriam," he called, "please come here."

On that afternoon in October one of the Nazis' radio signal detection vans was homing in on Merwede Square. The vans were daily prowling Amsterdam's streets. Residents found with radios could expect harsh punishment, with deportation of male family members the worst fear. Still, thousands of Amsterdammers chanced listening to radios. Their hunger for information and words of encouragement from the BBC and Radio Orange outweighed the attendant risk.

The phone call had alerted Otto Frank to the van's proximity. Its antenna was sniffing the air for signals and was seen heading toward his neighborhood. Moments after Miriam descended the stairs and listened to Samuel's whispered warning, the van braked in front of his shop. Samuel's customer saw it and hurriedly pocketed his change and left the shop, not eager to be seen in the presence of a Gestapo suspect.

The van's doors opened and three uniformed Gestapo exited. The first to enter the shop was Sergeant Walter Baemer. Without so much as briefly greeting Samuel, the sergeant ordered his men to search the shop.

"We know someone on this square has a radio. Maybe more than one. The signals are strong."

"Not us, I assure you," Samuel lied. "We have never owned a radio." He knew he couldn't claim to have surrendered one; the Gestapo's records would reveal that falsehood.

"We hear that often," Baemer replied caustically. "We have not always found it to be true."

Baemer joined in the search. "Nothing, Sergeant," one of his men reported.

"Up to their apartment," Baemer directed his men. "Search thoroughly. I will wait here." He watched for signs of anxiety in Samuel but detected none. "It would be pleasant if we could trust you Jews. But your reputation for deceit has followed you for centuries."

Samuel refrained from nibbling at Baemer's bait. His swelling anger notwithstanding, his face remained inscrutable. Instead he said placidly, "I wish there was something I could say or do to have you think better of us."

"You couldn't," Baemer said dismissively.

Upstairs in the apartment Miriam, Aaron, Mariah and Julia stood clustered in the living room. They were nervous and it showed. Julia was trembling and clinging to Miriam. Mariah stood at their side, hands clasped in front of her abdomen. Aaron was seething.

The two Gestapo men were pawing through cupboards, closets and drawers. They pulled books from shelves and let them drop to the floor. Below in the shop, the crashing books caused Samuel's jaws to clench in anger. The Gestapo pair pulled a sofa away from a wall and overturned chairs. They removed pictures and mirrors from walls, and the Follecks were grateful they weren't smashed or shattered. What was ignored was the ottoman. The Gestapo didn't so much as budge it.

The men descended to the shop. One shook his head.

"This doesn't mean we won't return," Baemer warned. "We know there are radios here in the square. We will search other shops and houses today. If we don't find one or more radios, we will continue coming back until we do."

Samuel, at six feet tall, three inches taller than Baemer, peered unblinkingly into the sergeant's angry eyes but said nothing. Baemer motioned to his men to leave, and he followed them from the shop. Samuel leaned forward, rested his hands against the sales counter and began trembling. I almost wish we had turned in the radio, he was thinking. Almost.

Later that autumn Seyss-Inquart moved to further strengthen his control over Dutch society. Apart from Anton Mussert's NSB, Seyss-Inquart banned all political party activity. He also arrested and incarcerated many former government officials. He deemed them inherently subversive and thus a threat. His heavyhandedness extended to virtually all aspects of Dutch life. One example: He oversaw the politicizing of cultural and social groups, including boys and girls clubs and chess clubs. If such groups were to endure they would be required to espouse Nazi ideology.

Seyss-Inquart's well-ordered view of Nazi-controlled Holland was dealt a blow on December 7. At home that Sunday night he turned on his radio at 9 p.m. The news of Japan's 8 a.m. attack on Pearl Harbor stunned him. What will this mean for America and Germany? he wondered. Japan is our ally, but I hope we don't go to war with America. That could prove disastrous. I am certain the fuhrer must be thinking the same thing.

In The Netherlands and elsewhere, millions were asking the same question Seyss-Inquart was posing to himself. No one as yet could provide a definitive answer.

At Joshua's home, he and Raluca were propped against pillows on his bed. He had fetched his radio from its hiding place above the closet ceiling.

"Your country will surely declare war against Japan," Raluca said.

"I agree. If it hasn't happened yet, I feel certain President Roosevelt will do it tomorrow."

"Do you think we should celebrate?" Raluca asked. "I am sorry. I don't mean celebrate a war against Japan. I know nothing about Japan. But it must be powerful to be attacking the United States. Such a strong country. People – Americans – will die. But I am wondering if this means America might try to free Europe."

"I don't know," Joshua said. "Going to war against Japan is one thing. But taking on Germany would mean many more deaths, and the American public might have no appetite for a second world war."

"Joshua?"

"What?"

"Do you wish you would have evacuated to America?"

He smiled affectionately. "I miss my family. But if I had evacuated, you wouldn't be part of my life."

They made love, slowly and tenderly. Joshua savored nuzzling Raluca's long, dark brown hair. Afterward they lay side by side, staring upward silently into the blackness. Several minutes went by before Raluca asked, "How much does it trouble you that I service Germans? Or any other man?"

"More than you can imagine. I wish you would stop and live with me."

Raluca sighed. "I am glad to know you feel that way. But Alicia, I still cannot abandon her. Even though she tells me I should."

Paul Bliss was distracted. It was after supper on December 7 before he and his parents, Noah and Goldie, heard the news about Pearl Harbor. Like most Americans they were stunned and angered. Paul slept little that night. Central to his thoughts was Joshua and what he might be enduring under the Nazi occupation.

On Monday, December 8, Paul arose before dawn, as was his custom. He went about his chores as usual but couldn't help pondering the news of the Pearl Harbor attack and how he might respond personally.

In Berlin that day, Adolf Hitler did what many Europeans, if not Americans, regarded as a favor. He declared war on the United States. So did Benito Mussolini in Rome. In London, after hearing the news, Queen Wilhelmina couldn't stop grinning. She was beaming, her eyes radiating hope.

At meals that day with Noah and Goldie, Paul initiated no conversation. Through breakfast and lunch Noah and Goldie said little, not wanting to intrude on Paul's thinking.

At supper though, Goldie said, "A penny for your thoughts."

"They might not be worth much more than that," Paul replied modestly.

"That's all right," Goldie said, smiling wryly, "I can make change."

Paul and Noah chuckled.

"Well," Paul said, "it seems America might be caught in a squeeze play. Japan already has attacked us in the west. And to the east Hitler has declared war. I'm trying to decide what to do. I was thinking I might talk to Ken Milligan tonight and see what he thinks." Milligan, a year younger than Paul, also was the son of farmers.

"That sounds like a good idea, son," said Noah. "It doesn't matter what you decide. I won't second-guess you. You will have our support."

"Thanks, Dad. I appreciate that."

The following morning Paul put on a thick, red and blue plaid shirt and blue denim overalls. He pulled on heavy blue socks and his brown work boots. Lastly he slipped into a brown cloth jacket. Then he left the house for the barn and the start of a day's work. After completing his early chores, Paul returned to the house and sat down with Noah and Goldie for a hearty breakfast of scrambled eggs, ham slices, oatmeal muffins and coffee.

"Umm," Paul mumbled appreciatively, "I'll bet the Army doesn't put out a breakfast like this. Absolutely delicious, Mom. As always."

"Does that mean," Goldie asked, "that you've made a decision?"

Paul finished chewing and swallowing a bite of muffin. "Ken and I talked it over. We're going to enlist."

"In the Army?" Noah asked.

Paul sipped his black coffee and smiled. "I'm not too fond of swimming, especially in deep oceans. That sort of rules out the Navy. The Army Air Corps could be appealing, but I'm not sure my frame would fit in one of those tiny cockpits. Besides, I'm thirty and probably should think about getting glasses. So it looks like the Army would suit me best." He ate another bite of muffin. "But not the infantry. Ken and I feel like we've done all the walking we need to do on the farms. So we're thinking of volunteering for the parachute service."

"Oh, Paul," Goldie said, alarmed. "Jumping out of airplanes. That sounds so dangerous."

Paul smiled knowingly. "I thought that's how you would react. But don't begin worrying now. I haven't even enlisted yet. And I don't know if the parachute service would accept me."

"To be honest I wouldn't be disappointed if it didn't," Goldie said.

"We'll see. Look, there is something else I want to discuss. You're going to need help working the farm. The way I see it, the Army will feed me, give me a uniform and a cot. So I'm planning to send my pay home so you can use it to hire help."

Noah reacted viscerally, eyes widening and chin rising. "That's very thoughtful, Paul," he said, feeling a rush of affection and respect for his first-born son. "But it's not necessary. We can manage."

"You probably could, Dad, but this is what I want to do. Let's not argue about it, okay?"

"Well," Noah grumbled, "I'm making no promises this morning. Your breakfast is getting cold, so chow down."

"I cannot believe it," Raluca said to Alicia. They were sitting in their apartment living room. Raluca was reading a Dutch newspaper – Nazi-controlled – dated December 13. Alicia was knitting a scarf that would be orange with blue border. "How could a man, any man, be so stupid? Insanity," Raluca muttered. "It must be a contagious disease. Especially among men. Even more so among dictators. First it is Hitler. Since Japan has attacked the United States and the United States has declared war on Japan, he must declare war on America. What was he thinking? Would a woman be so stupid? Or arrogant? Now Antonescu has caught the disease. That imbecile has declared war on America. Our little country."

"Perhaps," Alicia speculated, "he did it to make Hitler like him more."

"Oh, no doubt about that," Raluca concurred disgustedly. "But since he has already all but handed our poor country to Hitler, why be even more generous?"

"Maybe," Alicia murmured, looking up from her knitting, "he was worried that if he didn't, Hitler would replace him. Or assassinate him."

On December 12 Ion Antonescu had shocked his countrymen by declaring war on the United States. He didn't really expect Romanian troops to wage war on America. But he wanted to be on the winning side and genuinely believed that the combined forces of Germany, Austria, Japan, Italy and Romania would emerge from war as winners. He also saw an opportunity to expand Romania's borders and exact revenge on Russia for past transgressions.

To Antonescu, American retaliation against Japan would virtually eliminate any chance that America might try to liberate Western Europe. In the spacious living room of his Royal Palace quarters in Bucharest, Antonescu picked up a bottle of his favorite plum brandy and poured generously. He sniffed, sipped, smacked his lips, smiled and mused, *I don't think brandy has ever tasted better.*

CHAPTER 51

Father Brandsma was courting arrest and he knew it. He weighed the risk, ignored it and launched a new campaign that he was certain would incur Hitler's ire and likely draw his wrath. In early January 1942 Father Brandsma began trying to persuade Dutch diocesan Catholic newspaper editors to disobey Governor Seyss-Inquart's directive to publish Nazi propaganda aimed at poisoning attitudes toward Jews.

Father Brandsma also wrote a pastoral letter that he urged bishops to order their priests to read in all Catholic parish churches. The letter condemned Nazi anti-Semitic measures, citing as especially odious the arrest and deportation of Jews to concentration camps.

Joseph Goebbels, long ago given Hitler's green light to arrest Father Brandsma, now knew he had grounds – specious though they were – to move against the priest. After all, Father Brandsma was inciting fellow clergy to violate Third Reich regulations, and some of his disciples were acceding to his wishes.

Late one winter afternoon as the last glimmers of light drained from the western horizon, Father Brandsma was doing what he often did – praying while walking. He was beseeching God to grant him the courage to continue his war of words against Nazism. He was warding off winter rawness with a heavy black cape over his black cassock and gloves but no hat. His nose began to drip, and unconsciously a gloved forefinger reached up and dabbed away the mucous.

"Hello, Father."

Father Brandsma squinted in the fast-lowering gloom. "Oh, Raluca. How nice to see you. Another few minutes and I wouldn't have recognized you."

"I am glad you did. It is so nice to see you. But shouldn't you be wearing a hat?" Raluca was bundled against the cold – hat, scarf, gloves.

He chuckled. "I sometimes forget the essentials. At my age" – he was only seven weeks shy of 61 – "memories seem to be springing a few leaks." He chortled at his small joke and so did Raluca. "Where are you going?"

"To a food shop. Alicia and I need a few things."

"Well, don't let me interfere. It wouldn't do for a wordy priest to cause you to catch cold."

His use of the phrase *wordy priest* caused Raluca to feel a surge of anxiety. "Father, I...uh..."

"Go ahead, dear."

Raluca's eyes closed in momentary doubt. In the next instant she decided to accept his invitation to speak. "I admire your courage. The words you speak against the Nazis touch the hearts of many Dutch. Not only Catholics. Not only Jews. But that is what makes your words so dangerous – to yourself."

"You are quite right, Raluca. But I believe this is my mission, my sacred mission. I feel a duty to carry on." A pause. "Are you still wearing the cross?"

Raluca's left hand moved up and patted her coat-shielded upper chest. "I will never remove it."

"That is a touching sentiment. But if you ever feel the cross is jeopardizing your safety, please don't hesitate to remove it. Hide it if necessary."

His words caused Raluca's eyes to widen. He seemed to be saying that belief in the cross – faith in its protective power – might be insufficient to ward off harm. That might be true, Raluca was thinking, but if it is I still don't want to believe it.

Father Brandsma sensed her discomfort. "The cross is a symbol. A reminder of God's supreme sacrifice of His Son. But it need not make you a martyr before your time."

His bluntness penetrated her attempt at denial. "I will heed your words, Father – if," she smiled ruefully – "you agree to heed mine."

"I don't think I can promise that."

"Then you understand why I cannot pledge to remove the cross."

Sergeant Walter Baemer positioned himself and two of his men near Oude Kerk. He felt confident his prey would soon reveal itself. He was right. It was midmorning and Father Brandsma was striding purposefully west toward the medieval church. His breaths were crystallizing in the winter cold. His intent: Continue preaching his personal gospel of anti-Nazism.

Baemer waited until the priest began ascending the church's steps. Then he and his men hurried forward and intercepted Father Brandsma before he reached the doors. "You are under arrest. You will come with us now." Baemer's men each grasped one of Father Brandsma's upper arms.

Father Brandsma was tempted to ask, Where are you taking me? But he refrained, knowing the question soon would be answered.

Around a corner and on the church's north side, one of the men opened the driver's side rear door of a Gestapo staff car. Father Brandsma stepped inside. As the door closed, he looked at Oude Kerk. This could well be the last time I see you.

The next person Father Brandsma saw was Joseph Schreieder. He was the Gestapo's chief of counterintelligence in The Netherlands. He was seemingly an easy going Bavarian from Munich. In his case appearances were misleading. He happened to be a shrewd police officer. He assigned to himself the role of chief interrogator of high-profile detainees and known or suspected resistance members. Schreieder preferred kid glove questioning but was willing to employ harsher techniques.

Schreieder didn't rise from his desk chair when Sergeant Baemer escorted Father Brandsma into Schreieder's spartan office. For a long moment Schreieder studied the priest's placid countenance. Nothing remarkable about his features, Schreieder reflected. That is often true about leaders, Schreieder knew. The fuhrer is a classic example. He is hardly the paragon of the Aryanism that he espouses. Dark hair, dark eyes, nothing blond about him. Not at all handsome. But Hitler possesses undeniable vision, inner strength and perseverance. This priest would seem to possess those same qualities – and perhaps others as well.

At last Schreieder motioned to a guest chair and Father Brandsma sat. "I judge you to be a man of intelligence," Schreieder began, "so you needn't be told why you are here."

"For more than casual chitchat," Father Brandsma said pleasantly.

Schreieder chortled despite himself. "I see you are not suffering from wordless terror."

"I suffer terror. It is the terror of knowing what Adolf Hitler is doing to subjugate nations and peoples and eradicate Jews and others his warped psyche has deemed unworthy."

"Is that hatred you are harboring along with terror? I have thought a man of the cloth knows only love."

"A man of the cloth never ceases being a man with all of a man's flaws. I have many."

"Hubris is not one of them," Schreieder said, not trying to mask his admiration.

"You strike me as an intelligent man," said Father Brandsma. "Why do you follow Hitler?"

Schreieder sighed. "The answer is not a complex one. If you had lived in Germany after the First World War, you could answer your own question."

"But," Father Brandsma said without rancor, "following Hitler requires disposing of one's moral compass."

"Hitler's compass is taking us in the direction of prosperity and promise that is restoring German pride."

"Pride without principle."

A hint of a smile creased Schreieder's lips. "I can see why the fuhrer wants to see your gospel silenced. Herr Goebbels too."

"They have the power to silence me – as apparently they are. But I expect my gospel to endure."

"You might be right. But I doubt if others will preach it so publicly and so frequently."

"I don't think you feel you can keep me here in Amsterdam. Where are you sending me?"

"Initially you will be detained at Scheveningen." The prison at Scheveningen lay 24 miles south of Haarlem and just outside The Hague on the North Sea coast.

"Initially? It would seem Hitler would have me imprisoned farther from larger cities."

"Excellent deduction. Your next stop will be Amersfoort." The concentration camp there was intended to confine resistance fighters and criminals and lay only 15 miles northwest of Rhenen.

"Strange, isn't it?" Father Brandsma said.

"Strange? What is?"

"The way power and fear seem to be woven together so tightly. Hitler wields enormous military and political power yet fears a single priestly voice."

"I think what Hitler fears more than the words you speak," Schreieder said pensively, "are the thoughts behind them."

At Amersfoort Father Brandsma was forced to remove his flowing, ankle-length black cassock and white Roman collar. The sight of a detained priest could spark unrest among inmates. He was, though, permitted to keep his black-beaded rosary. He was glad he had given the small cross and chain to Raluca.

After the priest's arrest and imprisonment, Hitler wasted little time in signaling clearly that he would brook no outspoken critics in occupied Holland. Especially priests. The next 3,000 Jews to be arrested and deported from The Netherlands were all Jewish converts to Catholicism.

CHAPTER 52

If any Rhenen residents, apart from the Looten family, took note that the local occupation force had shrunk by two to 16, none commented publicly.

The soldiers themselves, of course, knew that Privates Billheimer and Melzer had disappeared. Sergeant Bohnenblust explained their unexpected absence by merely declaring that the privates had been disciplined for conduct unbecoming Wehrmacht troops. The newly promoted Bohnenblust's tone of voice – flat and hard – communicated effectively that questions would be unwelcome.

Mostly the remaining soldiers watched as Rhenen's people continued rebuilding their battered town center.

Lieutenant Kramer wrote daily reports that were necessarily short on substance but contributed to the spreading German reputation for meticulous record keeping. By war's end that penchant had resulted in records so voluminous and detailed that many senior Nazi officials were scurrying to destroy papers that they knew could put them in courtroom docks as war criminals.

Lieutenant Kramer didn't regard himself as obsessed with building and maintaining files, but one record keeping requirement he imposed would long live in the memories of Rhenenites who survived the war. Before the German invasion, Rhenen boasted a small, privately owned zoo. When the town was ordered evacuated on May 10, 1940, the zoo's owner managed to herd most of his animals aboard a craft that many locals joked was the second coming of the Noah's Ark – Rhine River style. Still, some of his animals were killed – for food – by both civilians and invading Germans.

Later, when Rhenen residents began returning, so did the former zoo inhabitants. They included a small flock of pigeons. Lieutenant Kramer had not witnessed a bird being used to carry messages but he was aware of the practice. He devised a record keeping system that, he hoped, would help thwart any nascent resistance movement. When a zoo pigeon reportedly died or was killed, the zoo's owner was required to deliver to Kramer one pigeon foot to prove that his birds weren't being used in resistance work.

Grudgingly, Rhenenites credited Kramer with creative thinking that headed off deadly reprisals and enabled townspeople to continue rebuilding their homes and businesses.

In Amsterdam Raluca and Alicia were part of a different kind of building effort. They were constructing relationships that they hoped would aid the city's resistance leaders. They knew the risks. Their bitterness toward the Germans, fed by invasions of Holland and Romania and deportations of Jews, grew more acidic after Father Brandsma's arrest.

Lieutenant Dettman groaned as his semen shot into Alicia's vagina. She took pleasure in orgasms and did her best to feign climax when Dettman failed to drive her there. He had become her steady client, and she didn't want to lose him. Dettman was gentle with her, but more important to Alicia his tongue was becoming ever looser as his affection for – and trust in – her continued increasing.

Alicia had another concern, one she shared with Raluca. Both prayed fervently that the possibility of pregnancy wouldn't become reality. Neither wanted to bear a child by a father they didn't love and perhaps couldn't identify. Neither wanted to give birth outside wedlock, and both sadly regarded marriage as a possibility as distant as the moon. Neither even wanted to think about abortion. Condoms were available but unreliable, and some clients including Dettman refused to use them.

Raluca also found herself with a regular client. Wehrmacht Major Juergen Henniger was first drawn to Raluca's dark beauty, slender torso and long legs. Eventually he began discerning her intellect. The combination proved powerfully magnetic. Raluca valued the relationship because it meant she was able to virtually eliminate liaisons with other customers. With Anna Clarbout's enthusiastic endorsement, Raluca charged the major a premium price.

In the spring of 1942 during post-coital whisperings with Dettman, Alicia learned of another Nazi policy change: Extended curfew hours. She knew she would be sharing this information with Raluca.

"You must miss your family and your home," Alicia murmured sympathetically.

"Yes, I would miss them even more if not for you. I have been here for more than two years but have been home only once."

"Where is your home?"

"Frankfurt. It is not far from here, but sometimes seems farther away than the stars in the sky."

"Will you be going home again soon?"

"I hope to receive another leave soon, but I am not sure. The longer curfew hours will mean more or longer shifts."

"When will the new hours begin?"

"The announcement will be made soon."

"Why make the hours longer?" She nuzzled against Dettman's neck.

"Longer curfews mean less time for the resistance to operate in darkness. It also probably means we will spend more time patrolling. That could mean delayed leaves or no leaves at all." A pause. "It also might mean I would not be able to see you as often."

Alicia, lying supine and staring up at the blackened ceiling, felt little fondness for Dettman but concluded she should express measured sympathy. "I hope you are able to return home soon." She chose not to feign sadness at the prospect of less frequent couplings.

Dettman had not quizzed Alicia on her personal history, but this conversation caused him to ask, "Is Amsterdam your birthplace?"

"No."

"Where then?"

"Far from here," she murmured. She then tried to stop that line of questioning by lying. "But I had an unhappy childhood and do not like to discuss it."

"I understand." Alicia's Dutch was sufficiently polished that Dettman hadn't previously considered the possibility that she was anything other than a native Netherlander. All Dutch were not blond and fair-skinned, he knew, but Alicia was darker than most. "Farther east?"

"Yes. A small farm."

Dettman's curiosity was aroused and he was sensing a need to know more. "A small farm where?"

Alicia was sensing that continued lying could lead to losing Dettman's trust. "In Romania."

"Romania! What brought you here?" he asked.

"The desire for a better life."

"Prostitution. Couldn't you have done that in Romania?"

"It is a poor country. Few men can afford to buy sex. And prostitution in Romania carries a stigma."

"In Germany as well," Dettman said. Romania, he mused, she is being very congenial for a woman from a country we Germans are controlling. Yet I don't sense hostility at all. But perhaps she resents me and hides it for my money. I wonder…No, she is but a whore. Whores are tolerated here but not respected. The resistance would not stoop to using whores. I am wasting my time on such thoughts. She is a whore, she is nice and I like screwing her. That is enough. Still…

"The Nazis are extending the curfew," Alicia confided to Raluca at their apartment. Raluca still was knitting a sweater for Joshua.

"What are the new hours?"

"Instead of beginning at midnight, the new curfew will start at eight. Instead of ending at four in the morning, it won't end until six."

"That is almost half a day. The Nazis must be getting worried about resistance activities."

"Are you going to tell Joshua?"

"He will want to know. So will the people on Corellistraat. They will want to caution their members. It would be like the Nazis to arrest curfew violators before announcing the new hours."

"I am glad we live so close to the brothel," Alicia said. "We should be able to sneak home during the curfew. If we couldn't, we would have to spend even more hours there."

"Has Lieutenant Dettman ever asked where you live?"

"No. Not yet. He did ask me where I am from. I am surprised he hasn't asked me more questions. Maybe he thinks I live at the brothel."

"Just as well."

"Yes. But if he asks, I don't think it would be wise to lie."

"You are very wise yourself, Alicia."

A spike in the number of sabotage acts throughout Holland before the new curfew hours were announced was causing Dettman to search his mind for an explanation. He was standing on a bridge spanning the Prinsengracht. Humidity was drenching the air. He tapped the bottom of a cigarette packet. He lifted the protruding cigarette to his lips and lit it. He inhaled deeply and exhaled slowly. Have resistance groups suddenly increased their membership? he asked himself. Have they accelerated training new recruits? Are they preparing for a major campaign? To Dettman the likely answer to all such questions seemed to be "No." What then is behind the uptick? The most plausible answer, he concluded, was leaked information. Dettman flicked ash from his cigarette into the canal. But leaks by whom? A disgruntled Gestapo officer? A member of Seyss-Inquart's civilian staff? To these questions, the same "No" seemingly applied. Then Dettman felt his cheeks flushing with acute embarrassment and his heart thumping with pulsing anxiety. He was recalling his boudoir disclosure to Alicia. If I am the source of the leak and she the conduit to the resistance, I would be mortified, and mortification could be the least of my consequences. If the leak was traced back to me through Alicia, I do not want to imagine Herr Rauter's reaction. Or Seyss-Inquart's. I need to watch what I say to Alicia. Or…Or perhaps I should confide something else of a sensitive nature and see what happens. Nothing, I hope. Absolutely nothing.

Alicia had listened to Raluca's description of Corellistraat and No. 6. Subsequently curiosity had been gnawing at her, and she decided to satisfy curiosity's appetite.

Raluca was food shopping. She had told Alicia that Corellistraat was only minutes away by bicycle. Alicia maneuvered their bike from the apartment building hallway outside into the mid-afternoon sunshine. She was feeling a building sense of excitement, much like a child anticipating her first look at Sinterklaas's largesse.

Alicia mounted the bike and began pedaling west and then south. She had an observer – Sergeant Walter Baemer. At Lieutenant Dettman's direction the sergeant was watching Alicia's movements, heretofore unremarkable. Baemer was standing on the northwest corner of Molensteeg and Oudezijds Achterburgwal. As with so many Amsterdam streets, Oudezijds Achterburgwal bore the name of the canal it paralleled. He flicked his cigarette butt to the pavement and hustled to a black staff car. He pulled open the passenger side front door, stepped inside and instructed the driver to follow Alicia at a discreet distance.

He needn't have been concerned with being detected. Alicia was lost in thought, seeing only what was in front of her. At Corellistraat she wheeled to her left and slowed. She saw No. 6 and its nondescript entrance. Immediately she sensed a heightened level of involvement. She hadn't met or even seen Kees de Heer but felt a satisfying bond taking hold.

Baemer's driver braked near the entrance to Corellistraat. The Gestapo sergeant watched Alicia taking in the street.

"I think the resistance will want to know about the new hours before they are announced," Raluca said to Joshua in her apartment. They were sitting on the settee. Raluca's lap was covered by blue and yellow yarn for the sweater she was making and her hands held the knitting needles.

"Agreed. They might have actions planned that would fall under the new curfew. Most of their work is done under the cover of darkness. These new hours could complicate their work, make it even riskier."

"Will you be going to Corellistraat?"

"I think I should."

"I would like to go with you." Before Joshua could reply, Raluca added hastily, "But I agree it is not wise for us to be seen together."

His head pivoted and he kissed her forehead. "If my faith in God was stronger, I would think he sent you as a gift."

She gazed up at his eyes. "So," she said mischievously, "I am but a gift of time and place."

"Quite right," he grinned, "and I am the grateful recipient. May it be so for a long time to come."

"But," Raluca added, turning somber, "not under these circumstances."

"What did she do after she got there?" Dettman asked Baemer.

"Stopped and looked around."

"Nothing more?"

"No, sir."

Dettman felt relief. He genuinely liked Alicia and wanted to continue using her to satisfy physical cravings. But he wasn't fond enough of the Romanian whore to chance risking his career or life. "Well," he said, "continue to shadow her and keep me posted."

"Yes, sir."

"Do we know anything particularly interesting about Corellistraat?"

"No, sir, but I will assign men to keep observing it."

CHAPTER 53

Tonight, Lieutenant Julius Dettman was musing as he lay beside Alicia in her brothel chamber, I will plant a seed. Not only in her vagina but in her ear. I detest doing this. But I need to be certain about her. I can't let my feelings for her ruin my career. Feelings, for a prostitute? Utterly ironic.

Alicia lightly caressed Dettman's bare chest with her left palm. "You have been awfully quiet tonight," she said softly. "I think your body is here, but your mind is not. Where is it?"

Dettman's reply was his right hand cupping Alicia's left breast. He rubbed the nipple twice and then slid his hand lower until it was brushing her thighs. In return she reached for his penis and began stroking. Soon Dettman was mounting her. Even then Alicia was sensing that the lieutenant had more on his mind than satisfying physical longing. She would not, she told herself, press him further. Not tonight. But if he should choose to reveal more, she would listen and respond gently.

After ejaculating Dettman was slow to disengage. He hovered above her. In the dim light Alicia could see that Dettman's eyes weren't focused on hers.

After withdrawing he rolled onto his back. He lay still and silent for long moments. When he began speaking his words were ones Alicia hadn't previously heard. "I am feeling pressure," Dettman said. "More and more."

"That doesn't sound good. What kind of pressure are you feeling?" She posed the question as delicately as she thought possible.

He answered with a question. "Do you have Jewish friends?"

"None. None of the girls here are Jews. I don't think I have done more than say hello to a Jew."

"Good."

"Why?"

"Because life is about to become more difficult for the Jews here in Holland."

"How?"

"They are going to be required to wear a yellow star on their clothing. The Star of David."

"I am sorry," Alicia said, her apology authentic. "What is a Star of David?"

"It is a symbol of Judaism."

"Why should Jews be forced to wear it?"

Dettman chose to reply with another question. "How can you tell if a person is a Jew?"

"I don't know that I can."

"Precisely. We want to be able to identify Jews easily."

"But why?"

"Nazi policy. We want Jews to feel isolated. Segregated. We want non-Jews to become used to seeing Jews as different and inferior."

Troubling questions immediately began bombarding Alicia's fertile mind, but she decided to ask – as innocently as possible – only one more. "Do you think they – the Jews – are inferior?"

"What I think doesn't matter. What does matter is what our fuhrer thinks."

Alicia couldn't recall ever seeing anything so clearly – at any time of day or night or in any place – as she now was seeing Julius Dettman in this dimly lit brothel chamber. This young lieutenant, Alicia was reflecting, seems so nice. Yet he is willing to put aside his own values, his own morals, and adopt the reality of a man who has shown himself to be a cousin of the devil – if not the devil himself.

"Do you think we should tell Joshua?" Alicia asked Raluca. She was referring to what she had learned from Dettman about the yellow stars. It was midmorning and they were sipping tea in their apartment. As was Raluca's custom when not knitting on the settee, she was sitting cross-legged on one of the violet chairs.

"I suppose so," Raluca replied.

"What about the people on Corellistraat?"

"I don't think Joshua would risk going there with this news. It doesn't seem like it would change any plans by the resistance. At least not right away."

"He might want to tell his Jewish friends," Alicia said. "Give them more time to decide if they will wear the stars or try to hide their Jewishness."

"Good thinking, my friend. I will get word to Joshua." Raluca fingered the cross Father Brandsma had given her. "And," she added, "I will be very careful about when and how I do it."

"Well," said Lieutenant Dettman to Sergeant Baemer, "I let slip to my Romanian whore about the yellow stars."

"Did she seem interested?"

"Not very. She asked a couple questions but then let the subject drop. Have you observed anything suspicious in her movements?"

"No. She has walked the short distance between the brothel and her apartment building but that's all. I haven't seen her speaking with anyone. Except her roommate and I have seen nothing suspicious in her comings and goings."

"Hmmm…We have learned that her roommate also is a whore and another Romanian. I think it best if you and your men continue the surveillance. Keep monitoring the movements and contacts of both whores." What Dettman was feeling but not revealing to Baemer was relief – relief that he wasn't compelled to order arresting Alicia for suspected resistance work.

"Do you plan to keep testing her?" Baemer asked.

"I think that would be best," Dettman replied. Actually, he thought that his reply was the only acceptable one. Any other answer would likely have Baemer doubting his ability to think objectively about his relationship with Alicia Domian.

By the end of May 1942 the Nazis had introduced a series of anti-Semitic measures. Jews in The Netherlands now were forbidden to ride bikes and trams. They couldn't enter hospitals and Jewish patients already in hospitals were forced to leave. Moreover Jewish physicians found it virtually impossible to obtain medicines. To compound Jews' isolation, they no longer were allowed to have telephones in their homes. Whereas young Jewish students already had been forbidden to attend public schools, older Jewish students now were forced to withdraw from universities.

Dettman had continued disclosing those pending sanctions to Alicia, but Baemer and his men had not detected anything to suggest she was betraying the lieutenant's trust.

Meanwhile, Holland's Jews were living in unrelenting, gut-wrenching fear. It wasn't only the mounting list of restrictions that was causing insomnia and – when sleep did come – nightmares. What was causing the most anxiety was the heightening prospect of arrest and deportation. Although arrests hadn't yet reached pandemic numbers, they were increasing. And an attendant reality of arrests and deportations was a central fact: No Jew arrested had been released.

One group of Netherlanders had so far escaped restrictions. As Raluca said to Joshua during one of their secretive trysts, "The Nazis have placed no restrictions on prostitutes. We are free to continue our trade as always. The Gestapo would have it no other way. Certainly Major Henniger wouldn't restrict me or Lieutenant Dettman Alicia. They pay us well and," Raluca smiled wryly, "they must be satisfied with the product."

During the same month in Haarlem, 12 miles west of Amsterdam, a smartly attired woman was carrying a brown suitcase. She was Jewish and was approaching the home of the ten Boom family. At the door the woman pressed the doorbell button.

Inside, Cornelia – known to family and friends as Corrie – heard the chimes, came to the door and pulled it open.

"Hello," said the woman.

"Hello," replied Corrie, looking at the woman's suitcase. "Are you lost and looking for directions?"

"My husband has already been arrested," the woman said tremulously, "and I have not heard from him since. Our son has gone into hiding with Gentile friends in the countryside." The woman, Corrie could see instantly, was frantic, terrified that she might be arrested, with detention amounting to a death warrant. "I am told you have Jewish friends," the woman continued. "Can you help me?"

"Come inside, dear," Corrie smiled. Thus began the harrowing saga of Corrie and her family as providers of haven to Jews, most of them strangers.

Corrie was born on April 15, 1892, in Amsterdam. At age 50 her visage was warm and open. Behind large lens glasses her eyes were bright with intelligence and kindness. Her smile was engaging. What wasn't obvious – at first to herself as well as others – were sizable measures of courage, resourcefulness and grit.

The ten Boom household included Corrie, her sister Betsie, older by seven years, and their father Casper. A married sister, Nollie, lived elsewhere in Haarlem, and a married brother, Willem, lived in Hilversam, some 15 miles southeast of Amsterdam and 24 miles southeast of Haarlem. Casper was a watchmaker who prided himself on the quality of his timepieces. For several years Betsie worked in Casper's shop as his bookkeeper. Later Corrie succeeded her and became a watchmaker herself. Betsie took over managing the household.

Corrie also kept busy outside the shop. For nearly 20 years she had been operating social clubs for girls ages 12 to 18. Activities included camping, hiking, gymnastics and music leavened with messages about God's love for all. She also had been running a club for mentally handicapped young people. They too heard Corrie's messages about God's love.

When the Jewish woman came seeking safety, the ten Booms already had taken in the owner of a nearby fur shop. In November 1941 German soldiers had barged into the shop, stolen all the furs, smashed windows and evicted the owner.

The ten Booms were, in fact, fond of Jews. Reasons: The bible characterized Jews as God's chosen people, Jesus was a Jew and Jews had authored much of the bible.

The ten Boom home was large with several spare rooms. Its location, however, was less than ideal as a hiding place for Jews; it stood only 100 yards from Haarlem's police station. That close proximity notwithstanding, the ten Booms were among Dutch families who had defied the Nazis' order to surrender radios.

When the Gestapo in Haarlem advanced the start of the curfew to 6 p.m., Corrie was compelled to close her girls clubs. That disappointment paled compared with a daunting challenge: Obtaining food sufficient to feed six Jews hiding on her home's upper floors.

To obtain food in occupied Holland people needed ration cards. While pondering this dilemma a name – Fred Koornstra – popped into Corrie's agile mind. His daughter had belonged to one of Corrie's girls clubs. More relevantly he worked in the Haarlem office where ration cards were issued.

Should I ask him for help? Corrie wondered. Could I trust him? Would he be willing to take on the risk?

That same evening Corrie decided to risk arrest. She began edging her way to Fred Koornstra's home. As much as possible she stayed close to buildings, ever watchful for occupation patrols. If caught she knew that lying would be futile. Detention would be certain, torture probable, transport to a concentration camp possible. On arriving at Koornstra's home, Corrie's heart felt as if it might explode through her dark blue shawl. Her right hand was trembling as it reached for the doorbell button. Koornstra came to the door, surprised to receive a visitor after curfew. He recognized Corrie and invited her inside.

If ever a man could be described as looking ordinary, it was Fred Koornstra. Short, balding and bespectacled, his paunch offered ample evidence that he was not stinting on securing ration cards for his own family.

Corrie explained her mission. "Will you help? Please?"

"Quite impossible," Koornstra replied with customary Dutch bluntness. "Those cards are counted over and over again. I have Gestapo looking over my shoulders every day. There is no way I could get away with taking any." Koornstra paused, his eyes closed in thought. "Unless," he said slowly, "there was a robbery. Now that I am thinking about it, perhaps I know the right man-"

"Do not tell me anymore," Corrie interrupted. "It wouldn't be safe. I should leave now."

A few days later Koornstra entered Casper ten Boom's watch shop. He now looked anything but ordinary. His left eye was blackened and his face badly bruised. He also was grinning slyly. Koornstra had, in fact, found the right man to inject realism into the feigned robbery. "Here," said Koornstra and he handed Corrie a fistful of ration cards.

CHAPTER 54

Near Amersfoort two Gestapo men escorted Father Brandsma from the concentration camp to a waiting train. No longer was he attired in his black shirt and trousers. Instead he now was wearing the black and white striped uniform of a prisoner. He still carried his rosary. Though having been underfed, his shoulders remained square, his back straight. His new voyage was about to begin. It would take him east. Destination: Dachau.

Queen Wilhelmina also was about to undertake a voyage, one that would take her west. On June 24, 1942, she was driven from her London home to Southampton. There she boarded a fast United States destroyer for America where she would be hosted by President Roosevelt. On arriving she first treated herself to a vacation. Her first stop was hardly a holiday mecca – Lee, Massachusetts. Then came stays in Boston, New York City and Albany, New York. Then on August 5 in Washington, D.C., she became the first queen to address Congress.

"Gentlemen," she began, "let me thank you for this opportunity to address you in this hallowed chamber of freedom and democracy. Freedom and democracy. Those two precious ideals are now difficult to find in many parts of the world, including my homeland. In your deliberations I beseech you to consider the plight of millions of innocent people – men, women, children – in Europe, Asia and Africa. They are, in fact, prisoners of the forces of evil. I know that America is reluctant to come to the aid of Europe. That is understandable. America did precisely that during the First World War, and that was barely more than twenty years ago.

"It almost seems presumptuous and unfair to ask the government and people of the United States for more assistance. But we in Europe now find ourselves trapped in the cold, heartless grip of Nazism. We need America's help if we are again to savor the fruits of freedom. We need…No, we desperately need modern weapons and equipment. We need medicine. We need doctors and nurses. Most of all we need your nation's fighting spirit as embodied in the hearts of your soldiers, sailors and airmen. I urge you to join forces with America's friends and help us defeat the monster who now has us in his jaws.

"Again, I thank you on behalf of beleaguered peoples, wherever they are suffering the oppression of Nazism, Fascism and Communism."

The only authorized long distance travel available to Dutch still in Holland was decidedly unpleasant. Arrests and deportations far to the east were increasing. They were forcing Jews to make life-altering choices. They could go into hiding and hope neither they nor their protectors would be caught. Or they could stay in their homes and hope they would be overlooked or go undetected as Jews.

The Franks – Otto, Edith, Margo and Anne – chose to go into hiding. Early in the morning of July 6, just as curfew was ending, the Franks made their way from Merwede Square to 263 Prinsengracht. Their new home was on the uppermost floor of Otto's place of business – and just a few doors away from Joshua's home. For their move the Franks dressed in layers. They carried small bags but no large suitcases that would draw attention from occupation troops or Dutch now serving the Nazis as informants. Otto's four employees on the ground floor were touched by his family's plight and were more than merely willing to support them.

The Follecks were slower to make a choice. So were their friends, the Sevels. Joshua was becoming increasingly worried about his Merwede Square friends and decided to visit them.

"You know the Nazis are arresting Jews every day," Joshua said in hushed tones in Samuel's shop, devoid of customers at this early morning hour.

"I know," Samuel replied. "But maybe if we stay long enough the arrests will stop. Surely the Nazis won't arrest every Jew."

Joshua knew his friend was mired in deep denial. "Samuel," he said sympathetically but firmly, "that is precisely what the Nazis will do. You know yourself Hitler wants to rid his Aryan empire of Jews. All Jews."

"We have so much here," Samuel said plaintively, alluding to the shop and the family's home above. "We would lose so much. And we already have fled once."

"Samuel, look around. You no longer see the Franks, right? Your kids are no longer playing with their kids, right?"

Samuel nodded. "But where would we go? We have no family in Holland. Our friends, most are Jews and those who aren't would probably fear hiding us. Who could blame them?"

Joshua drew in a deep breath. "You could stay with me."

"Joshua," Samuel said, clearly touched, "this is very nice of you. But-"

"But what? I live alone in a big house. Three floors. You and your family would have plenty of space, and you would have privacy."

"I...uh-"

"Good," Joshua said, brightening. "I'm glad that's settled. Now we must plan the move."

"Your home is large, but how will you hide us?"

"I've thought about that, and I believe I might have a solution. You get your family ready for the move, and I'll check into my idea."

"My friend, I don't know how to thank you for your generosity."

Joshua shook his head, shrugging off Samuel's gratitude. "You needn't thank me, not with words. Just letting me help will be thanks enough. Now, a word of caution. Do not tell anyone, not even the Sevels, that you are leaving. Be sure Miriam and your children understand this. Your closest and most trusted friend could say something accidentally and ruin your plans. And possibly cost your lives. After your move, I will get word to the Sevels that you have left and urge them to do the same."

On the morning of the move, Joshua arrived at Samuel's shop mere minutes after the curfew lifted. A light mist was falling. The streets were beginning to swarm with Amsterdammers heading to work.

The Follecks all had descended from their home to the shop. Like the Franks, they were dressed in layers and carried no large pieces of luggage. At Joshua's urging, Samuel and Miriam had prepared a list of small items that Joshua would retrieve later that day, filling his empty brown satchel that he would be carrying.

The family exited the shop. Samuel was last to leave. He locked the door and handed the key to Joshua.

The procession from Merwede Square north and east to Prinsengracht got underway. They were not wearing yellow stars. The family – Samuel, Miriam, Aaron, Mariah, Julia – were walking about 10 paces behind Joshua.

From a doorway to a hotel now serving as a barracks a uniformed Gestapo sergeant, Marcus Gunther, stepped in front of the family. He was smoking a cigarette. "Where are you going so early?"

"To work," replied Samuel. His armpits began springing leaks of anxiety-fueled perspiration.

"Your wife and children, do they work with you?"

"Yes, when needed."

Gunther decided to test his Gestapo-honed instincts. "I think you are lying. I think you are Jews – you look like Jews to me – and I think you are going into hiding."

Joshua looked back over his left shoulder and stopped.

"No, we are going to my shop," Samuel lied. "We need to arrive early to take inventory. It is very time-consuming."

At hearing Samuel's fabrication, Joshua turned and began edging back toward the group.

"You are going to my shop, so to speak," Gunther said, smirking. "We will do our own form of taking inventory." He dropped his cigarette butt to the pavement and ground it with his right boot.

Samuel's anxiety was giving way to a primitive surge of terror. His family was feeling the same cold dread. Interrogation and torture awaited; of that they all harbored no doubt. Could deportation be far behind?

"Excuse me, please," Joshua said amiably.

Gunther whirled to face the intruding voice's source. "You are not Jewish," he snapped. "I can see that. This is none of your business."

"Of course," Joshua said agreeably, "you are quite right. But I do have a question. Only one."

"Yes," Gunther growled, his voice abrasively impatient, "what is it?"

In a tone as flat as the Dutch countryside, Joshua asked, "Do you prefer guilders or marks?"

Gunther's eyes widened, then his jaws tightened with contempt. He verged on barking, You impudent twit. But Joshua's gambit and the way it was presented caused the sergeant to reconsider. "Marks go further."

"Agreed," Joshua smiled. "Let these people move along, and we need only settle on an amount."

Without turning to face the Follecks, Gunther extended his right arm and waved them forward. "Move along," he ordered testily, "and be quick about it." I can always track you down and arrest you later, he was thinking smugly.

The Follecks hesitated momentarily. They all grasped the jeopardy Joshua was risking on their behalf. Joshua nodded, slightly pivoting his head, and the Follecks began stepping around and past the sergeant. Mariah and Julia were holding hands, panic moistening their grip.

"Keep going," Joshua murmured. "Don't look back."

Silently the Follecks proceeded, slowly the first few paces, then a little faster.

"One hundred marks," Gunther said preemptively.

"A steep price," Joshua said in a tone devoid of emotion.

"Twenty marks per life seems a reasonable price," Gunther replied, his smirk again firmly in place and challenging Joshua to continue reining in his disdain.

"It still seems rather expensive for Jews."

"For Jews, yes," Gunther countered. He was enjoying this repartee with a fellow quick-witted Aryan. "But not for Jewish friends."

"Point made and taken," Joshua conceded readily. He unbuttoned his blue wool coat and with his right hand reached back to his hip. Gunther waited with self-satisfied expectancy to see Joshua's wallet – the quality of its leather and the thickness of its contents. Thick enough, Gunther was musing, and I might raise my price. Two hundred marks sounds better. When Joshua's hand emerged it wasn't holding a wallet. "What do you think of this price?" he asked coldly.

Gunther stared slack-jawed at the silencer-equipped .22-caliber gun. He gulped and his tongue flicked from his mouth gone suddenly dry. Frantically he tried to form and coherently speak a thought – one that might avoid what seemed unavoidable. Before the first word could reach Gunther's lips, Joshua shoved the silencer's snout against Gunther's midsection. Briefly, Joshua found himself thanking Kees de Heer for giving him the weapon. "Into that doorway," Joshua commanded through barely parted lips.

Gunther obliged, backing haltingly. Maybe I can survive, he thought fleetingly. No, he can't let me live. He knows that. I must act now. Gunther raised his hands to shoulder level, intent on pushing Joshua away and perhaps giving himself precious seconds to reach sanctuary inside the barracks.

Too late. As Gunther's arms began thrusting forward, Joshua squeezed the trigger. The bullet's force from point-blank range slammed Gunther against the door. His arms dropped to his sides, and his eyes rolled upward as he began slumping. Red began staining the center of his tunic. Joshua reached out with his left hand to support Gunther. He didn't want the sergeant falling onto the sidewalk. Still supporting Gunther with his left hand, Joshua secured the gun behind his belt. His right hand now freed, he felt for and found the doorknob. He twisted it and the door began opening. Gunther fell backward and inside.

Joshua inhaled, seemingly for the first time since the drama began unfolding. This will mean reprisals, he was thinking somberly. I've saved my friends' lives, at least for now. But other innocents will be killed in their place. Just lined up and shot. Joshua shook his head, trying to rid his mind of that grim reality. He backed onto the sidewalk and looked in the direction of the Folleck family. They were now about 80 yards ahead.

Samuel chanced looking back. Subtly, Joshua motioned to him to continue. He then began walking briskly, steadily closing the gap.

CHAPTER 55

July 26, 1942. Dachau. Evening roll call had been taken and prisoners had retired, filthy and still hungry, to their barracks. Father Brandsma, in his soiled black and white striped uniform lay wearily on his bunk. He closed his eyes and began his nightly recitation. He was praying for strength – both physical and spiritual.

Minutes later a Nazi guard arrived at his bedside. "Are you awake?" Father Brandsma's eyes opened. "Come with me," he said softly.

Father Brandsma said nothing. Slowly he swung his legs over the bunk's edge and stood.

The guard nodded toward the exit. Father Brandsma straightened his back and began walking toward the door. The guard was following.

The other prisoners were watching. They all knew Father Brandsma's reputation for fearlessly speaking out against Hitler. They found it easy to like and respect the modest Carmelite. Most were thinking what Father Brandsma was regarding as a certainty. He was about to be gassed or shot and then incinerated.

"Goodbye, Father," one of the prisoners, a Jew, murmured. "You are a good man."

"Bless you, Father," a second prisoner said quietly.

Father Brandsma nodded his gratitude.

Outside the barracks surprise awaited the priest. He expected to be ordered to a gas chamber or an execution spot favored by guards who fired bullets into prisoners' temples at point-blank range. Instead the guard said, "To the hospital."

Father Brandsma was puzzled. I am malnourished, he thought. We all are. But otherwise I am not sick. He summoned strength and began striding toward the camp hospital. Stay by my side, Lord. I ask nothing more.

Inside the hospital entrance, a white-frocked physician greeted Father Brandsma. He saw a look of compassion in the doctor's eyes, and he then could see clearly the coming denouement.

"This way," said the doctor.

Father Brandsma sighed and began walking down a narrow corridor. The doctor was at his side. The guard was following at a respectful distance.

At the doorway to a small examination room, the doctor said, "In there."

Father Brandsma stepped inside.

"Please. Lie down," said the doctor.

Father Brandsma complied silently.

The guard stood just inside the doorway.

The doctor reached down and pushed up the left sleeve of the priest's uniform. He then turned to a small table and readied a hypodermic cartridge. He inhaled and turned back to Father Brandsma. "There should be no pain."

Father Brandsma nodded slightly. "I understand."

"I am sorry."

"Just a moment, please."

"Of course." The doctor expected the priest to utter a prayer, perhaps silently. Instead Father Brandsma reached with both hands to his neck. Then, carefully, he lifted over his head the black-beaded rosary. His right hand held it out to the physician. "I want you to have it."

Raluca Johnescu was fingering the small cross Father Brandsma had given her. Head drooping, chest heaving, she was sobbing uncontrollably. Tears were running off her cheeks onto her dress. Alicia and Joshua were flanking her on the violet settee in the women's apartment. Each gently was holding and caressing one of Raluca's arms. They were saying nothing.

CHAPTER 56

October 1942. Governor Arthur Seyss-Inquart studied his stern visage in an office mirror. He straightened his black necktie. Then he stepped to his desk and penned an announcement: Henceforth all Jews in The Netherlands would be regarded as outlaws.

That same night in bed with Lieutenant Dettman, Alicia learned about the "final solution." Arrests and deportations would be accelerating. The Nazis' search for Jews would be intensifying. In confiding news to Alicia, Dettman expressed neither enthusiasm nor regret. To Alicia he appeared to regard this travesty as little more than the next step in the occupation business.

Later that morning at their apartment, Alicia shared the news with Raluca. "We should tell Joshua right away." He had confided to the women his decision to hide the Follecks. "And I think he will want to tell the people on Corellistraat."

"Joshua is away right now," Raluca said. "He didn't provide details, so I think it is resistance work. He said he would be gone for a few days."

Alicia slowly drew in a breath. She held it for a long moment before exhaling. "I am going to Corellistraat."

"Alicia-"

"I must. This is too important to keep from the resistance."

"Yes, but-"

"I will ride the bike and be back soon."

Sergeant Baemer and his driver followed Alicia in their black staff car. When she turned into Corellistraat, the car slowed long enough for Baemer to watch Alicia dismount the bike and slowly look up and down the street. What other reason would she have for returning to this street? Baemer asked himself. She is not whoring here. Baemer concluded he had seen enough to warrant arrest. "Go on," Baemer said to his driver.

"You know she can't be trusted," top cop Hanns Albin Rauter said to Lieutenant Dettman. "That is clear from your report."

"I know," said Dettman.

"You sound as though there is something personal between you and the woman." Dettman's lips pursed and his eyes closed momentarily. "If there is," Rauter said evenly, "I trust that duty will trump emotion."

The next morning several of Anna Clarbout's prostitutes were lounging in the brothel's ground floor sitting room. Their night's work ended, they were waiting for curfew to lift so that they could safely return to their homes. They were wearing shawls or sweaters to ward off the morning's autumn chill they knew would greet them when they stepped outside.

"I need to visit Oude Kerk," Raluca murmured.

"To pray for Father Brandsma?" Alicia asked.

Raluca nodded. "If there is a heaven I know he is there. If there is a God, I want him to hear my prayers in his house. I want him to hear me say this madness must end. Mass murder. How can a compassionate God tolerate such evil? I want to ask him that. I want an answer."

Alicia patted her friend's left shoulder. "If you get an answer, I will want to know."

"Of course."

"Do you expect one?"

"No."

Outside the brothel the women went their separate ways. While Raluca walked meditatively toward Oude Kerk, Alicia headed toward their Molensteeg apartment. At the building's entrance three Gestapo were clustered. They were chatting idly. Two were smoking cigarettes. The tobacco smoke caused Alicia to sniffle as she neared the men. "Excuse me," she said, stepping by them to pull open the door.

Sergeant Baemer flicked his burning cigarette to the pavement and grasped Alicia's left arm. "You are under arrest."

"We know you have connections to the resistance," Joseph Schreieder said so mildly that he almost sounded avuncular. "It will go better for you if you tell us what you know."

In his spartan office Alicia was sitting opposite his desk in an armless chair. Sergeant Baemer stood behind her. "You are mistaken," she said. "I am a prostitute. Nothing more."

Schreieder smiled. "I can see why men are drawn to you. You are very pretty. Young and pretty. And I sense that you are intelligent. Because you are, you cannot reasonably expect me to believe your denial, can you?"

"I work in a brothel. My home is nearby. That is my world."

"I know that your world is a little larger than that. I know that you are from Romania." At that revelation, Alicia felt the cold reality of betrayal. Lieutenant Dettman had given her up. "I also know that you know the way to Corellistraat. So you see," said Schreieder, "I know all that is necessary to conclude – reasonably – that you are more than a mere prostitute. Now, young woman, I suggest – suggest strongly – that you tell us more. Much more."

Alicia shook her head. "I cannot."

"Or will not."

"In this case," she said sharply, "I see that as a distinction without a difference."

"You are intelligent but you are also being foolish," said Schreieder. "I am trying to be kind to you. You have pluck. I will grant you that. But pluck will not serve your best interests. Names of others in the resistance will serve you much better."

"How was Father Brandsma served?"

"He died in a merciful fashion," Schreieder said. "Even though he was not repentant."

"Repentant? He was a hero."

"He was a traitor to the Reich. Now, give me names, and I shall see that you are spared."

Alicia gazed unblinkingly into Schreieder's eyes. Her head shook. "If I believed you, I could not betray others as I have been betrayed."

Raluca was worried. She had returned from Oude Kerk to their apartment. It wasn't like Alicia to leave their home so early in the day. The food shops weren't open yet. Ordinarily at this early hour she would be making tea. Raluca looked around the apartment for a note. Nothing. Where can you be?

The small interrogation chamber was even more barren than Schreieder's office. A small rectangular table. An armless unpadded metal chair on either side. One bare light bulb suspended from the ceiling. No windows. Along the far wall a bench with handcuffs, clubs, a whip, a box of matches, strips of white cloth. Above the bench and to its right, embedded in the wall, metal rings.

Three men accompanied Alicia into the chamber.

"Over there," Baemer said to Alicia. He pointed to the rings.

"No."

He slapped her left cheek with his leather-gloved right hand. She rocked back. He stepped toward her, spun her around and shoved hard. She went stumbling toward the far wall. Baemer's two men grabbed her arms and dragged her to the wall. They each picked up a pair of the handcuffs and connected Alicia to the wall rings. Wordlessly, using knives they began shredding and ripping off her clothes. Moments later she was wearing only her shoes.

"One final opportunity," said Baemer. "Give us the names and spare yourself."

Alicia remained silent. Seconds later she heard the whip's first crack. Nearly simultaneously she felt the first sting as the flailing leather tip bit into the flesh of her buttocks. Her scream erupted involuntarily and shrilly. More lashes followed. Blood began seeping from shredded skin. Sharp cries were mingling with moans. She remained wordless.

In the next minute Lieutenant Dettman entered the chamber. He was experiencing a welter of emotions – anger that Alicia might have been spying and helping the resistance, fear that her doing so could be jeopardizing his own well-being and enduring fondness for the woman who had shown him welcome tenderness. He willed himself to suppress those feelings. Without preamble he asked, "What about the other dark-haired whore? Another Romanian? What is her real name? Is she a spy too?"

Alicia didn't need to look back over her shoulder to know that the abrasive questioning was coming from her favorite – and favored – customer. Nor was she surprised, not given what she already had concluded about betrayal.

Baemer offered the whip to Dettman. He declined. "Take her down. Put her in a cell. Let her think about whether she wants more of this."

"Her clothes?" Baemer asked.

Dettman could see that Alicia's clothing had been reduced to rags. "She has no need of them."

Later that day Joshua returned to his home on Prinsengracht. He checked on the Follecks and then walked to Laura Reidel's apartment.

She listened while Joshua told her about giving haven to the Follecks. Her head shook and she smiled. "Joshua Bliss, I am many things but I am not surprised."

Joshua shrugged. "Right now the Follecks are living on my top floor. But they need a more secure hiding place. I need to build a wall. A false wall. Do you know anyone who could get the necessary materials to my house? Discreetly?"

"I do. They are shipping company people. They have an abiding hatred for the Nazis. I believe they can be trusted. They will know they are helping you, and they of course know about you and Meredith."

"Good." Joshua's relief was visible.

"Could you use some building help?"

"Yes. I don't have the skill to build the wall I have in mind. One that will be new but look old."

"I thought as much. The man who can get the materials has such skill. Give me the dimensions of the wall. His hatred for the Nazis runs deep. He lost a brother in the fighting in The Hague. That is why I am so certain we can trust him."

"Thank you."

"Can you stay a while?"

"Of course."

On his way from Laura's apartment to his home, Joshua used his and the Follecks' ration cards to buy food that he carried in his brown leather satchel. Bread, cheese, potatoes, apples, onions. He looked at his watch – the one given him in London by Kenneth Hixon – and decided he had time to reach the brothel before the curfew began.

When Raluca saw Joshua enter the sitting room, she sprang to her feet. She grabbed his right arm. "Come upstairs with me."

Her obvious urgency surprised Joshua. He glanced around the room and saw both sympathy and anxiety in the eyes of the other prostitutes.

Upstairs in Raluca's chamber they sat on the edge of the bed. He listened patiently while she told him about Alicia's unexplained absence. "I am fearing the worst," Raluca said. "Lieutenant Dettman has not been here to ask for her. So he must know where she is."

Joshua drew in a breath, nodded and rubbed his right palm across his bald head. He put his right arm across Raluca's shoulders and pulled her closer. You have every reason to be worried, he was thinking. "I will check with Corellistraat to learn what they know."

"Can you stay with me? Here? Tonight?"

Joshua looked at his watch. Curfew had begun. "Yes."

The next morning at Corellistraat the news confirmed Raluca's fear. Joshua then made his way from No. 6 to her apartment.

"What can we do?" Raluca asked plaintively. She knew Joshua's answer before he replied.

"Nothing," he said. "She has been interrogated" – and no doubt tortured, he was thinking. "If she has revealed anything, I think the Gestapo already would have arrested you." And possibly me, he was thinking.

Raluca's eyes welled. She, like Joshua, was thinking her friend had been tortured. Both had heard enough about Gestapo interrogation techniques to feel certain Alicia had not been spared harsh treatment. "I have never felt so helpless. I have never felt so far from home."

"You can't stay here – or in your apartment," Joshua said softly. "Sooner or later they – the Gestapo – will come for you."

"Do you still want me to come to your home? To live?"

"Immediately."

"But your friends are already living there."

"You will stay on the ground floor with me."

"But what if Alicia is released?"

"We will take her in."

"But you have said I shouldn't be seen with her."

"That's true. But I am constructing a hiding place. It should hold both of you."

"And your Jewish friends?"

"Yes." A pause. "I'm going to leave now for my home. Wait five minutes and follow me. When you arrive, the door will not be locked. Go inside and wait."

"What about my things?"

"Don't worry. Over the next few days, I will collect your things. Just give me the key and tell me what you want."

That evening at Joshua's home he led Raluca to the top floor to meet the Follecks. He introduced Raluca as a good friend who was in trouble with the Gestapo. He chose not to tell the family about Alicia. That would be, he concluded, a complication that would give the Follecks another reason to worry. Instead he chose to tell them about the wall he was having built. "It won't be pleasant if you have to hide behind it," Joshua said candidly.

"But if you think it best," Samuel said.

"I do. Raluca will be living downstairs with me. But she might have to hide with you."

Miriam shocked Raluca by stepping close and embracing her. "You will always be welcome to stay with us."

"They were so nice to me," Raluca murmured in wonderment. She was sitting with Joshua in his kitchen. They were sipping tea.

"Why shouldn't they be?"

"Because of." She stopped herself. "You haven't told them I am a prostitute."

"That's because you are not."

"What?"

"You were. Not anymore. You are my friend. That is all anyone needs to know."

"I can never thank you enough."

"Stop it," Joshua said with mock severity, smile barely visible but eyes flashing mirth. "Before you know it, you'll be making me out to be a saint. I am not that. I don't even want to pretend that."

"I want to go with you," Raluca said. It was nearing 10 a.m. "No, not all the way to my apartment. I know that would not be wise. But at least part of the way. I need to breathe some cold air."

Joshua nodded. "All right. As far as Oude Kerk. You can wait there or walk in another direction while I retrieve some of your things. I'll leave here first and you follow."

As Raluca was approaching Oude Kerk, she was surprised to see Joshua standing on the southern fringe of the church's surrounding plaza. She began gathering her wits to tease him when she halted, transfixed. In an instant she realized why Joshua was frozen in place.

Approaching the church from the east was a contingent of five troops – Sergeant Walter Baemer and four Gestapo privates. They were escorting a dark-haired woman. She was garbed in a coarse brown gown that appeared no more shapely than a burlap sack. Even from a distance Raluca could see that the woman had been abused. Her head drooped, her long dark hair was tangled and she was walking with a limp.

The men led her to the south side of Oude Kerk. Pedestrians were reacting variously. Some hurried past, scarcely looking at the bedraggled woman. Others, more curious and less fearful, stopped to observe.

The five men shepherded the woman to the church wall. Sergeant Baemer grasped her shoulders and turned her so that her back pressed against the wall. He placed his right hand beneath her chin and lifted. "Do you want a blindfold?"

"No."

"Alicia!" Raluca gasped nearly soundlessly.

Joshua saw Raluca and went rushing to her side. "Hush," Joshua muttered, barely audible.

"I need to go to her."

Joshua leaned toward Raluca, wrapped both arms around her, clasped his fingers and drew her close. "There is nothing we can do."

Baemer's four troops were armed with carbines. They formed a rank about 15 feet from Alicia. Baemer stepped to the side. He shouted no command. Instead he calmly directed his men. "Ready. Aim carefully at her chest. Fire."

Four triggers were squeezed simultaneously. Fire leaped from four muzzles. Four rounds slammed into Alicia's chest. She tilted quickly to her left and crumpled. Blood, seemingly black, began staining the coarse dark brown cloth.

Raluca pressed her face against Joshua's chest and wept. He could feel her knees buckling and held her firmly. His own eyes? He felt no tears leaking but did feel bitterness building. He gritted his teeth, attempting to suppress his outrage.

Another observer was standing on the eastern fringe of the plaza. Lieutenant Julius Dettman bowed his head. His shoulders slumped.

Most of the onlookers slowly dispersed. Joshua and Raluca were among the last to depart. They stayed until a Wehrmacht truck arrived to collect the corpse.

"Can you walk?" Joshua asked.

"Yes," Raluca replied. She sniffled and blinked.

"Go back to our home," Joshua murmured. "I will get some of your things. I am very sorry you had to see this."

Raluca turned away and began walking slowly. Joshua watched for a few seconds and then said, "Raluca." She stopped and looked back. "Our time will come," he said grimly.

CHAPTER 57

"I feel I should write to Alicia's parents but how?" Raluca was speaking to Joshua the next morning at his kitchen table. They had not eaten last night and still weren't feeling hungry. But Joshua had browned some bread in his oven, and they were chewing on it as they sipped tea.

"Your letter would probably be intercepted and censored," Joshua said. "The Nazis know Alicia was Romanian. Any letter addressed there would be likely to draw their attention. We've learned from de Heer that the Nazis arrested Alicia at the entrance to your apartment building. That likely means they know you were roommates. That you are Romanian. They could well be looking for you."

"What if I used our apartment as the return address?"

"It's not so much the return address as the Romanian address."

"I feel I must get word to her family. There must be a way."

"I can think of only one possibility that wouldn't put you or your friends in jeopardy. Write the letter but say nothing about the Nazis or

Alicia's arrest or execution. Just write that there was an accident and Alicia died. Say how sorry you are, but don't add that you will provide more details later. Maybe that kind of letter will get through."

Raluca nodded. "I will try to write such a letter."

Joshua stood to fetch paper and a pencil.

The next morning, just as curfew was lifting, Laura Reidel's friend arrived in front of Joshua's home. The man was driving a wagon drawn by an aging black horse. A tarpaulin was protecting the building materials from a steady drizzle. The man had counted on the wet weather as an ally. The man surveyed both sides of the Prinsengracht. In that weather at that early hour pedestrians were few. No occupation troops were in sight. Moments later Joshua was helping the driver unload the cargo and carry it inside. They went about their work wordlessly. When finished the men shook hands.

"Thank you," said Joshua. "You are?"

"Pieter." A pause. "That is all you need to know." Joshua nodded. "I am now going to drive my wagon back to my place of work. Later today I will return on foot to begin the work. It will be safer that way."

"Agreed," said Joshua. "I will be here."

That afternoon Sergeant Baemer came calling at Anna Clarbout's brothel. He asked for the owner, and one of the prostitutes tapped the door to Anna's apartment. On emerging and seeing a Gestapo uniform, Anna knew she must will herself to remain unflustered. She approached Baemer and smiled cordially. "How may I help you?"

"A Romanian whore works here. Where is she?" Baemer was being purposely abrupt, intending to shock and intimidate. He failed.

"You are referring to Alicia?"

"Alicia is dead, and I think you know that. The other one."

"I have not seen her in recent days," Anna said calmly. "Perhaps she has quit. My girls do that often," she lied. "But if you come back in a day or two, maybe she will be here. If she returns shall I tell her you called?"

Baemer sensed she was being truthful. An experienced madame would know the risk of lying to the Gestapo. "Yes, tell her Sergeant Baemer called and wants to talk about her friend. Your other Romanian." Baemer was certain Anna knew about the execution. Indeed, he felt certain word had spread to virtually everyone in central Amsterdam. That was the purpose of Alicia's public execution; demonstrate to Amsterdammers the folly of resisting the occupation.

The next morning Pieter was building the false wall with the Folleck family his rapt audience. Aaron volunteered to assist, and Pieter accepted the boy's offer. Two floors below Joshua was preparing to say goodbye to Raluca and leave for the bicycle shop when someone began rapping his front door.

"Who could that be?" he said to Raluca. She shrugged. "Wait in our bedroom," he said.

Joshua then stepped to the door and pulled it open. "Laura!"

"Good morning, Joshua. I would ask if you are surprised to see me," she grinned, eyes glistening, "but that much is clear. And no telephones anymore so…"

"Come in, please."

"Thank you. I can see you are leaving for work so I will be brief. No, I am not here to check on Pieter's workmanship. I have learned of another Jewish family – their name is Kaufmann – who need a hiding place. I am thinking you don't have space for more guests, but can you suggest someone?"

Joshua closed his eyes in thought. "Yes, I think so. From my contacts I have heard of a woman and her family who are hiding Jews. Do you think the Kaufmanns could manage to get to Haarlem?"

"I am not certain, but I think I could help with arrangements."

"Good. The person they want to connect with is Corrie ten Boom. Her father runs a watch-making and repair shop very near Haarlem's police station."

"Thank you, Joshua. The Kaufmanns will be most grateful – even if I do not reveal your name."

Joshua smiled. "Laura, you are one remarkable woman."

"Now that you say so," she grinned, "perhaps I am."

Later that day at the bicycle shop Joshua received his second surprise visitor.

"Can we talk?" Anna Clarbout asked.

"In our repair room," Joshua answered, motioning with his head toward the shop's rear. He shrugged as they passed Karel Veeder who crossed his hands in a waving motion as if saying I do not need to know.

Anna told Joshua about Baemer's visit and his asking for Raluca. In unhurried whispers, Anna and Joshua then devised a tentative strategy. Tentative because Joshua would need to discuss it with Raluca.

That evening while partaking of a simple supper of chicken soup, roasted potatoes, bread and tea, Joshua and Raluca discussed his conversation with Anna.

"This is risky for her," Raluca said somberly. "If she tells Baemer where he can meet me, he might press her for more information that could implicate you." Joshua shrugged. "Anna could be arrested. So could you. How many people in Amsterdam know you are American?"

"Not that many. You, Laura, Karel, Kees de Heer, Ernst Heldring, some of my former company colleagues."

"Because America is now at war with Germany, you are an enemy of the Reich. If the Gestapo even suspected you for any reason…"

Joshua sighed. "I know. But look, are you sure this is what you want to do? Absolutely sure?"

"Yes, Joshua. I must."

German U-boats were continuing their attacks on Netherlands-flagged vessels. On November 2, 1942, a U-boat torpedoed the Zaandam, another Holland-America Line ship, near the Brazilian coast. The attack killed 130 passengers and crew. The resulting headlines further inflamed enmity toward the Third Reich.

A day later Sergeant Baemer again visited the brothel.

"She has agreed to meet you," Anna told him, "but not here. She wants to discuss arrangements, including her price for services rendered, in a neutral setting. I am sure you can understand her thinking."

Fucking her no doubt would be pleasant, Baemer was thinking, and if that is what the whore and her madame think I want, that might be best. "Where?" the sergeant asked.

The first canal bridge after you walk onto Molensteeg."

"When?"

"Tomorrow night. Nine o'clock."

"After curfew?"

Anna shrugged. "You want her. Those are her conditions. I am sorry," which of course she wasn't.

In the blacked out night, Raluca could see the glowing orange tip of a cigarette on the canal bridge. She was watching that beacon from inside the entrance to her apartment building. She looked at Joshua's watch. Nine o'clock. She opened the door just wide enough to slip through. She walked steadily toward and onto the bridge. A westerly wind carried with it the salty tang of the North Sea.

Baemer, his eyes adjusted to the darkness, saw her form approaching. He inhaled his cigarette, flicked it into the canal and exhaled.

Raluca stopped about 30 inches away.

"I am surprised you agreed to meet me," Baemer said.

"I am a prostitute. I need money."

"Of course." A pause. "You know it was my squad that shot your friend."

"She was a prostitute," Raluca said in a voice as cold as the November night. "She made some poor choices. The resistance was her biggest."

"You are very understanding," Baemer said, clearly surprised by Raluca's forgiving attitude. "But I also think you a hard woman, a hard whore, and I understand you are willing to talk price."

"I am."

"What if I told you this meeting is not about fucking you?"

"Nothing you say would surprise me."

"Really?"

"Really."

"What if I told you I was going to arrest you? Would that surprise you?"

"Actually, I think the proper question is what would surprise you?"

"A witty whore. And, like your friend, Romanian. At least I now know that all Romanian whores aren't stupid. Well, I don't think anything you say would surprise me either."

"What if I told you that you are about to die?"

"What?"

"I believe you heard the woman," the voice from behind Baemer intoned flatly.

Baemer, startled, whirled. Before he could focus on the face that went with the voice he felt a small, hard surface pressing against his overcoat, chest high. "Who are you?"

"Someone you should wish you never met." Without waiting for a reply, Joshua angled the snout of the silencer slightly upward and squeezed the gun's trigger. He watched Baemer's eyes widen. Joshua reached up with his left hand to stifle any cry that might emerge from the sergeant's gaping mouth.

Raluca reached out, placing her hands in Baemer's armpits. "What do you think of my price?" she hissed lowly.

Joshua lowered his left hand and grasped Baemer's right lapel.

"Is he dead?" Raluca whispered.

Joshua squeezed the trigger a second time. "If he's not he soon will be." He jammed the gun in his jacket pocket. Then he grasped the other lapel. He and Raluca then turned Baemer so that his corpse was facing the bridge rail. "Okay," said Joshua, "now."

Together they let Baemer's torso droop over the rail. Then they reached for his legs, lifted and watched his body fall the approximate 18 feet into the cold water.

They looked in all directions. Apparently no one else was violating curfew, heard the virtually silent shots or the ensuing splash.

"Reprisals?" Raluca asked.

"If the Nazis find his body, yes."

"If?"

"With his uniform, shoes and heavy coat, perhaps his body will remain submerged, at least until it decomposes. Or maybe it will catch on something. Or be carried out to sea. We can only hope."

"There is one other thing we can hope for," Raluca said.

"Yes?"

"Justice for Lieutenant Dettman."

Raluca and Joshua spent the rest of the night in the Molensteeg apartment. They did not make love. Instead they lay side by side, awake, thinking their own thoughts, wishing their own wishes.

In the morning Raluca departed first, walking to Joshua's home. Joshua walked directly to the bicycle shop. Though unshaven, he was confident Karel Veeder would restrain his curiosity.

CHAPTER 58

Christmas was approaching. "This holiday season doesn't promise to be a very happy one," Joshua said. It was a Sunday morning in mid-December, and he and Raluca were lying in bed. "But I am glad you are with me."

Raluca turned to face Joshua. Smiling warmly, she said, "You are my gift. I do not know if I have ever had a better one."

Joshua edged closer and brushed her lips with his. "Do you know what? I have an idea."

"You always seem to have ideas," she teased.

"One of my more endearing traits, don't you agree?"

"How could I possibly disagree?"

Silence consumed the next two minutes. Raluca was first to break it. "Joshua, do you feel guilty?"

"About what?"

"Anything."

Joshua sighed, exhaling slowly. "Sometimes I still feel guilty about bringing Meredith here. She encouraged me, but I still feel some guilt."

"I feel the same way about Alicia. Only she didn't encourage me. I persuaded her."

Joshua stroked Raluca's left shoulder and upper arm. "I think we both will always feel some guilt about Meredith and Alicia. How many people can say they have no regrets? Not many. Most who say that, they are in denial. Or they are thinking shallowly – no deeper than a puddle after a summer shower."

"Do you feel guilty about anything else, Joshua?"

"Do you mean the killing?"

"Yes."

"Before the war began, I never envisioned myself killing anyone for any reason. I had never even killed an animal. I never had any desire to. But the killing I've done, the German soldiers in The Hague, that Gestapo sergeant who was threatening the Follecks, Baemer. No, I feel not a whit of guilt. I'm not saying I feel proud of everything, but not guilty. How about you?"

"The same. Not proud, but not guilty." A pause. "What about your new idea, Joshua?"

"This was a marvelous idea," Laura said exultantly.

"I simply could not agree more," Miriam Folleck said cheerily.

"Well," said Joshua, "I just thought my closest friends all should meet and get to know each other. The holidays seemed like a good time."

In addition to Laura and Miriam, Joshua had gathered with him in his living room the rest of the Folleck family, Raluca and Karel Veeder. He had confided his plan to Karel and in doing so had told him no resentment would follow a declined invitation. After all, Joshua had said, accepting could carry risk. Laura had heard much the same from Joshua. She and Karel both thanked Joshua for this thoughtfulness, and both accepted his invitation immediately.

Laura, Karel, Raluca and Joshua shopped separately, using ration cards to acquire the makings for this special party. Laura's cards included some purloined by what she termed "special contacts" to buy extra flour, eggs and sugar. And now, as the party was beginning Laura said, "Raluca, this is your home. Would you like to help me bake the cake?"

Raluca smiled affectionately. "Yes, I would. And thank you for asking me."

"Come, dear, let's go to your kitchen and get started."

"I have cigars," Joshua said, motioning toward Samuel and Karel. "Should we light up after eating?"

"Absolutely," Karel replied.

"I also have wine," Joshua said. "Miriam, Samuel, would it be all right with you if I poured a little for your children?"

Samuel and Miriam looked at each other, smiled fondly and nodded slightly, and then eyed their children. Aaron was now 16, Mariah 14 and Julia 11. They were watching their parents expectantly. "If they would like some, that would be fine with us. After all, they have endured much and this is a very special occasion." The children were beaming.

"Karel," Joshua said, "would you help me get the glasses and do the pouring honors?"

"My privilege and pleasure," he replied happily.

In Rhenen the wooden shoes that once had held Christmas gifts for Karin and Catherina Looten now were being worn daily. New leather shoes had become virtually impossible to find. Some children's parents had removed the shoes' wooden tops and replaced them with ropes or leather straps fashioned from harnesses and bridles attached to the wooden bottoms.

Rhenen's rebuilding campaign had stalled. The Germans now were confiscating all building materials for military uses. Fortunately for Rhenen residents, most homes and shops had been rebuilt largely if not entirely.

The party at Joshua's home went on for hours. After the cake had been baked and cooled and was ready for cutting, Raluca decided to tease Joshua. "You can see," she said mischievously to the assemblage, "that he has grown a mustache. And not a silly little thing like Hitler has crawling above his lips. But a manly, bushy one." Joshua was blushing but grinning. "Now, do we think he can eat a slice of this cake without getting icing on his mustache?" Everyone laughed, Joshua too. "Don't you think it contrasts nicely with his shiny head?" More laughter.

"Why did you grow a mustache?' Julia asked.

Joshua shrugged. "To look older."

"To avoid roundups of able-bodied men?" Aaron asked.

"Exactly," Joshua said.

"I think it accomplishes his purpose," Laura said. "He looks older but also, shall we say? more distinguished."

Isala Van Dyck had decided to go for a Sunday afternoon stroll. Joshua's party was ending as Isala turned into Prinsengracht. She saw two people exiting Joshua's home. How ironic, thought Isala, I know both of them. She had recognized Laura Reidel and Karel Veeder. Instinctively, Isala stepped into the recessed doorway of a bakery. Why should I care if they see me? she asked herself. The answer came quickly and clearly. It is because I am wondering who lives there. The only link I can think of between those two people is Joshua Bliss.

Isala returned to Prinsengracht again on Monday morning. From a doorway on the far side of the canal she watched Joshua leave his home. So that is where he lives. Probably going to the bicycle shop. As Isala was about to depart, she saw the door to Joshua's house opening again. A dark-haired woman stepped outside. She was coatless. Isala watched the woman stretching her arms upward and breathing deeply. Then the woman turned and entered the house. Who was that? Isala wondered. I have this vague feeling I have seen her before. She looks like she could be Jewish. Is Mr. Bliss hiding her? Could he be hiding others? It's a big house. Should I report him now or watch for more evidence? If I report him and I am wrong, I will lose credibility – and possibly business.

"Pieter did a very good job on the wall," said Samuel. "Let's hope we never have to use it."

"Moving the old cupboard in front of this wall was a creative touch," Miriam observed. "And cutting out a small door in the back and a matching opening in the wall was genius."

Pieter's false wall had created a 30-inch space between it and the outside wall. To enter that space, Folleck family members would have to lower themselves to their hands and knees and crawl into the cupboard and through the small door at its rear. No more than a minute or minute and a half would be needed for all five Follecks to complete the short passage. They felt confident they could scoot behind the false wall before any police could enter the house and climb to the third floor. Survival, they agreed, would provide incentive for fast action. Leaving nothing to chance, they rehearsed several times.

"Aaron, you did very well as Pieter's helper," Samuel said.

"I enjoyed helping him," replied Aaron, "and watching and learning. I might like becoming a carpenter."

"Perhaps some day you can," Samuel smiled. "It is an old and honorable profession."

Isala Van Dyck continued her surveillance. Two routines she observed heightened her suspicions about Joshua. She watched the dark-haired woman leave Joshua's house daily for short walks to food shops and bakeries. Would only two people eat so much? On Joshua's daily walks to the bicycle shop he carried a brown leather satchel. Why would someone working in such a shop carry a satchel? His lunch? But why a large satchel for a light lunch? Unless he was using it to carry larger quantities of food home after work. Additional surveillance confirmed for Isala that Joshua was buying food regularly. Still, she had seen no sign of anyone besides the dark-haired woman and Joshua living in his home. Perhaps, she thought, the best way to learn if he is harboring Jews would be to confront him when he is least expecting it. Catch him off guard.

Holland's largest concentration of Jews lived in Amsterdam. In February 1943 efforts to locate, arrest and deport them intensified when civilian governor Arthur Seyss-Inquart summoned Wim Henneicke to his office in the Binnenhof in The Hague.

Henneicke, a Dutch collaborator, had been working in the investigative division of the Central Bureau for Jewish Emigration in Amsterdam.

"If we are to rid The Netherlands of Jews within an acceptable time frame," Seyss-Inquart began, "we will have to accelerate the process."

"What do you mean by acceptable?" Henneicke asked. "Our efforts so far have been quite productive."

"They have," Seyss-Inquart agreed. "But we should see every last Jew removed from The Netherlands by the end of this year. If not from the entire country, then at least from Amsterdam."

"An ambitious goal. What do you propose?"

"I want you to consider the following organization. Form a small but highly motivated group. Their sole priority will be tracking down and arresting Jews in Amsterdam. I will pay a bounty – seven and a half guilders – for each Jew your group captures. There need be nothing secretive about your work. Employ local informants as you deem appropriate."

"I will report to you?"

"Directly and frequently."

On returning to Amsterdam, Henneicke's first recruit was Willem Briede. They formed a core group numbering 18 virulent anti-Semites and went to work with gusto. The 7.50 guilder bounty equaled approximately $47.50.

As word of their initiative spread, Joshua debated with himself a central question: Should I inform the Follecks? He sought Raluca's counsel. Her advice: Notify the family.

Joshua followed her recommendation and was glad he had done so. Said Samuel: "We would rather know the dangers than not." Miriam and their children echoed his sentiment.

During the next seven months Henneicke's group, dubbed the Henneicke Column, would hunt and arrest some 9,000 Jews. Most of them were deported to the Westerbork concentration camp in eastern Holland and from there to the death camp at Sobibor.

Isala had decided on what she regarded as the ideal time and place to confront Joshua with her suspicions. By now she knew his usual route from the bicycle shop to his home. From the shop on Barndestaag he would turn south for a block then west onto Sint Jansstraase. She would wait for him on the bridge that spanned one of the canals, the Oudezijds Achterburqual. February darkness would cloak her, adding to his surprise. With curfew about to descend she didn't expect to see many pedestrians. But if witnesses were nearby Isala would postpone her ambush to the next day.

Late in the afternoon on the first Thursday in February, Isala positioned herself on the bridge. She was eager to spring her trap on unsuspecting prey. Not only because she wanted to aid the fuhrer in his drive to cleanse the Reich of Jewry but also because she had learned of Joshua's condescension toward her and her beliefs. Yes, she admitted to herself, vengeance was central to her motivation.

She saw Joshua approaching the eastern end of the bridge. She had grown accustomed to his strong gait, his mustache and stocking cap. She waited until Joshua was within 20 feet and said, "Mr. Bliss, you are right on time."

"What? Who are? – Oh, it's you, Mrs. Van Dyck."

"Indeed, you remember."

"What are you doing here? And what do you mean by right on time?"

This is not the time for casual chitchat, Isala reminded herself. If I want to spring the trap, I must act now. "I believe you have a Jewess living in your house. The dark-haired woman. That as you know violates regulations. Jews are outlaws. I also have good reason to believe you are sheltering other Jews."

Joshua was startled. He hesitated before replying, his eyes narrowing, his mind racing.

"You see," Isala continued triumphantly, "you do not deny it."

"He doesn't have to," the disembodied voice said coldly.

Isala spun to see the source of the unfamiliar voice. "You," she spluttered. "What are you doing here?"

"Do you think you are the only woman who knows how to spy?" Raluca asked rhetorically. "You have been watching me, so I decided to return the favor."

"Your...Your friend is hiding you, a Jew. It is wrong."

In an instant Raluca chose not to correct Isala's wrongful conclusion. Instead, responding to her own protective instincts, she stepped around Isala, positioning herself between the woman and Joshua. Raluca's eyes narrowed, not in suspicion but in certainty. Her gloved hands rested against her slender hips. "You would inform on Joshua."

"I would," Isala snapped, "inform on him and you, the Jew – or Jews – he is hiding. If I had any doubts before, this meeting has erased them."

Joshua was watching this exchange with rapidly increasing admiration for Raluca. At the moment, he could see, she was beyond feeling fear. His own initial fright was ebbing rapidly.

"I see," Raluca replied. "Yes, I see the situation very clearly. Do you know the Nazis have murdered my best friend? My sister in fact if not in blood."

"But still another Jewess, no doubt," Isala snarled.

Raluca's lips pursed tightly. Her eyes penetrated Isala's. Then she raised her hands, grasped Isala's fur coat near the neck and turned her so that her back pressed against the bridge railing.

"Just what do you think you are doing?" Isala hissed. "Remove your filthy Jew hands from me." She tried – unsuccessfully – to bat Raluca's hands away.

"For the record," Raluca reconsidered, "I am not a Jew. I just thought you should know that."

"You are lying," Isala said contemptuously. "Jews lie."

"The devil must inhabit your heart." With that, Raluca, feeling strength previously unknown to her, pushed hard against Isala's shoulders. Her blond hair flew wide as she rocked back, teetering on her stylish high-heeled black shoes. She was struggling to regain her balance when Raluca shoved hard again. Isala's eyes widened in terror. She plunged screaming into the canal's murky water. She disappeared head first beneath the surface. Then her face rose above the surface once and she gasped. Her fur-covered arms flailed momentarily and then she submerged. Raluca and Joshua watched silently, without remorse.

Raluca was fingering the cross that Father Brandsma had given her. "Joshua," she said quietly after they had returned to his house, "I want to take a bath. I need to feel clean."

"Go ahead and fill the tub," he responded. "I'll soap your back."

CHAPTER 59

The summons was unexpected but not unwelcome. A brief, whispered exchange with a stranger at the bicycle shop instructed Joshua to report to No. 6 Corellistraat after work.

The stranger who had come to the shop was waiting outside the entrance to No. 6. He was smoking a cigarette and was bundled against the raw mid-February air. He nodded to Joshua, said nothing and, cigarette still burning, led him to Kees de Heer's office.

"Sit down, Mr. Bliss," de Heer said, motioning to one of the visitor chairs. He reached across his desk, offering his right hand. Joshua accepted it and they shook briefly but firmly.

"It's good to see you again," Joshua said.

"Yes, well, we all are looking forward to the day when we will not need to see each other again."

"Agreed."

"You know," said de Heer, "you are a lucky man."

"Oh?"

"Sergeant Baemer's body was never found by the Gestapo, occupation troops or the local police."

"But it was found by someone. Is that what you are saying?"

"One of our friends spotted it," said de Heer. "He was able to arrange permanent disposal. Discreetly."

"I see."

"The police did find the corpse of a blond woman in a canal. There was no sign of violence, no gunshot or stab wounds, so their conclusion was suicide."

"You disagree?"

"She was a collaborator. An informant. We knew that. Do you know who I am talking about?"

"I might."

"Yes. I thought you might. As I said, you have been lucky, but effective. That is the reason you are here this evening. I have a mission for you to undertake. It is particularly hazardous."

"Aren't they all these days?"

"Well put. And the reprisals are deeply distressing. Reprehensible. But we remain committed to doing what we can to complicate the Nazi occupation. To punish collaborators. To disrupt their work. To distract them. To cause them to re-deploy resources. In short to do what we can to free our nation and our people. You are not Dutch, but we believe you to be a fellow patriot."

"What is the mission?"

"I think it might go better if I join you," Raluca said. "He won't be expecting a woman."

"We should tell the Follecks," said Joshua. "Not the details. But if we don't return I want them to know the house is theirs for as long as they need it."

That night both Joshua and Raluca dressed in dark-colored clothing – browns and blues. Raluca pulled her long brown hair into a bun and donned a blue stocking cap.

Their first danger was exiting the house after curfew had begun. If intercepted they could offer no plausible excuse. Arrest and detention seemed a certainty. Snow was falling steadily, and that was a reason for choosing tonight. They regarded snow as a safeguard; fewer police and occupation troops would be patrolling vigilantly. More would be sheltering – against orders. But they were human. The occupation was nearly three years old, and a natural consequence was complacency. Wet snow on a raw Netherlands night was reason enough to seek comfort.

Joshua and Raluca proceeded cautiously, making their way east. Snow was collecting on their caps and coats.

Soon they were approaching P. Jacobszstraase. They turned onto the street and in the distance saw the tips of two burning cigarettes. They stopped and waited patiently until the pair of orange glows disappeared. Raluca's nose dripped and she dabbed the mucous with her gloved hand. They began moving again and soon were standing before the fashionable house that was central to their mission. They looked at each other and nodded. Raluca's right hand pushed the doorbell button. A minute later the door opened.

"Are you Mr. Seyffardt?" Raluca asked pleasantly. She smiled engagingly.

"Yes," said Hendrik Seyffardt, the former lieutenant general and head of the Dutch Army's general staff who had collaborated by recruiting Dutch for the SS and its occupation of Poland. "Who are you and what are you doing out after curfew?

"Us?" Raluca answered, shivering. "We are people who want to meet a traitor."

Seyffardt instantly felt the onset of anxiety. "I am no traitor," he stammered. He peered into Raluca's dark eyes. "You are a Jewess."

"Tonight," she said calmly, "I wish I was. This could be more satisfying."

"Leave!" Seyffardt commanded, his voice sounding less authoritative than he would have preferred. He began to close the door.

Joshua, standing behind Raluca's left, quickly reached forward and braced his left arm against the door.

In the next instant Seyffardt found himself staring in shock at the snout of a silencer-equipped .22-caliber gun in Joshua's right hand.

Joshua jammed the muzzle against Seyffardt's midsection and squeezed the trigger. As Seyffardt stumbled backward, Joshua fired again.

Seyffardt lay supine, groaning, hands clasping his abdomen. Blood was seeping from between his fingers. He began coughing.

Joshua and Raluca stood over him. They were content to let Seyffardt die slowly. Minutes passed. Seyffardt continued coughing and his eyes kept blinking.

"Should I put an end to his suffering?" Joshua asked.

"Why? Let him live long enough to reflect on the suffering he has caused others. His fellow Dutch."

Joshua nodded and he and Raluca left and began making their way back to Prinsengracht. The falling snow had not abated.

Seyffardt died the following day, and the luck of the resistance began thinning. Hanns Albin Rauter immediately ordered the execution of 50 Dutch hostages. He also ordered punitive raids on Dutch universities to beat disaffected students and dissuade them from joining the resistance. Rauter thought, correctly, that prime recruitment candidates for the resistance were the nation's educated youth. They were passionate and more easily aroused by injustice than older citizens.

Still, resistance actions continued undiminished. So did Nazi reprisals. In May, Seyss-Inquart ordered numerous summary court-martials – followed by immediate executions – of suspected partisans. He also imposed collective fines on Dutch banks and affluent individuals that totaled 18 million guilders.

CHAPTER 60

Almost precisely a year after Queen Wilhelmina arrived in the United States on June 24, 1942, she again found herself making a transatlantic crossing. Her arrival date in 1943: June 29. This time, though, her destination was Ottawa, Canada. And this voyage didn't have her traveling as a monarch but as a grandmother. She was journeying to attend the christening of her first granddaughter, Princess Margriet.

For a while Wilhelmina remained in Ottawa with her daughter, Princess Juliana and the baby. She was relishing her status as a grandparent before returning to England. "I wish I could stay long enough to properly spoil the child," mother told daughter.

During this same period in The Netherlands, the Nazis were rounding up more young men, Gentiles and well as Jews, for transport to Germany where they would work as slave laborers. As a result, thousands of young Dutchmen quickly went into hiding with family members and friends. Many of the men sought refuge in rural areas where the Nazi presence was much less pervasive.

In Amsterdam Joshua Bliss added to his disguise. In addition to his lush, drooping mustache, when outside he began walking more slowly and slightly hunched. He did, in fact, appear considerably older than his 28 years. Occupation troops and police, he could see, paid scant attention to a shuffling old man who was clearly unfit for hard labor of any sort.

Someone close to Joshua and four years older who appeared to be the picture of robust youth and endless energy was his brother. Paul and his hometown friend Ken Milligan had arrived in England as members of the 82nd Airborne Division. They had been given a rousing send-off in New York by a crowd of thousands. Most didn't know any of the soldiers. It didn't matter. One elderly man had pressed on Paul a box of R.G. Dun cigars and a bottle of well-aged Jameson's Scotch, a brand established in 1887.

Paul shook the man's hand and graciously accepted the gifts. "I lost a son on Guadalcanal," the man murmured unsteadily. Paul felt a lump forming in his throat. He pulled his hand away from the man, stepped back and snapped off a crisp salute. Then he slipped the cigars and Scotch inside his duffel bag and went striding up the gangway.

The throng stood alongside the transports, waving and cheering. Paul and Ken waved in return, grateful for the boisterous show of support.

Days later upon arriving in Southampton, Paul, Ken and every other GI was given a small, thin booklet measuring four by six inches and containing 40 pages. Its cover was brown with black lettering and its title was *Instructions for American Servicemen in Britain 1942*. It was a catechism of sorts, instructing young Americans on British culture and what the British regarded as appropriate – and inappropriate – words and behavior. Ironically since being published more than a year before, the booklet had become and remained a best seller among the British. The explanation proved simple to divine. For millions of British the booklet provided them with their first outside-in perspective on their culture and habits.

The airborne training was challenging, especially for 31-year-old Paul Bliss. "With all these kids around," he told Ken, "I feel like their older brother, if not their father. I now understand why the skills of so many major league baseball players begin fading after they reach thirty. The muscles, joints and hand-eye coordination of a twenty-year-old are like a race car. Plenty of horsepower and speed. But add ten years and our bodies are shifting to lower and slower gears."

While Paul and Ken and their 82nd Airborne comrades were training to spearhead a liberation, in Amsterdam Wim Henneicke's henchmen were busily tracking down Jews in hiding. To the dismay of many Dutch, the predators' chief hunting aides were fellow Dutch serving as informants.

An ominous knock at the door of a Gentile merchant family on Ververstraase brought capture to Guillermo Sevel and his family. The informants were their hosts who had been growing increasingly nervous about harboring "outlaw" Jews. The better part of valor, the hosts concluded, was betraying the Sevels. Guillermo, Juanita, Jorge and Maribel were sent to Westerbork in eastern Holland.

Joshua soon learned about the Sevels' arrest and deportation.

"I know you told me that you preferred to learn bad news," Joshua was saying to the Follecks. "I am afraid that's what I have today." He sighed, his lips pursed and eyes closed.

"Go ahead," said Samuel.

"The Sevels. They've been arrested and sent away."

Miriam gasped, then shuddered. Julia covered her eyes and wept. Mariah hugged her younger sister.

"Did someone inform on them?" Aaron asked.

Joshua nodded. "Their host family. They were afraid they might be found out and arrested."

Aaron inhaled deeply. "Shit," he hissed.

"Aaron!" Miriam cried.

"Sorry, Mother, but those people deserve to be arrested. They took in the Sevels and then turned on them. They are as bad as the Nazis. Despicable."

"Were they punished?" Samuel asked.

"Not so far as I know," Joshua replied. "And I doubt if they will be."

"Right," Aaron said bitterly, "the Nazis wouldn't want to chill anyone else from betraying Jews."

"That is enough," Miriam said more calmly.

"No, Mother, it is not. I am tired of hiding. Maybe I should leave here and join the resistance. I would like nothing more than to fight the Nazis."

Joshua looked questioningly at Samuel who nodded.

"I understand, Aaron." What Joshua was about to say next he knew would be hypocritical but nonetheless believed it appropriate. "But if you did manage to join the resistance and if you were captured, you could endanger everyone in this house."

Only Samuel among the Follecks sensed strongly that Joshua was active in the resistance, and he didn't intend to share that line of thinking with his son.

"I suppose you are right, Mr. Bliss," Aaron conceded. "But I can barely stand being penned up like this. Hens in a chicken coop have more freedom than we do."

"Aaron," Joshua said pensively, "if I gave you a journal, would you write down all your thoughts and feelings?"

Aaron hesitated. Miriam gazed expectantly at her son. "Yes, yes I would."

"After the war, after you are free again, perhaps your journal could become a book."

"Do you really think so?"

"If you write honestly and daily, yes I do."

"All right, Mr. Bliss, I will try it."

"Good."

"Aaron," Miriam said in a motherly tone, "you are forgetting something."

"Yes, of course. Thank you, Mr. Bliss."

On October 1 Arthur Seyss-Inquart again summoned Wim Henneicke to his office. His work had proved sufficiently fruitful for Seyss-Inquart to order the Henneicke Column disbanded. He was pleased with the column's results but was tiring of paying cash bounties that had totaled more than 67,000 guilders. His decision did not, though, end the daily hunt for Jews.

Afterward Henneicke gathered Willem Briede and the rest of his 18-man group in his office. "Governor Seyss-Inquart has told me to disband our column. Our job was well done. Some Jews remain in hiding, but we have cleansed our nation of about nine thousand of that subhuman trash.

On our own we will keep looking for the ones still in hiding. We don't need the bounty as motivation."

Joshua told the Follecks about Seyss-Inquart's decision to disband the Henneicke Column but didn't characterize it as good news. Doing so would have been disingenuous and given the family a false sense of lessened jeopardy.

He did, however, have good news to report. Corellistraat's connections to intelligence sources indicated a huge and growing buildup of Allied forces in England that was seen as the prelude to a major invasion of continental Europe.

"But when will they come?" Aaron asked impatiently. "We already have been prisoners in our own country for three and a half years. I haven't taken a breath of fresh air for sixteen months."

"I can only tell you this, Aaron," said Joshua. "We have a saying in America. Hang in there. I know it sounds crude but the meaning is anything but. We mean it to say better times will come. And I do believe they will."

"Why?" said Aaron, his dark eyes blazing cynicism. "Why should I hang in there? The Germans have a stranglehold on our nation and most of Europe."

Joshua shook his head. "Their grip is loosening, Aaron. Allied troops have taken control of North Africa. Our American General Patton has led the way to victory in Sicily and Italy will be next. The Russians have regrouped and will be pressing the Germans from the East. I'll bet there are plenty of Nazis who can see defeat coming. Perhaps even Hitler. What gives me even greater hope is the buildup of Allied forces in England. Aaron, if you had visited America and seen her industrial might, you would understand my optimism. Plus, American spirit itself is a powerful force – as I believe Hitler already is learning."

Part of that industrial might and spirit was being displayed in British skies that November. Paul Bliss and Ken Milligan were in the middle of the "stick" or line of 18 men standing, waiting to jump from the roaring Douglas C-47 transport. It would be their first practice jump.

"You ready, Paul?" Ken asked.

"As ready as my thirty-two-year-old body will ever be."

The red "ready light" flashed on, and Paul felt a tightening in his gut. The plane's starboard side door was open, and the rush of cold air signaled the first time Paul would willingly put 800 feet of nothing between his feet and earth. "I've jumped from the hayloft," he said wryly to Ken, "and that was exciting. But I've got a sneaking feeling this will be a tad more thrilling than a barnyard leap."

Ken balled his right hand into a fist and punched his friend on his right shoulder. "Hey," he joked, "when we get back to the States, you might take this up for a living. You know, barnstorm around the Midwest. Wing-walk and parachute."

The green "go light" flashed on and one by one in quick succession, fully equipped and armed paratroopers began their leaps. When Paul's turn came, his hands reached out and grasped the edges of the doorway. In the next instant he propelled himself outward. The rush of air and the jolt that accompanied the billowing of his parachute were far greater than when he had leaped, tethered, from the practice tower. "I'll be a son of a gun," he murmured to himself, "this is okay. Just maybe volunteering airborne was the right choice after all."

Choice was something long departed from the lives of the Sevel family. Later in November they and other inmates at Westerbork were herded from the camp to a waiting train. They were forced up ramps into windowless cars. Once packed as tightly as salted sardines in a can, guards pulled shut and locked the doors. The train's whistle sounded. Steel wheels began struggling for traction on steel rails.

Guillermo, Juanita, Jorge and Maribel were squeezed together in a corner. They wanted to believe what the Nazis had told them, that they would be resettled in the East. But it was hard to believe liars and criminals. The Sevels hadn't been told their destination. It was Sobibor, and they wouldn't be heard from again.

CHAPTER 61

In early 1944 Joseph Stalin still was badgering Franklin Roosevelt and Winston Churchill to launch an invasion of Western Europe. He was demanding creation of a second major front – Stalin didn't count as such the Allied push into Italy – to lessen German resolve against his Russian troops who were successfully counterpunching their way west toward the Vistula River and Warsaw.

Roosevelt and Churchill, with status reports in hand from Allied Supreme Commander Dwight Eisenhower, continued putting Stalin off. While the invasion of France and the Low Countries was nearing, Eisenhower persuaded Roosevelt and Churchill that rushing ahead prematurely with a cross-Channel armada would lead to disaster. Absent securing a strong beachhead followed quickly by a determined push inland, Eisenhower foresaw his troops being shoved back into the sea. That vision caused him more than one bout of insomnia.

The Allies' meticulous preparations, including rehearsals of beach assaults and airdrops, translated into continuing tensions – and worse – for occupied peoples.

On Wednesday, February 28, 1944, in Haarlem, Corrie ten Boom wasn't bookkeeping or helping Casper assemble fine watches. She was at home, sick in bed with the flu. Late that morning at the sound of the doorbell, Corrie dragged herself from bed. When she opened the door, a stranger said he urgently needed money to save some Jews from arrest. In short, he wanted money to bribe Nazi officials. Corrie felt uneasy about the request coming from someone outside her circle of 80 fellow Gentiles who were helping Jews. But she didn't want to risk jeopardizing the desperate. She handed cash to the stranger and returned to her bed.

Shortly afterward, about 12:30 p.m., the stranger returned. He was leading a group of Gestapo and another Dutch Nazi collaborator. They didn't sound the doorbell. Instead they burst into the house, intending to surprise all within, including Jews.

Corrie again rose from her bed. She entered the living room where the Gestapo were surrounding a group that included Betsie, Nollie, Willem and several Dutch who were unaware of hidden Jews in the house.

A Gestapo officer shoved Corrie into a small parlor and closed the door. "Where are the Jews?" he snarled.

"There are no Jews here," Corrie replied calmly. "There never have been." Corrie detested lying but regarded that a lesser evil than condemning Jews to death camps.

"Let me ask again," the Nazi growled. "Where are you hiding Jews?"

"Let me say again, there are no Jews here."

"Where is the secret room?"

"There is no such room."

The officer's gloved right hand slapped Corrie hard – once, twice, a third time. She could feel warm blood trickling from her lower lip. She felt faint but managed to remain standing.

The Nazi grabbed her and pulled her back to the living room. There he grasped Betsie's left arm and pulled her into the parlor. Behind the closed door, the process was repeated. Betsie proved strong. She endured a worse beating. When she was shoved back into the living room, her face was bruised and bleeding from cuts to her lips and left eyebrow.

Meanwhile other Gestapo men were searching the house for the secret room. After 30 minutes they called off the hunt.

"All right," their leader said, "take this lot to police headquarters and station a guard outside this house. If anyone is here they will starve to death."

At the nearby police station, Corrie and her fellow detainees were ordered to sit on the floor of a large room. After a while, a Dutch policeman named Rolf entered. "Let's have it quiet in here," he barked. "Toilets are outside at the rear. You may go out one at a time under escort." Rolf then shocked Corrie's brother Willem when he bent down and whispered, "You can tear up any papers you don't want the police to see and flush them down the toilet."

Willem promptly began passing on Rolf's advice to the others.

At the ten Boom home, Casper customarily had led his daughters in prayer. That night in the police station, he followed his custom for all the detainees.

The next day the group was trucked 24 miles south to Scheveningen Prison near The Hague. Each prisoner was put in a separate cell. That was the last time the ten Boom children would see their father. Soon after arriving all were released except Casper, Corrie and Betsie. Ten days later Casper died. The sisters would not learn of his death until weeks later.

Corrie and Betsie remained in separate cells for four months. Their guards – or warders – were women. They were strict and said little to

Corrie and Betsie. Still, news made its way into the women's cellblock where the prisoners called it out from cell to cell.

One day a surprise greeted Corrie. A warder opened her cell door, said, "Here," and tossed in a parcel. Its source: Corrie's married sister Nollie, now back in Haarlem. The parcel contained biscuits, a needle and thread and a bright red towel. Corrie noticed something odd about the postage stamp. It was affixed crookedly. She peeled it off and beneath saw writing: *All the watches left in the cupboard are safe.* Corrie's eyes brightened and her spirits lifted. The message was code. Its meaning: The Jews who had been hiding behind a false wall in the ten Boom home had escaped.

On a chilly morning in early May, Corrie was released from her cell and escorted to a hearing where her ultimate fate would be decided. She was expecting torture, at the least another beating. She prayed for strength.

"Sit down," a Gestapo officer said, not unkindly.

Lord Jesus, Corrie prayed silently, you were once questioned too. Please tell me what to say and do.

"I would like to help you," the officer said smoothly. "But you must tell me everything."

"I have already told the Gestapo all that I know."

The officer shook his head. "Tell me how you obtained the extra ration cards."

"They were brought to our shop. That is all I know," she lied.

The questioning went on for an hour. "Tell me about your other activities," the officer said, still calm.

"You mean my girls clubs and my work for the mentally ill." The officer didn't cut her off so Corrie eagerly discussed the details of her prewar work.

"But that is a waste of time," the officer spluttered, not in anger but incredulity.

"Oh no, not at all," Corrie replied, smiling warmly. "God loves everyone, even the weak and feeble. You see, the bible tells us that God looks at things very differently from you and me."

The repeated references to God and his goodness caused the officer's jaws to clench. "That will be enough for today," he said, bristling.

The next day the hearing continued, with the same officer. He surprised Corrie by asking her more about her beliefs. Lowering his voice, he confided that he had family in Germany and was worried about their safety amidst frequent Allied bombing raids.

Following the hearing the officer did what he could do to ease Corrie's incarceration. One example: He allowed her to see family members to learn the content of Casper's will. But he lacked authority to release Corrie and Betsie.

CHAPTER 62

Paul Bliss and Ken Milligan were pathfinders. As such they were among members of a contingent of 82nd and 101st Airborne and British 6th Airborne Divisions who would be jumping into Normandy behind the invasion beaches just after midnight on June 6. Their mission: Mark out landing zones that would be used by their comrades from those divisions beginning about an hour later. Their other principal job was to take and hold bridges and close off possible German escape routes from the Normandy beaches – dubbed Utah, Gold, Juno, Sword and Omaha.

As the lead aircraft in the fleet of husky transports passed over the French coast, word came from the cockpits to make ready. Paul and Ken and their 16 fellow pathfinders stood. A sergeant pulled open the fuselage door, and cold, bracing air came streaming inside. The men reached up to fasten their static lines to the overhead anchor cable that ran the length of the troop compartment. The familiar red "ready light" flashed on.

"Ready, Paul?" Ken asked.

"Too late to pick up a pitchfork and start throwing hay." He and Ken both laughed, a trifle nervously.

"Well, Paul, France isn't Holland, but this will put you closer to Josh in how long now?"

"About four and a half years since I last saw him. He did get a letter off to us after Holland fell in May of forty." What Paul didn't voice but what he and Ken were experiencing was lingering doubt about whether Joshua was still alive.

"Okay," shouted the plane's jumpmaster over the droning engines and roaring wind, "let's go."

The green "go light" flashed on and within seconds Paul and Ken were heaving themselves into the opaque void of a blacked out French night.

D-Day hadn't come quite soon enough for Corrie and Betsie. A few days later they were transferred to the Vught political concentration camp in eastern Holland. While waiting to board the train, Corrie saw Betsie and began pushing her way through the throng of prisoners. They hugged, thrilled to be together.

At Vught, instead of small, barren cells, the new prisoners were housed in barracks. They were promptly assigned jobs. For Corrie it was working in a Phillips factory that was making radios for Luftwaffe planes. It was delicate work and the Nazis assigned women to it because of their smaller, more dexterous fingers. Corrie and other prisoners used that dexterity to make sure finished radios were flawed. Not without risk.

If detected making assembly mistakes, the women endured brutal punishments. Severe beatings were common and numerous women were shot.

Buoying every inmate's spirits was learning that the Allied forces had invaded France.

As with other heads of European governments-in-exile, Queen Wilhelmina was overjoyed by the Allies' successful cross-Channel invasion. Her euphoria didn't last long. A few days after the landings, she was enjoying a change of scenery at a country house near South Mimms, a village just north of London. She was sitting at a desk, contentedly writing a letter to Juliana. In the distance she could hear the drone of approaching planes but paid them little attention and no heed. Then, without warning, a falling bomb exploded just outside the home. Queen Wilhelmina screamed, a reflexive reaction, as an interior wall of her office blew in and surrounding windows shattered, sending glass shards knifing through the room. The blast wave sent her chair to the floor and she found herself lying prone.

In the next few moments she began hearing cries for help. She did a quick inspection of herself. She saw no blood and could feel no pain from bones that might have broken. Slowly she got to her feet. She shook her head and blinked.

An instant later a Dutch soldier burst into the office. "Your majesty," he gasped, "are you all right?"

"I think so."

The soldier rushed to Wilhelmina and steadied her. Then he righted the desk chair. "Please, sit down. I will be right back with medical attention."

"Others are injured," the queen said shakily. "I can hear them. See that they are tended to first." The soldier hesitated. "Please do so. I shall last until the others are treated."

The blast killed two of her guards and wounded several.

Back in London, Churchill learned of the blast and casualties and phoned to ask Wilhelmina's condition. She laughed off his concern. "Hitler can't kill me in Holland or England. Each day he shows himself to be more incompetent – and more unhinged."

Churchill chortled. "If you feel up to it," he said, "I would like to bring you to 10 Downing Street. There is something I would like to present you."

A day later at the prime minister's residence just off Whitehall, Churchill inducted Queen Wilhelmina into the Order of the Garter. The honor was established in 1348 by King Edward III and had become England's highest award for chivalry. More relevantly in modern times, the honor signified a close bond between presenter and recipient. Origins of the term "garter" were fuzzy, but one possibility held that it referred to a small strap used to keep armor in place. Wilhelmina was only the second woman to be so recognized.

"Thank you very much, Prime Minister. I accept this great honor on behalf of the Dutch people."

"Winston from hence forward. I would prefer you address me much less formally."

"I believe I can bring myself to oblige – Winston. Wilhelmina here."

"A pair of W's," the prime minister grinned.

"We do make a stout pair, don't we, Winston? Of both frame and heart."

Churchill growled a chuckle. "There is something else I would like to show you."

"Oh?"

"It's my real office." Churchill was referring to his office and living quarters in a network of 21 rooms carved from below central London's Whitehall area. The Cabinet War Rooms they were called. They included a map room, a telephone center, broadcasting equipment, meeting rooms and others including Churchill's combination bedroom and office. Soundproofing and a ventilation system were installed. Their construction had begun in 1938 and become operational on August 27, 1939 – only four days before Germany invaded Poland, igniting World War II in Europe. Overlaying the rooms were five feet of concrete dubbed "the slab." By war's end Churchill had convened 115 cabinet meetings in the complex.

The Allied push into France began slowly, agonizingly so. Normandy's centuries-old hedgerows rendered progress arduous and perilous. The activation of General George Patton's 3rd Army on August 1 signaled a breakthrough and the sprint to Paris was underway.

Three days later in Amsterdam betrayal again was the order of the day. Early in the morning of August 4, police led by SS Staff Sergeant Karl Silberbauer barged into the hiding place of the Frank family. They were ordered down and outside 263 Prinsengracht. Before descending the stairs, Otto Frank showed Silberbauer marks made on a wall to record Anne's growth during 25 months in hiding. "You have a lovely daughter," said Silberbauer.

Joshua and Raluca watched forlornly as Otto, Miriam, Margot and Anne were taken away to Gestapo headquarters. Later they would be sent to Bergen-Belsen. Joshua knew he should tell the Follecks.

On August 15 the Allies succeeded with an amphibious landing on France's south coast between Cannes and Toulon. On August 19, as American and French forces neared Paris from the west, excitement – and organized resistance – were nearing a crescendo.

"It is easy enough," Queen Wilhelmina told Churchill, "to imagine the joy when our Dutch cities are liberated."

On August 25 in Paris' western suburbs, Patton's forces stepped aside to enable the French 2nd Armored Division, driving American-built Sherman tanks, to go rumbling into central Paris. General Charles DeGaulle who, like Wilhelmina, had until recently been based in England, led the way.

"With DeGaulle's nose," Wilhelmina observed wryly to Churchill, "the rest of him must always go first. He is patriotic, but his ego would not squeeze inside Notre Dame." Not that Wilhelmina and Churchill were lacking strong egos; they simply did a better job of managing theirs.

Dolle Dinsdag or "mad Tuesday." That's how September 5, 1944, would be remembered in The Netherlands. Allied forces were pushing north through Belgium and nearing Holland's border. Jubilant Dutch threw aside pent-up emotion and broke into riotous celebration. Orange was seen everywhere. Liberation seemed imminent.

"Are my prayers being answered?" Raluca asked Joshua. They were standing in front of their home on Prinsengracht.

"Let's hope God has answered his phone."

In Rhenen the Lootens joined townspeople in celebrating, albeit nervously. They would welcome Allied troops but were worried that the push north would again level their small city.

Lieutenant Karl Kramer and Sergeant Klaus Bohnenblust watched the celebrants – enviously. More than anything they wanted the war to end and to return to their homes in Freiburg and Frankfurt.

The celebration turned out to be premature for most Dutch. German forces were defending stoutly, and the Allied drive stalled in northern

Belgium. Certainly Dolle Dinsdag proved premature for Corrie and Betsie ten Boom. At the Vught camp German guards lined up and methodically shot 700 male prisoners. The remaining men and the women were loaded onto cattle trucks and driven to the Ravensbruck concentration camp in Germany. Some 35,000 women were imprisoned there. Corrie and Betsie found conditions deplorable to verging on inhumane.

Inside the barbed wire, their first two nights they were forced to try sleeping outside – in drenching rain. Then they were ordered into a barracks designed to hold 400 inmates. They were among 1,400 crammed inside. Their straw mattresses were swarming with bedbugs and fleas.

Corrie tried to remain cheerful. "When I am not praying," she smilingly told Betsie, "I am scratching."

Each morning at 4:30 the 35,000 women were assembled for roll call. If anyone was missing, the count was repeated. The process consumed hours. Women who slumped were whipped.

The women were slave laborers. Corrie and Betsie were put to work loading sheets of steel onto carts, pushing the carts to nearby destinations and unloading them.

One afternoon a guard screamed at Betsie. "You are not working hard enough or fast enough!" She knew better than to protest and braced herself for what she knew was coming. Nearly simultaneously she heard the guard's whip crack and felt the lash stinging her flagging back.

Corrie struggled to refrain from rushing to her sister's aid. Doing so would mean harsher punishment for both, perhaps execution.

The women's strength waned and weight dropped as they subsisted on a daily diet of potatoes, thin soups and black bread. The weakest women were put aboard trucks and taken to the gas chambers. Their corpses were cremated in the camp's ovens.

Corrie refused to give in to the daily temptation to let death embrace her and end her suffering. She had smuggled a small bible into the camp and began leading a group of women in nightly prayer. Her assemblage began growing. The guards did not intervene. Not because of kindness but because of their dread of the army of fleas.

"Dear Lord," Corrie proclaimed, "we thank you for our fleas."

In his small Rhenen barracks room Karl Kramer picked up paper and pencil and began writing to his wife.

Dear Hannah,

I cannot believe we can hope to occupy these conquered countries forever. It is too much to ask of any army. Sooner or later citizens will rebel en masse. History teaches that lesson. Will we have the will to fight? Will our army, so weary of occupation and homesick, refuse to shoot the occupied? Many of them we have come to regard as friends.

Of course as you no doubt are thinking, all of that could become moot. The Allies are winning everywhere and Germany's defeat is inevitable. What will it mean for us? I believe in large part our fate will depend on who conquers us. If it is the Russians I fear the worst. Everything I have been hearing tells me they are behaving like feral dogs. If it is the Americans or British, I have hope for humane treatment. That is the most we can hope for. Frankly it is all we deserve. May God show mercy on us.

I hope fervently that this letter makes it by the censors and finds you and Thierry in the best of health.

Your loving husband,
Karl

CHAPTER 63

Operation Market Garden was British General Bernard Montgomery's brainstorm. Employ the largest Allied airdrop of the war. From bases in England, use 1,500 planes and gliders to parachute 30,000 men and equipment from the 82nd and 101st Airbornes, British 1st Airborne and 1st Independent Polish Airborne Brigade. Their mission: Behind German lines, along a 60-mile stretch of a single road running north through The Netherlands, capture and hold a series of bridges, the last at Arnhem over the Rhine. Driving up that road would be 5,000 men and tanks from British XXX Corps' armor and infantry units.

Montgomery's vision: Cross the bridge at Arnhem in force, sweep east into Germany's industrial heartland, bypass the more difficult terrain to the south and end the war before Christmas.

"It is a bold stroke that General Montgomery is planning," Queen Wilhelmina said to Churchill. "If it succeeds my country will be eternally grateful to him."

"Montgomery has his doubters," Churchill acknowledged. "Let us hope their doubts are misplaced."

In fact Allied Supreme Commander Eisenhower was uneasy with Montgomery's plan. British General Roy Urquhart and Polish General Stanislaw Sosabowski were openly dubious, and General Patton detested it. Montgomery, with his dogged personality, prevailed with Eisenhower's imprimatur, and Operation Market Garden was scheduled to get underway on Sunday, September 17 – or only seven days after Montgomery first briefed his senior officers.

That short week was one reason Montgomery's plan had skeptics. Another was his belief that XXX Corps could penetrate those 60 miles in 48 hours. A third were landing zones near Arnhem that would require the dropped parachutists to cover several miles on the ground just to reach the bridge.

Each airborne unit was assigned a sector. Paul Bliss, Ken Milligan and others in the 82nd Airborne would be jumping into open fields between Grave and Nijmegen, two towns in the operation's northern sector or about 12 miles south of Arnhem – and only 12 miles southeast of Rhenen.

As the air armada neared landing zones, green "go lights" flashed on, and men began leaping into the void. From a jump altitude of only 700 feet, Ken made it to earth in one, unscathed piece. Paul didn't. During his descent he heard a scream. A second later he realized it had erupted from his mouth. A German bullet had pierced his left side. The pain was searing. He looked down and felt a stab of panic. His chute was drifting away from the landing zone. Moments later he crashed into a tree, its leaves beginning to take on autumn coloring. As his body dropped through branches, he felt consciousness slipping away.

Ken looked around for Paul. Seeing no sign of his buddy, Ken began moving with his comrades toward their goals – the bridges at Grave and Nijmegen.

An hour later Paul awoke to silence. The large stains on his field jacket and trousers told him that he had lost considerable blood. His tongue flicked dry lips. Well, he was thinking, let's see if I can get out of this harness without tumbling through branches to the ground. I'd really rather not break my neck. He reached for his knife and groaned from the effort. He unsheathed the knife and began cutting through parachute cords. He groaned again, the exertion testing his weakened body.

Paul heard muffled noises and peered into the thick stand of forest bordering the northeast side of the drop zone. A group of men armed with German machine pistols gingerly began emerging from the trees and stepping onto the fringe of the drop zone. Bright white among autumn's gold caught the attention of their leader. He led his men to the base of the tree and looked up.

Joshua looked down, not sure what he was seeing. Friendlies or unfriendlies?

"American?" the leader asked.

No use lying, Paul thought. "Yes."

"Good. We will help you down."

Two men handed their machine pistols to colleagues and climbed into the tree. They saw the blood stains, carefully freed Paul from his harness and gently lowered him into upraised arms waiting below. He was feeling relief.

On the ground Paul said, "Thank you. Do you mind if I sit? My legs feel like spaghetti."

The leader smiled and nodded, and two of his men eased Paul to a sitting position.

"We will see that you receive medical attention," said the leader.

"Thanks again. Who are you?"

"Resistance. Dutch."

Paul felt another wave of relief. I'm not in enemy hands, he thought, at least not yet. "What is your name?"

"Marcus. Marcus Schott." He smiled. "When I am not doing resistance work, I am a farmer."

Paul could see that a farmer's big hands accompanied Marcus' big smile. "That's what I was before joining the Army," said Paul, "a farmer."

"Well," Marcus grinned, "we farmers must be loyal to each other."

"Where are the other American soldiers?" Paul asked. "I'm with the 82nd Airborne."

"Your friends should be closing in on Grave and Nigmegen. They will meet German opposition. Strong opposition."

"We were told German defenses in this area would be light. Second-rate troops."

"You were misinformed."

In fact, British General Frederick "Boy" Browning was so intent on furthering Montgomery's grand plan that he had pooh-poohed low-level aerial reconnaissance photos that clearly showed a heavy concentration of German armor near Arnhem. He had deemed them dummy tanks and nonoperational.

"I will keep my fingers crossed," Paul said solemnly.

"Fingers crossed?" Marcus asked.

"An American expression. It means I am wishing them good luck."

"I understand."

"Speaking of luck, I have a brother here."

"In The Netherlands?" Marcus asked, visibly puzzled.

"Yes. In Amsterdam. He had bad luck. His wife died on the Simon Bolivar. He decided to stay in Amsterdam. I wonder what kind of luck he has had since then."

"You have not heard from him?"

"Not for more than four years."

"What is his name? What is your name?"

"Mine is Paul Bliss. My brother is Joshua.."

"Joshua Bliss?"

"Yes."

Marcus grinned again. "I think his luck has been good."

"How can you be sure?"

"He is one of us."

Paul's eyes widened in surprise. "Josh is with the resistance?"

"For a long time. I have not met him, but I know that he has accepted dangerous work. We respect him."

"Can you get me to him?"

"Most American soldiers," Marcus replied, eyes twinkling, "want to escape to England or Switzerland."

"Yes," Paul said, enjoying Marcus' wit, "but most American soldiers don't have a brother who is one of you."

"Touche. We are quite able to smuggle people into and out of Amsterdam. Are you willing to be a sack of grain?"

"I am a farmer, so being a sack of grain should come naturally."

As Operation Market Garden moved into its second day, the Germans were scrambling not only to hold cities and bridges but to mount counterattacks.

Hanns Albin Rauter, the Nazis' senior cop in The Netherlands, received an unexpected summons. He was handed command of a Wehrmacht combat unit. He would distinguish himself sufficiently such that later he would be promoted to general in the Waffen SS.

At Nijmegen, Lieutenant Karl Kramer hastily scribbled a letter to Hannah.

My Dear Hannah,

The Allies have launched a major drive from Belgium up through Holland. They are using parachutists – many thousands of them – to try to take bridges. Our unit's mission is to defend Nijmegen. I think the Allies will fail in this operation, but I now believe that the final chapter of this war soon will be written. I hope I am alive to read it. It would make a good history lesson for German students.

All my love to you and Thierry.
Karl

The ride in the horse-drawn cart was slow, smelly and jarring. Paul was grimacing from pain and gritting his teeth to prevent moaning.

"I am sorry for the rough ride," said Marcus, walking beside the cart. "We are almost there."

"Where?" Paul asked.

"A farm. Friends own it. We will hide you there and a doctor will come to treat you. When you are recovered, we will get you into Amsterdam."

"Okay," Paul muttered. He sniffed the air. Well, he reflected, it smells like farm land and that's not all bad. A little country cologne. Not bad at all.

Thirty minutes later the bouncing cart was approaching the farm. Its owner came forward to greet the resistance members, shook hands with Marcus and looked in the cart.

"American," Marcus told him. "He was shot parachuting. He landed in a tree."

"I will fetch a doctor," said the farmer. "Quickly. You can drive the cart into the barn. Make the man comfortable. He will have company. "

"Other soldiers?" Marcus asked, puzzled.

"Civilians." At that the farmer went running to a small enclosure near the barn. He lifted a saddle and blanket from a fence rail and opened the enclosure's gate. Moments later he mounted his black mare and went riding south to recruit a doctor.

Marcus motioned to the cart's driver who flicked the reins. The horse stepped forward. Two of the resistance men ran ahead to open the barn door.

On the evening of Day Three – September 19 – Ken Milligan was sitting on the ground near the Waal River at Nijmegen with other members of the 82nd Airborne. He remained puzzled by Paul's disappearance but was hoping he had connected with another 82nd company.

Nijmegen was the northern most city south of Arnhem. Its long bridge was the crucial link separating XXX Corps' armor from British Lieutenant Colonel John Frost's trapped and bloodied troops in Arnhem. Frost's men, charged with capturing both ends of the bridge, had managed only to seize its north end. Germans had blunted efforts to cross and take the south end. Moreover, German troops now were succeeding in crossing tanks from their end, penetrating Arnhem and surrounding Frost's vastly outweaponed men. It was a matter of British rifles and submachine guns supplemented by a scant handful of armor piercing shells fired from a handheld gun versus German tanks, other vehicles and supporting infantry. Making matters more dire for Frost and his men was the inability of the Allies to re-supply them. In short Frost's men were running perilously low on ammunition.

Ken Milligan was part of a unit commanded by Major Julian Cook. His mission: Cross the Waal and take the far end of the Nijmegen bridge. Mode of transportation: Boats of the flimsiest variety – coated canvas with thin wood struts. As his men stared agape at the rickety craft, Cook broke the awkward silence with a brusque challenge. "What did you expect? Destroyers? Let's go."

Ken was among the first to begin pulling the boats from the rear of delivery trucks to the ground and then locking in place the struts that gave the craft a semblance of stability.

"Okay, let's get them into the river," Cook shouted. "Go! Go!"

At that moment a line of XXX Corps British tanks on the road began lobbing smoke shells to the Waal's far bank to provide a screen for Cook's men. Ken grabbed the side of a boat with other men and began dragging it into the river. I've gotta admit, Ken mused, when I volunteered airborne, I never imagined becoming a riverboat man. Paul, wherever you are I hope you're keeping your feet dry. To Ken's surprise he found himself in the same boat with Major Cook.

The river's current was strong and Cook's men were rowing furiously to keep their tiny vessels from drifting away from the bridge.

Less than half way across the river, Ken felt a breeze strengthening, and he knew that meant trouble. The smoke screen began thinning. Almost immediately German mortar rounds began zeroing in on Cook's toy armada. One round scored a direct hit, sending 10 soldiers into the water. German machine gun fire raked another boat. Three soldiers at the front were hit, screamed and slumped. One slipped overboard. Men were thrashing in the water, screaming for help. In their uniforms with helmets, weapons, ammunition pouches and boots, they couldn't stay afloat and slipped beneath the surface.

"Row! Row!" Cook demanded, shouting above the tumult. "Keep rowing."

XXX Corps tanks resumed firing, targeting German gun positions near the opposite riverbank.

A few minutes later Ken's boat was nearing the sandy shore. Major Cook leaped into the shallows and began rushing ashore. Ken was trailing by only two steps.

Cook, Ken and other men made it to a road paralleling the river and immediately began running toward the bridge. Back on the other side, British troops also were nearing the bridge.

Lieutenant Karl Kramer had a birdseye view of the action but not one to savor. He shook his head slightly, thinking how different this reality was from occupation duty in Rhenen. Kramer, Sergeant Bohnenblust and a squad of 12 men were positioned as snipers high in the bridge's steel superstructure. The broad beams afforded advantageous shooting angles but only for soldiers not afraid of scaling to dizzying heights and with no safety nets below. If the Allies can take both ends of the bridge, Kramer was reflecting somberly, the bridge will be lost and I will be doomed. Up here the breeze is strong and the steel is cold. Far below he could see German soldiers running toward both ends of the bridge, trying to secure it. Their effort will be futile, Kramer thought, they aren't enough to stop the Allies.

As Cook and his men closed in, enemy firing intensified. Kramer looked at Bohnenblust, and they both signaled to the others to hold their fire. A German grenade detonated, and Cook's men went diving for cover. As they stood to continue their assault, two were hit, one screaming, the other uttering no sound. Cook kept pushing forward, shouting encouragement to his troops. Moments before the major and his men reached their end of the bridge, charging British troops began storming the opposite end.

"Now!" Kramer shouted and his men, sharpshooters all, took careful aim. In the next couple seconds shots began pouring down from the superstructure. Kramer watched several GIs fall or go diving for cover.

He then took aim himself and squeezed the trigger. His bullet slammed
into the chest of Ken Milligan, causing him to pirouette and fall, eyes open
in death before his body hit the bridge's surface.

Major Cook looked up. Kramer fired again and his bullet ricocheted
off a concrete pillar near Cook's helmet. Cook flinched and ducked behind
the pillar. He sucked in a deep breath. Then he exposed himself, aimed
quickly and squeezed. The round struck Karl Kramer in his midsection.
His carbine separated from his hands. As he began toppling forward the
carbine's shoulder strap snagged on a section of superstructure. Kramer's
head struck a beam and he felt consciousness slipping away. He was left
dangling, his body swaying like an abandoned marionette.

In the next few seconds Germans began dropping their weapons and
throwing up their arms in surrender.

Sergeant Bohnenblust acted on impulse. He waved tentatively at Major
Cook. Cook readied his M-1 rifle but held off firing. Carefully Bohnenblust
pulled his carbine strap over his head. Then he held the weapon in his
extended right hand and let the carbine go plummeting into the Waal. Next
Bohnenblust gestured to Private Max Thiessen. He followed Bohnenblust's
lead, removing the carbine strap and dropping his weapon into the river.

The two Germans nodded and began inching upward and toward each
other on a broad curving beam. Karl Kramer's body continued swaying,
now a human pendulum.

Major Cook and other Americans as well as Germans stood transfixed,
watching the drama unfolding above.

"What do you think, Major?" a young private asked.

"If that guy's alive, I hope they can bring him down. If he's dead, I hope
they cut him loose. No man should be left hanging up there."

Bohnenblust and Thiessen kept crawling until they were within arms'
reach.

"Lieutenant Kramer," Bohnenblust called, "can you hear me?"

A long moment of silence then, "Ungh."

"Lieutenant, we – Private Thiessen and I – are going to get you up. You
need to help us. Lieutenant, can you hear me?"

"Yes," came the barely audible reply.

"Can you raise your arms?"

Lieutenant Kramer had been ready to die. He had visualized Hannah
and Thierry, wanting them to be in his last thoughts. Pain fanning out from
his abdominal wound, he forced his arms upward.

Bohnenblust and Thiessen secured themselves as best they could, and
each grasped one of Karl's hands.

"Sir," said Bohnenblust, "when we pull you high enough to touch the beam, if you have the strength, try to grasp it. If you can grip it, we can get hold of your legs and pull you onto the beam."

"Go ahead," Kramer said and coughed. He gritted his teeth, knowing that pulling him up and stretching his midsection would exacerbate his pain.

Bohnenblust and Thiessen pulled and grunted. "Now, sir, try gripping the beam."

Kramer's fingers felt for a handhold.

"Good," said Bohnenblust.

"Let me go for this leg," said Thiessen, sweating despite the cool breeze. He reached down, firmly grasped Kramer's uniform trousers behind his knee and lifted.

Below on the bridge surface, a collective sigh could be heard. Most men, Americans and Germans alike, applauded. Major Cook touched the fore and middle fingers to the rim of his helmet.

September 22 came to be remembered as Black Friday by Polish Airborne troops and, if not black, certainly bleak to the people of Rhenen.

That Friday was Day Six of Operation Market Garden. The Poles' mission that night was to cross the Rhine and reinforce surrounded British troops. The crossing proved a disaster for the Polish brigade. Among those attempting the crossing in rubber rafts, only 52 made it to the Rhine's other side. The rest were killed by German machine gun fire or drowned when bullets punctured the rafts that quickly sank.

On Day Seven 150 more Poles would manage to cross. They weren't nearly enough to relieve General Urquhart's besieged men.

Meanwhile the Germans ordered the second evacuation of Rhenen. Abandonment was to take place immediately. It lacked even a smidgen of organization. All citizens were told they were entirely responsible for getting themselves away.

"Why are they forcing us to leave?" Catherina asked her father. "We don't present any harm to the Germans, and they can't have our safety or welfare in mind. Not now, not after all the suffering they have caused."

"No," Bert said, "they do not care a single whit for our safety. They simply once again want to remind us of their military might. They want us to remember they are still our masters."

"But they are losing the war, aren't they" Catherina asked plaintively. "Don't they see that?"

"Most of them probably do. But they know that saying so publicly could lead to immediate execution. I don't think any German dares stand up to Hitler, and he won't hear of defeat or tolerate retreat."

The evacuation order included an ominous warning: Any resident caught trying to sneak back into Rhenen would be summarily shot.

"Do you think they really mean that?" Catherina asked Bert.

"Oh, they mean it. But I don't think any of the handful of soldiers still here would shoot one of us. At least that is what I prefer to think."

The Lootens quickly packed a few things, left Rhenen and received shelter from a farm family some four miles to the southwest. Their host family already had taken in other evacuees, and their cramped house could accommodate no more. The Lootens' new residence was the white stucco-covered barn.

They wouldn't be alone. Inside, they saw a family of five huddled nervously in a corner, uncertain who would be entering their haven. The two families smiled at each other, mutual understanding and relief evident in their visages. Then Dora saw a lone man lying on straw under a blue wool blanket. He smiled and waved tentatively. Something caused Dora to walk closer to the man. His hair was cut close, and she could see his shoulders and exposed right arm were covered by what looked like a military uniform, although not German or Dutch.

"Hello," said the man in English. He held out his right hand. "Pleased to meet you. I'm Paul Bliss."

Two nights after the move, Dora and Bert were settling in for sleep in the barn's loft. Their bed consisted of straw and a blanket. Catherina and Karin were quartered in a stall below and likewise were arranging themselves on a mattress of straw.

"Bert," said Dora, "there are things we need. Clothes, pajamas, night gowns, blankets. We don't know how long we will be forced to stay here."

"I know. But I am afraid there is nothing to be done."

"Yes, there is."

"What?"

"I am going to ride Karin's bike to the edge of town and sneak back into our house. Tonight. Now."

"No. The risk is too great. You cannot."

"I don't think the Germans will be expecting anyone to return so soon. When Lieutenant Kramer left so did most of his men. As you told Catherina, there can't be more than a handful left."

"Dora-"

"I am going." A pause. "You are not the only one in the family who can be stubborn." She leaned toward Bert and pecked his left cheek. "And if we have an extra toothbrush, I will bring it for Mr. Bliss."

Dora rose, brushed straw from her dress and walked to the wooden ladder that was permanently nailed in place. Slowly and quietly she descended. She looked at her daughters in the stall. Neither was stirring. Then she glanced at the other family, sleeping, and Paul. He was awake and tossed a small wave. She nodded. In the darkness Dora moved the bike to the barn door and slowly pushed it open.

Outside, Dora paused while her eyes adjusted to the blackness. She looked up. Clouds were shading the moon but not entirely obscuring it. They seemed to be scudding by, clearing the way for moonlight to help Dora stay on the road. She mounted the bike and began pedaling toward Rhenen. Twenty minutes later she was dismounting and leaning the bike against a tree. On this clear night she was surprised that the light reflected by the moon was enough to cast shadows from trees and buildings. As much as possible she walked in those shadows.

At her home she inserted a key in the door lock and let herself in. Within minutes she packed a brown cloth bag tightly. I will have to make more than one trip to get everything we will need, she told herself.

Dora edged back through the front door and locked it. Momentarily, she froze. A faint sound caused her heart to begin racing. Germans? She listened carefully. The sounds ceased. An animal perhaps? She squinted and peered into the darkness. No sign of anyone. My Rhenen is now a ghost town, she mused sadly.

The next morning Karin approached Dora as she brought breakfast from the farmhouse kitchen. "Where did you go last night?"

Her question startled Dora, but caused Bert to smile.

"Uh-"

"No use fibbing," Karin interrupted. "You thought I was sleeping."

"If you must know, I rode back to our house to fetch necessities."

"Did you bring everything?"

"It wouldn't all fit in my sack. I will return tonight."

"I will go in your place," Karin said abruptly.

"No. Going was my idea."

"You can argue if you want," Karin said firmly, "but I am going."

339

"You are being hardheaded," Dora said accusingly.

"I am being Dutch."

Bert could see that accumulating stress was exacting a toll, and the price was flaring tempers. Though deeply worried about either his wife or daughter returning to Rhenen, Bert covered his mouth, barely able to contain his amusement.

"I will go," he said, trying to deflate the debate.

"No!" Dora and Karin snapped in unison.

"It is my bike and I insist," Karin said with unbending resolve.

Meanwhile, Catherina was staring wide-eyed, unaccustomed to Dora-Karin spats.

"You are sounding like your father," Dora blurted angrily.

"I could do worse," Karin retorted.

"Do you see the example you have set?" Dora snapped at Bert.

"Yes, dear."

"We both should be grateful for Father's example," Karin declared. "I am glad we all can agree on something at least."

Bert could contain his laughter no longer and quit trying. He guffawed – and tensions shattered. Karin began laughing, as much at herself as at the argument. First with tentative chuckles, then with jolly laughter, Dora and Catherina joined in the merriment.

Karin waited until after midnight to begin her bike ride to Rhenen. She was taking the same brown cloth bag Dora had used. As she pedaled toward town, she breathed deeply. This autumn air, she was musing, seems so crisp and dry. When I get back I should suggest to Catherina that we take a night ride through the countryside – after this battle is over. The night was still, the combatants – German, American, British, Polish – all having surrendered to the need for rest.

Karin arrived at the family home, unlocked the door and let herself in. She and Dora had discussed what she should collect. Scarves, gloves and caps were among the items Karin stuffed into the sack. She also slipped her winter coat over her dress.

The sack full, she exited the house and inserted the key into the door lock.

"Are you going somewhere?"

When hearing the words coldly spoken, Karin felt a hand touching her right shoulder. The surge of cold terror was so unexpected and profound she thought she might urinate. Slowly she turned.

"I-I forgot something."

"Yes, it seems that you forgot you might be shot," the soldier said smugly. "I could shoot you now," he said malevolently, "and be within my rights. What better way to teach this town a lesson?"

Karin tried willing her fear away. "We are living in a barn and," she said, gesturing to the sack, "we are cold."

"I suppose I could let you go," the soldier said, smirking, "but at a price."

"I have no money."

"You have something else."

"What?"

"What is between your legs."

Karin blinked. The shock of his suggestion – a demand? – found her fear giving way to anger. Images of the riverside assault by Privates Billheimer and Melzer and her rescue by Lieutenant Kramer and Sergeant Bohnenblust came flooding back. "You are pathetic," Karin half snarled.

"Yes," the soldier said caustically, "I suppose I am."

"I would," Karin said with unforced bravado, "rather be shot than raped."

Her words, spoken with the hardness of untempered steel, produced an unexpected result.

"Take your boney body and go," the soldier snorted. "Don't let me see you here again, or you will get your wish."

Lieutenant Kramer, once lowered to the Nijmegen bridge surface, had been tended to by an American medic. He had sprinkled sulfa powder into Kramer's wounds to ward off infection and pressure bandages to staunch bleeding at both the entrance and exit holes. Kramer was transported to an evacuation hospital back near the Belgian border where, much to his relief, he became a prisoner of war.

"Do you suppose," he asked a surgeon, "there is a way to get word to my wife?"

"I'm not sure, Lieutenant," the surgeon replied. "Why not write a letter, and I'll give it to our chaplain. Name is Captain Brecker and he is a resourceful man. You couldn't put a letter in better hands."

Defeat. On Day Nine, the last day of Operation Market Garden, the order to withdraw reached Generals Roy Urquhart and Stanislaw Sosabowski. Poles on both sides of the river helped to cover the retreat of remnants of the British 1st Airborne back across the Rhine – still another crossing in small boats and undertaken during a rainy night. The British 1st had gone into battle with 10,000 men. It came out with 2,000; 8,000 were dead, wounded, captured or missing.

General Bernard Montgomery claimed the operation was 90 percent successful. Dissenters were numerous. Among them: Roy Urquhart, Stanislaw Sosabowski, Julian Cook and thousands of Allied soldiers now in retreat or prisoners of war.

CHAPTER 64

The boat was long – about 40 feet – and narrow. It was gliding slowly through the canal's still water. Its cargo included brown sacks bulging with grain and one stuffed with Paul Bliss. He had bid farewell to the Lootens – and thanked Dora a second time for the new toothbrush – and the other residents at the farm.

Steering the craft was Marcus Schott. He was grinning. Smuggling people – usually resistance members – out of Amsterdam was a not infrequent occurrence. Sneaking someone in? He felt confident the Gestapo would show little interest in his inbound cargo. Like everyone else in Amsterdam they welcomed the arrival of new food stocks.

According to plan the boat was arriving midday. Marcus believed that the safest option for delivering his human load was precisely when German suspicions would be least aroused. In other words Marcus had told Paul, "right under their Nazi noses."

Paul was grinning when he replied, "This yankee farmer is happy to defer to this Dutch farmer."

Paul still felt twinges of pain but concluded he had recovered sufficiently to withstand the journey from the countryside into the city.

Now Paul could feel the boat slowing. He heard ropes being thrown and felt the boat's right side bumping against the stone wall bordering the canal.

"Here we are," Marcus said lowly. "We will unload some sacks of grain and load them onto carts that are standing by. Then we will pick you up and deposit you inside your brother's house."

"How close are we to his house?"

"About six meters," Marcus answered.

Paul quickly did the conversion from meters. A little longer than 18 feet, he figured. "Let's hope someone is home."

"Someone is," Marcus reassured him. "Not your brother. He is working at a bicycle shop. But someone is and she will not pry."

She? Paul wondered. This is more interesting than I imagined.

The unloading proceeded. After the carts had departed, Marcus pushed the doorbell button. Seconds later the door opened. "Yes?"

"My name is Marcus. I know Joshua. We both know Corellistraat. We have a delivery. Please do not ask questions. Not now. Not until Joshua returns from work."

Raluca studied her visitor, then nodded. "All right, I suppose."

"Step inside, please," said Marcus, "but keep the door open." He then turned and gestured to two burly colleagues. They and Marcus quickly surveyed both sides of the Prinsengracht and in both directions, north and south. Seeing no presence of Germans or local police, the two men hefted the special sack, stepped off the boat and quickly carried their load into the house and past Raluca. They placed it carefully on the floor.

Grain? she was thinking. How odd for Joshua to order grain and not tell me.

Marcus unsheathed a knife, its haft wrapped tightly in leather and its blade six inches long. He bent and carefully slit the sack.

Raluca was expecting grain to spill onto the floor. She reacted viscerally, staggering backward as Paul emerged and began rising to his feet.

"Hello, ma'am," he said, brushing grain dust from his army fatigues. "Nice to be here." Then Paul extended his right hand to Marcus. "Many thanks, my friend," he said as the two men's left hands covered their clasped right ones.

"I must leave. May our paths cross again."

"After the war," Paul said, "perhaps on your farm."

"Perfect," Marcus said, beaming, eyes glistening. "That would be perfect." He tossed off a casual salute, turned and left.

Paul looked at Raluca and grinned. "Not what you were expecting."

"Not at all." She promptly forgot Marcus' instruction to ask no questions. "Who are you and why are you here?" She could see he was a military man, although his olive green fatigue uniform was unlike any she had seen. It also showed numerous signs of hard wear.

"My name is Paul. Paul Bliss."

Raluca gasped. Then it struck her. "I have seen you before."

"What? When?"

"Soon after the death of Meredith. I saw you walking with Joshua."

"Oh, my God! You were with another woman. I do remember! I don't think I saw the two of you for more than a few seconds. Is that right?"

"Your memory is quite good."

"Amazing!"

"Yes, Mr. Bliss-"

"Paul, please."

"Paul, would you like some tea?"

"Very much."

"Good, then you can tell me how you got here."

"It's a long story."

"We have time," Raluca smiled. "Joshua will not be home for two more hours."

"Joshua is going to be shocked," Raluca said. Paul had told his story, with Raluca asking several questions. She found Paul to be as easy to converse with as his younger brother. He also told her about the youthful years on the family farm and Joshua's athletic exploits at Shelby High School.

"Your American football, I think it sounds like a very violent sport," Raluca observed.

"It's tough," Paul agreed.

"Our football is not so violent," said Raluca. "It is fast and there are collisions, but the players do not wear helmets."

"We Americans call it – your football – soccer."

"Oh, why is that?"

"I have no idea," Paul said. "And I must admit I've never seen a soccer game."

"Perhaps that will change if you stay in Europe after the war. Oh," Raluca said, glancing at a small kitchen wall clock, "Joshua should be arriving home from the shop at any moment."

"Should I hide and surprise him?"

Raluca laughed. "I do not want him to have a heart attack. I think it would be best if you waited with me so he can see you when he comes through the door. He will be shocked, but I think the shock would be greater if you came out of hiding. This will be a happy time."

They both heard the door handle turning. They looked at each other. Raluca smiled. Paul shrugged. The door opened.

"Hello, younger brother."

Joshua dropped his leather satchel and stared incredulously. What took place in the next few seconds wasn't so much a hug as a collision. Paul winced in pain. Joshua stepped back. "You're hurt?"

"Shot, but mending."

Joshua embraced his brother again, gently.

They clung to each other for long moments. Then Joshua tapped Paul's back twice and they separated.

Paul rubbed his brother's bald head. "Nice mustache too."

Raluca stood by, hands on slender hips, smiling and savoring this reunion between two American brothers, long parted by war and now brought together by that same war. I hope I get to tell my family about this, Raluca was reflecting. It is a story that deserves to be told and remembered.

"Damn!" Joshua's voice boomed. "It is so absolutely good to see you. Geez, you look good too. Despite being shot. Of course that uniform could certainly stand soapy water. Plus a needle and thread."

Paul chortled. "I haven't had much opportunity to do laundry."

"Tell me about it. Geez, Paul, tell me all about everything."

The supper that night was simple, filling and festive. Paul was introduced to the Follecks and was awestruck by their story – fleeing from Germany, settling and prospering in Amsterdam, accepting offer of refuge. Aaron saw in Paul a hero and Mariah and Julia were staring dreamily at him, all but swooning. Their wide-eyed gazing didn't go unnoticed by Samuel, Miriam and Raluca.

After the Follecks ascended to their third floor quarters, Joshua said, "Let's get you out of that uniform and into some of my civvies. And get you into our bathtub."

"Man," Paul said, grinning widely, "that sounds like the next best thing to heaven. Once in I might want to stay soaking forever."

"Take as long as you want, brother."

"I will start the water," said Raluca, "and put a fresh towel out for you."

In the bathtub Paul examined the entry wound. No sign of infection. After bathing and dressing in shirt, pants and socks courtesy of his brother, Paul said, "I can hardly believe I'm here with you."

"Could you stand a drink and a cigar?"

"Could I ever! Lead the way."

"You two enjoy some time together alone," Raluca said. "I am going to bed."

"Okay," said Joshua.

"Thank you, Raluca," Paul said. "You fixed a fine supper. And thanks for setting me up in the bathroom."

"You are welcome, Paul."

After she retired Joshua poured jenever, large quantities. "I don't have any fancy glasses," Joshua said, "but what do a couple of farm boys need with fancy?" Paul chuckled and they moved from the kitchen to the living room. There Joshua opened a small box and removed two cigars. He offered one to Paul. Then he produced a small box of wood matches. He struck one.

"Mmm, that's a mighty fine smell," Paul said, sniffing as the sulfur-fueled flame began burning the wood match. He clamped the cigar between his teeth and drew while Joshua touched it with the burning match. Paul let the fragrant smoke linger in his mouth before blowing it out. "Man, what a perfect way to end a perfect day."

Joshua laughed and lit his own cigar. He drew on it and formed a circle with his lips. He blew and the escaping smoke formed ascending gray circles. Then he and Paul sipped the jenever.

"She seems like a fine woman," Paul said, alluding to Raluca. "How did you meet her?"

"On a bridge."

"What's her story?"

"Let's put it this way. She's joined me in the resistance. Her best friend was executed for protecting the resistance."

"The woman I saw her with a few years ago?"

"The same," Joshua nodded. "Raluca couldn't stay in their apartment. The Gestapo would have come after her. I told her she should come here.

She has joined me in some resistance missions. There's more to her story, but I'd like to leave it for another day."

"Fine by me," Paul said. "I'm about talked out anyway."

The brothers continued smoking and sipping – and reminiscing about their time on the family farm. Frequent laughter punctuated their recollections.

In the bedroom Raluca could faintly hear their laughter. She smiled at the happy sounds and drifted into sleep.

CHAPTER 65

"Things seem a little crowded here," Paul said two days after arriving.

"How so?" Joshua asked. "You've got a room on the second floor."

"And I'm sleeping well. But I'm not really talking about beds. It's about food. I'm an extra mouth to feed, and anyone can see that food here is in short supply. I don't see anyone carrying extra pounds."

"We're getting by. I've got ration cards – and cash to grease my way in and out of the black markets."

"Yeah, well, I still think I should be figuring out how to get back to the Eighty Second."

"I don't think that will happen anytime soon," Joshua said. "From what I've heard the Allies have control of southern Holland. But the Germans have dug in and still hold the north. That includes the country's big cities – Amsterdam, The Hague and Rotterdam."

"So you're saying I'm stuck here."

"For the time being, I think that about covers it."

"Hmmm…Is there any way I can get word to my unit? And back to Mom and Dad? I'm thinking I'm now listed as missing in action. And they might be receiving a telegram that says that."

"I'm pretty confident the resistance can get word to your unit by radio. I'll get moving on that right away. Then the Army should notify Mom and Dad. But now that you've got me thinking about it, I might have a faster way to let Mom and Dad know about you. I should have thought of it sooner to let them know I'm okay."

"I'll bite. What are you talking about?" Paul asked.

"It starts with the resistance and asking them to make contact with a certain queen in London."

"A queen? You've come a long way from the farm, younger brother. It must be that Stanford education," Paul said, winking. "Either that or you took too many hits to your helmet playing football."

"That would explain a lot, wouldn't it?" Joshua said, grinning self-deprecatingly. "Anyway the queen thinks she owes me."

"Does she?"

"Maybe someday you can ask her."

"There's someone I'd like you to meet," Joshua said to Paul in mid-October. They were sitting, smoking cigars, in the living room. Both found the cigars therapeutic.

"Oh yeah? Who?"

"A friend. She's had it rough."

"She?"

"Yeah. I thought you might like to get to know some Dutch in addition to the Follecks and Marcus and his men. Broaden your perspective. Deepen your understanding of this country and her people."

Joshua's friend was only one of uncountable thousands of Dutch women who were having it rough. Not all of them still were in The Netherlands. At Ravensbruck in Germany, Betsie ten Boom had been growing progressively weaker. Hard labor, starvation rations, cold weather and persistent fever were combining to send her health into a downward spiral.

Now, in November Betsie's condition had deteriorated so perilously that she thought she might be gassed. Instead she was admitted to the camp hospital.

Corrie asked to visit Betsie. Her request was denied. But she wasn't forbidden from looking through a window into Betsie's ward each day as she walked by the hospital on returning from work.

Each night Corrie's prayer group beseeched God to spare Betsie and other desperately ill women. Daily more women died – or were gassed. All who perished were incinerated.

"Paul, this is Anneke Janssen."

"Anneke, this is my older brother, Paul."

The two shook hands politely. The introduction was made on a November Sunday afternoon in Joshua's living room. Looking on and smiling widely were Raluca and the Follecks.

"Nice to meet you, Anneke," Paul said.

"Thank you. Joshua has spoken about you and your parents."

"Well at least they haven't disowned me," Paul said. Everyone laughed.

"I am making tea for everyone," said Raluca.

"Let me help," said Miriam.

The next two hours were spent in pleasant conversation. All questioned Paul about his military experience – training and operations. Joshua shared the latest war developments as relayed to him by the resistance. Paul was heartened to learn that pincers were closing on Germany – the Allies from the west and south and the Russians from the east. What remained disappointing was Germany's continuing stranglehold on northern Holland.

As the afternoon was ending, Anneke said, "I must return to my grandparents' home."

"Let me see you out," said Paul. He accompanied Anneke to the front door. "I'm glad you agreed to meet me."

"I feel the same. Perhaps we can see each other again."

"I hope we do."

The Nazis continued to flex their military might in northern Holland. On November 10 and 11 in Rotterdam, occupation troops rounded up 50,000 men – mostly Gentiles – and transported them to Germany. There they began providing the forced labor needed to help keep the Reich's struggling manufacturing plants churning out weapons, planes and vehicles.

"Do you think it would be safe for me to get outside a bit?" Paul asked

Joshua. "I wouldn't say I've got a case of claustrophobia, but I could sure stand some fresh air."

"This is a big city," Joshua replied, "but you still could be spotted as a stranger." A pause. "Tell you what might work. We're into December, and it's getting dark early – before curfew starts. So if you went out for a walk around five and got back before curfew, you should be okay. It would probably be better if you were walking with someone. You'd be less likely to draw attention – or look less suspicious – than if you were walking alone. I could leave the bike shop a little early and be home before five."

"Or," Paul said, "could you speak with Anneke? See if she'd like to join me. We agreed we'd like to see each other again, and it would be nice to have some time together without an audience. You know, learn a little more about each other."

Joshua smiled. "Sure, I'll talk with her. But I want to be clear with her about the risk if she was with you and you were stopped by the Gestapo or local cops. And your dog tags, I know how strongly you feel about wearing them, but if you go out wearing them and are caught, well, you know what the Nazis do with spies."

"Good thinking, younger brother. Look, if she's not comfortable walking with me, maybe we could still talk here at the house."

"I'm not the world's greatest conversationalist," Paul said.

"When you are silent," Anneke said, "I will not feel uncomfortable."

"Good."

"Sometimes people speak more clearly with silence than with words."

"I'll keep that in mind."

They were walking along the Prinsengracht. Dusk was settling in. Both were bundled against the raw cold. In the dimming light they could see the vapors from their expelled breaths. Paul was wearing Joshua's blue wool coat and brown stocking cap.

"Life brings us much that we do not expect," Anneke said pensively.

"Lots of twists and turns."

Anneke looked up at Paul and smiled. "Yes, that is a good way to say it."

"Joshua has told me you lost your husband. I'm sorry."

"Thank you. He was a good man, a kind and brave man. Like your brother. And like you, I think."

Paul chuckled lowly. "Joshua for sure. I'm not sure just how brave I am. Maybe not so much."

"Even with one eye, I can see you are a good man."

"And I can see that with only one eye you take in much."

Anneke laughed. "As much as I want or need to. This way," she said, pointing to a bridge spanning the canal. "We can start back on the other side."

Ahead, with her one good eye, Anneke saw the orange tips of two cigarettes. Their smokers were standing in front of a café. "Police, I think," she murmured to Paul. "Ahead of us on the right." Quickly she reached up and removed her eye patch. "Let me hold your arm. Pretend we are lovers." Anneke didn't wait for a reply; she grasped Paul's left arm with both her hands and placed her cheek against his shoulder. "Continue walking slowly."

As they approached the two policemen, Anneke spoke softly to Paul. "This has been a most pleasant evening. Just right for walking."

Neither policeman interrupted their own conversation to so much as glance at Anneke and Paul.

"You think very fast," Paul said respectfully.

"The occupation has taught us certain lessons and helped us sharpen certain skills." Then with renowned Dutch bluntness, Anneke looked up at Paul and said, "You have never married."

"No. Came close once."

"You were promised?"

"You mean engaged?"

Paul couldn't see Anneke blushing in the darkness. "Yes, that is what I mean. Excuse my poor English, please."

"No problem. Anyway, the answer is yes."

"Why did you not marry?"

"She didn't want to be a farmer's wife. Couldn't blame her."

"Did she marry someone else?"

"A lawyer. They live in Cleveland – a big city with lots of lawyers."

"Do you think she is happy?"

"I hope so."

"Do you ever think about her?"

"Of course. I loved her."

"Could you love again?"

"I think I do." Anneke still was grasping Paul's left arm. He reached across with his right and covered hers. "One other thing, Anneke. I think you might be prettier without the eye patch."

On the afternoon of December 16 snow was blanketing the roofs and grounds at Ravensbruck. Corrie looked through the hospital window into the ward where Betsie had been confined. She had died earlier that day.

Another woman, an inmate working in the hospital, saw Corrie peering sadly and waved to her. The woman motioned to Corrie to look through another window into a room where the newly dead lay before being transported to the crematorium.

Corrie followed the woman to the window and looked in. She saw Betsie. Her face was no longer contorted in suffering. To Corrie her older sister now appeared as beautiful as she had been in her youth.

Early in the morning on the last day of 1944, Corrie and thousands of other women were assembled for roll-call. They were shivering, arms folded across their chests, feet stamping the ground, trying to get their blood circulating and warding off the worst of the cold.

"Prisoner ten Boom," a disembodied voice called out. "Report to registrations after roll-call."

Corrie's head snapped up. Is this my end? she wondered. Are they going to shoot me or gas me? Her shivering ceased. I am ready, Lord.

When roll-call was completed, she expected to be grabbed and dragged off. No one approached her. She went shuffling off to the camp's registrations office. She entered.

A sullen, bored clerk looked up and handed her a card stamped Entlassen or released. She was tempted – fleetingly – to ask if a mistake had been made. At Ravensbruck, death was the only release she had witnessed. In the next few minutes she was issued new clothes and given a railway pass that would take her back to The Netherlands. She walked toward the main gate and it swung open. She walked out.

Her friends and family in Haarlem were saddened to learn of Betsie's death. They were stunned – and thrilled – to learn Corrie had arrived at the local railway station. A joyous but subdued welcome ensued.

Later Corrie learned that, in fact, a clerical mistake had been made. She was not supposed to have been released. A mere week after her departure, all women approximately her age at Ravensbruck were gassed.

CHAPTER 66

"Grandmother, Grandfather, you must eat," Anneke cried, half ordering, half pleading.

"No," said Thomas Azijn, her grandfather. "We are old and you are young. It is you who must eat," he said calmly but sternly.

"If you do not, you...I will lose you," Anneke said, her throat thickening.

"Dear," said Lien, her grandmother, "we have lived a long, happy life. That is what we want for you. Please use our rations for yourself."

"Could we compromise?"Anneke asked lovingly. "You eat at least some of your rations? Enough to get you through this?"

As 1944 was ending, what would become known in northwestern Holland as the Hongerwinter was beginning. Before it ended an estimated 22,000 Dutch in that region would perish from starvation and malnutrition. Uncountable others would suffer severely.

Hongerwinter was a classic example of the law of unintended consequences. To help support Operation Market Garden and Holland's liberation, Queen Wilhelmina and her London government-in-exile appealed to Dutch railway workers to strike. They complied. In retaliation Nazi civilian governor Arthus Seyss-Inquart embargoed food shipments to northwestern Holland.

Foodstocks began shrinking. Exacerbating the dilemma was the onset of an unusually harsh winter. Systematically, Seyss-Inquart's administration began reducing daily rations for all foods, including bread and cheese. Meat coupons became worthless. Even black marketers were struggling to keep their dwindling stocks replenished. By the time the embargo was partially lifted, permitting limited food quantities to be delivered by water, canals had frozen over, becoming impassable for barges and boats. The affected area was home to about four and a half million Dutch.

Conditions were better in liberated southern Holland and in the east where Germany still ruled but food was more plentiful. Farmers everywhere were better provisioned, and that spared the Looten family from the famine's worst effects.

At his home where Joshua felt responsible for the Follecks, Raluca and Paul, he was able to acquire more than reduced rations by tapping his resistance sources. Still, hunger pangs were a nightly companion. Pounds began falling from frames, and faces were becoming haggard.

The visitor was a stranger in name if not in face. He appeared in Karel Veeder's bicycle shop about 1 p.m. and gestured to Joshua to join him at the door.

"Kees de Heer wants to see you in his office on Corellistraat," he whispered. "Can you come after work tomorrow?"

"Yes," Joshua replied.

"Good. He suggests that you arrange for the woman to be at the meeting."

Anneke was working in her grandparents' kitchen. She hadn't resumed wearing her eye patch. She had scrounged tulip bulbs – she wouldn't divulge where or how to Thomas and Lien – and was mashing them. She also had acquired – equally mysteriously – a handful of raw sugar beets. The culinary result was a stew of virtually indescribable taste and texture that caused noses to wrinkle and tongues to recoil with the first bites.

"I have prepared it," Anneke said, smiling wryly at her grandparents. "Now I insist that you eat it." The famine had not curbed her Dutch bluntness.

"Only if you eat a share," Lien said stubbornly.

Anneke nodded and smiled, and all three took plates to the living room that today was being warmed by flames in the fireplace. That increasingly uncommon happenstance was resulting from Anneke's having pilfered two railroad ties from a now unused rail line. She had paid – bribed – a merchant with a horse-drawn cart to deliver the precious fuel.

They spooned the unlikely stew slowly and chewed carefully. Lien gagged once. The meal required a full hour to consume.

"The war is going badly for the Nazis. It will be ending soon," Kees de Heer said to Joshua and Raluca. Once again they had arrived separately. "Even Hitler must be able to see that – if he is not totally blind to reality. His massive attack on the Allies in Belgium and France – they are calling it the Battle of the Bulge – has failed. But to us that doesn't mean that justice should become a forgotten priority."

Joshua and Raluca were sitting in de Heer's two armless visitor chairs. They were listening patiently. Thanks to Joshua's radio and broadcasts from the BBC and Radio Orange in London, he and his household members were reasonably current on war developments.

"So," Joshua said, "may we assume you have another mission for us?"

"If you are willing to take it on. As always, your decision will be voluntary. And with the war so close to ending, I will understand if you refuse. We want to undertake it because we see it as the necessary application of justice. Justice that is overdue already and might not apply if not administered before the war ends."

"In other words," said Joshua, "you think the bad guys might escape."

"Precisely."

"Go ahead," said Joshua.

They listened to de Heer describe the mission. When he finished Joshua and Raluca looked at each other. She nodded grimly but with no hesitation.

During the next several days, Joshua and Raluca began observing the movements and routines of their prey.

In the famine-struck area pets were disappearing. Desperately hungry people were eating cats and dogs along with horses, flower bulbs and anything else that could be swallowed to fill empty stomachs and possibly keep doors closed to the specter of death.

The fierce cold also saw people cutting down trees and breaking apart furniture for fuel. Most wood was removed from houses and apartments of deported Jews.

In Amsterdam wood became so scarce that none remained for building coffins, so bodies of the starved were being stacked inside the unheated Zuider Kerk.

Thomas and Lien had virtually stopped eating and no longer could any amount of petitioning by Anneke dissuade them from their chosen path. "When this war ends," Thomas told Anneke in a hoarse whisper, "we want you strong enough to celebrate."

Along with the elderly those most susceptible to the ravages of malnutrition were young children, and they too were perishing in tragic numbers.

One morning Anneke came to the bicycle shop. After a brief discussion with Joshua, the two mounted bikes to begin a long ride into the countryside. Each was carrying cash and empty cloth sacks. Their mission: Ride southeast and locate farmers with extra food to sell.

They weren't alone. Numerous other bicyclers were pursuing the same goal.

Joshua and Anneke succeeded. The roundtrip required pedaling more than 20 miles in the penetrating cold. Their facial muscles and jaws were stiff from riding against the frigid wind.

"Where are you and Raluca going?" Paul asked.

Winter's afternoon light was dimming, and Joshua and Raluca were pulling on coats, hats and gloves.

Anneke was visiting, as she was doing more often now that she and Paul were openly showing their mutual fondness.

"Out," Joshua said, stating the blindingly obvious. "It's better if you know nothing more." He purposely had refrained from saying anything in advance to Paul about a mission. Joshua didn't want to feel compelled to disclose details, nor did he want to have to fend off protests from his senior brother.

Paul nodded, anxiety tightening his face's open features. "How long will you be gone?"

"I'm not sure. If we don't return, you and Anneke do your best to take care of each other and the Follecks."

Paul closed his eyes, sighed and nodded. "Okay." A pause. "Joshua, whatever you are doing..." Paul stopped himself. He was going to ask if their mission was necessary. He knew better than to complete the question. "Be careful – and I feel silly for saying so."

Joshua chuckled briefly and lowly. "As older brothers go, you're a keeper."

Raluca fingered the cross Father Brandsma had given her. Then she buttoned her coat and opened the door. She and Joshua stepped into a gray, drizzly day quickly turning to night.

Inside the house Paul rose from a living room chair and beckoned Anneke to stand and come to him. As she rose and closed the distance between them, Paul reached out and wrapped her in his arms. Their lips met gently in their first kiss.

Raluca would serve as bait. The collar of her cloth coat was pulled up tightly around her neck. She was wearing a blue stocking cap. The ends of her long brown hair were brushing her shoulders.

Ten minutes later she stopped at the south end of the bridge she and Joshua had chosen. It spanned a canal that flowed westward and that their prey used on his evening walks from office to home. Raluca resumed walking and proceeded to the middle of the slightly arched span. Darkness was enveloping her and drizzle was soaking her stocking cap. She was sniffling and shivering, as much from fear as cold.

A few minutes later a man was approaching. Right on schedule, Raluca thought. I hope no one else comes. I do not want to delay this mission and have to go through this again. I think my luck is stretched thin. Raluca could see the orange glow of the cigarette the man was smoking. He started onto the bridge.

As he neared her, Raluca sniffled. "I need food," she said, sniffling again. "You can get me ration cards. I will do anything for them. Anything. Whatever you want."

The man stopped and peered into Raluca's dark eyes. Mere inches were separating them. "Anything? Do you mean that?"

"Anything at all," Raluca murmured convincingly. Now. In your home or your office. I am starving."

Joshua began moving. He was approaching the bridge from the same direction the prey had taken. He was wearing brown corduroy trousers and his customary blue woolen jacket and brown stocking cap. He would have liked to be wearing the orange scarf but knew that even in the darkness it was too conspicuous and memorable. The drizzle was running off the edges of his soaked cap and the ends of his mustache. He was carrying two lethal instruments – his silencer-equipped .22 caliber pistol and a less conventional weapon.

"I soon will be eating dinner," said the man. "You might make a tasty dessert."

"With payment in ration cards that I know you have at home or can get," Raluca said.

"So you know who I am?"

"I feel quite certain."

"I see. And are you one of the Jews who have escaped my hunt?"

"No," Raluca said through lips bluing from the cold drizzle, "but you are one of the slime who has escaped our hunt."

Henneicke took a half step back. "Young woman," he said, eyes glinting imperiously, "you are skating on very thin ice. Are you certain you know who I am?"

"Yes. You are a dead man standing."

"What?"

Joshua reached out and with his left hand tapped the man's right shoulder. "You heard the woman," he said in a voice as cold as the sinking temperature.

The man spun. "Who are you?"

"A stranger – but one you should wish you never met."

"Your accent. I don't believe you are Dutch, are you?"

"Does it matter?" Joshua asked.

"No. I will have you both arrested. And Dutch or not or Jewish or not, I will enjoy watching you both shot."

Joshua shook his head. "Someone might have me shot, but it won't be you." In the next instant Josh drove his right hand upward. It was gripping a long screwdriver he had borrowed from the bicycle shop. Joshua had honed the head to knife-like sharpness. Now he was driving it through Wim Henneicke's coat, jacket and shirt, penetrating his chest an inch below his heart.

Immediately Joshua clamped his left hand over Henneicke's mouth to muffle any cry. Henneicke's eyes widened in shock, then began slowly fading. Joshua lowered his hand and shoved Henneicke against the bridge railing for support. He and Raluca grasped Henneicke's coat lapels.

"I could have used a gun," Joshua said lowly to Wim Henneicke, "but that would have been too quick. You need a little time to think about your fate. We are going to drop you into the canal. If you don't break through the ice, we will learn soon enough if anyone cared enough to retrieve your body." Blood began dribbling from Henneicke's gaping mouth. "If you do crack the ice, I hope your cold heart rots below this bridge – or in the waters of the North Sea. If you have any last vision, I hope it's of the faces of the thousands that you condemned to early and violent death."

Joshua twisted and removed the screwdriver, wiped it on Henneicke's coat and put it in his jacket pocket. Then he nodded to Raluca. Together they lifted Henneicke up and over the railing. He fell head first. The ice cracked and groaned but didn't shatter. Joshua and Raluca knew it would be unwise to wait to see if Henneicke's body broke through.

CHAPTER 67

Queen Wilhelmina was grieving. Her insides felt as though they had been vacuumed out, leaving behind a throbbing shell. Her posture, usually as straight a flagpole, was sagging. "The people," she said, eyes misting, "my people. They are starving. They are dropping dead in the streets. We must," she told Prime Minister Gerbrandy in her London office, "find a way to relieve their suffering."

The prime minister, short in stature but strong in constitution, was at a loss for a solution.

Thomas and Lien Azijn died in their sleep. Lien went first, Thomas three days later. Joshua, with assistance from Laura Reidel, herself suffering severe hunger pangs, arranged for a horse-drawn cart to carry their corpses to the Zuider Kerk where they were stacked with others.

Back home on Prinsengracht, Joshua posed a question to Paul. "I don't like the idea of Anneke being alone. How would you feel if I asked her to move to Prinsengracht?"

"That would be fine," said Paul.

"If you two aren't ready to sleep together, we can make up another bed on the second floor."

"If Anneke accepts your invitation," Paul said thoughtfully, "tell her that's something we can discuss. Her and me."

"Okay."

"Before we go to bed together, there is something I want to say," Anneke told Paul forthrightly. She had brought clothing, toiletries and her grandparents' ration cards from their home on Gravenstraase. They were sitting alone in Joshua's living room. "You know I love you."

"And I love you," Paul said.

"That is good. Good that you say it."

"But I think you should remember what I am – and am not. I'm just a farm boy who got handed a rifle and learned to jump from airplanes. And," he smiled wryly, "with mixed results."

"You could not help being shot."

"No, I suppose not. But the fact is I'm no hero. Just a farmer."

"I am a city girl," Anneke said in her precise English diction. "But I have proved that I can adapt."

"To farm life?"

"How many eyes does it take to milk a cow?"

"In America?"

"I worked for Holland-America Line, and I always wanted to see America."

Paul's eyes narrowed. "Anneke, are you proposing to me?"

"There is still a war on, you know. Many things have changed. Even a one-eyed Dutch woman can fall in love with a yankee soldier. There are not so many men in Holland, so a woman must be bold."

"If that was your proposal, I accept."

"It was and I am glad."

"I'm not Dutch. You're not American. Getting you to America could be complicated."

"But anything is possible," Anneke said. "An American soldier who does not speak Dutch is forcing this Dutch woman to speak not so good English."

"Stand up," Paul said. Anneke stood. "Now we have to do this the American way."

"Do what?"

Paul genuflected in front of Anneke and took her hands in his. "Will you marry me, Anneke Janssen?"

"Yes, Paul Bliss. Now, I know this will be difficult," she said, grinning slightly, "but first you must follow Dutch tradition and sleep with me."

"You're teasing."

"Yes, I am."

CHAPTER 68

Kees de Heer rose from his desk chair and shook hands with Joshua and Raluca. "Sit down, please," he said cordially. "I asked you to come because I want to thank you personally for removing Henneicke."

"For me," Raluca said evenly, "it was a privilege to administer justice."

"Have there been reprisals?" Joshua asked.

"No. At least not yet, and I think they would have happened already if they were going to. If the Henneicke Column had not been officially disbanded, I feel certain reprisals would have come fast. There is one other factor that might be relevant. It seems that someone – not one of our people so far as I know – saw to it that Henneicke's body sank below the ice."

"Well, for the record," said Joshua, "I agree with Raluca. I was privileged to do my part, but I am not eager to take on another mission like that one."

"I understand. We have another similar mission coming very soon, but I have already assigned it to others. You both have accepted more risk than anyone should really ask." Joshua couldn't recall seeing de Heer smile but now he did. "Besides," the resistance leader added, grinning wryly, "even cats can run out of lives."

Late on the night of March 7, 1945, Hanns Albin Rauter was riding in a black BMW between Arnhem and Apeldoorn. Rauter was sitting on the right rear seat next to a senior staff officer. In front beside the driver was a junior staff officer. As the car slowed to round a bend, seven men dressed in German uniforms stepped into the road. Rauter's driver braked hard.

"Why are you stopping?" Rauter demanded roughly. Only two weeks earlier he had issued an order stating that German patrols should not stop any German military vehicles outside cities or villages. And who else, Rauter and his driver knew, would be riding in a BMW in The Netherlands but German military personnel?

"I am very sorry, sir," the driver apologized abjectly. "It will not happen again."

In the next instant the German-uniformed men leveled machine pistols and commenced firing. Bullets shattered the windshield and went tearing through the car. Two rounds hit the driver's face. Another hit the junior officer in his left shoulder. He, Rauter and the senior officer pushed open doors and scrambled from the BMW. They unholstered sidearms and began returning fire. The seven men, resistance fighters all, swiftly fanned out and threw themselves on the ground. The shooting lasted only seconds longer.

Rauter lay barely unconscious in a semi-fetal position on his left side. The two officers were lying supine, blood staining their uniforms in several places. One was missing teeth where a bullet had torn through his mouth and exited the back of his neck.

Marcus Schott and his fellow resistance members stood and approached carefully. Their guns were pointed downward, ready to fire. Their German boots kicked at the bodies. None stirred or moaned.

Marcus moved to the front of the BMW and emptied a clip into the radiator. Then he and the others left, disappearing into a copse of leafless trees.

Early the next morning a German patrol happened on the scene. Rauter, grievously injured, had feigned death. He would survive his wounds. With concurrence from Seyss-Inquart, Rauter also set about exacting revenge. His first reprisal took place at the site of the ambush. There Germans herded 117 political prisoners into the road and cut them down with machine gun fire. Soon afterward firing squads executed 50 prisoners in the Amersfoort concentration camp and 40 each in The Hague and Rotterdam. Why prisoners in Amsterdam were spared went unexplained.

When word of the mass reprisals reached Queen Wilhelmina, she was both crushed and outraged. In her mind, Rauter had sealed his ultimate fate. She concluded quickly that her people needed a major morale lift. In short order came a decision that caused stomachs to begin churning with anxiety among Prime Minister Gerbrandy, her daughter Juliana, son-in-law Bernhard and staff.

"Even if I agreed with you – and I do not – I doubt if the Royal Air Force would acquiesce," Gerbrandy told her. "And I simply cannot imagine Prime Minister Churchill consenting."

The queen phoned her British pal. She wasn't seeking consent. "Winston," she said without preamble or any exchange of pleasantries, "I need a plane. As fast as possible."

Churchill listened without interrupting or questioning. "I believe that can be arranged," he said dryly, grinning knowingly. This was another reason he respected and liked Wilhelmina. Her decision and demand reminded him of his three flights to Paris in 1940 in a futile effort to lend some spine to panicky French President Paul Reynaud.

The next day the borrowed plane, escorted by British spitfires, crossed the Channel and landed in Allied-occupied southern Netherlands. The queen visited Eindhoven and surrounding villages and received a rapturous welcome. Word of the queen's exploit was broadcast by the BBC and Radio Orange and produced the desired effect on Dutch morale.

A day later she was flying back to England.

At the same time in The Hague a husband and wife who would scarcely become an historical footnote were beginning a special project.

Before the Nazi invasion and occupation, William "Wim" and Joanna Toet ran a modest inn in The Hague. They provided suites for guests, including numerous Americans. One reason for their inn's popularity among U.S. visitors: The Toets spoke English.

A German soldier had burned a U.S. flag that the Toets had displayed.

Afterward Wim and Joanna began buying dye. Joanna and her daughter Hendrika began dying sheets red and blue and cutting them into strips. They began stitching those strips to strips of white and cutting other pieces of white into stars.

During that same month of March at Bergen-Belsen, Margot and Anne Frank died from typhus.

Miraculously, Otto remained alive.

In April with Allied victory seemingly imminent, Prince Bernhard made his own surprising decision. Acting on a brainstorm he appealed to General Eisenhower to negotiate a truce with the Germans that would permit imports of food to the starving millions in the still-occupied northwestern region of The Netherlands. Eisenhower possessed singular powers but lacked authority to undertake such a negotiation.

Bernhard was not deterred. He appealed directly to Churchill and Roosevelt who both gave Bernhard's initiative a thumbs-up.

Eisenhower then ordered planning to begin immediately. Allied agents started discussions with Seyss-Inquart and a team of Nazi senior officers. Central to the agreement: Allied planes delivering food would not be fired upon as long as they remained in specified air corridors.

Had Hitler been apprised of the negotiations he likely would have ranted until suffering another bout of apoplexy. Seyss-Inquart, seeing how the cards would be played, sensibly held his hand close to his navy blue silk necktie.

Both British and American aircraft would be ferrying food. The British mission, dubbed Operation Manna, was first to go. Inspiring the sobriquet was the Book of Exodus story in which food was miraculously provided to starving Israelites.

Two Royal Air Force Lancasters were chosen for the test flight. The first plane to lift off on the morning of April 29 was quickly anointed *Bad Penny*; the crew had in mind the expression *A bad penny always comes back*. Canadian pilot Robert Upcott led the seven-man crew. *Bad Penny* went wheels-up in bad weather and flew at only 50 feet above the Channel surface just in case any German gun crews hadn't received word of the truce – or would choose to conveniently ignore it and down a prize. At take-off, Seyss-Inquart had not yet signed the truce, but would do so the next day.

Operation Manna then began in earnest. More than 3,000 Royal Air Force planes – Mosquitoes and Lancaster bombers – flew 3,298 sorties. Because the precious cargo wasn't equipped with parachutes, the planes dropped their loads from as low as they could safely descend and regain altitude. Their designated drop zones included Valkenburg Airfield near Leyden, Duindijht horse race course near The Hague and Kralingsche Plas in Rotterdam and the city of Gouda.

A distribution system was quickly organized but some famished Dutch could not abstain from overeating immediately. An epidemic of retching and vomiting soon ensued as stomachs rejected unaccustomed quantities.

The American fleet swung into action on May 1. Army Air Corps officers dubbed their mission Operation Chowhound. During the next three days, the U.S. 3rd Air Division, using 400 B-17 Flying Fortresses, flew 2,268 sorties. They dropped 800 tons of boxed k-rations at Amsterdam's Schiphol Airport.

During the combined British-American operations, three aircraft were lost. Two collided and one fell from an engine fire. Meanwhile the effort saved uncountable thousands of lives.

CHAPTER 69

Joshua was driving a horse-drawn cart, once again supplied through the intercession of Laura Reidel. It was the afternoon of May 1, and the cart was heading northwest from Schiphol Airport to central Amsterdam, a little more than four miles distant. Sitting beside Joshua was Raluca. He had secured enough k-rations that would ease the hunger pangs of Laura, the Follecks, Paul, Anneke as well as his own and Raluca's for the next few days.

"Peace," Raluca said softly, "I think we should have peace very soon."

"Shouldn't be more than a few days now," Joshua said.

"It will seem strange to not live in fear," Raluca said pensively. "I can begin planning to return to Romania."

"Are you sure that's what you want to do?"

She shrugged. "Of course."

Joshua noisily sucked in a breath and blew it out forcefully. "You know I'm in love with you, Raluca. Have been."

"I do know certain things, Joshua. Yes, you are in love with me. Yes, I am a prostitute."

"Raluca, let me repeat. You *were* a prostitute. As far as I'm concerned, that's history."

"You would marry me?"

"That's what I'm saying."

"You are an educated man. I am not an educated woman."

"You've learned more than most people who go to college. And collected more wisdom much faster."

"You would take me to America? To meet your family?"

"That's what husbands do. Or fiancés."

"So, we are now engaged?" She smiled expectantly.

"Well, I haven't given you a ring which is customary in America. But I'm sure I can correct that deficiency as soon as the war ends."

"Deficiency?"

"A mistake on my part."

Raluca laughed. "I think I will never hear that American word again."

Joshua chuckled. "Maybe not that word, but I can guarantee you I will make more mistakes."

"I would be nervous to meet your family."

"You've already started. Paul thinks the world of you. So will my parents."

"But, Paul, he does not know I was a prostitute."

"Why should he? That's history only you and I need to know."

"I need to see my family, Joshua. Too many years have gone by. And I want to see Alicia's family."

"I have money saved. So do you. We will honeymoon in Romania."

The broadcasts on May 2 from the BBC and Radio Orange were the talk of The Netherlands. Queen Wilhelmina was flying back home – to stay. Her aerial chariot was a DC-3, and the reliable aircraft brought her down to an airfield between Tilburg and Breda, about 30 miles southeast of Amsterdam. Juliana and Bernhard joined her. From there they were driven to a stout country mansion called Anneville that bore the look of a miniature, turreted castle.

"How would you like to see the queen?" Joshua asked Raluca. They were exiting their house.

Although dangers had subsided, the Follecks remained inside Joshua's house on the top floor. It made no sense, Samuel and Miriam agreed, to leave their sanctuary and risk a senseless – and possibly fatal – act by a resentful Wehrmacht soldier or hateful Gestapo.

But Joshua and Raluca felt comfortable enough to go strolling along the Prinsengracht on a sun-splashed morning. Not far behind them followed Anneke and Paul.

"The queen? I know you are joking," Raluca smiled. Joshua eyed her but didn't reply. "Or are you?"

"I am not, Fiancee Johnescu. I feel a need – which I'll explain – to see Queen Wilhelmina, and I think you would enjoy meeting her."

"Meeting royalty? It is something I never dreamed about. And Alicia, she would not know what to think – or say. When will this happen?"

Thousands of Dutch were flocking to Anneville. They were exultant at the prospect of the war's imminent end and eager to pay homage to their queen whose faith in her countrymen never wavered. For hour after hour, Wilhelmina stood at an open window, waving gaily to the seemingly endless procession of adoring subjects.

Food still was scarce and luxury items nonexistent for the populace. "I will not eat food that is not available to my people," she instructed staff. When one admiring servant brought the queen precious strawberries, she politely but firmly declined the offer.

Joshua was riding Orange. When he and Raluca visited the stables where Joshua had deposited the horse five years earlier, he was shocked – and thrilled – to learn that the horse that had carried him from The Hague to Amsterdam had survived the war. The mount was gaunt, but Joshua and the stable owner were confident that food, water and exercise would soon restore Orange to his once-robust physique. Raluca was uneasy sitting a horse for the first time. At first she was content to let Joshua lead with the reins of the brown mare he had rented for her. Raluca was gripping the pommel.

It was nearing 4 p.m. when they reached Anneville. Joshua and Raluca dismounted and let the horses graze the lush spring grasses lining the sides of the gravel drive leading to the mansion. The horses snorted their pleasure over this fresh country repast.

"It looks like a palace," Raluca marveled. "I think I would get lost inside."

Joshua chuckled. "It no doubt has one or two rooms more than the typical family needs."

"I think most of the village of Apahida could live there."

She and Joshua took the horses' reins and led them to the end of the queue. By late afternoon it had shortened considerably.

From her open window Queen Wilhelmina spotted the horses and then focused on their handlers. Joshua was gazing up at her and jauntily snapped off an American-style salute, palms down. From Wilhelmina came a glint of recognition, faint at first but strengthening by the second.

She turned to her daughter. "Juliana, come here. Do you see the two people with the horses?" Wilhelmina was pointing toward them. "I think I know the horse and the man. Send someone down to bring him and his woman friend to me and someone to watch their horses."

Within minutes, a member of the queen's staff was leading a smiling Joshua and nervous Raluca inside the mansion. While climbing the flight of stairs to the second floor and the queen's chamber, Raluca's shoes seemed weighted with iron soles and heels. What do I say to a queen? she fretted. What should I do? I do not want to embarrass Joshua. She could feel anxiety tightening her chest.

When they entered Wilhelmina's chambers she was beaming. She offered her right hand to Joshua. He took it and they shook hands firmly. "Let me test my memory. It is Mr. Bliss, as I recall."

"Very impressive, your majesty," Joshua replied.

"It has been a while since you saw me off on the Hereward."

"Just short of five years."

"You know, Mr. Bliss, your reputation precedes you. I have been informed. I know what you have done for my country."

"I felt privileged to help."

Queen Wilhelmina nodded her understanding. "Your friend?"

"My fianceé. Please allow me to introduce Raluca Johnescu. She has worked with me in the resistance."

The queen surprised everyone in the room except Joshua when she offered her hand to Raluca. "Thank you very much, my dear."

Tentatively Raluca reached for the queen's hand. The firmness of Wilhelmina's grip surprised Raluca who smiled and bowed slightly.

"You have a lovely fianceé, Mr. Bliss. And I believe I still owe you a debt. As you know, I have not been able to repay it." She chuckled at her small joke, and Joshua chuckled in response. "Is there anything I can do for you?"

"As a matter of fact, yes."

"Anything at all, Mr. Bliss."

Joshua inhaled, then exhaled slowly. Raluca looked at him questioningly. "I want to marry Raluca who is not a Dutch citizen," Joshua began. He turned toward Raluca and saw her reddening. "Nor am I. My brother Paul is an American. He was a parachutist and was shot during Operation Market Garden. Marcus Schott brought him to Amsterdam, and he has been in hiding at my house. He wants to marry a Dutch woman and take her to the States. After I visit Raluca's family in Romania, we want to go to the States. It's all very complicated. Obtaining marriage licenses, passports, visas. We could use some help cutting through the red tape."

Queen Wilhelmina smiled knowingly. "I know about your brother, Mr. Bliss. As you'll recall, you asked Mr. Schott for help in communicating with your family. I was happy to oblige. Now, are you aware that I was in the States in 1943 as the guest of President Roosevelt?"

"I heard."

"Well, I also met Mr. Truman when he was vice president. If I put in a word with him, personally, I think you can expect the red tape to be cut in all the necessary places. I think you also can expect no delays."

"I can't thank you enough, your majesty," Joshua said.

"I too thank you," Raluca murmured.

"Well," said Wilhelmina with endearing self-deprecation, "even old queens can remember what youthful romance is like."

CHAPTER 70

May 5 brought an explosion of orange. What triggered it took place in the Hotel de Wereld (The World), a modest three-story rectangular structure in Wageningen, a small town barely three miles east of Rhenen. Settlements in the Wageningen area were mentioned in documents dating to 828. It received formal city rights in 1263.

On that May day German General Johannes Blaskowitz surrendered to Canadian General Charles Foulkes. The surrender document was signed the next day in the auditorium of Wageningen University – next door to the hotel.

Thus officially ended World War II in The Netherlands.

On Prinsengracht the Follecks descended from their third floor ayrie and ventured outside. "Sunshine!" Samuel shouted.

"Freedom!" Aaron exulted. He ripped a yellow star from his jacket and threw it in the canal.

Miriam began weeping, tears of happiness and relief mingling in the torrent pouring down her face. Mariah and Julia hugged her fiercely.

Paul and Anneke stood in front of the house, watching joyfully the Follecks' celebration of survival. Paul slipped his left arm around Anneke's back and drew her close. "Anneke," he said, "wait here." He turned and walked back inside the house. Moments later he returned, holding two glasses. "Jenever," he said, handing a glass to Anneke. "I would like to make a toast."

"Please do," she said.

"To the Dutch people and their will to resist and endure – and to Ken Milligan, my brave friend, wherever you are."

They clinked glasses and sipped.

The Lootens gave thanks but launched no celebration at the farm.

Instead they quietly gathered their belongings and began trekking back to the Rhenen house. Later that day Karin and Catherina flew their orange kites in memory of Luc.

In The Hague Wim and Joanna Toet draped their homemade American flag from an open window in their inn that they had reoccupied.

Laura Reidel began walking the streets of her hometown. She strolled by the offices of the Royal Netherlands Steamship Company and breathed deeply the salt-tanged air. She stopped in front of the memorial to Meredith and the others who perished with the Simon Bolivar. She dabbed at a lone tear that leaked from the inside corner of her left eye. Joshua Bliss, she mused, I believe Meredith would wish you and Raluca a happy life together. From today, she told herself, I must begin living to the fullest the next chapter of my life. I hope my story has several more chapters to be written. She smiled and continued strolling.

The next day, May 7, Joshua and Raluca rode the rented horses back into Amsterdam. At his home Joshua picked up two sheets of paper and a fountain pen and began a letter to his parents. When finished, he started another to the Forbes family. In both missives he related his engagement to Raluca.

On that same day Arthur Seyss-Inquart was hoping to slip into obscurity. He crossed The Netherlands into Germany. His escape was short-lived. In Hamburg he was arrested on the Elbe River bridge by two British soldiers. One, Norman Miller (birth name Norbert Mueller), was a Jew who had escaped to England at age 15 before the war. His entire family had been murdered in March 1942 at the Jungfernhof camp in Latvia.

On May 10 another celebration took place in Freiburg. Karl Kramer tapped on the door to his apartment. Hannah left the kitchen, wondering who might be visiting. Eight-year-old Thierry followed, tugging at the edge of her flower-print apron. Hannah pulled open the door. The boy looked in bewilderment at the man his mother was squeezing tightly, her tears spotting his uniform's tunic. She took no notice of the bullet hole.

EPILOGUE 1

Although the Dutch resistance killed numerous Nazis and collaborators, including Hendrik Seyffardt and Wim Henneicke, at the end of the war, many others had managed to evade justice.

Lieutenant Julius Dettman, the Gestapo officer who betrayed Alicia Domian, decided not to wait for justice to impose its will. His guilt weighing heavily, Dettman committed suicide, hanging himself on July 31, 1945.

Anton Mussert hadn't tried to escape The Netherlands. He was arrested at his office in The Hague on May 7, 1945. He was tried and convicted of high treason. He appealed to Queen Wilhelmina for clemency. She turned him down. On May 7, 1946, Mussert was executed by firing squad in The Hague at a site near the North Sea where the Nazis had murdered hundreds of Dutch.

After the war in The Netherlands, the Dutch tried and executed 39 other war criminals. Only one was a woman, Ans Van Dijk, and she was a Jew convicted of betraying other Jews. All 39 were executed by firing squad and most at the location where Mussert was shot.

Arthur Seyss-Inquart was tried at Nuremburg and found guilty of war crimes. Along with 10 other Nuremburg defendants he was hanged on October 16, 1946. He was the last of them to mount the scaffold. His last words: "I hope that this execution is the last act of the tragedy of the Second World War and that the lesson taken from this world war will be that peace and understanding should exist between peoples. I believe in Germany."

Seyss-Inquart's execution wasn't the last among convicted war criminals, and the Dutch hardly considered the execution of Hanns Albin Rauter a tragedy. On March 24, 1949, he was executed by firing squad near Scheveningen Prison.

Some criminals and collaborators many Dutch longed to execute escaped the gallows. Willem Briede who partnered with Wim Henneicke died from natural causes in 1962. SS Staff Sergeant Karl Silberbauer who arrested the Frank family was arrested as a prisoner of war. He was tried and convicted of meting out unnecessary brutality during interrogations and sentenced to 14 months imprisonment. He died in 1972 in his native Austria.

EPILOGUE 2

By war's end, about 270,000 Dutch men, women and children had lost their lives. That total translated into 2.36 percent of The Netherlands prewar population and the highest per capita death rate in Nazi-occupied countries in Western Europe. A major contributing factor was the fate of the nation's Jewish population. Of the 140,000 Jews living in The Netherlands before the war, only 30,000 survived. Among Gentiles who hid Jews in The Netherlands, one-third did not survive the war.

EPILOGUE 3

Professor E.M.Meyers whose summary dismissal precipitated the Nazis' closure of Leyden University and who went into hiding among friends survived the war. He was reinstated at the re-opened Leyden University.

EPILOGUE 4

After V-E Day Queen Wilhelmina chose not to return to Noordeinde, her palace in The Hague. Instead, for eight months she resided in a large house there. She continued traveling through the countryside, working to buoy spirits. Sometimes instead of traveling by car she rode a bicycle.

Her zest for life notwithstanding, she was tiring of politics, and her health began to fade. She decided to abdicate. On September 4, 1948, Wilhelmina ceded the throne to Juliana. At that moment Wilhelmina was the only survivor of the 16 European kings and queens who were ruling when she was crowned in 1890.

Wilhelmina retreated to Het Loo Palace, 42 miles east of Amsterdam and 65 miles northeast of The Hague. She died there at age 82 on November

29, 1962. At Wilhelmina's request and contrary to protocol – something that had seldom deterred the stout-hearted queen from following her heart's lead – the funeral was conducted with everyone wearing white. That choice was in keeping with her belief that death marked the beginning of life.

Corrie ten Boom also cherished the concept of eternal life. Hers, though, wouldn't begin for another decade. Her story was told in a book, *The Hiding Place*, that was published in 1970. A movie based on the book was released in 1975.

After the war Corrie established rehabilitation centers in Holland for concentration camp survivors and jobless Dutch who had collaborated with the Nazis. Many of the latter had been publicly humiliated after the war. Numerous women who had consorted with occupying Germans had had their heads shaved and been paraded among mocking Dutch citizenry. Some collaborators had suffered worse fates; they were lynched without the courtesy of a trial.

In 1946 Corrie began traveling the world. She spoke to audiences in more than 60 countries. Her core themes remained maintaining love for and faith in God in the face of adversity, God's love for all mankind and his forgiveness of the sins of transgressors. In 1977 Corrie was tiring of endless travel and moved to Orange, California. She died there on her 91st birthday – April 15, 1983.

EPILOGUE 5

Samuel Folleck started over – again. He and Miriam re-opened their clothing shop on Merwede Square. Their inventory had disappeared. They knew the occupiers had taken some and tried not to dwell on the possibility that Gentile neighbors had helped themselves to merchandise. What enabled the Follecks to restart their business soon after the war was the help of a private banker, of sorts. Through Joshua Bliss' intercession, Russell Forbes, still working at Chemical Bank, agreed to loan the Follecks the funds necessary to refurnish the store and replenish the inventory.

Samuel insisted that the arrangement be made legally binding in a contract, complete with a repayment schedule and a stipulated penalty for late payments. He repaid the loan ahead of schedule.

He and Miriam ran the shop until 1969 when they retired and Aaron took over the business. He had risen to an executive position in a large department store chain, but willingly left to take over the shop. He saw growth potential and planned to open more shops. He also saw an opportunity for his son Adam to learn the retail ropes in his own small shop – the original on Merwede Square.

EPILOGUE 6

"You have been a lifesaver," Joshua told Laura Reidel. "You are a beautiful woman – in every sense of the word. I learned more lessons about life from you than you can ever imagine."

It was a mid-May morning and they were standing in front of the waterfront memorial to Meredith. Joshua reached out, embraced Laura and drew her close. Her face pressed against his jacket, her eyes misting, Laura murmured a reply. "I do not believe I have ever had a friend – woman or man – who was more caring and more loyal. You pledged to stay in touch during the war and you did."

Gently she pushed away from Joshua. Her watery eyes peered up into his. "I do not know if this is our last meeting. If it is I will always remember you as my dearest friend."

Joshua's throat was thickening and he didn't try to quell the tears rimming both eyes. He smiled and semi-croaked, "Laura, I will now make you another pledge. After I return to the States, I will bring you there as my guest." Through his tears, he forced a grin. "After all, it is high time that you visited America and saw the roots of this once-upon-a-time farm boy."

EPILOGUE 7

After V-E Day, Queen Wilhelmina didn't procrastinate in beginning to apply her promised expertise in cutting red tape. Paul and Anneke were early beneficiaries. Anneke's passport and visa in hand, they sailed for

America and New York and there entrained to Shelby. They built a second house on the Bliss family farm and became parents to sons Peter and Henry. Eventually they took over running the farm for Noah and Goldie.

Joshua and Raluca were married in Oude Kerk. After the ceremony they asked to have their picture taken outside at the spot where Alicia Domian had been executed. They then embarked on their honeymoon, entraining for Cluj and there hiring a taxi to drive them to Apahida. Raluca's reunion with her family and Alicia's was bittersweet – the joy of reconnecting tempered with telling the Domians that their oldest child was buried in an unmarked grave somewhere far away in a land the family would never visit.

By the end of July Joshua had introduced Raluca to the Forbes family. They welcomed Joshua's bride warmly and thanked him for making the connection. Joshua accepted a job, managing an accounting group at Chemical Bank.

During the next few years Raluca and Joshua became parents to Alicia and Paul. She and Joshua built a summer cottage at the eastern end of Long Island near scenic Montauk Point. In bed they loved falling asleep to the soothing rhythm of Atlantic Ocean surf bathing the nearby beach. Sometimes, though, their sleep was plagued by nightmares of times past. The woman who first had sat a horse uneasily while journeying from Amsterdam to meet a queen became an avid rider. Well into their 70s, Raluca and Joshua could be seen riding, their galloping mounts kicking up wet sand and splashing through the low surf.

ACKNOWLEDGMENTS

Henk and Jeanne Deys were crucial to the creation of *Long Journey To Destiny*. In May of 2011 I interviewed them in Rhenen, The Netherlands. From his wonderful personal library, Henk gave me a book that describes WWII as it took place in and around Rhenen. He was born in 1932 in Indonesia and endured the Japanese occupation. He moved to Rhenen in 1946, eventually earned a doctorate degree and became a clinical pathologist. He also became the town's historian. Jeanne was born in 1933 in a village just outside Rhenen and later came to own and operate a pharmacy. She told me many war stories that I incorporated into this book. I am ever grateful to this charming, gracious couple.

This book would not have been written were it not for Peter and Jose Verveen. Peter is one of my Stanford classmates, and it was he who arranged my interview with the Deys. Peter flies his own plane and on the afternoon of the day my wife Lynne and I arrived in The Netherlands, he showed us the country from 1,300 feet in his 4-seat Cirrus. During ensuing days, he also showed us Amsterdam, The Hague, Rotterdam and much of the Dutch countryside. Twice Peter and I ate whole raw herring, right down to their tails.

Jose took it upon herself to locate several helpful articles published in Dutch and then translated them to English. She was helpful too in tracking down elusive facts and providing me with common Dutch first and last names. Jose and Peter have my eternal gratitude.

Bev Smith, former director of Stanford University's Executive Program in the Graduate School of Business and my Stanford classmate Ed Yang both provided valuable input that helped me create the look and feel of Stanford as it existed in the 1930s. Bev and Ed were particularly helpful in providing background on Palo Alto's two movie theaters, the Varsity and the Stanford. Ed even provided a list of every movie that played – including showing dates – at the Stanford in 1935.

Lynne, my loving wife of 42 years, began her career as an editor and did her usual stellar job of copy editing and proofing and curing flaws that otherwise would have populated this book.

Henk & Jeanne Deys

Peter & Jose Verveen

ROSTER OF REAL-LIFE PEOPLE

President Manuel Azana

Prince Bernhard

General Johannes Blaskowitz

Betsie ten Boom

Corrie ten Boom

Father Titus Brandsma

Neville Chamberlain

Winston Churchill

Premier Edouard Daladier

Admiral Karl Donitz

Father Albert Fate

A. Fournier

Lieutenant Colonel John Frost

Hermann Goering

Berta Grynszpan

King Haakon VII

Wim Henneicke

Adolf Hitler

Prime Minister Peter Gerbrandy

Fred Koornstra

Walter Lackner

President Tomas

President Wilhelm Miklas

Anton Mussert

Colonel Hans Oster

Vladimir Poliakov

Premier Paul Reynaud

Colonel Pieter Scharroo

Joseph Schreieder

Albert Speer

President Eduard Benes

Captain J.D. Backer

Willem Briede

Casper ten Boom

Willem ten Boom

King Carol

Colonel Dietrich von Choltitz

Major Julian Cook

Lieutenant Julius Dettman

Queen Elena

General Charles Foulkes

Francisco Franco

Joseph Goebbels

Hugh Carlton Greene

Herschel Grynszpan

Ernst Heldring

Rudolf Hess

Prime Minister Dirk Jan de Geer

Princess Juliana

President Paul Kruger

Princess Margriet

Masaryk King Michael

Norman Miller

Paul Nipkow

Constantin Perskyi

Hanns Albin Rauter

George Rignoux

General Rufolf Scshmidt

Hendrik Seyffardt

Cornelis van Geelkerken

Ernst von Roth

Chancellor Kurt von Schuschnigg

Sergeant Karl Silberbauer

Hendrika Toet

Wim Toet

Captain H. Voorspuiy

General Henri Winkelman

Major Bert Sas

Arthur Seyss-Inquart

General Kurt Student

Joanna Toet

Robert Upcott

Queen Wilhelmina

SOURCES

- American Heritage New History of World War II. Stephen Ambrose, C.L. Sulzberger. 1997
- Amsterdam City Guide. Karla Zimmerman, Caroline Sieg, Ryan Ver Berkmoes. 2010
- Cabinet War Rooms
- Diary of Anne Frank. BBC. 1987
- 82nd Airborne. Fred Pushies. 2009
- Europe in Flames: Understanding World War II. Harold J. Goldberg. 2010
- Interview: Henk & Jeanne Deys
- London Man. 1991
- 1939 – Countdown To War. Richard Overy. 2010
- Online articles:
  - Military History of The Netherlands During World War II
  - History of The Netherlands (1939-1945)
  - Titus Brandsma
  - Treaty of Versailles
  - Kristallnacht
  - Finland During World War II
  - Prostitution in The Netherlands
  - Spanish Civil War
  - Holland Schouwberg
  - Battle of Rotterdam
  - Rotterdam Blitz

- o Bombing of Rotterdam
- o A Jewish Story in Rotterdam
- o Kurt Student
- o P.W. Scharroo
- o Hitler's Office
- o Hitler in Paris
- o The Hague
- o Ernst Heldring
- o Freiburg
- o Dutch Government-In-Exile
- o Wilhelmina of The Netherlands
- o Noordeinde Palace
- o Het Loo Palace
- o Proclamatie Wilhelmina
- o Resistance
- o Dutch Resistance
- o Silencers
- o Stanford
- o Rhenen
- o Rhenen – Evacuation by Coalship
- o Evacuation by Coalship
- o Story of Mrs. Fietje (little Sophie) de Jong-Scheffer
- o Wageningen
- o Holland America Line
- o S.S. Statendam
- o Royal Netherlands Steamship Company
- o S.S. Simon Bolivar
- o The Ships List
- o Corrie ten Boom
- o February Strike
- o Dutch Famine of 1944
- o Operations Manna and Chowhound
- o Henneicke Column
- o Arthur Seyss-Inquart
- o Hanns Albin Rauter
- o Anton Mussert
- o Karl Silberbauer
- o Rudolf Schmidt
- o 23rd SS Volunteer Panzer Grenadier Division Nederland
- o Axis History Forum

- o South Mimms
- o Order of the Garter
- o Dodenaantal Tweede Wereldoorlog (Numbers of Death Second World War)
- Parade. A Grand Old Flag. July 3, 2011
- Rhenen: 1940-1945
- Site visits: Amsterdam, Brussels, Freiburg, London, New York, Palo Alto, Paris, Rhenen, Rotterdam, Stanford, The Hague
- Soldier of Orange. Erik Haselhoff. 1980
- Stanford Facts. 2008
- The Hiding Place. Corrie ten Boom. 1970
- The Story of Painting: From Cave Painting to Modern Times. H.W. Janson, Dora Jane Janson. 1970
- The Timetables of History. 1982
- World Book Encyclopedia

CPSIA information can be obtained at www.ICGtesting.com
Printed in the USA
BVOW062002290212

283634BV00001BB/1/P